By Vella Munn from Tom Doherty Associates

Daughter of the Forest
Daughter of the Mountain
The River's Daughter
Spirit of the Eagle

VELLA MUNN

SPIRIT
OF THE
EAGLE

FORGE®

A TOM DOHERTY ASSOCIATES BOOK
NEW YORK

SPIRIT OF THE EAGLE

Copyright © 1996 by Vella Munn

Cover art by Royo

A Forge Book
Published by Tom Doherty Associates, Inc.
175 Fifth Avenue
New York, NY 10010

Forge® is a registered trademark of Tom Doherty Associates, Inc.

ISBN: 0-812-53500-6
Library of Congress Card Catalog Number: 95-39745

First edition: February 1996
First mass market edition: March 1997

Printed in the United States of America

0 9 8 7 6 5 4 3 2 1

Acknowledgments

Without the timeless Modoc spirits which haunt the Land of Burned Out Fires, it would have been impossible for me to capture what I have of a unique culture and people. Yes, the National Park Service is responsible for preserving the Lava Beds of northern California and I am deeply grateful for their dedication to the past with its messages and lessons. I'm also indebted to the settlers, soldiers, reporters, and historians who documented their impressions of the war. Although the resultant books sometimes conflicted with each other, they gave me essential information. But it is the Modocs themselves who left behind the vital essence of their lifestyle, their understanding of the land, its seasons, and natural gifts. All I had to do was stand where they once stood and open my senses, my heart.

A special thanks goes to Gary Hathaway, acting Park Superintendent, for making his reverence for traditional Modoc culture come alive for me. His honesty about the Indians, army, and settlers has been invaluable.

Finally, I extend my own message of love to my husband, Dick, and my mother, Bonnie Palmer, for their willingness to explore and re-explore that wildly beautiful land with me. We learned lessons which will remain with us always.

"Once my people were like sand
upon the shore. Now I call but
only the wind answers."

—Old Schonchin, Modoc reservation chief

SPIRIT
OF THE
EAGLE

1

Northern California near Lost River, north of the Land of Burned Out Fires

The Modoc girl known as Teina sat huddled in the dark, staring at the dying coals from the fire that kept the winter storm from invading the small wickiup. The air on her naked body was no longer so hot that it made her sweat as it had when she went to bed, but she couldn't stir herself enough to reach for a deerhide blanket or her sagebrush bark dress. Nearby, her father snored.

Although she couldn't see the short, thickly built man, she easily imagined him sprawled on his back, arms outstretched, mouth open. He might reach for his wife, but tonight his possessive fingers would touch nothing.

Nena, Teina's mother, was gone.

A tule mat had been placed over the wickiup's roof opening as protection against snow and wind. If she added wood to the fire, the air would fill with smoke. Still, she wished she had something to do. Something to take her mind off her mother.

There was nothing.

Biting back tears, she repositioned her thin legs and turned her attention to the ladder that stretched to the opening. In her mind she saw her mother push aside the covering and descend. When she reached the ground, Nena would look around for her daughter and then, laughing a little in her excitement, tell her about the multitude of birds and other wildlife she'd seen while she was gone.

Only, tonight Nena wasn't out watching a long-legged crane pick its way through the swampy ground at the edge of Modoc Lake while hundreds of eagles patrolled the sky, their fierce cries seeming to echo against the distant mountains. Tonight Nena had gone out in a fierce storm because her husband had ordered her to go to the soldiers from Fort Klamath.

Unable to stop herself, Teina's hands tightened into helpless fists. She stared through the dark in the direction the snoring came from and imagined herself pummeling her father's face and chest, insisting he never again sell his wife to the soldiers.

But this wasn't the first time; she knew it wouldn't be the last.

A sound caught her attention, and despite the wind hitting what of the wickiup was above ground, she recognized approaching hoofbeats. Soldiers? Coming—coming for her? No! Although she'd seen twelve winters, her body was still that of a child, too small to accommodate a man.

Short moments later she relaxed. The horse was unshod and in that quiet time just before dawn, she knew it could only be her mother returning. She stood, waiting, needing her mother and yet unsure of what she would say to her. When the tule mat was pulled away, she saw first one leg and then another seek the log and fiber ladder. The wind howled; snow blew in through the opening. Her father snorted but didn't wake.

Nena was moving too slowly. Despite the sounds her father made, Teina heard her mother's labored breathing. Twice Nena sobbed softly and clung to the ladder as if too weak to continue. Stifling a cry of her own, Teina hurried over and helped guide her last few steps.

"Mother?"

"Home," Nena whispered and turned to embrace her daughter. Her arms and fingers felt frozen; snowflakes clung to her old elk cape. When Teina hugged back, Nena winced but didn't cry out.

"Mama, what is it?"

"They—fists—the soldiers . . . "

The soldiers had hurt her mother! Was it not enough that they used her body as if they had every right to it? Now they . . . they what?

"Don't go again, please!" The thought of what had happened between her mother and the soldiers was too much to bear. "Tell him—tell him you will no longer—"

"I cannot," Nena moaned and sank to her knees. Teina dropped beside her, cradling her mother's larger, heavier body.

Nena whispered, "I did as they said—spread my legs for them. Sickened on their whiskey breath. But they—"

Teina shut her mind to what her mother was saying; at least she tried to. But she wasn't a small child, living in her grandfather and great-grandfather's world. Her world had been invaded by the settlers and ranchers and soldiers who'd come to Modoc land—

"Wife? Where are the bullets?"

Teina was halfway to her feet before her mother grabbed her and pulled her back down beside her. "On the horse," Nena said. "I had—no strength."

"They paid as they said they would?"

"Yes."

"How many bullets?"

"I do not know." Nena's voice held an unaccustomed anger. "They forced me down, struck me. Laughed and hit and tried to make me drink their whiskey. I did not count the bullets, Wa'tcaq."

Teina watched her father's shadow come closer. "Hit?" he asked. "Did they have no use for you? You displeased them?"

"Stop it!" Teina gasped. "She is my mother! You cannot—I will not—"

She expected her father to slap her, knowing from past experience that there was no escaping his anger. The blow came so quickly that she didn't have time to duck. The side of her face flamed and her inner ear felt as if it might burst. She fought down a sob and continued to glare at him. "Do not raise your voice to me, Teina," he ordered. "I am your father."

And I hate you for it. "A father who trades his wife for weapons? Who forces her to—"

Wa'tcaq leaned down, not to strike her again but to yank her to her feet. She struggled, aware that her mother was trying to separate them but lacked the strength. "You are mine, Teina." His face was so close that her stomach lurched from his wretched breath. "My child and my responsibility and burden. You, my youngest, give me much grief."

Her father was no longer the man he'd been before strangers came to Modoc country and forced the People off the land that had been theirs since Kumookumts created it. "You sent her to them," she shot back. "They could have killed my mother, and you want me to remain silent? No!"

"Teina," her mother warned. "It is all right."

But it wasn't, and nothing her parents said would make her believe that. Her older brother and sisters had still been children in spirit when they were her age, but their world had been simple. Hers wasn't; she sometimes felt as old as her toothless grandmother. Knowing the folly of trying to free herself from her father, she stopped struggling and stared at his bulky shadow while fighting her sense of helplessness. "You are not a man, a warrior!" she sobbed. "You do not hunt or fish. Instead you send my mother to—"

"Teina!" Her mother reached for her, then grabbed her side, gasping in pain. Fear lashed at Teina. She pulled away from her father's loosened grip. When her mother swayed, she helped her sit down.

"I cannot see what is wrong. The shaman. I will—"

"No shaman."

Because Wa'tcaq didn't want Cho-ocks to learn what he'd allowed to happen to his wife. Filled with that knowledge, Teina somehow supported her mother's weight until her father—cursing—threw branches on the coals so shadows no longer claimed the wickiup. Nena seemed more asleep than awake now, as weak as a small child. Teina ran her hands gently over her mother's body. When she reached her thighs, she felt dried blood.

Sickened, she whirled on her father. He stared down at her, and in the flickering, growing light, she could tell he was keeping his weight off the knotted knee that prevented him from following deer or antelope as he once had.

She opened her mouth, not sure what she was going to say, wishing with all her heart that she had her grandmother's wisdom. What she saw in his eyes stopped her. He was staring, not at her face, but at her breasts. Since they'd become more than tiny nubs against her flat chest, she'd covered herself in his presence, hoping to keep what she was becoming from him.

"What is this?" He indicated her breasts. "You are a child no more. A woman?" He stalked toward his wife. "Has she had her first bleeding? You have kept this from me? Why has there been no puberty dance?"

"She *is* a child!" Nena's voice was thick with fear. "No bleeding. Not yet ready for marriage."

"Marriage." Wa'tcaq's lips thinned. "Ready for a man."

"No!" Nena struggled to sit upright. "You send me to the soldiers. I do as you order. But my daughter—"

"My daughter too. She is skinny with long arms and legs; the soldiers like—"

"No!"

The hard winter wind blew with an anger that threatened to rip the sage and dried grass from the earth. Snow, spat from black clouds, whipped and whirled like prisoners unable to break free. With nothing but low, distant hills to challenge it, the wind rejoiced in its freedom, a monster determined to play and punish.

A monster born of Tctuk, the rock squirrel spirit who had stolen snow from Kumookumts and set it loose upon the earth.

Modoc Lake no longer fought the unrelenting gale. The water, and fish that lived in it, lay trapped under a thick layer of ice. The ice groaned and even screamed sometimes, sounds that seemed spawned by something buried deep underground.

Teina snugged her heavy elk blanket around her shoulders and neck, then dropped to her knees behind a thick, spreading chunk of sage, protecting as much of herself as possible from the storm that kept the rest of her people huddled in their brush and willow bough wickiups. Because they couldn't fish with most of the lake frozen, the ducks and geese who wintered here hugged the ground or hid behind lava rocks to escape the wind and waited for calmer days when they could feed on swamp grasses. Only the eagles didn't care; only they defied winter during their relentless search for food. Even now, a number of them floated overhead; even more were perched on rises that ringed the lake. The distant eagles, fierce and watchful, made her slightly uneasy. Still, she gave no thought to leaving.

She would rather freeze or be eaten by birds of prey than return to where she would have to see her mother's bruised and swollen face, where her father sat counting the white man's bullets. As she'd done since she was old enough to walk on her own and first heard its ageless call, she'd sought the wilderness. Solitude.

Where could she possibly go? Who might give her shelter? The great god Kumookumts had disappeared from the earth, leaving behind only his footprints. Frog was powerful but lived in the water, where Teina couldn't survive. The immortal snakes might let her join them, or she could dwell with bears who, it was said, had human intelligence. Or maybe Eagle.

Eagle, the bringer of good fortune, the namer of all other animals.

The wind hurtled through the brush, slicing into the girl like a hunting knife. Yet she remained huddled among boulders that had been here since the great underground fire spewed its anger and waste over the earth, long before the first Modoc drew breath. The lake, so wide that she couldn't see to the other side, was home and shelter to more water birds than she could count. Thousands upon thousands of ducks, egrets, geese, herons, and eagles were born and died here. Many followed their instinct south in the winter, but untold others stayed. When the storms came, they found shelter so they could fly and swim and fish and hunt another time.

Maybe, if she prayed hard enough to Kumookumts, the birds would take her to their nesting places. She would spend her life safe on the top of a sheer rock ledge or in an ancient mountain pine. Alongside the great eagles she loved and revered and feared, she'd wait for summer with its warm breezes and long, hot days. In those wonderfully quiet places, no soldiers' horses would trample the delicate white and yellow and red flowers that found life in the thin soil.

The thought lifted her lips, but her smile didn't last long. She might love eagles, but she had to live with those of her own kind. She had to understand why strangers had come to Modoc land and why the old ways were blowing away like autumn leaves.

The wind took a deep breath, pausing so briefly that maybe she'd imagined it. When it threw itself again against sky and earth, she shivered and turned her head so the shards of snow wouldn't sting her eyes. She blinked back tears born of cold and anger and, again, asked herself why her mother allowed her husband to treat her like goods to be bartered. Why her father sacrificed her to his greed.

It was the soldiers. The tribe elders spoke of a time before foolish strangers crouched over streams looking for rocks they called gold, before white settlers came with their fences and livestock, before nearby Fort Klamath had been built. Once, the land in all directions had belonged to the Modocs. The meadows, hills, creeks, and great lake truly had been the Smiles Of God. Sometimes the fierce Klamath Indians ventured close and the Modocs were forced to fight for what was theirs, but those battles had been fought with bows and arrows and spears, not rifles.

Then the miners and settlers came, with their powerful weapons. And the fort. And the soldiers. The Modocs had been forced off the rich land given to them by Kumookumts the creator because the settlers wanted the meadows and hills and water for themselves. Her people had been ordered to live shoulder to shoulder with the Klamaths by men who would never understand that the Klamaths and Modocs were like cougars and deer, different—enemies.

When the wind paused for another breath, Teina leaned close to the snaggled sage and tried to breathe in its scent, but the storm had forced its pungent smell back into the gray green leaves and dark bark. Still, she marveled that this ancient shrub flourished where nothing should grow. If many antelope and rabbits and deer made the lava beds on the other side of the lake their home and wocus grew abundantly, her people could live out their lives there, but it was too desolate. Even when there was no storm, only a few songbirds and mountain sheep survived.

Only the birds and sheep and, maybe, someone who was not yet a woman but no longer a child.

Her legs cramped and she shifted her weight. Her knee landed on a sharp rock, and it was several seconds before she found a comfortable place to kneel. When she again looked out at the lake, she saw that a mist had begun to form over its frozen surface. Despite the wind, a dense, swirling cloud shape clung to the lake like snow on sacred Mount Shasta, only darker. Much, much darker. She could no longer see the eagles that guarded it.

Mist brought peace. She had always felt comforted by its cool, quiet blanket. The world slowed down then, lost its harsh edges. She would stand with water droplets on her face and in her hair and wonder if this was what it felt like to be a bear or squirrel in its winter sleep. Sometimes the fog's cold was so intense that she was forced inside, but even then, she felt the massive shroud just beyond her reach, waiting to envelope her with silence.

Maybe she could live in the mist. Then she shook her head at the idea of burrowing deep inside what had no substance, still staring at what the soldiers and settlers had named Tule Lake.

She wanted the newcomers gone, wanted the fog to swallow every pale skin and keep them there until the end of time. Maybe, she thought with a small laugh, the fog would force them deep into the earth where the great fire burned.

Fire. She held her numb fingers to her mouth and blew, but her breath did little to warm them. She wasn't a duck or an eagle, kept warm by its blanket of feathers. If she didn't leave soon, she would freeze.

But where could she go?

The answer, maybe an answer, came as if it had been waiting for her in the storm and fog. Chief Kientpoos, her mother's brother, had given her the elk blanket she now wore. He'd noticed that her father hadn't prepared her for the coming winter.

One day last summer she'd been standing in waist-deep water

watching tiny fish nibbling her toes while Kientpoos and the other braves fastened seines across the bows of their canoes so they could paddle about until the nets were full of fish. Just as they were getting ready to set out, a rifle blast caught everyone's attention. A moment later, a large doe burst into view and plunged into the lake. As they watched, the doe headed at an angle away from them, swimming powerfully. By the time the soldier who'd shot at the doe arrived, the creature was out of range. Still, the sweating, bearded man reloaded and fired again before slamming his heavy rifle to the ground.

Even with the wind raging around her, she remembered how she and her uncle had laughed together, the sound forever erasing the difference in their ages. After that, girl and warrior spoke frequently about the newcomers' foolishness.

"Captain Jack," he'd told her once, shaking his head in exasperation. "That is what the whites call me. Am I an army captain? No. But they say I look like a man named Jack who is a captain and they cannot pronounce my rightful name. That is how it is for all of us, it seems. Some accept their new names, embrace them even. I do what I must, but still I wish I had never heard anything except Kientpoos."

Reluctant to expose herself to wind and snow, she pulled her blanket tight against her throat and forced her legs under her. Still, she felt her long, straight hair being yanked away from her scalp and thrown into the air. As she stood staring at the fog now rolling toward her like a slow-moving bear, she fought the desire to spread her arms and wait to be lifted over the Earth.

For a moment, tears blinded her vision. She didn't know if it was caused by the cutting wind or her thoughts; she didn't care. She was so cold that it hurt to walk and yet if she stayed where she was, she would freeze and the fog would swallow her. She and her uncle Chief Kientpoos—not Captain Jack—would never again laugh together.

The thought that he was inside his warm wickiup maybe eating dried trout mixed with parsley roots put strength in her legs. If she had the courage to approach him, would he open his home to her, protect her from her father? She wiggled her toes inside her woven tule footwear, but couldn't feel them. Keeping her eyes half closed against the storm, Teina managed to make out the ancient deer path and started to follow it. After no more than three steps, she stopped. Between her legs, at her private place, she felt wetness. But she had no need to seek the bushes; it couldn't be that.

Wetness.

Bleeding.

Disbelieving, she tried to make herself start walking again, but her legs no longer wanted to obey her. Before she could put her thoughts to how different her life would be from now on, the puberty ceremony, womanhood, what her father might force her to do, something pulled her attention back toward the lake. The fog hadn't come any closer. It waited near the bank, so dark and lush she couldn't see the ice. Being swallowed by fog, freezing to death, anything was better than having to return to her father and tell him that she had left childhood.

It was now snowing with enough energy that the line between mist and snow no longer existed. The wind pushed at her and forced her to spread her legs and lock her knees so she wouldn't lose her balance. She was a fool for coming here. Even if the wild creatures lived in her heart and mind, she wasn't an eagle or a deer or a fox. Only, her anger at her father had been as powerful as a winter blizzard.

Not a woman! Not yet! I am not ready. Please, Kumookumts, help me!

A movement, the same as and yet different from the storm. Although her teeth chattered so that her head ached, Teina couldn't leave until she'd discovered the movement's source. It might be a soldier, but she didn't think so.

The mist seemed to sway and buckle, to move closer, then slide away. It covered the lake, blanketlike, sheltering, almost a part of it. Maybe Kumookumts had sent it here to protect the fish. If that was so, maybe the great, weightless mass would shelter her as well. She waited, shivering, curious, awed. The storm continued to attack. When she covered her chin and mouth with her blanket, her nose felt like a small chunk of ice. Her uncle would have to throw much wood on his fire before she thawed.

When what she'd been waiting for separated itself from the gray, cold cocoon of mist and started toward her, Teina's mind was so numb that at first she saw but didn't comprehend.

An eagle had been born of the mist, not simply emerged, but born. His hunter's body looked so heavy that he shouldn't have been able to rise above the earth and yet with his great wings outspread, he seemed as graceful as an antelope racing across the plains. Unable to breathe, she craned her head upward so she wouldn't lose sight of him. Even when she nearly lost her balance, she kept on staring. Snow slashed at her lids and lashes.

An eagle—*Eagle*—coming her way.

As the elegant bird soared and dipped, in love with the wind's current, she knew he had spotted her. More than that, he sought her.

She was longer aware of the cold and yet she continued to shiver. The eagle was huge and his wingspan far greater than her height. His talons and beak were made for ripping at flesh. "Eagle?" she managed to whisper. "Eagle? Do you hear me? What . . . "

Although the storm tugged at its feathers, the eagle continued to fly with lazily outstretched wings as if he was certain that his strength far outstripped any blizzard. He seemed intrigued by each new gust of wind, riding it out, conquering winter. His beak was slightly opened. Teina imagined that Eagle was smiling, and the last of her fear fluttered and died.

"Eagle."

As he soared overhead, the huge bird dipped his magnificent snow white head. She saw—a momentary glimpse—that a thin, dark streak ran back from his beak to where his feathers turned dark at the shoulder. His small, red eyes locked with hers. A silent scream tore through her, not a sound of terror but one of awe. She struggled to remain standing, felt the push of air along the side of her head as Eagle's wings came within inches of her.

The bird turned immediately, as mobile as a tiny songbird, and again swept over her. This time his right wing dipped even lower, brushed her temple and seared her flesh from forehead to the top of her head. Heat flowed through her as if she'd been touched by a great fire.

Eagle.

She wanted to lift her arms in reverence, to see if the eagle had injured her or simply left its mark, but she knew if she did, she'd lose hold of her blanket and expose herself to the ice and sleet. Weeping, she waited for the eagle to make another pass and wondered at his incredible grace and power. When he was again so close that she could see the center of his eye, he all but stopped in midair. Hovering, wings barely moving, the winged predator blanketed her. Although he hadn't touched her, Eagle now completely shielded her from the storm. Her legs nearly gave out, but she forced strength back into them.

Eagle.

After beats of time that slid off into the mist, the great bird again tilted its body and brushed his wing along her shoulder. This touch left no molten imprint. Eagle's talons were so close that Teina could have touched them. They were like knives sharpened for war, hard and dark and deadly, yet she didn't fear them.

Eagle had touched her, run his feathers over her, warmed her. Seared her from forehead to temple.

With a cry that set her nerves to shaking, the great bird soared upward and she understood that even this magical creature needed to seek currents of air or it would fall. She watched it head for the heavens and wondered if her heart would break.

Eagle again descended. His beak was still open, still laughing. His eyes seemed less red now, more like one of the dark caves that dotted the Land Of Burned Out Fires. He didn't come quite as close this time. Still, the tip of his right wing touched her cheek like a mother's caress. Then he flew in a tight circle around her, pushing away the storm, making Teina wish she could climb on his back and be lifted to the heavens. At his nearest, she could again see the strange and mystical dark mark flowing along its white head.

Then Eagle was leaving, nearly gone. She stared as he reentered the mist as silently as he had come. For a long time she stood and shook and cried. Had it been a dream, a product of her storm-frozen mind?

No.

Eagle was much more than a winged predator. She believed that, never doubted the legends told in poetry and song. The first Eagle, even before the first Modoc, had lived on the Sprague River. From its perch on the mountains, he could see clear to the salt chuck that the whites called the Pacific Ocean. Eagle, created by Kumookumts, had given all other animals their names and in gratitude those animals even now freely gave their flesh to him.

Eagle kept the Modocs safe.

One eagle, a magnificent loner, had blessed her.

And she was, heart and soul, a Modoc.

Sobbing, she stumbled closer to the mist that had swallowed her spirit. "Tell me of what will be—of what my children will know—of . . ."

But Eagle had gone back to the mist where he belonged. She was left with nothing except the feel of his wing on her cheek and shoulder and the still-burning heat on the top of her head.

And a feather.

The large black and white feather rested on the fur that covered her shoulder. He had placed it there for her, a gift. A message? Maybe a blessing. Awed, she closed her frozen fingers around it and tucked it against her budding breasts.

She was no longer a child, no longer Teina. Unlike those who traveled as far as Mount Mazama during their spirit quests, she'd only had to open her wild heart to find peace. To be touched by Eagle.

When she looked again, she saw that the mist no longer clung to the lake's boundaries. A low, rolling mound was now so close that it lapped at her feet, teasing, beckoning, comforting.

Eagle had left behind something of himself in the mist, in Luash.

Luash. Mist.

It hurt to smile, but she gave the gesture freedom. When she laughed, the storm instantly swallowed the sound. She didn't care.

On this bleak and yet wonderful winter morning, the child known as Teina had ceased to exist.

In her place was Luash, a woman blessed by Eagle.

2

Near Fort Phil Kearny, Wyoming Territory

Four days 'til Christmas.

"On the first day of Christmas my true love gave to me . . . "

True love? Christmas? Hell in a cold, God forsaken, tree-choked land.

It hurt to be this scared, hurt the top of Jed Britton's head and the back of his neck clear down to the base of his spine, chewed at his gut the way the curs around the fort attacked the deer bones the cooks threw their way.

"On the second day of Christmas my true love gave to me two turtle doves in . . . "

Hell.

Jed's horse wheezed and stretched its neck in an attempt to pull more air into its lungs. Although he was barely seventeen, Jed knew the old gelding was nearing the end of its wind, but word had just come down the hard-riding line that Crazy Horse had been spotted, running like the dog he was from the well-armed cavalry and infantrymen hot on his tail.

Nothing else mattered.

Jed leaned low over the gelding's neck, taking a nugget of courage from the animal's muscle and sweat. His ears rang from the violent clamor of hooves, squeaking leather, cursing men. When he stared beyond the mass of horses and soldiers, he saw nothing except winter grayed pines and brooding hills. Felt trapped by them. His throat and nose and lips were raw, scraped by the frozen air. He tried to look ahead, to where the others had pointed, for a glimpse of the Sioux war chief, but he rode in the middle, surrounded.

Next to him a soldier a few years older than himself clung to both his horse's mane and his too-slack reins. If the animal stumbled, the rider would be thrown and maybe trampled. Jed thought to yell a piece of advice, but now wasn't the time. Once they were back safe at the fort, he would take the soldier aside and show him how to ride.

Jed had all but been born on horseback; there'd been close to twenty head on his father's plantation. If the army hadn't issued him this broken down nag, he would be galloping beside Captain William J. Fetterman, chasing the small war party that had attacked a party of woodcutters earlier in the day. Instead, he was hampered by—

By himself. After all, he hadn't told a soul about the awards he'd won showing his father's fine Tennessee Walkers.

Because he was so damnable scared. Because it hurt too much to think of everything he'd lost.

The gelding wheezed again, the air around its muzzle clouding white. The sound came from deep in its thick chest, and Jed knew what that meant. His mount was blowing itself out. How much more the animal had inside him, Jed couldn't tell, but he knew it was not enough.

Someone shouted, a rebel yell. For maybe a half second he lost his fear, and in its place sprang a boy's memories of righteous southern men.

"Jed? Jed!"

He swiveled, still listening to his horse's breathing. Up behind him came Charles Grant, who always informed folks in no uncertain terms that he held no kinship with the president who shared the same last name. Charles was, by both their reckoning, no more than fifteen years older than Jed. Still, whenever Jed thought of him, Charles and his dead father nearly became one in his mind.

"What?"

"They're not putting up much of a fight."

" 'Cause they're stinkin' cowards!" Jed yelled back, full of uneasy courage.

"Maybe." Charles's breath billowed white, mixing with the spent air of eighty horses and men. "And maybe that's what Crazy Horse wants us to believe."

"What do you mean?" Careful not to get too close to the mount directly ahead of him, Jed ran his hand low on his horse's neck as if his warmth and youth and health might help keep the beast going.

"Maybe nothing. And maybe—" Charles stood in his stirrups and strained to see ahead. "Just don't close your eyes for one second, you hear? Those Injins start shooting and you find yourself a tree to hunker down behind."

"I can't do that. Captain Fetterman says we're—"

"The captain's a damnable fool!" Charles shouted, unmindful of those around him. "He thinks he can run through the Sioux single-handed. If they was that easy to kill, don't you think the army woulda done it by now?"

Nearby, someone laughed. Still, Jed wished Charles wouldn't talk that way about their commander. Charles had been busted at least four times because he wouldn't keep his opinions to himself. "It don't worry me none," he'd told Jed. "Long as the army keeps clothes on my back and food in my belly, I don't care what rank they slap on me."

Jed didn't either, but since he'd been seventeen for less than a month, it wasn't likely anyone was going to make him a general.

Besides, he had other things to worry about. His horse was dying. Maybe it already knew that; maybe it was still trying so hard to keep up with the others that it hadn't realized its heart was breaking.

Jed could tell the gelding what that sounded like. It came on the tail of a mother's sobs, a father's helpless curses, a boy's terror and despair and, then, bone-deep loneliness.

"On the third day of Christmas my . . ."

Lodge Trail Ridge was behind them. The relative flat of the wagon road beyond the fort had made it easy for the calvary to gain on Crazy Horse and his few thieving followers. Now they were approaching the fork of Pano Creek where—

Indians!

Everywhere!

Jed stared in disbelief, his ears nearly shutting down under the assault of hundreds of war cries. He yanked on the reins so hard that his gelding shuddered, then stumbled, tossing its head.

Men yelled as they frantically reined in and struggled to aim their rifles. Jed followed suit, not that killing one Sioux would make any difference, but he was being swept along by the frenzied action all around him. Out of the corner of his eye, he caught a glimpse of Charles, who suddenly looked old and vulnerable. When Jed fired, the unwieldy rifle kicked his shoulder; he couldn't tell whether he'd hit anything.

Sioux warriors, mounted and armed, their faces deadly with hate and war paint, kept shouting. The sound came from hell. Jed's head rang so, he thought it would split, and he desperately tried to remember his childhood prayers. He wanted to clap his hands over his ears and scream so he couldn't hear anything except his own voice and know he was still alive.

The ground rumbled under the assault of more than a thousand unshod hooves as the Sioux charged from where they'd been hiding. Near him, a man cried out and without looking, Jed knew he'd been hit.

Hit! Killed! *Now I lay myself down to sleep. If I should die—*

Fear lashed at Jed's belly. Already some of the calvary had dropped rank and were running hard out toward any and all cover. Mindless of his wrecked horse, Jed spurred it, even though he had no idea where he was going.

A second ago it seemed the Sioux had been sweeping toward them like a fast-moving hurricane. Now the savages were in the middle of the disorganized and frantic calvary, swinging clubs and shooting arrows. A warrior, his cheek painted with a jagged streak of lightning, was so close that Jed could see a gap where a tooth should be. The warrior was intent on a soldier frantically trying to reload. As Jed watched, the warrior lifted a spear over his head. Jed focused on a dark, unbelievably muscular forearm, heard a cougar-like snarl. Even before the spear was released, he knew it had been thrown with enough force to send the weapon through a man's chest.

A scream, a cry, an oath.

Helplessness and, not soon enough, death. *I pray my soul to keep!*

Jed's heart bucked frantically, as if trying to escape his chest. His arms had become so heavy he didn't think he could lift them. He needed to retch.

Charles! Charles would—

Sweat ran down his sides and back. If the icy wind cooled it, he didn't notice. His horse was moving without direction, lurching sideways as much as forward.

An army was supposed to be organized and proud. This one wasn't. When he saw a man jump from his wounded horse and start running, Jed could tell the man had lost control of his kidneys.

"God in heaven!"

"Run! Someone—the fort! Get help!"

As his horse's legs went out from under him, Jed felt a hot poker stab into his side. He stared disbelieving at an arrow that had somehow become caught in his uniform. When he tried to yank it away, he realized that his flesh, not the fabric, held the arrow in place. Bile rose inside him. His face flushed. He wanted to scream. Maybe he did, and just couldn't hear the sound for all the other screams.

His horse was on its knees now, head stretched forward, body shuddering. Jed stumbled off it, somehow holding onto both his side and his spent rifle. Every damn one of the Sioux was on horseback. Only a few had rifles, but it didn't matter because there were hundreds of them and the ambushed and terrified white men might as well have been unarmed.

Jed desperately wanted to see if someone was heading toward the fort for help, but from what he could tell, no one could think beyond trying to stay alive. Not knowing where he was going, he started running toward some low lying hills where there might be a tree or boulder to hide behind. His side had come alive with pain, yet fear kept it from overwhelming him.

The look on other pale faces, fury and stark terror, set his belly to grinding. These men had taught him how to curse and brag, that it was natural and right and manly to hate the Sioux. One had even eased a little of the loneliness inside him. Today, with the weak sun struggling to break free from a haze of clouds, the uniformed soldiers made him think of chickens routed by foxes.

Jed stumbled, surprised by his weakness, but managed to right himself. He'd just dodged to escape a riderless horse when something hit his leg and he pitched forward onto his knees. *Lord* . . .

For a moment he crouched with his fingers digging into the cold ground and his rifle half under him. Then, although the top of his head was threatening to explode with pain and he was scared to look, he did.

An arrow protruded from his right calf.

Lead me through the valley . . .

Thunderclaps of screams and curses and war yells rolled over him like a spring swollen river. He groveled on the ground, unmindful that he was tearing his nails on the rocks. He couldn't stop shaking, couldn't stop the puppylike whimpers coming from deep inside him. Finally, fighting dizziness and terror and helplessness, he rolled onto his good side and tried to blink away the red curtain someone had thrown over his eyes.

The Sioux hadn't gone away. Their sweat-streaming horses were so close that he didn't know why he hadn't yet been struck by a hoof. He saw underbellies and dark, naked legs and knew hell couldn't be any worse than this.

He must have touched either his leg or his side because his hand was wet with blood. This time he did retch. When it was over, he felt so spent that all he could do was lie next to his waste and try to remember how to breathe.

He'd just begun to lift his head when he heard a laugh. No. It couldn't be a laugh. Surely no one, soldier or savage, could find anything funny about this nightmare. But the sound must be awfully close for him to hear it in the midst of this. . . .

Someone grabbed his hair. He felt his head being yanked up and to the side and looked into the eyes—the eyes of hades. The warrior had painted his face black and red so that his white teeth stood out in horrible detail. He leaned so close that their noses nearly touched. Jed smelled the man's breath and sweat and hate. His own body was filled with the stench of fear. He struggled to free himself, but he was no stronger than a small child.

The warrior held a knife high in his free hand, making sure Jed saw it, then screamed something. Although Jed didn't understand the words, he knew he was being condemned to hell.

Didn't the savage know? This battlefield was hell.

As he continued to struggle both against the Sioux and his own terrifying weakness, the knife descended, slowly, tautingly. He was vaguely aware that men continued to fight and die all around him, but nothing mattered except that he was going to be scalped.

He screamed, tried to kick and bite. The knife touched his forehead so gently that he had a flash of his dead mother's caresses. The impression didn't last. The knife became pain.

His scream joined the hurricane of sound around him, loud enough, he prayed, that he wouldn't be able to concentrate on being scalped.

The savage laughed again. Jed felt blood run down the side of his face and frantically tried to wrench away. His wounded leg had no strength and his side was on fire.

Suddenly the savage's laugh turned into a gurgle, a funny, choked sound. Although he continued to crouch over Jed, he was no longer trying to scalp him. He gurgled again from deep in his chest, then shuddered and flopped almost gracefully onto the ground with his face plastered into the cold dirt. Jed saw that his naked back had turned red.

"Jed! You alive?"

He tried to answer Charles, tried to thank his only friend for saving his life. Instead, he whimpered and nearly threw up again.

Charles ran toward him, his rifle banging uselessly against his leg. He'd just begun to reach for Jed when his body spasmed as if a giant had attached ropes to his limbs. Charles stared at Jed and despite the heat and hell around them, for one, maybe two seconds there was only the two of them and terrible regret for what they'd never share.

Jed shouted when Charles crumpled to the ground. He'd known the Sioux was dying. Now he knew the same about his friend. Charles lay still, a pocket of quiet in this storm from the earth's underbelly. Despite the pain, Jed began dragging himself toward Charles. *God in heaven, please don't let this be.*

Only God wasn't on the battlefield.

Tears now dry, Jed stretched out his hand. He was too far away, couldn't touch . . .

Why . . . this dark . . . *on the fifth day of* . . .

Pounding hooves. Curses. Leather squeaking. So . . . so many hooves.

Were the Sioux back?

Concentrating, Jed opened his eyes. It took so much effort that he was forced to rest for several minutes, his vision still blurred. He smelled winter cold and blood. His body was both numb and so racked with pain that he felt as if he was drowning in a whirlpool of agony. He thought that his scalp had stopped bleeding but was too weak to lift his hand toward it.

The sound of approaching horses became a tidal wave, and he could no longer ignore it. Blinking over and over again, he managed to chase the film from his eyes. He lay with his head on a knot of ground higher than his body, which made it possible for him to see a great deal.

Charles hadn't stirred from his crumpled position. Because his mind refused to deal with his friend's death, Jed strained to make out the approaching horsemen.

"Oh my God! I don't believe—"

"It's not possible! God in heaven . . . "

The words were American. The horses now prancing nearby wore shoes. As the fear of even more Sioux coming to finish him off faded, Jed fought his body's weakness and managed to lift his head. His side and leg and head throbbed; he ignored them.

Soldiers from the fort had arrived. They were armed and if there were any murdering Sioux still here—

He didn't think so. Otherwise, wouldn't their hellish war cries be assaulting the air?

"They're dead. All of them."

No. Not all. I'm—please, not all.

He tried to sit up, but he'd lost too much blood. His head weighed at least a thousand pounds. Still, he refused to lie back down and die. "Help me." His words sounded like they came from a baby. He didn't care. "Please help me."

Someone on a dark, healthy breathing horse rode so close that he could see the individual hairs on the horse's fetlocks. The soldier dismounted and dropped to his knees beside Jed. "This one's alive!" the soldier screamed. "Where's the med' ? Get the—God, what happened?"

"Ambushed," Jed got out. "The others?"

"I don't know," the soldier said, not meeting Jed's eyes. "We came as soon as we could, but the devils were already gone. I pray—" He touched Jed's scalp and his face blanched. "Oh my God. They nearly—why didn't they finish?"

"Charles killed him."

"Charles?"

"My friend." *My friend.* "Look after him, please. Right over there. He's . . . "

The soldier was staring at Jed's leg now, and at the arrow still in it. Two other calvary men joined the first, their voices heavy with disbelief. Although they quickly knelt beside Jed, they kept looking around. Jed wasn't sure whether they were on the lookout for Sioux or if something closer held their attention.

Something in this nightmare from hell.

When they rolled him over onto his back, he sobbed. He wanted his mother beside him, his father holding his hand. He needed Charles ordering him to stop whimpering like a baby, Charles pouring brandy down his throat.

"It's a massacre. A—massacre."

"We'll get 'em. Hunt down the bloody devils and kill every one of 'em."

"Shut up! We ain't doing that right now. Soldier? Soldier?" One of the men poked his face close to Jed's and spoke loudly as if Jed was deaf, or dead. "We'll get you back to the fort. You're going to be all right, you hear? This was one time God—"

"God?" Jed barely got the word out.

"Yes, God," the man repeated, his head bobbing up and down, his eyes showing too much white. "The Lord was with you today, boy. Saved your life when all the others—saved your life. You can spend the rest of your years thanking Him."

Another man joined those around him. This one didn't waste time staring but immediately began cutting at his uniform. He thought he recognized the fort doctor, but his vision had started to blur again. "You listen to what Henry says, boy. Listen and be grateful. The Lord was surely riding on your shoulder today."

"God—had nothing to do with it." His voice was failing; maybe he was dying.

"You don't know what you're saying. He—"

"No!" He reared up, fell back gasping. "It's taken me seventeen—seventeen years to find out. But I know. Know . . . there's no God."

3

Morning nibbled at the edge of Luash's mind, but she pushed it away. She had been up most of the night, talking to old Aga about summers past, when the Modocs wandered from Goose Lake to distant Mount Shasta while hunting deer, antelope, and mountain sheep, about the sweet taste of wild plum and choke cherries and fields of camas waiting to be dug.

Now the woman lay near her snoring softly, twisted fingers curled under her chin. When she woke, they might talk again of when Aga's body was young and strong. But maybe Aga would be deep within herself, thinking of the death-sleep that waited for her.

Luash hoped there was yet more time for talking. Aga's memories of summer valleys filled with rabbits, sage hen, squirrels, and woodchucks were so vivid that they nearly made Luash forget the seemingly endless cold and her fear that she and the others would be forced back onto the reservation. There whites demanded they give up their ancient ways, ways her people had embraced from the beginning of time.

Warmed by the thought of harvesting water-lily seeds while standing in a sun-heated lake, Luash snuggled under her heavy blanket and listened to the wind's rhythm as it knocked gently against the large, crowded wickiup.

The sound put her in mind of a mother's humming as she rocked her baby. Once her own mother had sung to her like that, long before she knew the meaning of such words as *rancher* and *soldier*, long before she'd followed her mother's brother Chief Kient-poos and the other rebel Modocs back to this place. She'd grown up here, but the army men said it no longer belonged to them. Half awake, Luash pretended she was a newborn, secure and warm in her mother's arms, her belly full of milk, eyes drooping. . . .

Rifle!

She had bolted to her feet and was trying to kick away the deer hide still tangled around her before her mind made full sense of the sound. She heard others yelling, but in the gloom, she couldn't make out the individual figures of the four families that had found shelter under one roof. Aga called out weakly, but Luash couldn't concentrate on her because another rifle shot had followed the first, and then a third. Unconsciously, Luash ran her fingers from her forehead to the top of her head, along the streak of white hair that had been there since the first day Eagle touched her.

One of the braves hurriedly pushed aside the willow-bough door and let in a little of the dark winter morning.

"Soldiers," he announced flatly.

A woman sobbed. From out of the corner of her eye, Luash saw Nau'ki clutch her child to her breast. Aga muttered again, her voice thick.

Another brave joined the first; both began speaking rapidly. Because horses snorted and pounded the ground just beyond the entrance, Luash couldn't hear what they were saying. Not taking time to slip on her footwear, she grabbed her sleeping blanket and threw it over her shoulders.

Soldiers.

"Luash, don't!"

Ignoring Aga's warning, she hurried forward so she could stand in the doorway. Thick fog rolled in from the nearby lake, making it all but impossible for her to see beyond the hastily constructed, close-bunched village. Several other women pressed around her, and even though they shook and cried, she took comfort in their presence.

The braves stared at the armed men in uniform, who yelled and gestured. In three heartbeats, Luash realized the bedraggled look-ing soldiers were demanding to see the man they knew as Captain Jack, her uncle. Over and over again they insisted that if Captain Jack didn't show himself, everyone in the winter camp would pay. She wasn't sure what *pay* meant, just that it was a threat.

"He is not here," Cho-Cho, who the whites called Scarface Charlie, insisted. The brave's hands were knotted at his sides, and he shook his head from side to side as if not yet comprehending that a sleeping village had been surrounded. The large scar on his right cheek was pulled tight by his clenched teeth.

"You lyin' red skin," a soldier said in heavily accented Modoc. "Montgomery seen him just yesterday. Spotted him sneaking 'round his ranch; slaughtered one of his prime bulls."

"Montgomery is the one who lies."

If she hadn't been so uneasy, she might have laughed at the army man's reaction. His cold-whitened mouth tightened; he looked to be in danger of breaking his jaw and his big ears all but flapped. He shivered violently. "You better keep quiet, Scarface. Your squatting time's come to an end. Like it or not, you and the rest of this outlaw bunch is heading back where you belong."

She wasn't surprised by this. For months now, the army had been saying that those who followed Kientpoos had no right to win-ter here. But what else could they do? The Klamaths had all but chased them off their shared reservation. Kientpoos, Cho-Cho, and the others were men, not animals to be kept in pens. Neither were their families.

Although she didn't look behind her, she knew most of the women and children had joined her. They spoke in whispers, sounding more disbelieving than afraid. Someone said she couldn't remember seeing Kientpoos since yesterday. Luash thought he might have left Lost River with his old wife Spe-ach-es, but remained silent. She couldn't imagine speaking a word to the soldiers, some of whom had frost in their beards; all looked half frozen. Frozen and angry.

"We have told you this before," Cho-Cho was saying, "told your leaders why we came here. The army has not kept its word to make the Klamaths leave us alone. Until there are promises we can believe, we will not return to the reservation."

"The army doesn't make deals with renegades, Scarface." The man with ears too large for the rest of him aimed his rifle at Cho-Cho's chest. "If the rest of your people can live in peace with the Klamaths, your bunch can by God learn to do the same."

Cho-Cho spat, then expanded his chest as if daring the man to shoot him. His wife begin to cry. "The others are cattle, small burrowing animals. They have lost their hearts and their courage and no longer look at the world through the eyes of a Modoc. We have no need for them, no use. We—" Cho-Cho tapped his chest "—we are men."

"Men hiding behind their women's skirts. Damnit, where's Jack?"

"He is not here. Are your mule ears broken, army man?"

Even before the words were all the way out of Cho-Cho's mouth, the soldier's ears began jiggling again. Ignoring the warrior, he yelled for Captain Jack, then, in English, ordered the men with him to round up all the Modocs.

Luash watched, barely aware of her icy feet, as the shivering soldiers tried to herd the men, women, and children into a circle. Several of the women glanced anxiously at her. Whispering, Luash translated what the soldiers had said. Many of the women and children hurried back inside and flattened themselves against the underground dirt floors, where bullets would be less likely to find them.

From where she stood, she heard the army men arguing with Cho-Cho and the other braves; the argument seemed to go on forever, with the soldiers demanding the Modocs surrender their arms while the braves continued to refuse.

Across the meandering river, where the hot-tempered Ha-kar-Jim had his camp, Luash could hear a few more army men and some settlers trying to convince those Modoc to give up as well. When a scuffle broke out between Ha-kar-Jim and a white man, Cho-Cho and two other braves dove for their wickiups. They emerged a moment later, rifles in hand. Most of the soldiers simply stared; she wondered if they were so frozen that even their minds had filled with ice.

"Leave!" Cho-Cho ordered. "This is our land. You have no right!"

"Put that thing down, Scarface. You don't want to start a war," a deep-voiced man insisted. Luash didn't care who had issued the order; she knew it wouldn't be obeyed. Already, several braves had taken advantage of the fog and the disorganized soldiers to hurry out of sight. None of the armed braves fired at the army men, who didn't seem capable of making up their minds whether to chase the fleeing warriors or remain in the village.

One of the soldiers barked an order at her, and Luash felt hatred build in her belly. When Eagle first came to her, she hadn't fully understood what it meant to have white settlers and an army fort on land that had belonged to her people for all time. Now, six years later, she did.

It meant the end to freedom.

"You get going, now! You hear me, squaw?"

She wheeled, ready to fight, but the soldier was no longer speaking to her. Instead, using his horse's bulk, he'd backed Cho-

Cho's wife against the side of the wickiup. Angry, Luash hurried over, clamped her hand around the man's ankle, and yanked. "Do not call her squaw!" she warned in English. "Her name—"

"You think I give a damn what her name is?" He kicked out, but Luash was too fast for him. She ducked, then straightened. The man spun his horse around, looking as if he wanted to run her down. A rifle shot rang out.

"They're attacking!" one of the soldiers yelled.

Luash stared at the barely visible low hills where several of the soldiers were pointing but couldn't see anything. It seemed to her that the rifle blast had come from somewhere much closer, maybe from one of the army men themselves.

"Kill the thieving—"

One shot followed another, echoing in the icy air. Several dogs who'd cowered near the wickiups now ran among the prancing horses. Their excited yapping and growling caused two of the soldiers' mounts to buck and throw their riders. Luash saw several more Modoc men grab their weapons, watched in horror as the soldiers pushed their way through the knot of women and children to get to the armed men.

Three soldiers remounted and tried to crowd their horses into a single wickiup. When others joined them, even more braves ran for their houses. Moments later they emerged, rifles held in strong hands. They aimed at the closest soldiers, but instead of firing, began backing toward the corral that held the Modoc horses.

"Stop them!" the army man who'd been yelling for Kientpoos earlier bellowed. "Don't let 'em—"

Luash didn't wait to hear the rest. Ignoring her now frozen feet, she ducked behind several women. Taking advantage of the deep gray shadows, she managed to reach the corral without any of the soldiers spotting her. She unlatched the gate and held it open, yelling at the already nervous horses. They charged past her into the middle of the confusion and were quickly mounted by their

Modoc owners. As soon as the warriors were mounted, they began galloping toward the hills.

Cho-Cho was among the last to leave; somehow he'd taken advantage of the confusion and slipped past the soldiers who'd thought they'd trapped him. He extended an arm to Luash, indicating he wanted her to climb aboard behind him, but his horse was moving too fast for her to take a chance.

"Shoot! Stop—"

"No! Get the women!"

She whirled around, looking for whoever had spoken. At that moment she felt a horse push into her and lost her footing. On hands and knees, she stared up—up into a pair of deep gray eyes framed by long, windblown hair nearly as dark as hers. "Don't try anything, squaw," the man ordered. "Get with the others, now!"

She stood her ground, not because she was not afraid of him, but because she was protected by Eagle. She would not grovel before this soldier with hate in every line of his too strong body.

Although she felt as if she'd been speared by his dark glare, she took a moment to settle her blanket around her before slowly starting toward the few women and children the soldiers had managed to round up. Only when she was next to Nau'ki and her screaming baby did she allow herself to search for the braves. They were nearly out of sight, galloping hard for a willow thicket fed by a spring creek. In a moment the fog would hide them.

Several of the army men had taken off after them but were now turning around and coming back. Without exception, they looked to be at the end of their strength, their cheeks scraped red, eyes sunken. Even if they hadn't just finished the long, cold ride from Fort Klamath, they wouldn't want to risk being caught out in the fog by braves who knew the land's secret places far better than they ever would. Across the river much the same scene was being played out; she prayed that soon the two scattered villages would be able to join as one.

"We've got our orders," Wiggling Ears was saying in English. "And chasing after a bunch of half naked runaways isn't one of them."

"They shouldn't have gotten away. If someone had kept an eye on the horses—"

"I told Murray and Rich." Wiggling Ears looked around, then jabbed a finger at two men. "What the hell were you doing?"

Luash didn't listen to the answer. She cared nothing about foolish men who had ridden in to capture an entire village but instead had allowed armed and mounted Modoc warriors to slip away. As she waited, wondering what the soldiers planned to do next, she forced herself to look at each and every one of the mounted enemy.

Some of them she knew—at least she recognized their faces. She'd seen them when they came to the reservation and more frequently since Kientpoos's band left it and set up their village here. None of the soldiers had ever spoken to her except to try to buy her favors with trinkets and to call her names that brought back memories of what her mother had endured. She'd been careful not to be alone where one or more of them might grab her. Even now, several were looking at her in a way that made her flesh crawl.

Didn't these men, these strong and stupid soldiers, know she would kill them—or herself—before she let them touch her?

"I'm asking you squaws one more time," Wiggling Ears said in broken Modoc. "Where's Captain Jack?"

Where you can't touch him. It was all she could do not to laugh at Wiggling Ears's stupidity. Did he really think Kientpoos was huddled nearby, waiting to be found and dragged to Fort Klamath? "He will not speak with you," she told the soldier in her practiced English. "He has heard all he wants of army lies."

"He's got no business leaving the reservation. He knows that. Why he thought he could get away with it—come on, squaw. You and the rest of your people are only going to get yourselves into more trouble this way. Can't you see that?"

Although several of the women warned her to remain silent, she faced Wiggling Ears. Despite his obvious agitation, he shivered and tucked a hand under his armpit to warm it. In this weather, the journey from Fort Klamath must have taken most of a day and a night, leaving the soldiers so cold and hungry that the will to fight must have been frozen out of most of them. If this was what the army's leaders looked like, they would never bend the Modocs to their will. She would remember to tell Kientpoos that.

"I am not Squaw," she said forcefully. "My name is Luash. And before you came, *his* name was Kientpoos. I still call him that."

"Do you think I care?" Wiggling Ears urged his horse closer, but she refused to back away. She sensed that everyone was looking at her now, her people with love and concern, the army men with hatred and lust. "I'm tired of this nonsense. Listen to me, Luash. You tell your leader—whatever you call him—that his running, thieving days are over. All of you are going back to the reservation. I've got my orders."

Never. She wanted to throw the word back at the man, but she was only one against more mounted and armed soldiers than she dared take time to count. Just as she started to fold her arms over her chest, powerful fingers clamped around her wrist. Startled, she tried to jerk free, but the grip became stronger. She turned, thinking to order whoever had grabbed her to release her. The words died inside her.

She'd seen those dark gray eyes before. The man who'd called her squaw when she freed the horses was now staring down at her in a way she couldn't understand. A way that made her even more wary. "Get back in line," he ordered. "You want to stay alive, you do as you're told."

Ignoring the cold fingers that were now cutting off her circulation, she returned the soldier's unrelenting gaze. His short-whiskered face was young, only lightly touched by wind and winter, but his eyes had seen a great deal. Those experiences had made him hard and old before he'd had time to be a youth. The wind captured his long, black hair and lifted it off his forehead. She spotted a jagged scar at the hairline and without being told, knew how he'd gotten it. His hatred of her and her people must be part of his very soul; she would be wise never to forget that.

"You do not own my heart, white man," she told him in his own tongue, the lessons of the one settler she'd befriended serving her well. "Nor my body."

"You think you can hold off the United States Army? If you do, you're a fool."

"You are the one who does not understand." In her mind she saw Eagle. Even now he might be flying high overhead, hidden by morning clouds and mist, protecting her. "There are forces—"

The soldier jerked her arm in an attempt to herd her back to the other women. She glanced toward where the warriors had gone. As soon as they could, they would return and punish the man who wouldn't let go of her. The man who'd nearly been scalped once and carried that experience deep within him.

When she looked at her captor again, she saw that his attention was no longer on her but on several of the soldiers. As she watched, they picked up some branches that had been left near last night's council fire and plunged the ends into the smoldering coals until the branches burst into flames.

"What are you doing?" the man holding Luash demanded of Wiggling Ears in a voice so deep that his entire body seemed to rumble with it.

"Giving the squaws a choice. Either they tell me where Captain Jack is or their village goes up in flames."

"He is not here!" Luash struggled to keep her voice under control. "Do you not understand? You cannot—"

"Don't tell me what I can and can't do. I'm not going back empty-handed. You got that?"

"He is not here!"

"I don't believe you, squaw."

Why was she arguing with a man who would attack a sleeping village? Although Wiggling Ears continued to glare at her, she simply glared back, silent. Finally he cursed and yelled an order at one of the men who held a burning brand. The man started toward the nearest wickiup.

"No!" All the women shrieked as one. "No!"

"Get 'em out of here!" Wiggling Ears ordered. "They're going to march until their feet fall off if that's what it takes to get them back to the reservation. And when their men come looking for them, we'll disarm the bunch of them. Maybe then they'll understand the army means business."

"No!" Frantic, Luash struggled free and spun away from the man with eyes like a winter hawk. But she was too late. The wickiup burst into flames, dried brush and willow boughs easily catching fire. "No!"

Out of the corner of her eye, she saw another soldier hurry forward and plunge his flaming stick through the open door she'd come out of a few minutes ago. She'd already started to run toward where she'd left Aga when someone caught her from behind and held her against his hard body. "Aga!" she screamed. "She will—"

"There's someone in there?"

The gray-eyed man. "She is old and sick. She is too weak to escape!" She twisted from side to side, but freeing herself from this man's strength was impossible. Smoke filled her lungs; her eyes began to burn. She heard women and children crying, soldiers cheering.

"Damnation! Stop fighting! You can't help her!"

Stop? Let Aga die? No! Even as denial washed over her, she knew the man was right. The wickiup burned as if it had been made of dried pine needles and pitch. Unable to stop herself, she began to weep, shaking. She heard her captor's quick breathing and wondered if he'd somehow absorbed some of her horror.

The ragged sound of her sobs blended with the *snap* and *pop* of flames. She trembled in the soldier's all-encompassing grip and watched the wickiup turn into a mass of dark smoke and flames redder than an eagle's eyes. Aga's time for dying had come. No shaman would be called to her side. If the tribe moved on, she would be left behind. It was wrong. Death should be met with dignity, not in fear.

"No!" Spurred by the inferno before her, Luash began fighting again. "No!"

"Stop it!" The man squeezed tighter, his grip hard and insistent. "It's too late."

"Did you hear me, Jed?" Wiggling Ears demanded as he rode up. "I told you to get those women on the move."

"You don't outrank me, *Captain* Jackson. You don't even know what you've done, do you?"

"We've got those thieving Modocs on the run. They'll—"

"Unless she's lying"— he indicated Luash—"you just burned a woman to death."

"Serves her right."

The man called Jed swung around to face the other man. "Don't you *ever* question me again, Jackson."

Jackson jabbed a thick finger at her. "If you're taking that squaw's word—"

Luash felt herself being pushed forward. Her feet were numb; she nearly lost her balance and had to rely on the army man's bulk to keep her from falling. He was staring down at her, waiting for her to repeat what she'd told him. Still, she forced herself to remain silent until she'd gained control over her loathing of everything he stood for.

His eyes had indeed taken their color from the hawk. He seemed older now than he had earlier, but it might be a trick caused by flame-shadows, by what she'd learned from an old scar. She waited for him to demand more from her, to raise his rifle against her, but instead, he held her firmly in front of him and she returned his intense gaze until she forgot everything except his presence.

This man who wore his hatred like a war shield was trying to look inside her until he'd exposed her heart, until there was nothing she could keep from him. Didn't he know that a white man would never know certain things about a Modoc? Still, she had no wish to hide the truth from him.

Yes, she said with her eyes. *Yes. You have killed Aga. Robbed her of a dignified death.*

"Damnation."

"Are you listening to me?" Captain Jackson demanded, his voice a harsh intrusion. "We've got to get these women and children out of here before their braves return."

Jed's mouth settled into a hard, straight line like a cougar stalking its prey. She could see in his eyes that he wanted to say something neither man would ever forget or forgive and was struggling against those words. As he opened his mouth, flames shot up nearby. Cursing, he spun around, still dragging Luash with him.

A third wickiup had caught fire. Whether it had been set or sparks from other fires had reached it didn't matter. In that instant of distraction, she ripped free of his grip and sprinted toward the sobbing women. A burst of sound like something from the underworld drowned her cry as the flames spread to yet another house.

Some of the soldiers' horses, frightened by the quick-moving inferno, began to fight their numb-fingered owners. At the same time, rifle shots cut the air, telling her that the braves had stopped running and were firing at the soldiers. She grabbed a small girl so her mother could more easily carry the baby in her arms and raced toward the willows.

"Look out! The whole damn village's going up!"

She didn't care who the soldiers were yelling at. The only thing that mattered was that she and the others were running away from their burning homes, toward freedom. All except for Aga.

The little girl clamped her arms around Luash's neck with such strength that she could barely breathe. Her feet felt like stumps and she tried to keep from stumbling. She'd lost her blanket; the cutting wind sliced at her flesh.

Behind her the village the Modocs barely had finished building burned.

"Would you look at that! Just like tinder. Whoa! Whoa, damn you!"

"Let it burn. Serves 'em right."

Whoever said that laughed. He was immediately joined by others. Despite herself, she stopped running and whirled around. Although several soldiers glanced at the fleeing women and children, no one came after them. Instead, they watched the village burn and laughed.

A knife twisted in her heart, opened it to pain and grief and hate heavier than any emotion she'd ever imagined. The little girl started to sob, but what Luash felt went too deep for tears. She wanted to scream, to draw back a bow string and plunge an arrow into a white chest.

One man stood apart from the others, silent, staring at her instead of into the deadly flames. It was the too-strong soldier with the winter hawk eyes, the scarred flesh and soul.

The one called Jed.

4

No one could live in this godforsaken place where once the Earth had spewed its fiery innards over everything for miles around.

True, the first time he'd come out to the lava beds, he had spotted a couple of antelope nibbling on sage and the tough, sparse grasses that somehow found enough soil for their roots, proof that some kind of life could be sustained. But that had been a month ago, before he'd accompanied Captain Jackson and thirty-eight soldiers to Lost River on a fool's mission. Since his last visit, winter had set in for good, and as far as he could tell, even the antelope had taken off for more hospitable territory.

When his horse dropped its head in an attempt to drink from ice-encrusted Tule Lake, Lieutenant Jed Britton dismounted and climbed a nearby rise, his boots crunching on the few inches of frozen snow with every step. He stood, legs spread to counteract the uneven surface and strong wind, his breath drifting white around him.

He hadn't told anyone he was coming here, which might have been a mistake. But if he was going to comprehend the enemy and convey that comprehension to military commander of the Department of the Columbia, General E.R.S. Canby, he had to stand where the Modocs stood, listen to the same silence that wasn't silence at all. He had to stare into the naked horizon and try to grasp why the Indians clung to this nothingness. Besides, sometimes a man needed to get away from noise and confusion and endlessly unproductive so-called strategy sessions, even if it meant some distant warrior might spot him.

Jed fixed on the deceptively level land near him, looking for movement, for stealth, his nerves tuned to messages of danger. He concentrated so fully that he forgot the wind attacking his cheeks.

When he got right down to it, his life wasn't that important. Despite the deadly attacks on unsuspecting settlers that had taken place in the hours and days following the burning of the Modoc village, he wasn't running scared—unlike nearly everyone else. If the time to die came, he'd face it squarely, not cower like the terrified kid he'd been a lifetime ago.

Driven to absorb as large an impression of what was happening as possible, he hadn't taken particular pains to hide while making his way here from where the rapidly growing army forces were setting up near Crawley's Ranch in anticipation of further trouble. If any Modocs were nearby, there was no way he could hide because the terrain around the lake was so open. But if the scouts and settlers could be believed, the renegades were holed up in some nearby lava caves.

Still, was he, like his friend Wilfred said, courting death?

Instead of trying to find an answer to the question he'd been asking himself for years, he walked back to his horse and absently scratched the animal's neck. He ran his fingers up under the mane to warm them and briefly laid his cheek against a thick-haired, muscled shoulder. Unless he wanted to risk death by freezing, he'd keep the shaggy animal near him.

The damn fog had a choke hold on the lake, effectively hiding the geese and ducks he knew were out there, along with the eagles he'd noticed his first day in this part of northern California. The predators' voices, discordant and yet in harmony, echoed like cries from the underworld. The days had all run together in his mind, the miserable cold sweeping down off the mountain until he couldn't remember what it felt like to be warm. Longtime ranchers like John Fairchild said that sometimes the fog stayed for the better part of a month, all but blotting out the sun, and that a man better stop thinking about that if he didn't want to go crazy.

Jed would have to tell Fairchild it was already too late for him. He, a southerner, had no business—

Modocs! Even the name added to his restlessness and discontent. They were nothing but a small bunch of hard-headed braves—little more than fifty by most accounts—squaws, and children who'd defied a fort full of soldiers by walking off their reservation and squatting where the settlers didn't want them. If they'd been left alone at Lost River, or if either Major Green or Indian superintendent T.B. Odeneal had thought to warn the local ranchers before the attack on the winter village, he wouldn't be here, attempting to gather information to take to General Canby.

Since the disastrous attempt at rounding up the Modocs, a number of innocent and luckless ranchers had been brutally killed by revenge-seeking braves such as Hooker Jim, Curley Headed Doctor, and Slolux. Rumors ran rampant about what the widow Boddy had seen when she found what was left of her husband's body. Even Henry Miller, who'd long supplied the Modocs with food and ammunition, had been shot through the heart by bucks hell-bent on scalping every white man they could.

This desolate chunk of land should have been left to the buzzards. Instead, orders had gone out to send all available Oregon and California soldiers here. To subdue fifty braves? Damnation, didn't anyone know anything about fighting Indians?

Jed jammed his hands in his coat pockets and paced to the edge of the lake. The Black Hills. Sitting Bull. He could taste his need to be back there with Lieutenant Colonel George Custer and his troops, pitting himself against the savages who'd left him for dead. He knew how to fight Sioux; he'd go to his grave happy if he could run every last one of them into the ground.

He sure as hell didn't want to be stuck in the middle of this—what did the Modocs call it—the Land of Burned Out Fires. But he'd been ordered here by none other than Custer, who'd agreed with the secretary of war that those at Fort Klamath needed a seasoned Indian fighter acting as advisor while they dealt with the Modocs.

Jed had advised them, all right. He'd suggested surrounding the two small villages separated by an icy river, slipping in and grabbing the horses, sinking canoes so the Modocs couldn't take off across Tule Lake. But Colonel Green had been hell bent for sending Captain Jackson's troops straight into camp—and look what had happened. Worst of all, Jed's insistence that nearby ranchers be warned ahead of time had fallen on deaf ears. As a consequence, innocent men were dead and war was staring everyone in the face. Hopefully General Canby would heed Jed's argument that it wasn't too late to avoid more bloodshed, but with pressure coming from both area residents and the United States government, he wasn't sure.

When he turned from the lake to stare out at the seemingly endless lava flow, he had to admit the Indians had been right when they named the land what they had. If there was such a thing as Hades—which there wasn't—it would look like this.

Why in damnation had the Modocs taken refuge here? How were they going to keep from starving? All the army had to do was wait until the Modocs' empty bellies forced them out of hiding. That was what he intended to convey to General Canby.

Something pricked at the back of his neck and spine. With his rifle cradled in his arm, he stared into the winter gray afternoon. Nothing moved and he tried to tell himself he was a fool for feeling uneasy. Still, he hadn't stayed alive by being stupid. He wished he had a blacksmith's bellows. That way he could blast away the fog and know for sure if anyone was watching him.

Nearby, his horse searched for something to eat, his breath a white rhythm. He laughed in an attempt to force himself to relax. If anything was out there, it was probably no more threatening than an eagle.

An eagle or a woman.

The thought glided into him, not for the first time. As he'd done before, he tried to shake himself free, but she wouldn't go away.

She. Damnit, he shouldn't be thinking about the young squaw. All he'd done was stop her from running into the blazing shack. He'd wrapped his arms around her slender yet unbelievably strong body because he didn't want to see her, an Indian, risk her life. Just because her long hair had somehow touched his neck and throat and he'd felt her heart pounding against him didn't give her any call to leave something of herself behind.

Didn't she know he hated her kind and everything they represented? They'd killed the only person he'd given a damn about and scarred both his body and heart.

He should have let her go. What did he care if she turned into cinders and smoke? She hadn't wanted him to stop her, had fought like a wildcat—had left a part of herself imprinted on him.

No she hadn't! The only reason he couldn't get her out of his mind was that it had been too long since he'd so much as touched a woman.

Angry, he again concentrated on his surroundings. Not content with encompassing the lake, the fog had spread to the lava beds themselves. The thick, heavy mist, with its ability to muffle all sound, put him in mind of some great starving creature. If he wasn't careful, the fog would wrap around him and swallow him whole.

He looked down at his legs, surprised to see only a faint wisp instead of the monster of his thoughts. Damnit, what was he doing here? Just yesterday, he'd been with the other officers while they reviewed everything that had been done or remained to be done in order to insure the safety of the remaining ranchers. If they didn't do things right, folks like that slovenly, long-haired reporter H. Wallace Atwell would write more scathing articles about the army for the *San Francisco Chronicle* and *New York Herald* and half the world would know what was happening here.

He still couldn't believe it; here they were in the middle of hostilities with the Modocs and the damn reporters were writing down everything they said or did, getting much of it wrong.

"We don't have the rest of our lives," Jed had interrupted Lieutenant Colonel Frank Wheaton just this morning. "Give the Modocs one chance to come in for peace talks and if that doesn't work, we starve them out."

The colonel, who was the district commander, had glared and again reminded Jed that he was following orders from President Ulysses Grant and the secretary of war General Sherman—orders that often contradicted each other and changed constantly. In the meantime, Jed was stuck here with a brain full of knowledge of Indian fighting and no way to use it unless he managed to convince General Canby of his course of action.

Something caught his attention. After a moment he spotted an eagle gliding in and out of the fog, its heavy body floating effortlessly. The bird, in his prime by the look of his pure white head, hung over the blasted and burned landscape as if he owned it. What the bird found of interest, Jed couldn't say. Just the same, it was strangely comforting to realize there was a creature out there that didn't give a damn that fog and wind and cold could suck the warmth from the Earth itself. The eagle was partly shrouded in gray, so he couldn't be sure, but there seemed to be something on the top of its head, a thin, dark streak of some kind.

His horse pawed the ground and whinnied impatiently. "What's the problem?" he muttered. "Maybe you think that bird's going to take a bite out of you?"

When the horse started to wander away, he reached for the reins and held them in his numbing fingers. Once the weak sun set, he'd have to get to the dubious shelter of a tent before night froze his limbs. "We'll go back pretty soon," he whispered. "Soon."

The eagle had disappeared, not, he told himself, that he cared. Still, he couldn't help wondering where it had gone. He supposed it lived in one of the distant cliffs with others of its kind although the idea of birds of prey co-existing gave him pause. Maybe they were solitary creatures, like him.

The sound of the wind sliding endlessly down off the distant mountains seeped into him. The cold bore through his bones. Weary, his eyes blurred. He couldn't remember what it felt like not to be here, or why he'd been so damn eager to leave Crawley's Ranch, where army tents were cropping up like spring flowers. Even his horse seemed unreal, a dark, life-affirming chunk against a background of nothing.

Still, he couldn't make himself mount and get the hell out of there.

After tying his horse to a sage bush, he again walked to the lake. He squatted, his rifle still held in his right hand, and dipped his left fingers into the icy liquid that had been exposed by his mount's restless pawing. He didn't know if the lake froze clear over in the winter, but he wouldn't be surprised. What did the eagles and other birds do if they couldn't fish?

And why should he care whether some stinking eagle starved?

Something chased down his spine. Pulled to his feet, he spun around and started toward his horse, but before he could reach it, he caught a movement he knew wasn't a figment of his imagination.

He wasn't alone. Someone had emerged from a distant jumble

of rocks and was walking slowly, deliberately toward the lake. The person was so far away he couldn't tell if it was Modoc or rancher or soldier, just that the stranger wore a heavy cape of some kind.

The newcomer continued his purposeful steps. Twice, whoever it was looked toward him, but the glances didn't last long. Either the Modoc—if that's who it was—didn't set any more store by his life than Jed did, or the Indian's reason for reaching the lake made risking his neck worth it.

Jed brought his rifle to the ready position. He might be able to hit the intruder at this distance, but that would take as much luck as skill. If this was some chief, Jed would be doing the army a favor by sending one of the Modoc's leaders to the happy hunting ground.

Just the same, it didn't seem right to bring more death to this place that already felt dead.

The fur-draped newcomer reached the lake, faced into the fog, and slowly lifted his arms to the heavens. Long, dark hair streamed out behind the figure like a scarf.

A woman?

A Modoc?

Her?

Step by slow step, as if he was approaching a skittish antelope, Jed began closing the distance between them. She seemed unaware of his presence; maybe all she heard was the sound of ducks and geese, who had been chattering for several minutes. He hadn't gone far when something high above the woman caught his attention. The movement quickly sorted itself into an eagle. Motionless, not believing, he could only stare.

It *was* an eagle, maybe the one he'd seen earlier.

As the great raptor dipped lower, he nearly cried out a warning, but if the woman wanted to become eagle food, that was her affair.

When he started walking again, his progress was even slower than before, not, he told himself, because he didn't want to disturb the woman and bird, but because until he knew what was going on, he'd be a fool to take chances. Twice he glanced behind him to make sure his horse hadn't been spooked by the creature. When he turned back to the woman, she was staring at him, her wide stance a silent warning.

She didn't want him to come closer. Well, that was just too bad. After all, he was the one carting a loaded rifle.

The eagle had wheeled away and the fog had swallowed it. Now it returned, its flight bringing it much closer to the woman. Instead of ducking or trying to run, she extended her arms even more. He thought he heard her say something, but the other birds were now making so much noise that he couldn't be sure.

He stopped. Once again, the eagle soared away, but not back into the fog. Instead, it seemed to be playing with a breeze, momentarily distracted from the woman. She stood, still and patient, her hair floating weightless behind her.

Her robe slid off her back and landed in a heap on the ground, but she didn't seem to care. She wore some kind of fiber shift that ended at her calves, leggings, and some kind of moccasins as protection against the cold. The wind flattened the shift against her breasts and waist and hips, revealing a young, slightly built woman whose body nonetheless had enough substance to carry a child.

For the third time, the eagle pulled its wings close to its body and descended—slowly. The woman threw back her head and stood on tiptoe, actually calling the huge bird to her.

Fine. Let it kill her.

Only that wasn't going to happen.

The eagle dipped one wing toward the ground, nearly touching rock and soil and hiding the woman from view. Trembling a little, Jed sucked in a breath but couldn't remember how to let it out. That damn bird was bigger than the woman, at least it was if its wing span was taken into account. And yet she'd walked out into the open so she could call it to her.

Call it to her? Impossible! Yet, he couldn't shake the thought, the growing conviction that that was exactly what was happening. He needed to blink, to turn and walk away, damned himself for believing what he was seeing.

The bird didn't long remain hovering over the woman. Before its heavy body could pull it to the ground, it soared upward again, seeking freedom and mobility in the sky. The woman laughed, the sound soft and alive.

He lost track of how many times the young Modoc and the bird of prey danced their impossible dance. He marveled at the eagle's agility, which defied both gravity and logic. Yet, that paled before what he was learning about the nameless Modoc. She loved the eagle; there was no other way to express the bond between them. The joy in her laughter, the enthusiastic way she reached out to briefly caress a wing, made him rawly hungry to experience the same thing. She lifted her face so she could feel the press of air the eagle pushed toward her, and he envied her. Once her long fingers brushed the eagle's head as if tracing the ribbon of dark against a white background. A moment later, she caught a strand of her own hair and he saw that in the middle of that black mass was a thin, white streak.

Eagle and woman, sharing—sharing what?

"Go! Fly free! Take my gratitude and heart with you."

He hadn't heard her speak before. The sound was as musical as her laugh, strong, filled with life. And she was speaking English; for his sake?

"Eagle. I thank you."

She wasn't shrieking with helpless disbelief today, but he knew that voice. This *was* the woman he'd prevented from running into the burning hut. The one who'd been hovering at the edge of his emotions ever since.

Although she continued to stare after the eagle, the creature didn't return. Finally, she reached down for her blanket, wrapped it around herself, and faced him. It was then that he saw she held a large, dark feather in her bare hand.

He must have come closer without knowing it because he could now look into her big, dark, shining eyes—eyes alive with a message so deep he couldn't begin to understand. She didn't say anything, but her stance told him everything he needed to know.

She wasn't afraid of him or the weapon he held. But neither was she comfortable with his presence. She simply watched; there was no other way of describing it. He wondered if she would try to run if he charged her. Maybe. If her long legs were any indication, he would be hard pressed to overtake her. And if he aimed his rifle at her—he almost did that just to see what her reaction would be, but he'd been privy to something incredible between her and the eagle and didn't want to ruin the impossible thing they'd shared.

"What are you doing here?"

Her English was accented, but he had no trouble understanding her. "I have every right," he shot back, surprised because he suddenly felt defensive.

"This is Maklaks land, Modoc land. It has been since the beginning of time."

"Not anymore, squaw."

She straightened, pulling her blanket closer against her. "You do not call me squaw, white man."

He nearly told her he could call her whatever he wanted, but if he did, they'd argue and that wasn't what he wanted. "What's your name, then?" he asked, when what he wanted was an explanation for the impossible thing he'd just witnessed.

She didn't answer right away. He sought through his memory,

trying to remember whether he'd ever had an honest to goodness conversation with an Indian woman. He didn't think so. "Do you remember me?" he asked. "At your village—I stopped you from burning to death."

She shook her head, her eyes seeming to fill with wisdom and beliefs he couldn't grasp. "Aga would have left this world in peace and dignity if the army had not attacked sleeping women and children. I will never forget that. And yes, I remember you, white man."

The way she said the last two words made them sound like a slap. Jed knew she didn't want him to come any closer, and because he didn't want her running away—for reasons he couldn't begin to understand—he stayed where he was. "I'm Lieutenant Jed Britton of the U.S. Army."

"Jed Britton. Lieutenant Jed Britton." She tapped her chest. "Luash."

Luash. The name was music, a whisper on the wind. "That's your Modoc name. What do settlers call you?"

"I have no other name, white man."

"Not white man. Jed."

Something that might be a smile touched her lips. "Do you understand?" she asked. "You are called one thing, and want no other name. It is the same for me."

So he'd blundered. It was just that the settlers and soldiers had given the Modocs names, names like Captain Jack, Hooker Jim, Shacknasty Jim, and Curley Headed Doctor. "Luash." Jed tried out the word, liked the way it felt on his tongue. "Does it have a meaning?"

"Mist."

That fit. "Who named you?"

"I did."

"You did? Not your father?"

"My father does not own me, Lieutenant Jed Britton."

"Your husband?"

"I have no husband."

Not married? But she was fully grown. Most Indian girls took a husband shortly after their puberty ritual—at least that's how things used to be. Nowadays, with everything changing for the Modocs, he wasn't so sure. Maybe her husband had been killed or had run off with another woman. No. Not that. A man would have to be crazy to want a different body to curl up against.

"What are you doing here?" he asked, remembering he wore the uniform of the U.S. Army, or at least most of a regulation uniform. "I could have killed you, you know."

"No. You cannot."

No. Were her menfolks hiding nearby, waiting for him to make a wrong move? Slowly, cautiously, he lifted his rifle until it was aimed at the ground just ahead of her. "It's loaded."

"Is that what you do, Jed Britton? You kill a Modoc simply because she speaks to you?"

"A lot of folks would call me a hero if I did." He took a frigid breath. "You and that eagle. What was that about?"

Luash had been waiting for the now clean shaven, too broad-shouldered soldier to ask her that. She shouldn't tell him, at least not give him an answer that came from her heart. Yet she spoke honestly. "Eagle and I are one." She touched the mark Eagle had left on her, and then indicated the feather her spirit had gifted her with today.

"One? What are you talking about?"

"You will never understand. You do not belong here, Lieutenant Jed Britton. This is my people's land; it does not want you standing on it."

"I hate to tell you this, but rocks don't give a damn what happens to them."

He was wrong. Kumookumts had created everything, even the smallest piece of sand. But whites believed in other things. They spoke of God and Christ, of a woman called the Virgin Mary. Many reservation Indians had turned their backs on their ancestors' teachings and prayed to the white man's gods, but she never would.

Not with Eagle spreading his wings over her.

"You are so wise that you know everything?" she threw at him, not sure why she was standing here with the cold buffeting her instead of returning to her people. "If that is so, then surely you know why Eagle came to me."

"If I knew that, I wouldn't be asking, would I? It makes no sense."

Why had she let him see her meeting with Eagle when she'd always believed that only her people should know of what existed between her and her spirit? When she first spotted the soldier, she hadn't been sure he was the man from the morning of the attack, but it hadn't taken long for her to recognize him. And that, for reasons she didn't understand, was why she'd still lifted her arms to the sky and answered her spirit's silent call. "You are not Maklaks—Modoc. You will never understand."

"Maybe," he said after a silence that lasted so long she stopped being comfortable with it. "What I do know is that what I saw couldn't happen."

"But it did."

"Yeah. It did." There was an expectancy to his voice and she knew he wanted her to explain. But what happened between her and Eagle was for them alone. She'd given the lieutenant all she could, more than she should have. Enough that he would be forced to acknowledge the truth about someone he considered little more than an animal.

Maybe that was why she'd let him see Eagle, why she'd spoken in English.

He hadn't taken his eyes off her, but his rifle now hung by his side. His knuckles were white, and he shivered slightly. If Eagle touched him, he would be able to better withstand the winter, but of course that would never be.

"This rebellion of yours isn't going to work," he said when neither of them had spoken for a long time. "There isn't a chance in hell that a handful of Modocs can hold off the army, especially one that has the government behind it, as behind as they ever get that is. You'll starve."

"We were starving on the reservation."

"If you'd gotten along with the Klamaths—"

"Could you do that, Jed Britton?" she interrupted. Rage flowed through her like fire; she didn't try to stop it. "If you were forced to live in the same valley with the Modocs, would you put down your rifle and your hate and sit with them? Would you embrace those who have turned their backs on their ancestors, the old ways?"

"If it came down to that or dying . . . "

"If you say you can make your peace with my people, I will believe you lie."

Jed shook his head. "It's the Sioux I'll never forgive."

She'd heard of the Sioux, a warlike tribe that had long defied white man's government and army. But the Sioux were far away. What did this man care about them? "Is that why you are here? Because your hate for the Sioux is so strong that it might kill you if you remain near them?"

His features darkened, and in his narrowing eyes, she realized he was closing a part of himself off from her. "What I do or don't feel for the Sioux is none of your concern."

"You make what is happening here your concern. Why can it not also be the other way?"

He glared at her; his fingers tightened around his rifle until his bones showed. His breath escaped in a steady stream. Still, she didn't regret saying what she had. "Before the settlers came, Modoc and Klamath walked in a wide path around each other. We cannot do that anymore. Instead, we are told we must lie down together. We are told we must learn to write and read the white man's words and forget our own. That we should build houses, no longer live in wickiups. That our ways are wrong."

"I don't make the laws. I'm simply here to carry them out."

The gray in his eyes seemed lighter today than when they'd first met. Still, there was nothing soft or giving about the man. The white, jagged scar over his right temple seemed a natural part of him, a memory proudly carried. He was, she sensed, someone who had learned not to trust or care. She couldn't imagine wanting to be like that. They were nothing more than strangers staring at each other across a deep canyon. And yet she'd let him see what no white man had before—her and Eagle together.

"You never question those laws?" she asked, wondering why she cared about his answer.

"Oh yes, I question. But not on this."

"You believe the Modocs have no right to the land where their ancestors' ashes are scattered? That the yainax—the mountains and valleys and streams and lakes created for us by Kumookumts— are no longer ours?"

"If this Kumookumts is your deity, I can tell you, he doesn't exist."

Suddenly angry, she threw back her shoulders and refused to blink despite the cold weather. "You have never heard of the Creator and what he did and yet you say he does not exist. How can that be?"

"Because I know what I'm talking about."

She watched his hard and expressive eyes and waited for him to break the silence. He didn't. "You are as wise as Grizzly?" she asked.

"Grizzly? Another of your so-called deities? Look, unless you ever lose everything and everyone you care about, unless you're so scared you think you're going to die and you pray until you can't pray anymore and those prayers aren't answered, until that happens to you, don't tell me what to believe or not to believe in."

She hadn't known he had that much anger in him, yet now that he'd opened himself to her, she realized she'd sensed the rage lurking deep in his eyes. "You are a bitter man, Jed Britton."

"If I am, it's because I have a right."

"You have a right not to believe in anything beyond yourself?"

"A reason. A damn good reason." He glanced up, drawing her attention to the fact that the weak winter sun would soon slide out of sight. The unseen birds continued their ceaseless noise, would sing through the night and join their voices with those of the owls. "Look, I've got a piece of advice for you to take back to Captain Jack."

"Kientpoos."

"What?"

"All his life he was called Kientpoos—until the ranchers and soldiers gave him another name."

"Whatever." He shrugged. "You tell him this. There's no way, absolutely no way the Modocs can hold off the army. We'll run over you—starve you out—"

"You are wrong."

"No I'm not. Do you have any idea what a howitzer is? As soon as they get here, they'll blow those beds apart."

"Can a howitzer fly?"

"What?"

"I have seen the army's cannons. They are foolish weapons. What will you do? Put them on wagons and pull them over endless sharp rocks? Your wagons will break down; your horses' legs will shatter."

"Then maybe we'll just wait until the Modocs run out of water."

Thinking of the ice river trapped underground but accessible from one of the caves, she nearly allowed herself a small smile.

Melted, the ice would supply enough water for everyone. But Jed was right about one thing: if the army prevented them from hunting and foraging, the Modocs would have to surrender.

That was why she'd sought Eagle today. Only a shaman could heal and protect. But although Cho-ocks was doing magic so the Modocs would have the power to defeat their enemies, Luash had needed Eagle's message. Her spirit had blessed her as he'd done so many times before and she prayed she had her answer. Eagle's strength and courage meant the warriors would continue to feed their families' bellies.

"You are very sure of yourself, Jed Britton. Perhaps I will take you back with me and the Modocs will make you our chief. When you say all should surrender, they will not argue."

"Only if you explain why the hell your warriors slaughtered innocent ranchers."

"I do not know," she whispered, suddenly wishing she didn't understand a word of what he was saying.

"What's the matter, Luash? Don't tell me you think your people were wrong?"

"Not all my people," she said with her head held high. "Only a few braves who took their anger and turned it into revenge."

"A few? Rumors are that every Modoc man was in on it."

She wasn't sure what the word *rumor* meant. What she did know was that she couldn't let Jed think revenge ruled everyone. "That is not so. Only—" She wouldn't tell this army man who was responsible. "Only—a few."

"Curley Headed Doctor. Slolux. Hooker Jim. That's the stories anyway."

"Cho-ocks, not Curley Headed Doctor. Not Hooker Jim, Ha-kar-Jim. They acted alone, without Kientpoos's blessing."

"Maybe. Maybe not." He shifted his weight, the movement startling her. "Damnit, the army isn't going to let these killings go unpunished. The only way you're going to save your necks is by sur-rendering."

"Is that what you want to do? Force me to go back with you so your leaders will call you a great warrior?"

His mouth twitched, but she couldn't tell whether she'd angered or amused him. As she'd done before, she waited for him to say something. Instead, he looked at her with his gray, deep eyes until she no longer saw his rifle and uniform, until he became nothing except a man—tall, strong, and straight, blessed by sun and wind and rain.

Shaken, she tried to make her legs turn and run, but the fog had wrapped itself around them and she couldn't move. Couldn't tear her gaze from his.

He was a soldier, a man who hated who and what she was, and yet today, she couldn't make herself hold onto that.

His arms were filled with strength. His voice carried power and determination. He came from a world she didn't understand, had seen and done things she never would.

But he was a man; this winter blasted afternoon, nothing else mattered.

"Why aren't you afraid of me?"

"Maybe I am."

"If you were, you'd be back among those rocks. You knew I was out here; still, you came."

"Eagle was waiting for me."

"Eagle? That doesn't make a damn bit of sense." He drew his fingers through his hair.

"Because you do not understand."

"There's nothing to understand! Look, I don't believe any of that nonsense about what's his name, Kumookumts, so don't try to tell me he had something to do with what that bird did."

"If not Kumookumts, then who?"

He didn't answer, but in his silence she found his unspoken reply. He had no explanation. "Ask your own god, Jed. Maybe that is who sent Eagle to me."

"I don't have any god."

Although he'd thrown the words at her, she sensed an awful loneliness behind them and wanted to know what had happened to bring him to this. But if she asked for the truth, he might not be satisfied until she'd given him the same thing—told him about a despairing girl in search of something, anything, and how that call had been answered.

She didn't know him well enough for that, would never trust him with what was in her heart. "No god? Then I feel sorry for you," she said.

"Don't!" he spat and lifted his rifle.

She stared at the deadly weapon. "Why do my words anger you so?"

"You don't understand, do you? You and I are at war. Nothing else matters."

She didn't say anything, didn't move, hung onto a spent breath long after she should have released it. *At war.* He might be wrong about a great many things, but in that he spoke the truth. Why then had she revealed herself to him and let him see what was private to her?

The answer she'd given herself earlier slipped off into the fog. She cared nothing whether others of his kind ever understood what it meant to have a Modoc heart.

Only he mattered.

And she didn't know why.

5

The everlasting wind slapped noisily at canvas. Tents that had been erected only a few days ago already were covered with snow crystals and debris. Smoke and sound hung in the air as if incapable of escaping the frozen earth. Despite the large number of soldiers, volunteers, and reservation Indians, there was surprisingly little movement as most of the men clung to what heat they could get from the campfires dotting their night-darkened world. From a distance, the still-growing army camp looked like silver and gray blisters protruding from the flat land, vulnerable despite their number.

Troops were being sent from everywhere to help quell the hostilities. Their sheer number was responsible for the sense of disorganization, the lack of unity. The Twenty-first Infantry, all the way from Fort Vancouver, was still resting up from its arduous journey through rain and mud. The weary soldiers muttered that they'd better not have to spend much time here, cursing the miserable conditions, the bone-chilling cold.

Rancher Oliver Applegate, who'd argued that there hadn't been enough troops to force the rebel Modocs to leave Lost River, and had been proven right, had organized sixty-eight men on his own, most of them Warm Springs Indians, who camped as far from the troops as they could. Obviously, they trusted the soldiers as little as the soldiers trusted them. Volunteers from local ranches had come to guide soldiers unfamiliar with the area. So far, all they'd done was sit and wait, none too patiently.

A couple of times, Modocs had ventured so close to Crawley Ranch that their taunts had rankled everyone within earshot, but Lieutenant Colonel Wheaton had given strict orders not to engage in battle before the campaign began in earnest. In the meantime, men waited and grumbled and cursed both the damnable weather and Captain Jack's Indians.

His head down to protect his eyes, Jed walked from the hastily erected rope corral where he'd left his horse toward the filthy, oversized cook tent. From the looks of things, the other officers and most of the enlisted men had eaten already, which meant he'd have to be content with whatever the cook scraped from the bottom of the pot, but years of army food had hardened his belly. What he needed was strength, not a culinary experience. After the silence of the lake, the din caused by too many voices, carelessly handled weapons, and livestock set his head to pounding.

There was no design to the military camp. Everything from bedrolls to stockpiled ammunition had been dropped carelessly wherever the whim struck. Jed slowly threaded his way around the many knots of men and equipment. A number of them looked up at him expectantly, pausing in the middle of their endless card playing. Obviously, they'd identified him as an officer and were hoping he'd have some information to impart to them. He didn't, and kept walking.

Although his mind felt overloaded from trying to make sense of what lay all around him, the sounds, the heavy smell of smoke and unwashed bodies, a movement to the side caught his attention. Second Lieutenant Wilfred Ellenshaw, a long, lean rope of a man half hidden under a heavy wool coat motioned for Jed to join him near one of the campfires. When Jed reached him, Wilfred handed him a tin plate with a meat and potato stew rapidly cooling on it.

"I saw you ride in," Wilfred explained. "Thought I'd better grab you something while there was something to grab. Don't ask me what the meat is. It tastes like old dog. My grandfather could cook better than this and he nearly starved to death after my grandmother died. You missed yet another strategy session, this particular one about whether we can spare enough men to place guards at all the ranches hereabouts. Lieutenant Wheaton's so upset over what the ranchers are charging for grain and hay that he doesn't much care whether they get any protection."

Jed leaned forward and let the fire start to warm him, glad that he and Wilfred were a small distance from most of the activity. He stared through the gloom at the officers' tents but saw no sign of movement there, just the shadowy flickering of lanterns burning inside. "I've heard. They're asking more than enough, and the grain's not that good."

"It's a crime, that's what it is. It doesn't help things that the ranchers are nervous and angry as hell. They aren't going to hold with being put off much longer and aren't interested in hearing that there's no saying when those two howitzers and more ammunition are going to get here from Fort Vancouver. They just don't understand what it takes to support an army."

"So that's what the session was about, trying to appease the ranchers?" Taking his attention from the tents, Jed studied the horizon, or rather what he could see of it in the dark, which was damn little. Crawley's Ranch had been built in a small meadow with a creek running through it. There'd once been a number of trees. Now nothing remained except for stumps, one of which he was sitting on.

"Mostly. They also want the army to explain why so few soldiers were sent to round up the Modocs. Wheaton has started an inquiry, but I doubt if that's going to satisfy anyone. Major Green keeps pointing the finger of blame at that Interior Department Superintendent Odeneal, and Captain Jackson says he was just following orders. They're both trying to protect themselves, never mind the truth. Where you been?"

Jed wanted to shrug off the question, but Wilfred would only keep after him until he had an answer. "If I'm going to see General Canby, I want to be able to give him as clear a picture of the situation as possible. I decided to look things over." It was still noisy, men shouting, horses milling about, the clang and clatter of weapons and other possessions. He needed the lake's silence—a silence that in reality was something else.

"What things? Where?"

Jed stabbed a potato chunk and popped it into his mouth. The indistinguishable meat had already begun to congeal, the fat as pale as the potatoes. What, if anything, was *she* eating tonight? "The lake."

"Clear around by the lava beds. That's what you're saying, isn't it?"

"Yeah."

"Are you looking to get yourself killed?" Wilfred asked heatedly. He leaned back as the wind swirled smoke around him. "Or if not that, busted? I don't suppose you told Jackson where you were going."

"No need. If I see him before I take off tomorrow, I'll give him my impressions."

"Sure you will; you and Captain Jackson are that thick." Wilfred snorted. "Especially after you called him out. You and he nearly came to blows during the attack, unless you've forgotten."

"I haven't."

Wilfred snorted again; it turned into a brief coughing spell. "Then you tell Lieutenant Wheaton he's a fool for spending so much time with those damnable reporters and he starts muttering he wishes you'd never been sent here. Now you're riding out alone like you're asking the savages to take a shot at you. What is it? You think you've been alive too long?"

"Look, my ultimate responsibility is to General Canby. He can't be here right now. He's depending on me to keep him informed. That includes letting him know what I think of what his officers are doing, or not doing."

"Even if that means alienating Jackson and Wheaton and a half dozen others?"

"Maybe so." Jed stared at the other man. "What do you care? You're not my father."

Wilfred swatted at the smoke still circling him. "Thank God. And even if I did have kids, they wouldn't be as old and ugly as you."

Jed ignored that. "Any update on when the howitzers might arrive?"

"What do you think? I've gotten so tired of hearing different answers that I've stopped asking." He coughed again and stood up. "My opinion? No one knows. But when and if the guns do get here—"

"It isn't going to make a lick of difference."

Wilfred glanced around as if making sure no one overheard, then sat down as the smoke spiraled upward. "What makes you say that?"

"The land; look at it. It's too rough and rugged. We'll never get the cannons close enough to where the Modocs are holed up to do any good."

"You tell Wheaton that. I'm sure as hell not going to."

"He won't listen. I've already tried," Jed said, as what he'd told Luash about the big guns settled inside him. She hadn't been afraid of howitzers. When he tried to impress her with talk of their power, she'd said exactly what he just had.

But then, nothing seemed to frighten her.

For several minutes Wilfred sat beside him while firelight painted his friend's features, his attention seemingly on the nearest campfire, where a number of enlisted men sat huddled close to what heat they could get, but Jed knew what was coming.

"I thought you might have asked me along," Wilfred muttered. "We practically go back to the beginning of time, you know. Or maybe you think you're invincible now that you're a hot shot advisor riding on Custer's coattails. A twenty-three-year-old first lieutenant. Next thing, they'll make you general."

Jed ignored that. Although their individual assignments often separated them, the friendship that had begun six years ago—when Wilfred had kept him from bleeding to death after the Fort Kearny massacre—still held strong and had resumed quickly when the two of them wound up at Fort Klamath. Jed knew Wilfred continued to mourn his bride, who'd been dead for almost ten years, and would go to his grave regretting that they hadn't had time to become parents.

Wilfred, who'd been with the troops who'd found Jed and his dead companions, had done more than bind his wounds. He'd held Jed for nights afterward when the younger man's nightmares threatened to tear him apart. Neither spoke about the past, but they were bonded in ways no one else would ever understand. Having a friend here felt good.

Jed grunted and shifted his weight in an attempt to find a more comfortable position and watched, bemused, as a surprisingly well fed looking dog wandered close, sniffed in the direction of his plate, then turned away. He'd seen the lop-eared mutt before and knew it belonged to the Crawleys. Obviously one member of the Crawley family didn't mind having his land overrun by strangers.

The corralled horses were moving restlessly about and their collective breath made the air around them look like a low hanging cloud. Jed took it as proof that they hadn't been fed, yet another sign that the whole operation was disorganized. If he knew General Canby as well as he thought he did, the Civil War veteran would insist on returning from Yreka with him so he could oversee the operation. "I didn't tell you where I was going because I needed to concentrate on this miserable stretch of nothing. I wanted to try to figure out why anyone, Indian or white, ever laid claim to it. If you'd been along, I'd have had to listen to you yap about nothing."

"Nothing? If it wasn't for me, boy, you wouldn't know enough to stay alive. You're crazy. Poking around looking to see if you could get an arrow in your back."

"Not likely an arrow. I'm guessing every one of those braves has a rifle."

"Probably." Wilfred dug at the frozen earth with his cracked and worn boot. "So, what did you see?"

"Nothing."

"You were out there all day looking at nothing?"

So he hadn't fooled Wilfred. It wouldn't be the first time. "Actually, I found a rich plantation tucked away in those miserable rocks. Hot, humid air, a rich cotton crop. Fine ladies in hoop skirts and parasols."

"Will you shut up!" Wilfred picked up a log and tossed it onto the fire. Sparks spat in all directions. "It's bad enough being stuck here without having you going on about God's country. Nothing, you say. What were you doing all those hours then, looking for a send-off to the happy hunting ground? Disappointed because no one accommodated you?"

Wilfred knew the answer to that, better than Jed wished he did. Although Jed didn't go out of his way to court death, neither was he like a lot of the men around them, shaking in their tents, if they were lucky enough to have one, scared sick they'd wind up scalped. When men asked—when they stared at the scar that angled up into his hairline and figured out how it got there—he told them scalping wasn't the worst thing that could happen to a body, but they didn't believe him. Most times they said the Sioux had lifted his brains along with his hair.

Maybe they had.

"You know what it's like near the lake," he said. "Flat and tree-less. I'd have to be blind not to see an Indian approaching."

"There's blind and then there's just plain stupid." Wilfred eyed Jed's plate, then grabbed a piece of fat laden meat between thumb and forefinger and jammed it into his mouth. He chewed for the better part of a minute before swallowing with a grimace. "We've got three so-called cooks now, not a one of them worth a lick. Did you see anyone?"

"A woman."

Wilfred whistled, then, slowly, his expression turned to one of disbelief. "What woman's going to be wandering out there where the Modocs could grab her? Even a whore's got more sense than that. You've been drinking too much of that week-old whiskey." He indicated a knot of men who were passing around a jug with no concern for whether an officer saw or not.

"A Modoc woman."

That, finally, put Wilfred at a loss for words. Jed stared at the firelight until his vision blurred and he couldn't remember the color of anything except red. "And she wasn't alone."

"Her brave was with her?"

"No. An eagle."

"An eagle? What the hell are you talking about?"

I don't know. "I'm just telling you what I saw." *Maybe that way it'll start to make some kind of sense.* He ate, no longer tasting.

"Are you going to tell me the rest?"

"There is no rest. While she was standing there, this eagle flew over her."

"The hell you say."

"Then it came back, so close she was able to touch it."

"The hell you say."

"She talked to it, laughed with it. As long as she wanted it there, it stayed around."

"The hell you say."

Jed glanced at what was left of his meal—if it could be called that—put down the plate, then went back to staring into the fire. Out of the corner of his eye, he spotted a hay wagon being pulled into place near the corral. The horses' restless movements became almost frenzied. "Believe me or not. I don't give a damn."

Wilfred didn't say anything. Jed could hear him breathing, but the sound wasn't loud enough to distract him from his thoughts.

She was beautiful, more wild looking than any Modoc he'd seen in his short time here. While most of them dressed partly or completely in what they'd bought or stolen from whites, what she wore had been fashioned from natural fibers, her shoes made from tule reeds and then stuffed with fur to keep her feet warm. Her hair was so long and glossy he couldn't help but wonder what it felt like. The white strand in it had held his attention for a long time, then he'd gone back to looking at the rest of her.

A lot of the reservation Modocs and Klamaths lived on little more than bread and tobacco and looked rather sickly, but if her healthy skin was any indication, her diet was gleaned from the land. She carried herself as if she took pride in her body, and although he didn't want to be thinking this way, he ached to feel her against him.

She wouldn't be feeling the same about him.

"The two of you talked?" Wilfred prompted.

Jed nodded, still trapped by memories. He cleared his throat and tried again. "She wasn't afraid of me. I asked her how come. She said something about her spirit."

"And that's when you told her there's no such thing, just as there's no God."

Wilfred knew him too well. "Something like that."

"What'd she say to that? Wait a minute. You don't understand Modoc."

"No, I don't," he said as several of the closest enlisted men glanced his way. One came close to smiling. The others nodded.

"So she knows English. Where'd she pick that up?"

"We didn't get around to that. It's—it was unbelievable. Maybe she was waiting for me all along, waiting until I was there to see. I don't understand it, not at all. It was so cold I could hardly think, but that didn't seem to bother her. There she was, alone. Hating me and yet . . . I know she hated me. And yet—why the hell did she let me see what I saw? What did I see? Damnit, what . . . "

He shouldn't have said a word. If he hadn't, he wouldn't be remembering the way she looked, sounded, the easy, competent way she handled her slight yet strong body. He'd begun casting around for a way of changing the conversation when the men who'd been watching him stood and started his way. He didn't recognize any of them, but that didn't surprise him. He'd never looked that young or inexperienced.

"Lieutenant Britton?" the tallest asked. He glanced down at his chapped hand but didn't offer it, and Jed sensed they were green recruits who didn't know how they were supposed to approach an officer. "We was talking, trying to figure out what's gonna happen or if anything's ever gonna happen. Someone said you've been fighting Injins fur a long time."

"Years," Wilfred answered for him. "Twenty or thirty, ever since he got too old for farming and his teeth fell out. The lieutenant here's the only man Sitting Bull's scared of."

Jed glared at Wilfred, but it was too late. Although none of the men had ever been to the Black Hills, they'd obviously heard of the fierce Sioux war chief and were suitably impressed. "I've never been face to face with Sitting Bull," he corrected. "Not many men who are still alive have. But I've seen what he's capable of."

A couple of the men stared at him, but none asked for an explanation; he figured they didn't want to know the details. "What we was wondering," the tall man continued, "was what you think's going to happen. Or if anything's ever going to happen. This waiting is 'bout to drive us crazy. Those savages snuck up on God-fearing white women and children and slaughtered them in their sleep. They've got to—"

"No one was asleep and there weren't any women killed. No children either, least wise not little ones." If there was one thing Jed hated, it was gossip run amuck.

The men glanced at each other as if not sure whether to believe him. "The army's got to assume responsibility for some of what happened after we tried to take them at Lost Creek," he continued. "Burning their village—letting them get away because we didn't have enough troops or know what we were doing—a man would have to be a fool not to figure there'd be trouble."

"Murdering and mutilating innocent ranchers was wrong."

"Yeah. It was. And the army can't let that go unpunished."

"That's why we're here. We know that. But, well, what we're asking is, are we in danger of being scalped? None of us have ever fought an Indian, never thought we'd have to. It's hard sleeping for thinking about what they might do."

Jed sighed. He didn't want to feel responsible for these wet-behind-the-ears kids who were probably only a couple of years younger than him, but he did. "Look around," he said. "If you were an Indian, would you walk in here?"

"Maybe not right here, although they've come pretty close—but what if we're out on patrol?"

If they were on patrol, they'd better keep their eyes and ears open the way he'd done today. "What do you want me to say? That you've got nothing to worry about?"

"What we want is the truth. The other officers, they keep saying there's no way less than a hundred Indians, half of them women and children, can hold out against all these soldiers, but we've been

here for weeks now, and we aren't hunting them down. Is that because—" the young soldier glanced around as if reassuring himself
that no one else was listening "—because Lieutenant Colonel
Wheaton's afraid of what's going to happen?"

Whether fear entered into Wheaton's thinking Jed couldn't say.
What he did know was that the lieutenant was hamstrung, waiting for the necessary equipment and his final orders. Part of the
trouble was, it took days to wire word from one end of the country to the other and hostilities by a handful of Indians wasn't the
only thing the government had with which to concern itself. The
rest of it was that General Canby outranked Wheaton, and the general didn't want anything to commence until he was here to oversee it personally—which was why he'd asked Jed to ride down and
brief him while he was meeting with the business leaders of Yreka.

"I can't tell you what's going to happen," he said when the men
kept studying him, their eyes wide and uneasy. "Just don't ever take
anything for granted and always keep your rifles with you."

"They're savages. Murdering savages."

Savages. He'd spent the last six years of his life believing very
little except that. Tonight, he wanted, needed, to hold the word in
front of him so he could again stare at what drove him.

But today he'd heard a Modoc woman laugh.

Called her Luash and learned what the word meant.

Seen her touch—and be touched by—an eagle.

Morning and sunlight never reached the boulder-strewn cave's far
corners. At night, when people gathered in it, their voices and occasional laughter echoed off the solid walls, but now all she heard
were the gentle and not too gentle snores of those who were still
asleep. Cold penetrated everything. Even if there was enough firewood for a blazing fire, the rock walls would have rejected the heat.
Needing light, sound, and warmth, Luash clambered to the surface
where ice encrusted sage and bunchgrass grew before turning

around and looking back at where she, Kientpoos, and a half dozen others now lived.

A shadowed cavern should be nothing but shelter during a storm or a place for children to explore, not a Modoc home. Her feet weren't used to the harsh, uneven ground, the lifeless chill of rock, the unending dark that daily sent her in search of the weak winter sun that showed itself only infrequently.

But in the caves her people were safe; there were no other places left to them. Looking back only brought heartache, and she had had enough of that.

Before she was fully awake, she'd seen Kientpoos climb out of the cave. Now she spotted the short, solidly built man and several other braves sitting on the large rocks that circled the newly made dance ring, their shoulders hunched against the cold. Their clothes were a mix of Modoc and white, boots and pants that had either been bought or stolen from settlers, heavy hide blankets and bead necklaces.

Already two shaman dances had been held at the dance ring, but this bitter morning Kientpoos and the others weren't watching the reservation-forbidden ceremony. Instead, they spoke quietly and seriously among themselves, barely noticing her. Cho-ocks wasn't with them. She didn't have to endure the shaman's dark, hostile stare.

Leaving the men, she wandered away so she could take care of her needs in private. When she was done, she tried to make herself walk back to the cave so she could help Whe-cha with morning meal preparations, but she'd been without sunlight for too many hours. Even if she and the men were the only ones about this early, being alone with clean, cold air in her lungs was better than inhaling dark, trapped air while she listened to children endlessly ask their parents when they could go home.

In the distance, she could see that fog still draped Modoc Lake, but it didn't reach as far as the cave, giving her a clear view of her surroundings. Even the wind hadn't yet stirred and in the awesome quiet, she was able to concentrate on the endlessness of her world. The land in all directions buckled and jutted, stark and hard, as if fashioned by an enraged shaman. Even now, with ice glimmering on everything like countless stars, the harshness remained. Still, she loved the contrast between white snow and midnight lava rocks, the few wind-buffeted trees that managed to cling to life here.

Elizabeth Campbell, the rancher's wife who'd traded beans and corn for Luash's waterbird eggs and berries and taught her English, had tried to understand why the Modocs considered this unkind land sacred, but she'd had no more success at that than Luash had had in understanding why Elizabeth wanted to return to the eastern city from which she'd come.

Luash sighed in relief as she thought of Elizabeth and her children safely back in that place called Boston, maybe unaware of what had happened between Modocs and whites. Still, although she knew Elizabeth was happier now than she'd ever been here, she missed their fragile friendship.

Wandering aimlessly, she slowly circled the cave, taking note of the winter gray sage and grass, of the tiny holes where mice and other creatures would remain until spring. Not far away were the few cattle some of the braves had stolen. Once they were gone, there might be no more meat for a long time. Her lungs burned from pulling in frozen air; her face became numb. Still, because she'd known seventeen winters here, she would wait patiently for the return of warmth.

Cho-ocks might be nearby, hidden from her by the rough terrain as he went about making his magic. Would he ignore her presence or remind her, as he so often did, that she wasn't a shaman and thus incapable of drawing true power from her spirit?

She could make out the fogbound lake from where she was, its hidden surface promising endless water. Jed had been wrong; so far the army had made no attempt to cut her people off from what always had supplied them with water and food. She needed to break a hole in the ice and dip her tule basket into the lake so those in her cave would have enough to drink.

She also needed to sort out what had happened between her and Lieutenant Jed Britton. There was something about the man she couldn't begin to understand. He'd made the army his life. He had killed her kind; she only needed to look into his eyes to know that.

Still, when they talked and she looked deeper into those endless gray depths, she forgot about his hatred and thought only of the hollowed-out places deep inside him.

Her thoughts were pulled from Jed when she saw an old man emerge slowly from one of the other caves. From this distance, she couldn't tell who he was. She thought he might walk into the sage so he could relieve himself. Instead, he stood with his face uplifted as if studying the sky. It worried her that his coat was torn at the shoulder and he didn't have something over his head, but it wasn't her place to look after him.

He looked lonely and sad. Studying him, she saw that he'd clasped his hands in front of him. After a moment, he stopped staring at the sky and looked down at his hands. Then, the gesture tearing at her, he let his arms drop by his side. His back bowed and his head sagged. His breath spread out around him like fine white feathers.

"Luash."

She started but quickly recovered when she recognized her uncle's voice. "You are done talking?" She indicated where Kientpoos and the others had been sitting.

"For now. Cho-Cho has spotted more cattle not far from here. He is taking several men with him."

Luash nodded, her head suddenly heavy. "If they are successful, the ranchers will have even more reason to hate us."

Kientpoos's attention strayed from her to the old man who'd

lowered himself to his knees on the icy ground. "They are foolish to let their cattle roam. And this is our land."

Again she nodded, then lovingly touched her uncle's arm, pulling him away from the old man's sorrowful prayers. "I know. I should not have said anything."

"No. You have every right." Kientpoos briefly cupped his leathered hand over his reddened nose. "I do not want this; I want you to know that. To be at war . . . last year I was welcome in Yreka. Now I would be shot if I went there, all because I want to live my way."

She gripped his wrist. "You tried to explain we were being asked to do the impossible. How dare they say we must turn our backs on a shaman's wisdom and healing and take up their religion!" She imagined she could hear the old man chant as he prayed to his guardian spirit and sent out her own prayer that his plea would be rewarded. "Again and again you went to the officers. Only—"

"Only they did not listen." Sighing, Kientpoos settled himself on a rock and stared off into space, a solitary figure surrounded by harsh vastness. She sat near him, her own gaze following the same direction. Ever since that first time, when Eagle left his sign in her hair, her people had walked in a wide path around her. The men didn't understand why she should be blessed by Eagle when many of them had no spirits despite repeated quests; the women didn't understand how she had gained a spirit before her puberty dance. But nothing had changed between her and Kientpoos. They could still open their hearts to each other and he treated her not like a root-gathering woman, but like someone with wisdom.

"That is behind us. We cannot change what happened," she offered, all the while wondering if her words were enough.

"That is what I keep telling myself." His smile lasted maybe two heartbeats. "I must look forward; everyone expects that of me—

except for those who say I should have already attacked. But to declare war against many armed soldiers . . . "

"Ha-kar-Jim, Slolux, Ki-esk," she spat. "Especially Cho-ocks, our shaman. They are men of war. Men who attack unarmed settlers and spill their blood in retaliation for what was done to us. They say they did right, but my woman's heart says they condemned us."

"Condemned? Is that how you see it?"

She'd wondered why Kientpoos had sought her out when his two wives were waiting to feed him. Now she understood. "I believe that, even after the army attacked, there was still a chance of peace. They did not come to kill. Aga's death was an accident." She paused, working through her horror at the senselessness of what had happened—thinking briefly of Jed Britton's role. "But some of our braves let themselves be ruled by revenge. Now the army will never forgive or forget."

Kientpoos continued to look at her but said nothing. "Ha-kar-Jim, Slolux, and the others are young men full of themselves," she went on. "Quick to anger, slow to think."

Her uncle's deep sigh left a white puff on the air. "I told them that, but they anger again and call me a frightened old man. Luash, I tell you this. I believe the Modocs will survive only if we are one. If we fight among ourselves . . . "

He took another deep breath. "Will any of us be alive in the spring?" The question seemed wrenched from deep within him. "My niece, I do not understand this blessing Eagle has bestowed upon you. Still, I see you with him and know it is good that your spirit protects you from all danger."

"Safe." Her mind floated into the past and embraced memories as vivid today as when they took place. "Yes."

"Because of Eagle, your father has not tried to use you."

"Nor does he speak to me," she said as a child's laughter cut through the air. Glancing in that direction, she spotted a couple of boys, one chasing the other into the sage. The praying warrior didn't acknowledge their presence.

"Do not mourn what cannot be changed," Kientpoos said kindly.

"I try not to, but sometimes it is hard."

"No one can walk that journey for you. Luash, I must ask you something. Eagle is your guardian, but does he look with favor on all Modocs?"

She pulled her lower lip into her mouth and held it firmly in place. She'd been asking herself the same question for days and nights now, praying she'd find the answer her heart needed. Yesterday, she'd been so distracted by Jed's presence that she'd barely remembered what else had happened. Now she reached under her blanket and pulled out a great, dark feather. "Eagle gave me this the last time I saw him." She handed it to Kientpoos. "It is my gift to you, a promise from my spirit. Whoever holds it may be blessed as I have been. He and those who look to him for guidance and leadership."

Kientpoos gently ran his fingers over the feather's glossy surface. He smiled a little and she wondered if it was because the boys, both of them laughing now, had reappeared. "I want to believe."

"My thoughts were full of you when I called Eagle to me. Why else would he leave a part of himself, if not to lighten your heart?"

Kientpoos tucked the feather inside his white man's shirt but said nothing, only looked up at the still-growing day. Thinking he needed to be alone with his thoughts, she started to stand, but he stopped her. "The children—it is still a game to them. They do not understand, but they will. You do not have to remain here. You have no husband who wants you by his side. If you return to the reservation—"

"Never! My home is with you, with everyone who will not be treated like cattle."

"If you were married—"

"I have no husband because I will not be a slave like my mother!" Her words sent shards of pain through her head, and she forced herself to calm. "And because too many Modoc men forget what it is to walk the old ways. Even if I wanted to live with a man, I am set apart. You know that."

"A husband is mortal, not a gift from Kumookumts. But a man can give you things even Eagle cannot."

Despite what happened between her parents, she knew Kient-poos was right. His young wife Whe-cha loved him; the affection between the two simmered like boiling water. And Kientpoos's old wife Spe-ach-es didn't seem to mind sharing her husband with another. "What man wants a wife who would rather chase after wind-blown eagle feathers than gather roots, camas, and wocus?" she teased. Then: "I cannot give my heart to a man who forgets his Modoc name."

"Our world has changed; we must change with it."

She turned her attention from him to the massive clouds. Eagle was out there somewhere, living his life of freedom, waiting for the next time when one of them would seek out the other. "Not all change is right; there must be wisdom behind it."

"Wisdom and caution; I know." He pushed himself to his feet and shook his head in response to the boys' uninhibited yells. "It is good that we are so far from the enemy. I need to hear children, want them to laugh without fear. At least they have that. Luash, a lifetime of no one next to you is a lonely thing. I think—" he held out his hand and helped her stand "—that there is a man for you. When you find him, you will know."

"They're attacking!"

Jed found himself standing without being aware of moving. He stabbed around in the dark for his boots and jammed his cold feet into them. At the other side of the tent, Wilfred was doing the same.

Not bothering to speak, he grabbed his rifle a half second before Wilfred reached for his. Shoulders colliding, they bolted through the opening, all but taking the canvas with them.

"Attacking!" someone yelled. "Injins, attacking!" His cry was repeated immediately by countless others. Jed tried to make sense of what was happening, but the dying campfires did nothing to take away the night. Gradually, he became aware of frantic activity as several hundred men milled about. He'd returned from Yreka with General Canby just yesterday. If the Modocs had seen—if the general was in danger—

"Where?" he hollered as a man on horseback pranced nearby. "Where are they?"

"I can't see 'em! Oh God, they're going to slaughter us all. Murdering—murdering—" Whatever else the rider might have said was lost in the sound of a rifle shot.

Trusting Wilfred to follow him, Jed took off on the run toward General Canby's. Because someone had placed a lantern on a nearby rock, he was able to spot the Department of the Columbia commanding officer, his trousers unfastened, speaking earnestly to one of his aides. Jed didn't try to deny his heartfelt relief at seeing the man safe.

"Who sounded the alarm?" Canby demanded of the violently shivering youngster at his side.

"I don't know, sir. I was—I was—"

"You'd fallen asleep, damnit. What the hell's going on?"

Another shot sounded, followed by another. Cursing the dark, Jed was forced to trust his other senses to tell him what was going on. One thing he already knew: if it had been an Indian attack, he would have heard shooting before the cry of alarm had been raised. "Sir, I don't think—"

"What don't you think?" Canby interrupted before he could finish.

"Listen. Do you hear fighting?"

"You're right," Canby breathed after a moment. "Jed, where are the Modocs?"

Although he wasn't sure that was as important as calming everyone down, he started to assure the general that if the Indians had been on the move today, the scouts would have known.

"Unless they'd fallen asleep like this fool." Canby pointed at the shivering young man. "What'd they do, wait until I got here? Where's my horse? And Lieutenant Colonel Wheaton—where the hell is he?" Canby grabbed his aide's arm and shoved him toward the corral. "Check on the horses, and bring mine as soon as you get him saddled."

Turning toward Jed, he continued, his voice loud so he could make himself heard over the continued shouts and occasionally discharged rifle, "This is Wheaton's responsibility. He should be taking charge. Where the hell is he?"

"I'll look for him, sir."

"You do that. And while you're at it, tell the men not to fire unless they've got something to shoot at. We don't have enough ammunition, and they know it. In this dark, they'll only hit each other."

An hour later, Jed was back at the general's tent. It had taken most of that time to get the word to everyone that whatever had happened, it wasn't an ambush. A few of the soldiers and volunteers had gone back to bed, but most continued to mill around the now brightly burning fires as they reassured themselves that they were safe. Wheaton had appeared before Jed had had a chance to search for him, leaving Jed and Wilfred free to concentrate on other matters, namely making sure the ammunition didn't disappear completely.

Now, waiting for General Canby to begin speaking, Jed couldn't help thinking that if Canby had taken a half second to put things together at the start, he'd have realized that the Modocs would have to be total fools to try to take on this many troops. Dawn had begun to make itself known. General Canby had combed his thick, well-trimmed beard. His drooping lids all but covered his dark eyes and emphasized his bushy eyebrows, putting Jed in mind of a kindly bear. Canby was in full uniform, his appearance commanding respect.

"I think the best we can do is put this incident behind us," he said. He jerked his head at Lieutenant Colonel Wheaton, who stood with his hands locked behind his back. "The lieutenant colonel has assured me that adequate guards will be in place tonight, so there won't be a repeat of this performance. Much of the problem, I'm convinced, is that the men are tired of inactivity. They know I'm here; they're anticipating action."

"They should be," Wilfred spoke up before Jed could warn him to keep his mouth shut and his opinions to himself. "They came to fight, not wait."

"I know that," Canby snapped. "However, they don't understand how complicated this campaign is."

Jed knew what the general was talking about; after all, he'd been the one to brief him. Much of the food was uneatable. Mules sent as pack animals had turned out to be half wild and useless. A wagon load of whiskey brought from Jacksonville had been a bitter disappointment; most of the jugs' contents had leaked out. Although Jed had been relieved that they wouldn't have to contend with a camp full of drunken men, the incident had put everyone in a foul mood. Maybe that, and not Canby's arrival, had been the catalyst for the mass hysteria that had taken place during the night.

"I've been thinking on this," Canby continued. "And I'm ready to admit that I, and you, the officers, are partly to blame."

Jed waited.

"Starting today, the men will know why they're here." He glared at Wheaton. "There will be regular briefings. The howitzers are now at Van Bremer's ranch and ready to be brought here. It's time to put our plan into action, or at least make it clear that there will be action, soon. Lieutenant Colonel Wheaton, I want the men assembled this afternoon; I intend to personally address them. In the meantime, I expect my officers to draw up their final opinions on where each outfit should be stationed when we attack and give me a timetable on how long it will to take to get the troops into position. Gentlemen, this is a war."

Did Jed want to throw his life away? Was that what he was asking to have happen by going back to where he'd seen Luash? No matter how Jed tried to turn his attention to something else, it insisted on returning to the same damn question.

In the distance, he could see dark clouds gathering and guessed it was snowing on massive Mount Shasta, a hundred miles to the south. If the storm reached here and snow again blanketed the beds, their ugliness would be hidden beneath white quiet, but that hadn't happened yet.

Today the air felt of tension, hostilities, years of co-existence between white and Modoc thrown away.

Still, here he was.

He hadn't always had so little regard for his life. Growing up on his father's plantation had instilled in him a deep respect for what the land was capable of producing. But his father was buried next to his mother on land that no longer belonged to the Britton family. Why he hadn't died along with his parents he couldn't say, except maybe he'd been too young to have his heart broken.

That's what had killed them. Their neighbors, most of them ruined too, believed that fever had taken his mother and his father had died of infection after cutting his leg, but Jed knew different. He'd seen it in their eyes as they struggled to make a go of things after the war. But the carpetbaggers had come down from the North and with the government behind them, the newcomers had managed to wrestle what was left of Britton Plantation away from his parents.

History. The past.

It took several hours to reach the lake and then work his way around to where he'd seen Luash. By then, it was spitting snow, but it didn't look like a full-blown storm. If he was wrong, he'd get cold and wet, nothing new for a man who couldn't remember the last time he'd slept inside walls. As long as he remained near his horse and the horse didn't break a leg, he'd get back to camp in one piece.

He'd heard from a couple of local ranchers that the Modocs had taken off for Mount Mazama, leaving the army protecting folks from ghosts. A half Klamath roustabout was adamant that he'd seen a trail of Modocs on horseback heading toward Mount Shasta. He didn't believe either of those stories any more than he did the one about how several Modocs had dressed up like soldiers and were living in the middle of camp, but neither could he be sure that Captain Jack's bunch was still deep in the beds. That, he told himself, was why he was here.

That and because he didn't want to hear any more about how the army was determined to end the Modocs' miserable excuse for resistance.

Dismounting, he hobbled his horse's front legs so it couldn't roam. He spent several minutes wandering around, trying not to look over his shoulder—trying not to call himself a fool. He kept his eyes peeled on the sky, but saw no sign of an eagle.

When he'd satisfied his curiosity about the lake—yes, it was still iced over—he returned to his horse and pulled some jerky and hard bread out of his saddlebags. Taking pity on the animal, he shared the bread with it.

"You think I'm crazy, don't you? I don't suppose it's a lot of comfort to have me point out that it's not snowing as much as it was awhile ago."

The horse pushed its nose against his chest. Barely aware of what he was doing, he started scratching between its ears. "It doesn't make sense, does it? Even if we leave right now, it'll be nearly dark by the time we get back. What do you think about spending the night?"

The horse went on shoving, its eyes half closed.

"I don't suppose it makes that much difference to you. You've got your winter coat, but all I brought for myself are a couple of blankets."

A couple of blankets. He really had done that, hadn't he? When he tied the blankets behind his saddle, he'd told himself that only a fool would go out in the winter without some kind of protection, but in the back of his mind, maybe, he'd known what he was willing to do if it meant, maybe, seeing Luash.

Luash.

Mist.

A woman who spoke with eagles and believed herself safe from all harm.

The woman now emerging from the lava beds.

6

Lieutenant Jed Britton stood in the drifting snow with his horse dozing nearby. Luash studied the man, noting his heavy winter coat and the rifle by his side. He looked lonely but not vulnerable and she guessed he wasn't a man to concern himself with vulnerability.

She'd been waiting for him for days. She'd told no one, not even Kientpoos, what she was doing. If she had, she would have been asked questions she couldn't answer, not even for herself.

She walked slowly toward Jed, acutely aware that he closely watched her every move. She felt the cold, strangely gentle touch of snow on her face but couldn't think how to lift her arms to wipe away the moisture. The storm blunted his impact, but not her reaction to him.

"You should not have come," she said when she reached him.

"Am I being watched?" He didn't take his eyes off her.

"Our scouts are near Crawley's Ranch; it is an easy thing to hide from many enemy eyes. If someone saw you leave it, they saw only a single man and paid you little attention. Still, your life is in danger."

"I imagine it is."

It was her turn to say something, but for a long time, she didn't try. Behind him brooded the great lake that had fed her people for as long as Modocs walked this land. Jed didn't belong here; this was her place—her people's lake. And yet, perhaps because his coat and hair were snow-dusted, he had begun to blend into his surroundings.

"Some of your braves have been stealing cattle." His eyes were relentless on hers. "The ranchers are demanding that the army do something about it."

"Are they going to?"

His mouth twitched in that quiet, unexpected way of his. "I'm a soldier, Luash. I can't tell you that."

"No, you cannot."

"Then what are we doing here together?"

"There are things we need to say to each other. Once we have done that, it will be over between us."

"It better be." He frowned. "Where did you learn English? You speak it so well."

"I had a patient teacher."

"It had to have taken a long time. Why——" His voice thinned; he didn't seem to know how to finish the question.

"Why did I want to learn white words? Because no matter how much I prayed to Eagle to take away the newcomers, I knew they would not leave. Eagle's wisdom was that I study all that I could about those who had moved onto Modoc land."

"Eagle's wisdom? Ha!"

"You laugh at what you do not understand. I got to know a settler's wife. Elizabeth. We each had things the other needed. Sometimes I think we were friends." She fell silent, remembering her visits with Elizabeth.

"How did you know I was here?"

"I was watching."

"For me?"

"Yes."

"Why?"

"I do not have the answer to that," she said and walked around him to run her hand over his horse's neck. Despite her blanket's bulk, she felt Jed's heavy coat brush her arm and faced him. "I understand not enough of what happens when I am around you, Lieutenant. All I know is, we had to see each other again."

"Why?"

She wished he would not keep asking that question over and over again, forcing her to dig deep inside herself for the truth. "You are here. So am I. I say it is because something is unfinished between us. Why did you risk your life today, Lieutenant?"

"Jed." She nodded. He said, "I can't stop thinking about what I saw between you and that bird. Isn't that enough of a reason?"

No, it wasn't. Still, she didn't want to talk about the forces that had propelled them toward each other. She knew she should hate him. How much simpler things would be if she felt that way. But this soldier who made war with her people was not just an enemy. He was also a gray-eyed man with a body made for fighting and survival, a man with loneliness in his heart.

"Why aren't you afraid of me?"

His beautiful gray eyes were less sheltered, less distant than they'd been the first time, as if he was letting go of a little of himself. Still, so much of him remained beyond her touch. She sighed. "You do not know what Eagle is to me; until you do, you cannot understand."

He shook his head, rejecting her words.

"I have never met a man like you. Someone who surrounds himself with bitterness and yet finds beauty in what is around him."

"Beauty?" He indicated their surroundings. "This isn't beautiful."

"The wind touches you; you sense its message," she said as the distant howl of a wolf drifted to her. "Your words say there is nothing to embrace about this land, but your eyes say another thing." She looked up at him, felt his spirit pulling at her, glanced away. "I see loneliness there. And questions. A wish that tomorrow would come and take away the loneliness."

She'd barely gotten the words out when he grabbed her and yanked her so close that his features blurred. "The way I live is how I want it!"

"No. It is not." She easily pulled free, told him with her eyes and stance that she didn't want him to touch her again. "Listen to me, army man. Once I was a child known as Teina. Something happened—something that showed me I could no longer live with my parents. I could have become bitter, as you are, but my soul did not want that. I went to live with my uncle." She straightened, looked him in the eye. "You call him Captain Jack."

"Captain Jack?" He reared back, teeth clenched. "Why didn't you tell me that before?"

"Then, it was none of your concern. I no longer have any wish to keep that from you."

"No more secrets? All right, I'll tell *you* something—the reason I came looking for you today. The army isn't going to go away. We're stronger, larger. Damned determined. War has been declared, Luash. Tell your uncle he's going to get himself and everyone else killed if he doesn't give up."

War. "And if he gives up, what happens then? Will he be taken in chains to some white man's prison?"

"That's for the courts to decide."

"White man's courts!"

"Yes," he insisted. "White man's courts, because there's no way a handful of Modocs can win. Look, we've got a general here now. A general! The army's determined to roust your people out of the lava beds. They're not going to go away until they've accomplished that."

"Why do you hate us so?"

"Why do I hate you?" He looked furious but determined. "All right, I'll tell you. And once I have, maybe you'll understand."

"I will not want to hear this, will I?"

He breathed out, long and slow, his warm breath just brushing her forehead. "Years ago the Sioux damn near scalped me." He pressed his fingers against the scar on his forehead. "Shot me full of arrows and left me more dead than alive. I was the only one not killed. Out of eighty good and decent men, the only one . . ."

He was still speaking, but she couldn't concentrate. She had good reason to have no love for his kind. Hadn't they treated her mother as if she was less than human? Hadn't they forced the Modocs who'd followed Kientpoos to flee their burning homes like frightened antelope? But what she felt was nothing compared to what ruled him.

Turning away, she slowly walked as close to the lake as she dared. The unseen birds made so much noise that she couldn't hear Jed, but she sensed that he was right behind her. She wasn't afraid of turning her back to him. Still, his scar was a memory of that horrible day when the Sioux had tried to kill him; he would live his entire life with that reminder.

"This—" she indicated the lake "—is a gift to my people. Everything, sun and clouds, even the winter storms are sacred. There would be no Modocs if Kumookumts hadn't scattered seeds over the world. He and the other gods lived with our ancestors and spoke the language of the Modoc. He left behind his footprints, so we would know and understand, and always be reminded of his blessings. Some Modocs have forgotten that, but not those of us who want to live at Lost Creek. That is why we will not surrender— because Kumookumts lives in our hearts."

"Why are you telling me this?"

"When you speak, I hear a man who believes that Sioux and Modoc, that all Indians, are the same, just creatures to feel your hatred and bitterness and be destroyed. Those emotions have twisted you."

She heard him suck in a quick breath and waited for his anger. But although she could feel it pressing against both of them, he didn't say anything. The birds momentarily quieted, and in the near silence, she heard the wolf again. As she struggled to gather her thoughts, she continued to stare out at the frozen lake. Why had this soldier, this complicated, contradictory man, touched her life?

All she could give him in return was a piece of herself— understanding of who and what she was. Later she would face the question of whether she'd given him too much. "I cannot look inside your heart and feel what it feels. You say you want me to know about your scar, what you survived, but I say that is a bad thing. Your heart stands in yesterday, Jed. Only you can bring it into today."

From out of the corner of her eye, she watched his hand become a fist. His fingers had already turned colorless from the cold, but now they became so starkly white that she could see the strong bones and dark veins beneath his flesh. Blood pulsed through him; his body was young and powerful. A man like that should be embracing his tomorrows, not lost in what had been.

"You are not like most soldiers," she continued. "You do not stay safely in camp. Instead, you ride out here to tell me that my people will die if they do not do as the army says. Maybe—" She glanced his way, then forced herself to go on looking at him. "Maybe it is because Bear has called to you and you cannot pretend you have not heard."

"Who's Bear? Another of your spirits?"

"Not mine, no." She tapped the side of her head. "Bear has the wisdom of man. Maybe he came to you in your sleep and whispered his wisdom to you."

"You're talking nonsense, Luash."

"Modoc beliefs are nonsense, you say. Are we to embrace the

words of your Sunday doctor simply because he carries an old black book? Tell me something, Jed. This world of your god, who supposedly created the world in six days, are the Modocs in it?"

"He isn't *my* god."

She wrapped her arms around herself and rocked back on her heels. "Then who guides you?"

"No one."

That could not, should not be, but if she told him he was wrong, he would only argue with her. "I cannot say why Eagle chose me, but my gratitude and joy will last as long as I live." She slipped her fingers through her hair and held up the white strand for him to see. "This was his gift to me. Would you call it nothing, Jed Britton?"

"I don't know." His voice was heavy and dark. He made a move as if to touch her hair, and then pulled back. Still, his attention remained on what she'd shown him. "That's the hell of it, I don't know. But there's one thing I'm damn sure of."

He stood so close that if he wanted—if she wanted—they could easily be in each other's arms. "And that's that no matter who your deity is, he can't stop the army from running over you."

Sudden fear sliced through her. "Because you have so many soldiers?"

"Not just that. They're set to stay until they've starved you out. Worn you down. Killed you, if need be."

She'd been wrong. She wanted nothing to do with him after all. "So much has been taken from us already, why not everything?"

To her shock, he placed his arm lightly on her shoulder. She tensed, nearly broke free again. When he didn't say anything, she stared up at the snow and fought what he was doing to her senses.

"Long ago, before the first white man, there was only us and the Klamaths and Snakes," she told him. "In those times, Kumookumts walked among the Modocs and showed them where to hunt for antelope and deer and mountain sheep, how to hide from our enemies. We were children who cared about nothing except gathering enough camas, wocus, chokecherries, and wild plum to see us through the winter. We celebrated when the men trapped elk. Great fish came to the rivers and we celebrated that too. Although the elk and fish and wild plum will always be here, there is little to be joyful about now.

"So much has changed," she continued when he said nothing. "Mistakes were made by Modocs as well as whites. Long ago, my grandfathers killed and scalped. One winter many Modocs living at Lost River were ambushed by settlers. That time Modocs were scalped, and there was hatred on both sides. We cannot go back to being children; I know that. But knowing does not stop me from wanting what my ancestors had."

"I want back my parents' plantation. Only, it isn't going to happen."

"Plantation?"

"Fertile land ripe for growing. So rich you wouldn't believe it. It was the only place my parents ever wanted to live."

"But they lost that, the way the Modocs have lost their land?" she asked.

His fingers on her shoulder contracted. "There was a war between one half of the country and the other, over things neither side could understand or accept about the other. It was so complex, but it doesn't matter anymore. Our side—they called it the South—lost, and those who won forced my parents off their land." Before she could brace herself, he turned her around and stared down at her. "I don't know why I'm telling you this."

"Maybe we are not so different after all. We both understand the power land has over us, how rich the gift."

"Land my parents bought with their sweat and work. The Yankees had no call to take it from them."

"Bought?" The wolf called again; she tried to hold it to her, think of nothing else. "The word has little meaning to me. What you see here, and even what you cannot, was created by Mother Earth. Her offspring are the mountain peaks and lakes, and a mother does not sell her children."

"You really believe that, don't you?" Jed asked, his question both gentle and hard edged. "You're convinced that some entity that goes by the name of Mother Earth is responsible for everything?"

"Why does what I believe bother you so? I would think it does not matter."

"It doesn't," he snapped and she knew it was a lie. "All right. So Mother Earth and Kumookumts created Mount Shasta. What in the hell good is it? What do the Modocs, or anyone for that matter, need with a massive chunk of rock covered with snow?"

"Eagle and Sun God live there. Without Great Eagle, all animals, birds, and fish would be without names. Great Eagle gifted Bear with the wisdom of humans and made Snake immortal."

"Oh Luash, no."

"That is our belief. It was right and true before your Sunday doctors came and said we were wrong."

"Belief?" he whispered, "Do you have any idea how long it's been since I've had belief?"

She didn't have to be told; she'd seen the answer in his eyes. "Then I cry for you, Jed Britton. You will never sit at a temescal and offer up prayers to those who gave you life. You will never add your own prayer stone to the piles alongside trails, never make an offering of food to the spirits."

"You're talking crazy. This is nonsense."

"Nonsense? You, who have never walked in our footsteps, would take away our belief?"

"If you had lived through what I did—it sure as hell wasn't God's hand."

"You were spared. Your god—"

"If there had been a god, he wouldn't have destroyed my parents. Don't you understand?" She saw in his eyes a hopelessness, a frustration, questions that went as deep as his soul. "What happened, happened. The Sioux who was trying to scalp me was killed by my only friend. Then Charles—I watched Charles get shot. Listened to him die. If God had a hand in any of that—no. I can't accept that."

His fingers had continued to bite into her as he spoke, and yet despite the pain he was inflicting, she couldn't bring herself to pull away. She'd never seen such agony in another human being. Even when she had realized her father was capable of selling her body to satisfy his greed, she hadn't known despair that deep.

"I cannot say why those things happened to you," she whispered, not sure she was using the right words, or if any would reach him. "But to condemn your god—"

"He condemned me."

Wondering if a spark of belief remained in him, she stared deep into his eyes, but what she saw made her pull back. He was challenging her with words, throwing his anger at her. Speaking straight from his wounded heart.

"To walk through life alone, to never know peace, is a terrible thing."

"What makes you think I'm not at peace?"

"It is in everything you say. If you were Modoc, true Modoc, you would look at Mount Shasta and feel awe because that is the home of Sun God. The great mountain is a gift, a blessing, the work of hands beyond our understanding. That is what true belief is, Jed. Beyond understanding."

"Damnit, Luash. How can you swallow this?"

She jerked free. He reached for her again, but she held up a warning hand. The wolf had been silent; now he howled again, a drifting, lonely sound. "Do not touch me. I do not want to feel you on my flesh."

"Why? Because I'm making you face the truth?"

"Because you have lost the truth."

He blinked, and in the gesture's aftermath she saw that she'd both angered and hurt him. The anger she understood, but the other . . . "You tell me I am wrong to believe that life springs from Kumookumts, but if not from him, where then?" He opened his mouth, but she didn't give him time to speak. "I will tell you something and then maybe you will understand."

"What?"

"I would be dead if Eagle hadn't come to me."

Again he blinked, and in the vast amount of time that seemed to take, she realized she was going to tell him something she never thought she would tell a white man. How he'd been able to wrench that out of her, and why she believed he should know, had a great deal to do with the look in his haunted eyes and the anger in his voice, but it went beyond that.

In a voice that stumbled and hesitated, she told him why she'd fled her parents' wickiup in the middle of a storm, all those years ago. He regarded her gravely, but said nothing. "For many nights after I returned home, my father acted as if I was dead. He stared at the mark Eagle had left on me, but I did not know whether he believed. Then his greed overcame him. I looked up from my work one day to see several soldiers approaching. Although I did not understand their words, I knew what they wanted of me. I knew my father was responsible."

"What did you do?"

"I wanted to run." She should be watching Jed so she could see his reaction, but even after all these years, the pain of that day remained, and she was forced deep inside herself. "My legs danced with the need to flee. But they were on horseback; I could never have escaped them."

"Your feelings meant nothing to your father?"

With her eyes closed, she shook her head. "Not long after my oldest brother was born, my father fell while hunting mountain sheep. The shaman's magic made it possible for him to walk, but he never hunted again. My mother made baskets which she sold to the settlers so we would not starve. Still, his heart became as twisted as his knee."

"I'm sorry."

She wanted to believe him. "I wish I had known him before. My mother is a gentle woman. Surely she must have once felt affection for him."

"Is she afraid of him?"

"Yes. She—once she ran. Another took her in, but my father threatened to kill that man, and his children. She returned."

"Luash, the day the soldiers came for you—what happened?"

She opened her eyes, but her vision was too clouded to make out his features. "They grabbed me. I fought, screamed. That only made the soldiers laugh more. I was alone, fighting. Alone." Despite the years that separated her from that day, the memory of the terror she'd felt hadn't faded. "One slapped me, but I couldn't stop screaming."

"Didn't your people hear?"

"I was in the forest, searching for piñon nuts. My father must have known where I was going and sent the soldiers after me. Great fear filled me. I knew what my mother had endured. I was afraid I would die."

"And then?" he prompted when she couldn't make herself go on.

"And then Eagle came. Only, you don't believe that, do you, Lieutenant Jed Britton?"

He stood before her, his body so still that she wondered if he had turned to stone. Still his voice, his surprisingly gentle voice, brushed over her like a feather. "Just tell me what happened."

She could do that. "I heard a great cry, a scream unlike any other. Maybe Eagle had been in the clouds, watching over me. I do not know. Suddenly he was among the men, tearing with his beak and talons. They shrank before his fury. Some tried to fight him, but they had set down their weapons. Eagle buried his talons in their faces. When they lifted their hands to protect themselves, he attacked those as well."

Jed didn't say anything. She waited, barely aware of her ragged breathing. In her mind, she saw the three men cowering before Eagle's attack, their faces and hands and arms stained with their own blood.

"And you've never been bothered again?"

She shook her head. "The soldiers must have told him, because when I returned home, my father was waiting for me. He was furious, demanding to know what had happened. When he tried to strike me, Eagle attacked him."

"No."

"Yes. Eagle slashed at my father and tore a great gash in his head. Since that day, Wa'tcaq has not touched me, not tried to sell me to the soldiers. Not spoken to me. It was then that I asked my uncle to take me in." It was not the end of Luash's story, but it was all she needed to tell Jed.

She wrapped her arms around her waist, surprised to discover that her robe was covered with flakes. Still, she didn't feel cold. She glanced up at the steadily falling snow, stared at Jed who was rapidly disappearing underneath a white coating, his head cocked to one side to let her know he too had been listening to the wolf. The world around them had faded, leaving just her and this army man who hated and killed Sioux and had come here, maybe, to kill Modocs.

"Then I feel sorry for you, Lieutenant Jed Britton. To be without belief . . ."

"It isn't your concern. It will never be your concern. What is is this: Convince your uncle to surrender. Otherwise, none of you are going to be alive to see spring."

It was nearly dark by the time Luash returned to the lava beds. Although two older women were still some distance away, carrying heavy loads of dead sage for their morning fires, she didn't see any children. The rich aroma of roasting beef wafting in the air told her that dinner would soon be ready. She spotted Kientpoos's young wife Whe-cha sitting outside their cave staring up at the sky.

"I am a foolish woman," Whe-cha said, laughing softly. "I grow cold waiting for the stars to show themselves."

"Maybe tomorrow."

"Maybe. I heard Wolf earlier and told myself that he was welcoming the stars." She sighed and stared behind her at their cave-house's dark entrance. "It is as if life has stopped here, as if spring will never come."

"Spring will return," Luash reassured her. "It always has."

"I know, and I must not tell my husband how hard it is for me to live this way, but there are times when I feel as if I am nothing more than a rock."

"Whe-cha, you are young!"

"Am I?" she whispered, and kicked at a chunk of lava rock at her feet. "Luash, you know how much I want my husband's child, but it still does not grow inside me. Maybe—maybe the fault is with me. Or maybe my husband worries so about what will happen to our people that his body is incapable of anything else."

Luash leaned forward and kissed the top of Whe-cha's head. "You worry too much. Worry is not good for a woman's body."

"So the shaman says, but knowing that and changing what is inside me is not a simple thing."

"I know. Whe-cha, I will sleep elsewhere tonight. If you and my uncle have privacy—"

"It does not matter." Whe-cha pointed without looking up. "He is with Cho-ocks again. I fear he will not come to me tonight."

Wondering if Whe-cha was right, she gave her friend a comforting hug before picking her way over the rock-strewn ground to the sentry outpost where Kientpoos and the shaman who whites called Curley Headed Doctor knelt as they looked out over the land. These days there was always a guard stationed there, since from that vantage point, the Modocs would know if the enemy was approaching long before anyone got close enough for an accurate shot.

Wishing she dared wait until she and Kientpoos were alone, she forced herself to walk up to her uncle and the shaman. Cho-ocks, looking barely older than a boy, glared at her, as she expected. His little eyes, which seemed out of place with his broad temple and generous mouth, hardened. "What are you doing here, Luash?" he demanded. "This is men talk, nothing to concern you."

"I think different." The wind hit her and she shivered. "The army general is at the soldiers' camp."

"I know," Kientpoos said.

"You do? How?"

"Cho-Cho was near their camp last night. He saw things, heard things that make him believe the army men are scared rabbits running from shadows."

Although she didn't believe that, she nevertheless nodded to give herself time to think. If she told her uncle and the shaman that she'd been talking to a soldier, they would demand to know why. But she had to tell them about Jed's warning.

"Eagle came to me today and gave me his wisdom. The general has told the soldiers that it is time for war," she said. "They will never turn their backs on us, never leave us alone."

"What would you have us do?" Cho-ocks challenged. "Surrender? Walk up to them like cattle ready for slaughter?"

"I did not say that. I—"

"Enough, Luash!" Cho-ocks interrupted. "The army men call

me a murderer, me and other braves. They may simply take you back to the reservation, but they would hang me."

The image of Modocs she'd known all her life swinging from a rope sent a spasm through her. "You should not have—"

"They burned our village. We sought revenge."

Although she would always believe that killing unsuspecting ranchers was wrong, it was too late to argue that. "Uncle, you were not one of them. They do not hate—"

"Luash, please," Kientpoos warned. "The time for arguing, and for peace, is behind us. Look around you. The army will never be able to overrun us here. We are safe."

"But—"

"What is it?" Cho-ocks sneered. "Have you become a frightened old woman?"

"No! Never." Clinging to what Kientpoos had just said, she reminded herself that the Land of Burned Out Fires indeed protected the Modocs as surely as the frozen lake protected the fish. Forcing tension out of her body, she smiled at her uncle. "Whe-cha waits for you."

Grunting, Kientpoos got to his feet. "Alone?"

"Alone."

"That is good." He took a few steps, then stopped. "Cho-ocks, you will spend the night here? You do not want me to send another to watch for the enemy?"

"There is no need," Cho-ocks said. "My eyes are keen, my magic strong. We are safe."

Luash wanted nothing more than to believe him.

7

JANUARY 16, 1873

"It isn't going to work. The terrain's impossible. Fighting the weather's like fighting another enemy—one that will demoralize these unproven troops."

"I've had enough of your opinion, Lieutenant!" Captain David Perry glared at Jed through eyes closed to mere slits against the harsh wind. Behind them, some two hundred soldiers and volunteers gathered behind a series of low bluffs in preparation for tomorrow's attack. "You've already expressed yourself more than adequately," the captain continued. "We all know you believe we're on a fool's mission. However, this is the United States Army. The general, the other officers, and I have made our decision based on tried and true battle strategy. As soon as the Modocs see the extent of our strength, they will surrender."

Jed snorted. "They're already aware of our so-called strength. Who do you think fired at us yesterday? They're taunting us. More importantly, they know this land; we don't. It's been almost two months since they fled into the lava beds. If they didn't believe they could outlast us, they wouldn't still be there. Believe me, they're not going to turn over their weapons simply because we march on them." *Try* to march on them.

"So you insist, which I heartily dispute. Our numbers alone will demoralize them. However, should those miserable cowards attempt to flee, they will find that impossible."

Jed grunted, frustration boiling inside him. If only he was back with Custer! Instead, he was trapped here without a troop to command or any decision-making capacity. He could offer advice—but that advice, more often than not, was ignored, even by General Canby, who was under incredible pressure to put an end to what politicians called a minor uprising.

Damnit, hadn't he offered to ride out with a couple of reservation Indians to try to talk to Captain Jack about surrendering peacefully? Although he had a strong suspicion he would have been turned down, because the Modocs who'd murdered settlers were afraid of reprisals, he hadn't even been given the chance to see how the offer would be received.

Instead, the war campaign had begun. Colonel Bernard had sent troops to capture the Modoc canoes so the Indians couldn't escape by water as they'd done at Lost River, but so far there had been no word that they'd achieved their objective.

Thanks to the dense, bone-numbing fog that clung to everything for miles around, Bernard's men had probably missed the canoes altogether. Not that that would make any difference, since the Modocs obviously had no intention of fleeing their stronghold. Why, he'd asked over and over again, would well-hidden Indians desert their natural cover and expose themselves on the flat land beyond the lava beds?

The answer he'd been given was so naive that he nearly laughed. Superior forces and weaponry would win the day against a handful of savages.

Damnit! The only thing that would be gained by forcing half-frozen soldiers to ride closer to the Indian fortress was that the exposed skirmish line the officers insisted on would give the Modocs a clear shot at their enemy. Ride! What a joke that was. Horses were less than useless on this uneven, treacherous ground.

Although Captain Perry looked ready to continue the argument, Jed turned his back on him and made his way to the edge of one of the bluffs that overlooked the distant stronghold.

Those few infantrymen not huddled around sagebrush fires lay on their bellies staring out at where they expected to fight tomorrow. The fog, which had shown some signs of dissipating earlier, had settled once again over the ground. The short day was ending, making it impossible to get a decent look at the lay of the land. From here, the country appeared perfectly flat, an easy march for the men. What they couldn't see was that the terrain was hard, uneven, and frozen, calling for a torturously slow march.

Ignoring the cold, Jed found a mound of shale to sit on and stared out at what looked like a shallow, quiet lake but in reality was the blanketing fog. Hidden by lava outcroppings were countless caves, narrow channels, stone hills, and valleys, and beyond that, the relatively flat stretches of land where the Modocs kept their few remaining horses and the cattle they'd stolen.

Luash was living in one of those caves. Maybe she'd left its shelter and was staring this way. Maybe she was thinking of him. Rightly calling him her enemy.

"Your pessimism only serves to demoralize the privates and volunteers. If that was your attitude at the Black Hills, I can see why Custer sent you here."

"My military attitude has never been anything but appropriate," he told Captain Perry without looking at him. "However, as you have so frequently pointed out, I have not been put in command of any troops. Thus, morale for the green recruits and untrained volunteers is your responsibility."

"Morale could not be higher," Captain Perry hissed. "Perhaps you did not see the letter Lieutenant Colonel Wheaton sent to the War Department. As he pointed out, the troops are in better condition for hostilities than any he has ever seen. He ended by praising how well the regulars and the volunteers work together."

Jed hadn't seen the letter, not that it surprised him. The more he expressed his opinion that the officers were underestimating the tenacity and determination of the Modocs, and overestimating the determination of the troops, the more he found himself excluded from both casual conversations and decision-making meetings.

But, damnation, he couldn't sit back and nod approval at the endless delays, lack of planning, inexperience, and ignorance. "Tomorrow we will see how well they carry out their orders," he muttered. "One thing I know; by nightfall either you or I will be right." He took a long breath. "I hope it's you, because if not, we'll be burying some of these boys."

To a man, the sentries turned and stared at Jed. For a moment, he wanted nothing more than to order these youngsters to run for their lives. But he was a soldier; he couldn't remember having been anything else. And in his world, dying walked side by side with living.

"Keep your eyes and ears open, boys," he said. "That's the way you stay alive."

"We shouldn't even be here," one of them muttered. "Look at this land. Hell couldn't be any worse. Let the savages have it; it ain't fittin' for anyone else."

Captain Perry ordered the sentry to be silent, but Jed found nothing to argue with in the boy's statement. Surely the ranchers who'd been clamoring to have the Indians removed could have found more fertile ground for their cattle. This place was worthless to everyone except the Modocs.

To Luash.

* * *

Turning her back on the vast stretch of land that surrounded the stronghold, Luash stared down at the red rope made of dyed tule fiber which extended in a wide circle around the Modoc camp. Cho-ocks had placed it there after much making of magic, declaring that the rope would protect all who remained inside its shelter.

Now, as the shaman ordered tail feathers from a great hawk, an otter skin, and several white-haired dog skins to be attached to his medicine pole, she carried yet another armload of sagebrush close to the magic fire. If Cho-ocks saw her, he would insist that her presence angered his spirit, but she couldn't sit back and do nothing when tomorrow weighed on her heart like a great rock.

She'd heard the braves taunting the Klamaths who'd helped guide the army here. She understood that few Modocs felt their lives were in danger. She knew that the army was too slow and awkward and noisy to catch her people. Still—a shudder surged through her at the thought of how close the army had come already, of war.

Cho-ocks left his medicine pole and walked over to where the musicians, seated on rocks around the sacred dance circle, were already beating their drums. He was soon joined by the rest of the men, all with their faces painted red except for two black lines down each cheek. The droning song of courage and victory began while the braves stood and stared at each other, their bodies motionless. Then they began moving slowly around the fire, alternately stepping and sliding their feet.

The drumbeats and monotonous chanting continued until she could no longer remember hearing any other sound. Even though she kept to the shadows with the other women, she felt herself being caught up in the ghost dance. Movement blurred as the dancers became more and more involved in what they were doing. Even the berdaches, those who sought pleasure with other men and were not wanted in battle because their magic was said to be weak, had been allowed to join in.

Many of the nearly fifty dancing warriors moved with their eyes closed. Some mouths hung slack. More than one began to tremble as if a spirit had taken hold of his senses. Finally, after fearsome jerking motions that became more and more frantic, Cho-ocks fell to the ground. His arms and legs trembled violently; his eyes rolled back-in his head, and sounds that made no sense spat from his mouth. Despite herself, Luash half believed the shaman had been possessed by his spirit.

When she began to sway in time with the dance, to feel its growing control over her thoughts, she forced herself to slip away from the others. The deep, hypnotic sound followed her into the frozen night.

In the distance, she could make out the glow from a number of fires where the soldiers waited. Surely the frigid air sent the ghost dance song to those waiting to attack them. Kientpoos and the others had said the army would probably try to approach from several directions, but it was a fool's effort. Even if the army men marched one hundred across, they could not possibly draw a circle around where her people waited. Escape would be as easy as turning and running where the army wasn't.

But running meant leaving the shelter and safety of the caves. Cho-ocks's medicine. That would be done only when and if the shaman said.

A soft sound of rushing air reached her and she imagined Eagle flying above her in the dark. She touched the top of her head in a wordless prayer of thankfulness, then continued to pick her way over the iced earth. She'd placed fresh stuffing in her footwear today and pointed out to Whe-cha that sagebrush bark held up better against sharp lava than white man's boots, which stiffened and sometimes made the wearer stumble. Whe-cha had agreed, sticking out her feet to reveal a well-worn pair of deerskin moccasins. Although Whe-cha had protested, Luash insisted on helping her stuff them with dried swamp grass and fur.

As she moved beyond the last of the light cast by the ghost fire, she deliberately kept her thoughts on Whe-cha. Her uncle's second wife was so young, barely past her puberty dance time. Although she had been sleeping with Kientpoos since the ceremony, the girl was still without child. Luash had done what she could to allow Whe-cha and Kientpoos time together, but in her heart she believed it was better that no babies be born during this uncertain time.

Made uneasy by her thoughts, she turned her gaze toward the sky, but the clouds blanketed the stars as they had done for so many nights. Behind her, the ghost dance continued. She heard the beat echo off rocks, imagined it sliding off into the distance. Jed was an officer, a lieutenant. He had told her he hadn't been sent here to lead men into battle, but she couldn't imagine what he would do if he didn't fight. When the army advanced on the lava beds, he would be among them, wouldn't he? If he showed himself, a Modoc warrior might aim his rifle at Jed and—

A sob rolled up from somewhere inside her, and although she struggled to deny that she'd made the sound, she knew the truth. She would weep if Kientpoos or Cho-Cho or Whe-cha were killed, and the thought of losing any children made her shudder; children made the journey into tomorrow. Even Cho-ocks's death would bring her sorrow. But until she'd stood before the gray-eyed white man and told him about Eagle, until she'd sensed the turmoil inside his heart, until they'd listened to a wolf together, she had never imagined she would grieve over a white man's death.

It was too dark to see the magic rope, but she knew it lay behind her. Now she stood with her arms wrapped around her, her hair blowing across her face in the freezing air, and sent out a silent prayer to Eagle. She entrusted her safety and life to him, and knew her faith would be rewarded. She could walk into the middle of a battle and be safe from harm. If Cho-ocks's medicine continued to be strong, the Modocs would be protected. Even if he told them to leave the Land of Burned Out Fires, his medicine would go with them.

But who would protect Jed? Would he live to see another night? She was still asking the question when she heard first an owl's hoot and then a coyote's cry.

JANUARY 17, 1873

"They come!"

Luash sat bolt upright, the nearly sleepless night forgotten. It was barely dawn. Hearing her uncle's deep curse, she slipped her blanket over her shoulders and made her way toward Kientpoos and Whe-cha's sleeping place near the mouth of the cave. By the time she reached it, Kientpoos was already gone.

"Luash!" Whe-cha called out. "Stop him!"

"I cannot. He knew this time would come. We all did."

"But if he is killed—" Whe-cha grabbed her wrist with surprising strength. "Where are they? Here?"

She couldn't believe the army men had managed to reach the stronghold without the sentries being aware of their approach. Still, until she saw with her own eyes, she couldn't reassure either herself or Whe-cha that they were safe. Without waiting for the younger woman to get dressed, Luash scrambled up and into the fragile light.

Braves seemed to be running everywhere, yelling, laughing even. They were all armed; some carried more than one rifle. She looked around for her uncle but couldn't find him. Most likely he was already at one of the overlooks. She headed toward the one with the best view of the army encampment. Before she reached it, she heard excited Modoc voices, her uncle's among them.

"They are snails," he laughed. "Snails who believe that numbers are more important than wisdom."

"Even snails will reach their destination," someone pointed out, "unless they are stopped."

"Then we will stop them."

Stop. By killing. Although she'd long known it could come to this, it was all she could do not to call out to Eagle to take her away from this. But although Eagle might spread his wings over her, he could not change her from what she was, a Modoc deep within the Land of Burned Out Fires.

It seemed that every brave wanted to see the approaching army, but finally she managed to sneak close enough for a look. The approaching army was so far away that they appeared to be ants, but there were so many of them, a disturbed anthill of soldiers swarming closer. Slowly closer.

"Do they think we will sit here and wait for them?" Cho-Cho asked sarcastically. "What is this thing the army does? Surely it is not fighting."

"Perhaps," Kientpoos said slowly, "they wait for us to come to them."

"Do they?" Cho-Cho was laughing now. "Then I say we will make them happy."

"What are you talking about?" she blurted, although it wasn't her place to question what the braves did.

"We are warriors," Kientpoos answered. "We go out to meet our enemy."

"No! There are so many!"

"Hush, my niece! Numbers do not matter. Wisdom does. Wisdom and cunning."

Be careful. Please, be careful! With several of the braves now staring at her, she knew better than to speak her thoughts aloud. She was a woman, and women did not go into battle. They remained behind to care for the children and wait for their warriors' return. Still, there was one thing she could do.

"My spirit goes with you today," she told her uncle, glad to see the eagle feather she'd given him braided into his hair. "He will fly over you and keep you safe. You and all Modocs." *Only Modocs.*

What was he doing here?

As Jed made his slow, awkward way on hands and knees, he tried to ignore the wrenching knot in his belly, but it was too deeply entrenched. Besides, without a healthy dose of fear, he might lose the fighting edge that kept him alive. How many hours they'd been "marching," he couldn't say. All he knew was that the advance, if it could be called that, had begun before dawn, and now it was late afternoon. The worthless horses had been left behind before they'd gone more than a quarter of a mile. The howitzers hadn't fared any better.

They had covered maybe three miserably slow miles in the better part of a day, first toward the stronghold and then east because a frightened volunteer had brought word that Major Green's troop was pinned down and in desperate need of help. After too long a hesitation, Captain Perry had ordered his command to change course and head for the lake so they could meet up with Captain Bernard's troop and hopefully rescue Major Green. ·

Jed had argued that placing a large number of soldiers in one place would only allow the Modocs to escape to the south, if they were so inclined. Perry was in no mood to listen to Jed.

Jed swore under his breath. The land here was all but impenetrable, a never-ending series of rocky chasms, some as deep as thirty feet, followed by steep outcroppings that taxed a man's strength and wore out both his clothing and resolve.

The Indians were phantoms in the ice-choked fog, appearing out of nowhere to fire at the laboring soldiers before running back to safety among the countless gullies that were their home. He'd known this was going to happen. But knowing that he and the others were in for an unequal fight and living through it were two different things.

The first could be argued impassionately and endlessly and philosophically. That debate delighted eastern politicians who had never seen battle and didn't know the taste of fear. The second meant struggling against dense, paralyzing fog and a churning belly while fighting for every miserable, frozen inch of land, all the while waiting for that next hostile rifle shot—the one that might end a man's life.

Although he was cold to the bone, Jed was driven to keep moving by more than the weather. He could have remained behind. After all, his value here didn't lie in his ability to lead troops into battle. But if he did that, he would have to live with what the troops said and thought of him. Only a man who walked, or crawled, into danger would be listened to, and if he survived today, by God, General Canby—who was back at Crawley Ranch—had better listen the next time he addressed him.

"I'm going to die here," a nearby soldier whimpered. "I know it."

"You don't know anything of the kind," he whispered back.

"It don't matter. I just want it to be over."

"It'll be dark soon," he tried to reassure the man. "The Modocs won't have anything to aim at then."

"Maybe it's not Modocs," someone else said. The man grunted sharply and Jed imagined him forcing his body over rocks capable of tearing flesh. "Maybe it's ghosts. There's got to be thousands of them. Everywhere. Playing with us. Laughing . . ."

After a short pause, the soldier began speaking again. His words were disjointed, hatred and fear interspersed with comments about the hard but safe pack train job he'd left in Redding so he could fight ignorant savages. Only, it looked as if the Modocs weren't the savages; after all, they weren't crawling on their bellies like dogs.

"Fighting this way isn't working," Jed hissed. "By tomorrow, there's going to be no doubt of that."

"Tomorrow? I can tell the general that right now."

Another man laughed harshly and then dropped his voice. He was ready to argue with anyone here that, bad as the waiting and noise of last night had been, this was worse. Not only were the Modocs making the army look like bumbling fools, but they were toying with them, slipping close to fire at exposed and trapped targets before scurrying back to whatever hellhole they'd come from.

Jed, who'd given up trying to sort out the sounds whispering down the narrow ravines, agreed. If he'd been in charge, not a single man would be here. Instead, he would have waited until he had enough troops to surround the stronghold and then done what he'd been advocating for all along, cut the Modocs off from food and water.

Captain Jack was no fool. Eventually, he would have turned over the young bucks who'd slaughtered innocent ranchers. If it took hungry babies crying themselves to sleep to bring about peace, that would be better than forcing any more soldiers to risk their hides.

Babies crying with hunger. Men and women helplessly watching their children grow weak.

Jed clenched his teeth and forced his frozen fingers into fists, but that did nothing to erase the unwanted image that had formed in his mind. The Modocs were human beings, people who laughed and loved and—

What was happening to him? Until he'd met Luash, he hadn't once thought of an Indian as someone with emotions no different from his.

A nearby rifle blast echoed off the rocks and froze Jed where he crouched. He tried to swallow, but his mouth was too dry. A man cried out in pain. It wasn't the first time; the Modocs had killed one man already and injured at least three more. But this voice— damnit, the man sounded so young!

When the injured soldier kept up a high-pitched sob, Jed scrambled toward the sound, concentrating on trying to get his heart back to something like a steady pace. Fog lapped at the rocks. That plus the deepening shadows of afternoon forced him to crawl at a maddeningly slow pace. At least the soldier's voice was filled with strength as well as pain, and Jed took that as a sign that the wound, although painful, was probably not fatal.

Straining, he spotted a uniformed figure plastered against the ground. After inching forward a few more feet, he recognized Captain Perry. The two men stared at each other. The wounded soldier's cries had become a childlike sob impossible to ignore. Leaving Perry, Jed covered the remaining distance as rapidly and quietly as possible. The writhing soldier stilled at Jed's approach and turned frightened eyes on him.

"Are you hurt anywhere else?" he asked.

"My leg! Just my leg." The soldier gripped his calf. "Oh God, it hurts! I—I thought everyone had deserted me."

"I haven't, son," Jed whispered, feeling a thousand years old. Careful not to bump the young man, he closed his hand over his shoulder in what he hoped was a comforting gesture. "You're going to be all right. No one dies from being shot in the leg."

"But—what if I lose it?"

Although Jed couldn't promise anything without having seen the wound, he told the man that no doctor would cut off a leg simply because there was or had been a bullet in it. "I have to get you to safety," he whispered. "I'm sorry, son, but it's going to hurt."

"I don't care! I just want out of this hell before they finish me off."

He nearly warned the man to keep his voice down so the Modocs wouldn't hear him, but what did it matter? Surely the warriors had heard the sobs. In all likelihood, whoever had shot the youngster was just out of sight. He might never know why the brave hadn't finished off his victim.

Damn you, Luash. They're your people.

Keeping his tone as light as he could, he complimented the

wounded man on the spot he'd chosen to fall. Because he was in a depression, the rocks on all sides acted as a natural shelter. "Still, it's safer back there. We've got to move."

"I've been trying. But it hurts too much."

"I know, but you don't have a choice."

"If they get their hands on me, they'll scalp me, won't they?"

Your people, Luash.

Cursing the lack of anything to secure the man's leg with, Jed explained that he was going to grab him under his arms and as carefully as possible drag him closer to relative safety. The man, who had told him his name was Mason Robert Wilson III, tensed but nodded. "I don't want to make no noise. I kept telling myself to be quiet, but I couldn't stop."

Because fear had the upper hand. He wished he had the time to reassure Mason before taking hold of him, but with every second, the danger grew. After telling the boy that his job would be to keep hold of the rifles and protect his bad leg as best he could, Jed began pulling him toward where he'd seen Captain Perry.

Mason sobbed, then fell silent. His body was so tense that Jed felt as if he had hold of a log, but he could hear the youngster's teeth grinding together. He wheezed, his breath coming fast and hard.

Your people, Luash. They put this boy through this.

Jed was sweating by the time he left the gully. If he thought there was any advantage in waiting, he would have remained with the boy until darkness gave them needed cover, but anything was safer than where they'd been.

"Jed."

Captain Perry had spoken so softly that at first he didn't recognize the voice. He had to hand it to the man; he'd somehow overcome whatever emotion had kept him rooted to the ground and had slipped closer.

"What?"

"You're going to need help."

Jed settled himself onto his hip, supporting Mason against his chest. "You're offering?"

"I've already lost one man today. I don't want to bury another."

The sun was setting; the fog shadows had become even thicker. The rocks and depressions, the caves and cracks had lost all form. Jed was fairly sure where the others were, but it wouldn't take much for him to become disoriented. Every breath he took washed the air around him in white. He could no longer feel his ears and nose and mouth and he had begun to shake. His feet, inside his stiff boots, could have been wooden stumps, and if he hadn't worked himself into a lather hauling Mason, his fingers too would have been useless by now.

How could *she* live here?

"Ready?"

Jed nodded. Perry had hold of the wounded man's left arm. His face determined, he straightened. Before Jed could warn him not to expose himself, a burst of sound shattered the pulsing silence and Captain Perry pitched forward, screaming.

Jed managed to grab Perry and ease his fall. He felt blood on his hands and knew Perry had taken a bullet in his upper arm. In the freezing air, the blood smell quickly faded.

"Are you shot, white man?" an unseen Modoc sneered. "Maybe you no longer be so sure of yourself." Jed clutched Perry against him, comforting the wounded captain with the only thing he had— his body.

"I'm hit. I'm hit," another warrior echoed Perry's cry. Trapped by both Perry and Mason's needs, Jed frantically tried to make out where the voices were coming from, but the shadows, the land itself was against him. The private trembled. Perry's body twisted first one way and then the other as pain had its way with him. The sense of isolation dug into Jed. Isolation and vulnerability and hatred.

"You no man," the hidden Modoc taunted. "You squaw."

Damn you to hell, Luash.

8

Van Bremer's ranch, usually home for a single family, overflowed with soldiers. They camped in small groups clustered near the house. Although it hadn't been dark long, most of them were curled up on the ground wrapped in blankets, three smoldering fires the only warmth.

Luash had never been this close to an army stronghold, had never guessed she would crawl on her belly to the edge of the bluff that looked down on men, weapons, and horses. But ever since the army's attack and retreat, she'd battled emotions that could only be calmed by coming here.

An officer had been shot. Ha-kar-Jim, who claimed responsibility, hadn't known who he'd hit. What he did know was that the officer had cried out and fallen to the ground where two of his companions, one of them already wounded, lay.

Full of himself, Ha-kar-Jim had insisted that no white could stand before him and that those who tried would watch their blood seep into the ground. Hadn't he already killed more white men than there were fingers on both his hands after the burning of Modoc homes at Lost River?

Jed was an officer. Maybe he'd been out there two days ago while she watched what she could see of the battle from her rocky vantage point. When the soldiers began retreating, taking their dead and wounded with them, she had tried to bury her thoughts in the sounds of the victorious scalping dance that lasted through the first night. The next day she'd helped the other women prepare beef and camas stew while the tribe's children noisily replayed the battle around them, but early this morning, feeling sick, she'd ventured out onto the battlefield where chilling silence had replaced the sounds, sights, and smells of fighting.

She'd come across several bodies stripped of clothing and weapons, and despite her horror at what had been done to them, she'd sent Eagle a prayer of thanksgiving that no Modoc blood had been shed. Cho-ocks had taken full honor for that, saying his powerful medicine was responsible for the Modoc victory. Maybe he was right, and maybe Eagle had spread his protective wings over all her people.

By afternoon, Luash had reassured herself that Jed's body hadn't been left behind at this horrible place, but that did nothing to quiet her fear for him. She'd seen wounded soldiers being lifted onto horses' backs and led away. Jed could have been one of them.

There was a full moon, and although clouds and fog often covered it, she was grateful for the faint light cast by it and the fires burning near the sleeping men. Over and over again she traced in her mind the route she had to take if she was going to get any closer, but every time she started to leave her shelter, her body froze; the sensation had little to do with the bitter cold or cutting wind.

She shouldn't be here. What did she care what happened to a gray-eyed man who hated her people and lived for little other than to fight them? She should wish him dead. If he was, he would fade from her mind and she could go back to who she'd been before he touched her with his words.

But she didn't know whether he was dead or alive and the question ate at her the way a spring swollen creek attacks its banks.

Calling herself crazy, she drew her blanket up around her neck to ward off what she could of the night and slipped away from her shelter. Ha-kar-Jim said the soldiers had crawled on their bellies like snakes. Now she was doing the same as she made her way to the sleeping men. She heard loud snoring. While the soldiers kept their rifles near them, none stirred the way a man does when his sleep is light. Ha-kar-Jim had laughed that many of the fleeing soldiers had fallen asleep on their horses. Unless she walked into their camp beating a drum, there was little danger she would be spotted.

Lantern light glowed from within the Van Bremer house, and she was careful not to walk where anyone inside might spot her. A soldier, a sentry she guessed because he was near the horses, sat slumped forward, his face nearly touching the rifle resting on his lap. Despite her reason for being here, her eyes strayed to the corralled horses. If she could bring them back to her people, even Choocks would have to acknowledge her courage.

A horse that had been sleeping standing up lowered itself to the ground and stretched out, sighing deeply. Although she had ridden several times, she had no idea how she would make the animals follow her back to the beds without waking the soldiers.

Besides, horses hadn't brought her here.

After waiting behind a stack of rough-cut lumber for several minutes, she forced herself to leave its protection. Although her lungs burned with the need to take a deep breath, she was too close to the soldiers to take the risk.

She was insane for coming here.

She stared at the cabin. When the shadow of a man passed in front of the window, she dropped flat against the ground, then lifted her head. Another man came to the window and stared out of it, but she was too far away to make out his features. In there, she reminded herself, were men who were not overcome by exhaustion, or were so consumed by thoughts of revenge that sleep wouldn't come. Surely they were talking about her people, cursing them, maybe planning their next attack. If they knew she was out here, they would kill her, or worse.

Despite her faith in Eagle, the thought nearly overwhelmed her, and she had to concentrate on calming her pounding head and heart before she could go back to trying to locate Jed.

Jed. A man who challenged everything she believed about those of his kind. A man tied by his own hatred. A man who had seen her with Eagle and had reached past her defenses to touch—to touch—no!

The frozen ground bit at her hands and forced her to stop so she could tuck them against her body. As she waited for her fingers to warm, the tug she'd sensed coming from the cabin returned, stronger this time. She didn't want to go any closer; those men were armed, angry and armed. A man lying a few feet from her groaned and tucked his body closer in upon itself. She stopped breathing, then slowly relaxed. This man, who looked so young that it tore at her resolve to hate the enemy, had rolled so that his blanket no longer covered his back. It wouldn't be long before he stirred. She knelt, with the cabin to her left and motionless bodies surrounding her, and wondered at the insanity that had taken hold of her.

The cabin, full of life and men, called to her in some unfathomable way.

She was still on her knees when she again spotted movement at the window. Whoever it was stood motionless for a long minute. Because the lantern was behind him, all she saw was his silhouette. He looked to be Jed's size, but she'd never seen him without his heavy coat, and this man wore only a shirt. Finally he turned as if distracted by someone behind him and moved out of sight.

The night held silent and still, a pocket of time without beginning or end. Sometimes night gave her comfort, a chance to be alone with her thoughts. And sometimes night filled her with a restlessness so raw that she wondered if she might shatter.

Tonight beat with restlessness.

The door opened and a large form filled it. The breeze blew toward her; she caught the sound of men's voices but not their meaning. When the door closed, the man remained outside, standing with his back only a finger's span from the heavy wood. He carried a rifle.

Then he began walking and she knew. Jed walked like that, strong and purposeful, yet as if his body weighed no more than that of a fawn.

She shouldn't have come here; she didn't want to see him after all.

He made his way toward the nearest campfire and after propping his rifle against a rock, piled wood on the coals. When fresh flames pushed heat toward the sleepers, he retrieved his weapon and walked to the second fire. When he'd replenished all of them, he stood with his back to the last one, his attention not on those at his feet but the darkness beyond.

Could he possibly know she was out here?

After a seemingly endless stretch of time, Jed moved toward the barn and slowly walked around it. When he was where she couldn't see him, she hurried toward the corral and crouched deep in the shadows. Now she was closer to the hills. If he tried to stop her, she might be able to escape into the night before he overtook her.

But if he shot at her—

No. Jed wouldn't kill her.

Reappearing, he started back toward the cabin, his steps slow as if he was reluctant to go inside. Before, his attention had been on the men and fires. Now he kept his gaze on the night and when he looked in her direction, he stopped for two, maybe three heartbeats.

Pain shot through her numb legs as she straightened, but she dismissed the discomfort. Maybe he didn't need sight. Maybe something else held him to her.

And her to him.

He began walking toward her. She told herself she should turn and run like a swift-legged deer, but she simply stood and waited, her mind overflowing with him. Her heart felt like a drum being beaten with angry fingers.

"I knew I'd find you here," he whispered. "Somehow I knew."

He'd stopped far enough away that his presence didn't make her uneasy. She was grateful for that and wondered if he knew how much courage and insanity it had taken for her to come here. "I thought you might be dead," she told him.

"And that mattered to you?"

He didn't have to tighten his grip on his rifle. Surely he knew she was no threat to him. But the movement reminded her that they were enemies. In a strange way she was grateful for that. Grateful and filled with regret. "Ha-kar-Jim said he shot an officer," she explained with the night and his presence lapping at her senses. "I had to know if it was you."

"Did you?" Anger and a soft confusion flowed through his words. "Where were you during the fighting? Did you see any of it?"

"A little."

"And?"

She hadn't come here to have him throw his words at her, but if he'd asked, she wouldn't have told him what had compelled her to risk her life for this meeting. She couldn't because she didn't understand herself. "Your soldiers know nothing of fighting in the Land of Burned Out Fires. They were lost, like small children far from their mothers' sides."

Although she thought that might anger him, he only grunted. She wished she had the power to chase away the night. Daylight would expose her to even more danger, but at least she would be able to look deep into his eyes for the emotions buried in him.

This was the first time she had seen him without his bulky clothing. She realized he had been created with generous hands. His broad shoulders left no doubt that she couldn't pit her strength against his and yet she wasn't afraid of him.

His chest was so wide that his buttons strained slightly. His waist was narrow, his belly flat. Strong hips flowed into thighs made for a lifetime of riding and walking. If she tugged his uniform off him, he would keep no secrets from her, and she would know everything about him—the muscles that roped his body, the sun-baked color of his flesh, whether—as she had heard about white men—he had hair on his chest and belly and back, and covering his manhood.

Her mind snagged on that part of him, but she felt no sense of shame. Still, in attempt to keep her thoughts from him and his power over her, she tried to remember what they'd been talking about. She'd made fun of the soldiers; he'd said nothing in turn.

"Did you think we would be easy to defeat?" she asked. "That we would flee the only home left to us?"

"No. I didn't. But I seem to have been the only one who did. However, because of our miserable showing, the others have come around. What about your warriors? We heard them singing. I imagine they're pretty full of themselves right now."

She wasn't quite sure what he meant by "full of themselves." "There has been much boasting and the scalping dance lasted a long time."

"There wasn't any scalping."

"No." She tried to ignore his harsh tone, then reminded herself that the truth and what she wanted were worlds apart. "But the dance fills our braves with courage. They have much to celebrate, much to boast about. Jed? Why did you come out here? The others—" She pointed. "They sleep like the dead."

He placed the wooden end of his rifle on the ground and leaned against it, looking comfortable and yet not comfortable with himself. "I knew—no. I couldn't have known. I can't say what it was. Some sense . . . those poor exhausted youngsters almost let their fires go out. It's a good thing I checked up on them."

He wasn't saying her presence had touched him in any way. Fine. Now she didn't have to tell him she'd known he was inside—that something of him had reached out to her. "What about those in the house? They speak of making more war?"

"There isn't much else to talk about."

He was far enough away that she could stretch out her hand in the space separating them and not touch him, and yet the distance wasn't nearly enough. He called himself nothing but a soldier and yet there was something about him, a power nearly as strong as the underground force that once spewed fire over the land. She felt like a fragile plant caught in the path of molten lava; if he touched her, she might be destroyed. "I do not want it to be like this. To fight, to kill may be a man's way, but my woman's heart seeks peace."

"It's too late for that. Look." He ran his hand through his hair, the gesture both angry and helpless. "I'm not going to tell you about what's being discussed. I won't betray the army."

She tried to speak, but he didn't give her time. "There's one thing you can take back to your leader and that's this—the army doesn't give up. We've got more troops, hundreds more, on the way. It'll cost the government a bloody lot of money to fight this damnable war, but in the end we're going to win."

"You have said that before."

"The question is, do you believe me?"

"Jed, you speak of more troops. Earlier you told me of great weapons, howitzers, that would bring the Modocs to their knees. But that did not happen."

She thought he gave a brief nod, but it was so dark that maybe it was nothing more than her imagination. "No, it didn't. They're all but useless on this ground, like you said."

"I will tell you something." Her thoughts boiled inside her, dangerous. "When we saw the army approaching, I went far into the lava beds where no one, Modoc or white, could see me. My mind was full of the sight of soldiers slowly coming closer, many weapons. Our shaman had done much magic to protect us, but there was something I had to do."

"And that was what?"

"I sought Eagle." He couldn't look into her eyes and see what was inside her. Still, she kept her gaze trained on him and hoped he might feel, might believe. "I prayed to him to shelter and protect my people. He came, hovered over me for a long time, then flew off in the direction of the soldiers."

"I don't want to hear this."

"Then he returned, bringing in his beak a soldier's hat. He let it drop to the ground, then tore it apart. When I saw that, my heart was filled with joy and peace."

She waited for him to tell her she couldn't have possibly seen what she had and even if Eagle had attacked a soldier's head covering, it didn't mean anything, but he didn't. "I speak the truth," she insisted.

"The truth? Luash, you said you came here because you thought I might have been wounded, or killed. That mattered to you?"

"I do not hate you, Jed Britton. I wish I did. It would be easier if . . . "

"You don't want this any more than I do, do you?"

She didn't have to ask him what he meant by "this." Although what she felt was without form, it filled her and made her feel young and alive. "No. I do not."

"Then you should have stayed away."

"And you should have remained inside."

This time she was sure of his short nod, followed by a deep and yet quick sigh. "You have to leave," he whispered. "If someone sees you . . . "

The men nearby were like the dead, and if someone emerged

from the house, she could run away before they saw her; Eagle would protect her. "Maybe you are that someone," she challenged. "You are armed. I have no weapons. Shoot me, Jed Britton. Then you will never have to look at me again."

"Damnit, I wish I'd never laid eyes on you."

"I know."

"Do you feel the same way?"

"Yes."

Yes. Luash's admission echoed inside Jed. He tried to tell himself that was exactly what he wanted to hear, but it wasn't the truth. Tonight, the only truth was that she stood before him looking part human and part wild creature, surrounded by the night, caressed by it. What she'd told him about her spirit bird had sent a chill through him, but with her voice flowing around him, he hadn't been able to concentrate on anything except the fact that she'd risked her life because she'd had to know whether he was still alive.

He'd been full of her yesterday. Even when Perry was hit and he wondered if he might be next, a small corner of his mind had remained under her control. Hating her power, he told her what had happened when he realized he was responsible for two wounded men. He said nothing about the curses he'd hurtled her way.

"Your warriors laughed at the captain," he challenged. "Damnit, the poor man had been shot."

"Your soldiers came to kill us."

They couldn't say a word without it being about the differences between them. Why the hell then had he walked outside? The answer was as simple and as complicated as why she'd let him approach her.

"Jed?" she said softly. "What happened? Both men, they lived?"

After telling himself that as soon as he answered her there would be no more reason for them to go on talking, he explained that he'd ordered all soldiers within earshot to make their way to him. Then he deployed several to move the wounded; the rest were put to work defending their position. He put no emotion in the telling, said nothing about the anger and fear that had been churning through him.

Still, before he was done, he felt her fingers on his forearm. Warm. Alive. Both challenging and comforting. "You were alone with two injured men for a long time," she said softly. "The captain and the private looked to you for comfort, and there was little you could give them. It was a hard thing."

The only thing she hadn't mentioned was the cold sweat that had filmed his body, and yet he guessed she knew about that too. "I didn't run. I thought about it, but I didn't."

Her fingers became more than a whisper-touch. "No. You would never think of yourself only."

This woman, this so-called savage, knew too damn much about him.

"Life is precious to you, Jed," she whispered. Her hand was back by her side; he wondered if she regretted the brief contact. "You say it is not, but that is not the truth."

"I never—"

"You say you believe in nothing, that you live only to fight, but I say you have too much heart for that."

"Do I? I cursed you yesterday. Wanted you dead. When I had a man's blood on my hands, I wanted it to be yours."

In the distance, a horse pounded its hoof against the ground. Another responded by whinnying loudly. The sounds briefly turned her from him, and yet she didn't appear to be startled. Why should she? She believed some bird rendered her everything but immortal. "I do not believe you," she said. "It would be easier if I did."

"Leave, damnit. You got what you came here for; you found out your braves didn't finish me off—this time."

"You hate me."

"There's dead men over there, one barely old enough to leave his mother's side."

"I killed no one."

"You know what I'm talking about! The boy didn't want to be here. He was probably so scared he couldn't move."

She took a backward step. He told himself he was going to let her go. Still, his hand snaked out and caught her wrist. She jerked, forcing him to grip tighter. "Let me—"

A sudden shard of light distracted him. Someone had opened the cabin door; the glow from the lantern spilled into the dark. Before he had time to react, someone called out his name. Instantly, Luash's arm became like a taut bowstring.

"Don't!" he hissed. Although there was no need, he pulled her around and clamped his hand over her mouth. Fear hammered at his heart, stark terror for this woman. "I'm out here," he responded as loudly as he dared, hoping none of the soldiers would wake, hoping the night hid both him and her. "What do you want?"

"What are you doing? It's the middle of the night."

"Some things a man's got to do in private. I'll be right there."

"You'd better. Perry's awake and asking for you."

"I told you, I'll be there." Luash was still, her body both soft and solid against his. The man, Lieutenant Colonel Wheaton, muttered something Jed didn't catch. He stood with his shoulder braced against the doorjamb as he peered into the night. Wheaton was director of the command against the Modocs. The last two days had been a nightmare for him, and his endurance and patience had been stretched nearly to breaking. What he might do if he spotted Luash turned Jed numb. After a minute, the lieutenant colonel cursed softly, then stepped back inside, closing the door behind him.

"He didn't see you," Jed whispered.

She twisted against him, yet there was nothing frantic about her movements. Even more of her warmth flowed into him. She felt so light; he marveled that there was so much strength in her slight form, such softness beneath the thick layers of clothing.

"Jed. Let me go."

"Are you going to leave?"

"I do not know. Let me go."

He couldn't do that, not yet, but he knew that a few more moments of her body against his wouldn't still his need. In fact, it would only make it worse. Slowly, cursing himself for not turning his back on her when he first realized who was out there, he drew his hands off her. He waited for her to jerk away, but she simply took a half step and spun around so that she was looking up at him.

He didn't need morning or light from the campfires to know her eyes were filled with questions, distrust, and secrets kept from him, maybe a tiny opening into her soul—even if he didn't believe in souls.

He laid his fingertips on her cheek. She pulled in a quick breath, but didn't move. *Stop it. Don't.* . . . He couldn't hold onto the rest of the warning he needed to give himself, but then how could he, with the sound of her breathing in his ears?

He explored her face in the dark, a blind man seeking answers in brush strokes of sensation. She had no spare flesh over her narrow nose and strong chin. Below her eyes, he discovered warm velvet that made his fingers feel like roughened wood by contrast. He turned his attention to her lashes, to the bones which sheltered her huge dark eyes. That she allowed him to touch her so intimately seemed the greatest of miracles. He knew the spell could be easily broken, wondered at the reason for this small measure of trust, then decided trust had very little to do with it.

He could still hear her breathing. In his exploration, he'd discovered that her nostrils were flared. There, simple and basic and primitive was the reason why she hadn't let the night envelope her.

He sensed her tremble, guessed that her response came from

that place where sensation and little else dwelled. He wanted to tell her he understood, but when he tried to form the words, they jumbled inside him. They now stood apart from each other, but he remained imprinted with her and need crawled over him like a hungry animal.

"You were afraid of the man who called to you," she whispered. "Why?"

"Not for me. For you."

"You should not care what happens to me."

"No. I shouldn't. I cursed you yesterday, wished you into that hell I don't believe in. But I did that because—because I was scared and angry and sick. I knew the army wasn't going to win that attack."

"Because my spirit is strong."

"Stop it! That damn bird of yours has nothing to do with this! You think you're invincible; someday that's going to get you killed."

Her laugh was short and musical, a soft brush of sound that reminded him of why her life had become precious to him. "There are going to be other battles," he forced himself to say. "And your people are going to lose them."

"If that is so, then hiding me from your soldiers is foolish."

"Go, Luash. You don't belong here."

For too long he didn't think she was going to speak, and when she did, her voice lacked strength. "You are right, Jed. I no longer have any right to stand on this land."

"That's not what I meant. I'm talking about—"

"I know what you are saying, Jed Britton. And I have no wish to be here when your soldiers wake. But there is something I leave with you. Our spirits remain on this land; you cannot order Sun God to leave Mount Shasta. You say Kumookumts is not the creator, but your words do not change what I know. Listen to the night, Jed Britton. When you hear a coyote howl, when owl sings his song, you will know that death will again visit your kind."

"Coyote? An owl? You can't believe that."

She stood before him, her body motionless, touching him only with her words. "You have no spirit, Jed Britton, and mine is powerful. That is what I know."

No! he wanted to throw at her, but a distant wolf had caught the night breeze with his ageless call and she was looking up at him. Smiling a little.

Listen, he heard her say although her lips didn't move. *This sound belongs; only this sound and those who understand it.*

9

Five days after the abortive attack on the stronghold, Captain Bernard, under orders from General Canby, abandoned Land's Ranch. He took with him several wagon loads of supplies and a small number of men, their destination the Applegate Ranch to the west. As they approached Scorpion Point, they were attacked. Although none of the fleeing men were hurt, the Modocs burned all the wagons plus the badly needed grain.

Shortly after, some Modocs fired at the military camp at Van Bremer's ranch, nearly causing a panic there. Other Modocs did the same at the Dorris ranch, their intended victims this time some Indians who hadn't joined them in the lava beds.

While reports of that attack were still coming in, a small number of Modocs attacked a group of volunteers who were moving horses along the lake's north shore. As a result, volunteers began deserting, along with some of the reservation Indians. The soldiers who would replace them hadn't yet arrived.

When he received word that General Canby wanted to meet with him, Jed was certain he knew why. Although he expected other officers to join them for an update on what had happened over the last few days, except for the general's aide, they were alone at an isolated spot some five miles from the stronghold. They had an unbelievable view of an entire valley clogged with black, lifeless rubble and rocks, proof of what a volcanic eruption could produce.

"Incredible. Absolutely incredible," General Canby said from where he stood overlooking the valley before Jed had had time to dismount. "And not just the land. The Modocs know no fear. They're like ghosts; no one knows where they'll show up next. I'm certain they're not out here. Nothing, not even an animal, would have any reason to be, and yet I keep thinking I'm going to see some warriors."

Leaving his horse with the aide, Jed joined his general. Although he'd heard of this spot, this was his first time here. Incredible. Vast. Nearly incomprehensible. Both lifeless and compelling. "This humbles me," he admitted. "No matter what civilization accomplishes, it can't match this."

"I agree, Lieutenant," General Canby went on. "I've fought Seminoles and taken part in the removal of Seminoles and Cherokees to Indian Territory. I thought chasing Seminoles through the Everglades had tested me in ways I never would be again, but I was wrong. These Modocs—I am inclined to believe you have been right all along and that cutting them off from all hope of food or escape is the only way to bring an end to this war. However, and this is between the two of us, that is not what is going to happen."

"I don't understand."

With an impatient finger, General Canby motioned for his aide to join them. The scruffy-looking young man handed Jed a telegram. Reading carefully, Jed learned that the newly reelected President Grant had decided to dispatch a peace commission to deal with the Modoc situation. Grant was under considerable pressure from religious groups and pacifists to end the hostilities without further bloodshed. Head of the commission was to be A.B. Meacham, the former Oregon Indian superintendent.

"I want the truth from you, Jed," the general said. "I'm beginning to think you're the only one who will tell me what I need to hear, not just what you might believe I want to hear. Do you honestly believe a peace commission has a chance of bringing things to a close?"

"Where is Meacham?"

"In the capital, unfortunately. It'll take him several weeks to get here, and I'm not at all convinced that he and whoever is appointed to work with him will succeed in defusing things peacefully. I'm well aware that the relationship between Meacham and Captain Jack is not the best. However, the president has made his decision, and I am bound to honor that. In the meantime, I have decided that Lieutenant Colonel Wheaton must be relieved of responsibility for the entire campaign. The soldiers have lost confidence in him. If we're going to prevent any more desertions, any more demoralization, we *must* have new leadership."

Was General Canby thinking to give him that position? Before Jed could remind his commanding officer that there were others who outranked him and who wanted the position, the general smiled, the grin barely visible through his beard.

"I believe I know what you are thinking, Lieutenant. However, you can rest your mind on that matter. You have the reputation of being a bit of a rebel; when you believe you are right, you don't care who hears. I'm concerned the men might not look to you with the degree of respect needed. We *must* present a positive, united front to the troops and volunteers, something that's sadly lacking at this point. Beyond that, if you have to answer to me for everything you and the men under you do, you might be less honest than you are now."

"I might," he acknowledged.

General Canby laughed. "And I need that honesty, even if I don't always act on it. To lay my cards on the table, much as I would like to do as you've advocated and simply trap the Modocs until they are forced to give up, this is *not* what the president and his advisors want. They are adamantly opposed to anything less than a massive show of force, so that when the peace commission is ready to begin work, the Modocs will have full understanding of and respect for our strength. Don't fail me, lieutenant. What are your impressions of Colonel Alvan Gillem?"

"Gillem? I don't personally know him."

"Hmm. But you know of him."

Yes, he did. Dividing his attention between the general and their surroundings, Jed planned his reply. It would be easier for the future of his career to plead ignorance, to keep his opinions to himself, but General Canby had turned to him because he needed honesty. "He's a southerner, but he didn't support the Confederacy during the war."

"And your family did?"

"Yes, sir."

"Which means you might not be kindly disposed toward Colonel Gillem?"

"That's not it. I mean, that's not the reason for my reservations."

"And you have reservations?"

Maybe he should feel backed into a corner, but he didn't. Instead, he welcomed the opportunity for honesty. "What I know about Colonel Gillem comes to me secondhand. However, I have heard the same stories over and over again. It's my impression that Colonel Gillem's treatment of both enlisted men and officers is erratic and sometimes downright unfair."

"I see."

"I also understand that other officers resent him because he has advanced through the ranks more rapidly than most. They believe that wouldn't have happened if he hadn't been a personal friend of President Andrew Johnson."

"Do you believe that?"

"I don't know, sir."

"Hmm. If you were in my position, what would you do?"

Was that why General Canby had asked for him, so he could get an honest opinion? Hoping that was the case and hoping it meant the general would give his observations more serious consideration from now on, Jed gave him as complete an answer as possible.

"Confidence in Lieutenant Colonel Wheaton has been seriously eroded, probably fatally so, thanks to the dismal results of our so-called assault on the lava beds, followed by the recent Modoc attacks. There are other officers already serving here who might be capable of taking over Wheaton's responsibilities, but the question is, do those officers honestly believe the Modocs can be defeated? There's no denying that the January seventeenth attack was a disaster."

"Yes, it was."

"And since then, the Modocs have been toying with us, flaunting their superior knowledge of the area. Perhaps you need new blood, a West Point man with influential political connections, a man who can get the government to provide us with the manpower and arms necessary to defeat the Indians."

"Yes." General Canby drew out the word. "Perhaps that *is* what this campaign needs." Swinging away from him, the general turned his attention back to the massive lava field. "Thank you, lieutenant. I trust we will be speaking again soon."

Jed and the other officers met with Colonel Gillem at the newly formed Lost River headquarters on February 9. Afterward, Jed told Wilfred that the tension between Gillem and the outgoing Wheaton had been palpable.

"Gillem's already riding roughshod over what's been going on so far," he explained as they watched a blacksmith at work on the horses corralled at the Van Bremer house. "When he heard that freight companies from Jacksonville and Roseburg have been charging twice what it would cost to bring supplies up from Redding, he immediately cut off all Oregon freight. The teamsters are up in arms over the lost revenue, but there's not much they can do."

"Except hope the Modocs win; they'd probably call it justice."

"It's not going to happen. Gillem's soon going to have nearly seven hundred troops at his disposal."

"That many?"

"More. There's at least another hundred forty at camps Warner and Harney just waiting to be called into service."

"Do you think that's going to make an impression on the Modocs?"

"I'm about to find out," Jed said, his attention fixed on the blacksmith's fire. The erratic wind lashed the flames in first one direction and then the other. It hadn't snowed for several days, but unless he was wrong, more would be here before nightfall.

"What do you mean?"

"Gillem doesn't have the patience to simply sit back and wait for the peace commission, and General Canby has turned responsibility for the campaign over to him."

"Already?"

"Unfortunately," Jed said, honestly, because Wilfred was the one person he could confide in. "You've been at Fairchild's ranch. You know what the word from Captain Jack is."

Wilfred grunted. "That he wants peace talks. At least that's what he says, not that I'm inclined to believe him, given how successful the Modocs have been so far. So, what's Gillem got up his sleeve?"

"He wants someone to go into the stronghold. Probably hopes he'll be able to convince Jack that the peace commission was his idea. A politician to the end," he finished sarcastically.

"You're going to volunteer, aren't you. Why the hell would you want to do a fool thing like that?"

"Because General Canby recommended me."

"You and the general are that close?"

"We understand each other. And maybe . . ." Jed's gaze strayed in the direction of the stronghold. "Maybe through Luash, I can get Jack to listen to me."

"Jack's going to hear what he wants, and do what he wants. I don't for a minute believe he's thinking about rolling over and giving up."

"Maybe. Maybe not. Someone's got to find out what he's thinking, that's for sure. Look, if he is so inclined, and if he still has the support he did back when his group walked off the reservation, he ought to be able to talk the lot of them into surrendering."

"Not too likely," Wilfred insisted.

"You think not?"

"So do you; admit it. Damnit, Jed, the Modocs have to have heard that the grand jury in Jacksonville indicted some of the braves for the deaths of those settlers. The likes of Hooker Jim and their shaman aren't going to risk getting their heads put through any nooses. They'll hold out, try to talk everyone into doing the same. Put pressure on Captain Jack to stay right where they are."

"That's what I want to find out, how much power and control Jack still has. If they're fighting among themselves, it might change things, make it easier to defeat them."

"Maybe. Who's going with you?"

"No one."

"The hell you say. You trying to get yourself killed before spring?"

"Whether I approve of the man or not, Gillem is giving the orders. Neither he nor General Canby want to risk more lives than absolutely necessary. And you and I both know there's no guarantee this so-called peace commission is going to accomplish anything. Hell, we don't even know who's going to work with Meacham, when and if he gets here."

"So they're offering up your life, and you're letting them. After what happened to you" —Wilfred looked pointedly at the scar on

Jed's forehead—"I'd think you'd be looking for excuses to add to your collection of Indian scalps, not the other way around."

"I never took a scalp! Never!"

"Calm down, will you? You just ain't got no sense of humor."

That, Jed admitted, was something he couldn't argue with. He hadn't had to tell his friend what he'd agreed to do. If he'd wanted to keep from being asked a lot of hard questions, he'd have kept his mouth shut until he'd gotten back—if he got back. But he'd confided in Wilfred. Maybe he wanted Wilfred to talk him out of this insanity.

Only, he wouldn't listen to the argument, he acknowledged as Wilfred handed him a half empty jug of whiskey. He was leaving for the stronghold tomorrow because he didn't want to carry any more wounded boys off a battlefield.

And because he hadn't seen Luash for nearly two weeks.

"Soldier coming!"

Luash jumped up from where she and Whe-cha were smoking the fish the men had caught at the lake last night after breaking through a thick layer of ice. Ignoring disapproving glares from the women scrambling for cover with their children and from the men who'd already lifted their rifles to their shoulders, she hurried over sharp lava rocks and stared down at the approaching mounted army man. He carried a small white flag and wore a full cape which spread over his horse's flanks. Because he was bareheaded, she easily recognized him.

Jed Britton was coming her way, his horse stepping carefully over new-fallen snow already hardened into ice.

"What is this?" Cho-ocks insisted. "A trick. Kill him!"

Ha-kar-Jim pressed close to the shaman. Like Cho-ocks, the hot-tempered young brave was well armed. "His scalp will fly from my horse's tail," he boasted. "When the other army men see, they will shake in fear."

"No. There will be no killing today." Kientpoos, flanked by Cho-Cho, stepped in front of the two. "This is one man; there is nowhere for others to hide. My niece, stay with me."

"What?" Cho-ocks protested. "You would have a woman speak with the enemy?"

"Speak, maybe. Listen, yes," Kientpoos insisted. "She understands the white man's language far better than the rest of us. She will know if he uses words meant to confuse, lying words."

Uneasy, Luash moved a little closer to her uncle. Since fleeing to the lava beds, her skin had become dry and it was nearly impossible to keep her hair clean. On this windy, clear, and bitterly cold day, the long strands flew about her head and tried to wrap around her neck and face. She was acutely aware of her often repaired footwear and didn't know what Jed would think when he saw her wearing a blanket that had once belonged to the army.

When Jed swung off his horse and made his slow way up the trail she and the others had worn between the stronghold and Modoc Lake, hesitancy was replaced by anger so hot she forgot her frozen cheeks. *He* had forced her to spend the winter like some burrowing animal. He and the rest of his kind. Let the shaman kill him. Let Ha-kar-Jim finish the job a Sioux had begun years ago.

"What are you doing here?" Kientpoos demanded once Jed was close enough to hear. "Maybe you come to buy food? If you have, we have much to sell. Deer and rabbit, ducks and geese. Many fish, all gifts from the lake."

"Only because the army hasn't seen fit to cut you off from it." Jed's voice was calm and even. Still, his eyes had turned from gray to black, making her wonder how much emotion he'd knotted inside himself. "Also, if the ranchers are to be believed, you continue to steal cattle."

Kientpoos shrugged. Sitting, he indicated to Luash that he wanted her beside him. Jed seated himself on a rock opposite them. Cho-ocks, Cho-Cho, and Ha-kar-Jim remained standing nearby.

"We cannot help it if a few foolish strays wander too close." His comment was followed by loud laughter. Even Jed smiled.

"Maybe you and I will roast some beef and speak of peace," Jed said.

"No peace!" Cho-ocks interrupted. "This is our land! My magic will keep all Modocs safe."

Luash waited for Jed to tell the shaman he was wrong. Instead, he shifted his weight and looked slowly around him. His hands were folded on his lap. Because the cape fell nearly to his knees, she couldn't tell whether his fingers were relaxed or fisted. The wind caught the cape and blew it tightly around him, then released its grip. He looked so incredibly brave and alone that the hot anger she'd felt a minute before faded. He'd glanced at her as he was sitting down, but his gaze now held on Kientpoos. "You remember Alfred Meacham?" he asked.

"Oh, yes," Kientpoos acknowledged, his mouth a hard line. "When he became Indian superintendent, he said there could be no more shamen, that gambling was wrong. He would not meet with me when I asked him to. It is good that he is no longer here."

"He's coming back."

"Ah." A cold smile twisted Cho-ock's lips. "Maybe he would like to give me his scalp."

"I doubt that." Jed's look was grim. "He's been far away, talking to our great chief."

"President Grant. I know your chief's name. I am not as ignorant as you think."

Jed gave the shaman a quick nod. "President Grant is very concerned about what's happening here. He doesn't want any more bloodshed."

"Maybe he should come to Modoc country."

"Maybe he should," Jed muttered. "But he doesn't have time. That's why he let Meacham and others talk him into trying a peace commission. Fighting isn't proving anything."

Ha-kar-Jim, who'd leaned over to sharpen his knife on a rock, straightened. "So Meacham wants to talk peace. I say it is because your president knows how powerful the Modocs are. He fears us, knows that even if there were more army men than there are birds in the sky, they would not be enough to beat us."

"You're wrong," Jed said, the words little more than a whisper. He turned so that he was now facing Ha-kar-Jim. "Fighting costs a great deal of money and folks aren't going to want any more men risking their lives. That's why they're looking to find a peaceful way to end these hostilities." His gaze returned to Kientpoos. "I've heard that you feel the same way. Is it the truth?"

"Ha!" Ha-kar-Jim jabbed his knife in Jed's direction, the gesture making Luash's heart lurch. From where she sat, there was no way she could stop the brave from attacking Jed. "Why should we surrender when we are wolves who hunt and kill at will? Are you part of this, the peace commission?"

"I don't know. That hasn't been decided. I'm here to tell you why there's been no more attacks on the stronghold."

Cho-ocks laughed. "There have been no attacks because the army men know my magic is powerful. Your soldiers are like newborn puppies with their eyes still closed. They stumble over rocks and bite themselves and each other."

That caused the standing Modocs to snicker. As they muttered among themselves, Luash kept her gaze on Jed. For no more than a heartbeat, he took his attention off Kientpoos and glanced her way. She couldn't tell what he was thinking or whether he was glad to see her; she barely had time to send him a silent message of admiration and warning.

"You are a brave man," Kientpoos said once the others had calmed down. "Either that, or you are so foolish you do not know your heart may stop beating before nightfall."

"Believe me, chief, I'm no fool. What I'm saying is, if you want out of here before you're forced out by more soldiers than you've ever seen, you have to listen to what Meacham and the others say. In fact, there's nothing General Canby and Colonel Gillem would like more than to have this matter resolved before Meacham gets his commission going."

"Matter resolved? What is this?"

"The end to war," Luash supplied. "Surrender. That is what you are saying, is it not, Lieutenant?"

Jed didn't move so much as a muscle, gave no sign of what he was thinking. "Yes."

For a long time no one spoke. She was terrified that Jed had so angered the shaman or one of the young braves, maybe even her uncle, that they would vent their anger by killing him. "What will happen to me?" Ha-kar-Jim asked. "Will I be allowed to join the others who speak with Meacham of peace?"

"You?" Jed said slowly. "I don't know. You're wanted for murder. You and several others, including your shaman."

"If I am not promised land and freedom, I will not leave this place," Ha-kar-Jim insisted with a glance in Kientpoos's direction. "My chief gave me shelter when our enemies sought vengeance. He will not abandon me."

Luash hated hearing Ha-kar-Jim say that. She hadn't been there when he, Cho-ocks, and the other braves returned from their raids on the settlers and didn't understand why Kientpoos had allowed them to stay here. When she'd asked him about it, he'd said the Modocs were one and had to remain together, that they could not live without their shaman, but since then, Ha-kar-Jim and Cho-ocks had protested every time Kientpoos spoke of a peaceful end to the conflict.

"Tell me about these peace talks," Kientpoos said, ignoring Ha-kar-Jim. "When they are over, will the Modocs be allowed to return to their land?"

Despite the sun glinting off the frozen snow that surrounded them, Jed's eyes darkened. "You know the answer to that. The settlers have the weight of the army and government behind them; things will never go back to what they used to be."

"Then—"

"Hear me out. There's another place. The president's been talking about sending your people to the coast. They'd set up a reservation—"

"No! This is our land, not the coast! This government of yours forced us to live with the Klamaths. There we felt like rabbits being hunted by wolves. I say it: we are done being rabbits!"

"You may not have a choice."

That one unarmed man could ever silence four Modocs struck Luash as impossible, and yet it happened. "No choice?" Kientpoos said finally. "You said you can make no promises for Ha-kar-Jim and those who followed him. What about me?" He pointed at Cho-Cho. "What about him? My friend walked beside me when I took my people off the reservation. What will the army do with us?"

Jed's mouth tightened. Despite her tangled emotions, Luash longed to put her arm around him. But he'd come here knowing what questions would be put to him—knowing he was risking his life. "I'm not going to lie to you, chief," Jed said. "And I don't think the peace commission would either. You will probably be sent to prison."

Prison. Luash forced herself to imagine Kientpoos sitting inside the stockade at Fort Klamath while the seasons played themselves out where he couldn't feel or smell or see them. She would rather plunge a knife in her uncle's heart—in her own heart—than allow that to happen.

"Prison." Kientpoos spat the word. "No."

"Would you rather be dead?"

"Maybe," her uncle said, as Luash had expected. Kientpoos stood. With a sharp nod of his head, he indicated he wanted Ha-kar-Jim and Cho-ocks to follow him. Cho-Cho started to join them, but Kientpoos ordered his lifelong friend to keep an eye on Jed.

Cho-Cho stepped toward Jed, then stopped, as if not sure whether Jed was a prisoner or a guest. Ignoring the curious and sometimes hostile gazes from the men, women, and children who had slipped close during the conversation and were still staring openly at Jed, she joined Cho-Cho. "He will not run," she told him.

Cho-Cho grunted, his scarred cheek not moving with the rest of his grimace, but said nothing. Instead, he indicated he wanted Jed to follow him. After a glance in her direction, Jed did so, his boots making a dull crunching sound. Several children giggled; a woman ordered them to be quiet. Her command was followed by even more giggles. Luash went with Cho-Cho and Jed, only a little surprised to realize that Cho-Cho was leading Jed to his cave. Cho-Cho climbed down the rock stairs, then held up his hand to help her descend. He didn't ask what she was doing here, only waited for Jed to join them. Although she'd often come to Cho-Cho's cave, today she tried to see it through Jed's eyes.

The small underground opening was narrow. At the back where Cho-Cho and his wife had placed their tule bed, it was utterly without light. They'd shifted rocks from the middle of the cave's floor to the sides, so their children had a flat place to play, although most of the children at the stronghold preferred to be outside whenever it wasn't storming. There was a fire pit near the entrance, unlit today because fuel was scarce and only used at night or for cooking.

Jed, his eyes constantly moving, stood with his arms by his side and took a deep breath. Luash imagined the feel of the cold, dry air entering his lungs. She wanted to scream at him that he and the rest of the army were responsible for making her people flee to this lifeless place. Then he looked at her with eyes that said he understood how much she missed the valleys and mountains, and once again she stopped hating him.

"Luash? Why are you here?" Cho-Cho asked.

She turned toward the handsome young warrior who, as a

child, had torn his cheek while trying to climb onto a settler's wagon. "I know him," she said.

"Know?"

She nodded but didn't try to explain herself. Instead, she sat on the nearest rock and waited while Jed chose another for himself. He took several minutes to take in his surroundings, including a careful study of the figures and symbols Cho-Cho's oldest son had painted on the wall above his sleeping place. Finally, he turned his attention to her. She felt herself begin to shudder and wondered if it was because she didn't want him looking at her or if the days and nights of not knowing whether she'd ever see him again had been harder than she'd allowed herself to admit.

"You're looking well," he said, ignoring Cho-Cho.

"So are you."

He laughed at that, the sound soft and low. "I might not be before the day's over."

"No," she told him honestly. "You might not be. Why did you come here?"

"Why?" he repeated and she wondered if he was asking himself the question. "A lot of reasons. It's my job. And there's more to it than that."

"Is there?"

"Yes. I kept thinking about the first time I saw you. You and your spirit."

"What is this?" Cho-Cho interrupted. "You let him see you and Eagle together?"

She nodded but didn't take her eyes off Jed—Jed who looked so strong and brave and alive. "You have not gone back to fight the Sioux?" she asked.

"This war isn't over. Until it is, I can't leave."

"Why not? Does your president order you to stay here?"

"No, I want to stay. Is that what you want to hear? I'm not ready to leave."

She'd seen something hard and sudden in his eyes. "You are a brave man. Not many would have ridden into an enemy's camp."

"You did."

She could all but hear Cho-Cho's silent question and guessed that everything she and Jed said would be relayed to Kientpoos. She shrugged. "The army is too stupid to know when a Modoc is in their midst."

"And because you wanted to see how I was."

She'd sensed he was going to say that, and even though she didn't know what to do with his honest words, she was glad they could be like that with each other. "Kientpoos will never agree to being sent to the coast," she told him. "We do not know that land; it is not ours."

"You might not have any choice."

She was so weary of hearing that that she wanted to rip the words from Jed's throat. "What will you do if Ha-kar-Jim and the others refuse to let you leave?"

"Do? I won't have any choice." He held up his hands as proof that they were no defense against a Modoc rifle.

"Then why—"

"Why did I come, knowing the danger? I don't know, Luash. That's the hell of it. I don't know."

10

They live in here.

The stone roof over Jed's head hung so low that he couldn't stand upright. Closer to the opening, the ceiling rose so steeply that neither he nor the man he knew as Scarface but Luash called Cho-Cho were in danger of tearing their scalps on the jagged projections. The air, cold and slightly stale, hung around him like a barely living thing, and the rock walls were a breeding ground for endless shadows.

He didn't understand how anyone could remain in here without becoming claustrophobic. True, the Modocs were accustomed to living in dark wickiups, but those were made from brush and twigs, tule and willow, not centuries-old lava. From infancy, the Indians looked up at a sky that went on forever, vast and free.

The army had forced them here. And yet if what he'd seen of the men, women, and children was any indication, they seemed to be thriving. It was obvious that they knew how to use every resource available to them, no matter how meager.

He had been in enemy camps before, including once as part of a peace party at a Sioux hunting camp. That time, too, he'd wondered whether he'd live out the day, but at least then there had been other soldiers with him, and everyone had sat out on the prairie with a warm breeze tickling their flesh.

Here it was terribly cold. He glanced at Scarface, who stood near the fire pit. The faintest whiff of smoke rose from the blackened coals, but although both Scarface and Luash wore several layers of clothing as protection against the winter, no attempt had been made to keep the fire going. When he saw the small pile of sage brush beside the pit, he understood why. What little fuel they'd found had to be carefully parceled out.

A doll lay close to his feet. Made from tule stalks tied with twine at the neck, waist, arms, and legs, the figure wore a scarf of faded calico. He'd sensed and heard several Modoc children watching him while he was talking to the braves, but hadn't dared turn his attention to them. Now he all too easily imagined a little girl clutching that doll while her parents entertained her with stories about Modoc history—stories Luash had given him a glimpse of. How did that child's parents answer her questions about why she couldn't go to the river that had always been her home?

"Sqa'o Jane's mother made that for her when she wouldn't stop crying after the army burned her home," Luash said, her voice so void of emotion that it made more of an impact than if she'd screamed at him. "Sqa'o Jane. A girl who is half of the old way and half new."

He wished she was closer so the dark interior of the cave didn't hide so much of her features. This way, he kept being distracted by the endless weave and buckle of the cave's walls. The structure seemed to hang over and around him, taking him back thousands of years to when molten lava burst from deep within the earth to pour its hot energy over sage and manzanita. The walls and roof were silent; still, he imagined what it had sounded like when flame and gases screamed their way to freedom.

I wish you weren't here, he wanted to tell her.

"You could be killed," she whispered. "The truth. Why did you come?"

Because of you, he nearly said, but trapped the words inside him. "It's my job."

"So you say, but I do not understand, Jed."

"Jed?" Scarface said. The large, V-shaped scar under his right eye briefly held Jed's attention. Even with it, the man was somberly handsome. "How well do you know this soldier?"

"Not at all; not enough," she replied, then explained that Jed was the man who'd prevented her from running into a burning wickiup after a dying old woman. She added that she'd seen him near Van Bremer's ranch following the abortive attack on the stronghold. Jed wondered what, if anything, she'd told anyone about the other times they'd met—the things they'd said to each other.

"What's going to happen?" he asked Scarface.

"They will not kill you today, white man. Kientpoos will not allow it."

"Maybe Kientpoos no longer leads."

Scarface stared intently at him, and he wondered if the warrior was reacting to his use of Captain Jack's Modoc name or surprised that he understood so much about the Modoc chain of command. "All are weary of living here," Luash spoke for him. "But they know that it is not Kientpoos's doing."

Although he wanted to ask her how much longer that sentiment might last, he couldn't. She'd shifted her weight so that the winter sun slanted over her, and despite himself, he was losing himself in her. Her dark hair lay tangled around her face and throat. She looked like a woman awakening from a night spent in her lover's arms. He knew that wasn't true; she'd told him she hadn't shared herself with a man and he believed her. Still, the thought of how she would look and feel in his bed stirred his senses.

Although she still wore her blanket coat, she no longer held it tight against her chin. He could see a few inches of soft flesh, imagine a fragile vein beating at the side of her neck.

A boy who looked to be about eleven or twelve appeared at the cave opening and informed Scarface that Kientpoos wanted him. The boy then pointed at Luash. "Our chief says you are to stay with the army man and that he is not to leave."

Luash didn't stir as Scarface scrambled to the surface and disappeared. "You've been well?" Jed asked cautiously. Being alone with Luash made him feel very uncertain.

"My heart is sad but my body strong."

"And Eagle? You've seen him?"

"Not so much."

Not so much. The simple words chilled him. "Maybe you haven't been able to get away. I imagine you have a lot to do here."

"A lot, white man. Every day we see more soldiers coming to our land. Wagons and tents. Weapons. Sometimes it is dangerous for me to leave, to be alone so Eagle can hear my words."

"I told you that was going to happen. They're setting up a permanent camp."

"They have no right."

"They have every right, Luash. They outnumber you and they have more weapons."

She didn't react, but he guessed she was assessing what he'd just told her. "So, your leaders say the Modocs are to be moved to the coast," she said without a trace of emotion.

"It's either that or risk being annihilated."

"Annihilated. I know that word, white man. Killed, all of us. Many of your people would be happy if that happened."

At seventeen, with his scalp torn open and bleeding and arrow wounds in his side and leg, he'd hated enough to want the entire Sioux race wiped from the Earth. He couldn't say when he'd stopped being driven by rage; maybe, until he'd met a Modoc woman named Luash, nothing had mattered except the fighting.

He'd seen things that haunted his nights—a wagon train after an attack, two settlers' homes burned, scalpings—but he couldn't keep any of those memories with him today. "It doesn't have to happen, not if the Modocs agree to the peace terms."

Although she didn't say anything for a long time, he sensed that she was carrying his comment through to an undeniable end. If her people surrendered, they would have to comply with whatever their white captors decided to do with them. If they continued to resist, maybe not even the owner of the tule doll would leave the Land of Burned Out Fires alive. Would Luash chose death over the alternative? "Can the white man's words be believed?" she asked, splintering his thoughts.

"I don't know."

"You do not know? You have been part of many treaties. Surely you know the answer."

Damn, she was hard. Hard and direct. "I've seen them work and I've seen them broken. Mostly broken."

"Because Indians defied the rules?"

"Not just Indians," he told her honestly, not at all surprised when she nodded, a small, cool smile touching her lips.

"It is not easy, is it?" she asked as several high-pitched voices from unseen children reached him.

"What isn't?"

"This thing between you and me."

Her words touched him, no stronger than a small bird's feather and yet so powerful that he felt buffeted by them. "No," he said. "It isn't."

By Jed's reckoning, the Modoc men met for the better part of an hour. During that time, he and Luash said little to each other. Occasionally children poked their heads in the opening and stared down at him. He tried to look beyond their large eyes, round faces, and ragged clothing to their individual thoughts and emotions.

Most giggled and hurried away when he acknowledged them, but the boy who'd come for Scarface spoke some English. He told Jed that he'd been riding horses ever since his father had bought one from a settler. He was convinced he could outrun the wind. Jed smiled at the boy's boastfulness and was pleased to see Luash relax enough to smile with him. Neither of them said anything about whether the horse, or the boy, would survive the winter.

Finally Captain Jack sent word that he was ready to see Jed again. This time, Jed was surrounded by close to forty men, probably the entire fighting force within the stronghold today. The rest he guessed were either out scouting or hunting. Jack explained that although Ha-kar-Jim, Cho-ocks, and the others who'd attacked the settlers still objected to having anything to do with the whites, he and Cho-Cho had asserted their leadership. They were willing at least to meet with the peace commission. "What I will think and do once the peace people have stopped talking I cannot say," Jack explained. "But I am weary of fighting; I want to take my family home."

Although he should have pointed out that "home" would no longer be where Captain Jack had always lived, Jed simply promised to carry that message back with him. Given the way the shaman and Hooker Jim and several others were glaring at him, saying as little as possible seemed like the wisest decision.

"When the time comes for peace talking," Captain Jack added, "I want you there."

"The president didn't appoint me. I don't—"

"I believe your eyes, Lieutenant. I know what they say, and I will know if we are being lied to."

He digested that. "I'll tell the general. I don't know how he's going to react."

"There is only one way," Jack said with a small, cold smile. "If your peace people want to meet with me, they will keep you with them."

"Why me? It has to be more than my eyes."

Jack's smile grew. He looked older and wiser than he had a few minutes ago. He nodded in Luash's direction. "There is lightning between the two of you. Lightning and thunder. It is like the energy which accompanies a storm. When I speak with your peace people, my niece will be by my side and your eyes will say the truth to each other."

Energy? Studying Luash, he noted that her only reaction was to continue to meet her uncle's gaze, her expressive eyes sober.

"Go with him," Jack told her. "Make sure he is safe."

"What does he mean?" Jed whispered after the Modoc chief and his warriors left. They were still surrounded by women and children, prompting him to keep his voice low. "He can't want you to go clear back with me. It isn't safe."

"Not to the soldier place, but to where there is a line on the ground. What do you call it, a boundary? If I stay with you until you have crossed it, no Modoc will attack you."

Hearing that made Jed wonder, again, just how close he'd come to getting his scalp lifted today. Still, knowing he didn't yet have to leave her made it difficult for him to think of anything else. Barely acknowledging him, Luash led the way down the narrow but well-beaten trail. Once they reached his horse, she said something in Modoc to the old man who had been looking after it. Grunting, the man handed the reins to Jed and hobbled away.

Jed started to swing into the saddle, then asked if she wanted to ride behind him. He wasn't surprised when she shook her head. In truth, he was relieved, because if she placed her arms around his waist and he felt her breasts pushing into his back, he wasn't sure he could handle it. He decided not to mount.

They walked side by side, the horse to his left while, inch by inch, he allowed himself to believe that he wasn't going to be killed today. Luash was closest to the lake, but although a large number of eagles were near the shore, they didn't hold her attention. "They've been bunching a lot lately," he observed. "I take it they're going to be migrating before much longer."

"I am always sad when they leave. When they come in the winter, it is as if they have taken over the world. When they fly, the sky is dark with them."

"What about your eagle? Will he leave with the others?"

She shook her head, eyes on the horizon. "He is not like his kind in that way. This is his only place."

Because of the bond between the two of you?

When he said nothing, she pointed south to a distant, mounded butte. Her lips parted slightly and he waited for her to speak. Still, it took her a long time to break the silence. When she did, her eyes were back on him. "From there, one can see the morning sun spread itself over the center of the world. Why would Eagle not want to spend his life here?"

"The center of the world?"

"We call that peak Spirit Butte. Those making their vision quest have always climbed it; it is a place of great wonder and peace. I wish—I would like to go there now."

But she couldn't. The army wouldn't let her. "Tell me about it."

"This matters to you?"

"Yes," he said without explaining further.

She took a deep breath. "I should say nothing; this is sacred to the Modocs. And your Sunday doctors tell us we are wrong to believe as we do."

"I've heard some of those preachers. They don't have the answers any more than anyone else does."

"Remember something, Jed. My heart rejects the words of the Sunday—the preacher. It also rejects your words when you say it is wrong to believe in anything."

Just then, a large flock of geese rose off the lake, their wings making a loud whirring sound. He felt all but buried under movement, watched intently as, eyes shining, she followed their flight. "What about Spirit Butte?" he pressed when he could make himself heard.

She glanced over at him; then her attention fixed on the horizon. "When the sun rises, it first touches Mount Shasta and turns the snow on it into fire. Little by little, sunlight blesses the rest of the world as if a blanket is being pulled away. It is like golden rain, clean and beautiful, waking animals and birds, finally reaching the lake. Everything is warmed and brought to life. Everything except the caves."

"The caves." He was barely aware that he'd spoken aloud. The wind blew freely here and because she made no attempt to tame her hair, it whipped around her like a soft, black cloud. "You're lucky you've got them."

That made her laugh and spread her arms as if to encompass everything they could see and even beyond that. "Lucky? You do not have to live in them." She pointed at the ground. "Down there, everywhere, are caves and tunnels. It is said that a strong man could spend his life exploring what exists beneath the surface and not know it all. It is another world, a dark, cold, lifeless world."

Breathing in sweet air, watching the unbelievable number of birds on the lake, hoping for a glimpse of her Eagle, he found it hard to concentrate on what she'd just told him. "Do you ever explore them?"

"No. I want to be where the sun lights my way."

"I understand."

"Do you?" There was a sharp edge to her voice that he'd been waiting for without realizing it.

"Yeah. I do. When I was in Scarface's cave and saw that little doll, it hit me. Your people didn't have any choice but to take shelter there. Or maybe the truth is, they've cut off all other options. If they'd stayed on the reservation—"

"Enough! A person cannot go back in time."

She was right. Too damn right. "I have to ask something. Do you really believe Captain Jack—"

"Kientpoos."

"All right, Kientpoos. Do you believe he can keep the others, like Hooker Jim and the shaman, in line?"

"I do not know."

"But he's going to try, isn't he? I mean, the Modocs need unity."

"What do you care about unity? It would be simple to defeat us if the Modocs fought among themselves, if Cho-ocks lost his medicine."

"Yeah, it would. But I'm trying to understand some things, so I can judge the success or failure of the peace talks."

"If you believe Kientpoos is not strong, will you tell your general to wait until the Modoc have fought among themselves and have no leader?"

"That's not my decision to make, Luash." The moment he'd spoken, he was sorry. She'd asked for an honest answer and he'd given her an evasion. "What I do know is that the president's getting a lot of pressure from folks wanting this war over before it gives other Indians ideas."

"Ideas?"

"If a handful of Modocs continue to defy what's soon going to be close to a thousand troops, the Sioux and others will go on fighting."

"I would like to see that."

For some reason that made him laugh. They were nearing that imaginary line in rock and earth beyond which she wouldn't step. When he'd crossed over it, she'd return to her people and maybe he'd never see her again. "You're warm enough?" he heard himself ask. "There isn't much wood for—"

"Do not ask whether I shiver at night, white man. You put me here; your army says I can no longer travel into the mountains for what I need to keep me warm."

He wanted to throw arguments and denials at her but nothing he said would shave away her sharp honesty. Although he'd long known that the basic problem between whites and Indians was that they both claimed the same land, always before the enemy had been braves painted for war, fierce warriors who killed and flaunted their scalps and believed that without honor there was no life. Who wanted him dead. Today the enemy was a beautiful, soft-spoken young woman who'd snuck into an army camp because she needed to know whether he was still alive.

When he stopped, his horse immediately dropped its head and began searching for grass beneath the ice and snow. Luash continued walking, her gaze fixed on the silvery gray lake. She ran her hand along the back of her neck, drew her hair off her blanket, released it so the wind could play with it again. Maybe thirty feet now separated them. For a moment, he thought she was going to turn back toward him and readied himself for her dark eyes. Instead, she lifted her arms toward the horizon. As she did, the blanket slid off her shoulders and pooled at her feet. Her deerhide dress wasn't heavy enough to protect her against the chill and didn't have enough body to prevent the wind from pressing it tight against her body.

She swiveled toward him, arms still outstretched. Behind her, the clouds that had begun building on the horizon shifted from gray to deep purple. She seemed unaware that her small waist was sharply outlined, that the top tie was missing from her neckline. The teasing wind caught the loose fabric and lifted it, giving him a glimpse of dark flesh.

She was no longer looking at him. He felt lost, angry, and relieved. If there were any sharpshooters about, she would have made a perfect target, but there were few lava outcroppings along the lake shore and thus nowhere for someone to hide.

Even before he saw the eagle, he guessed what had captured her attention. How she'd sensed its approach didn't matter. Like the silent communication that brought the Modoc woman and eagle together, certain things were simply beyond his comprehension. As the great bird drew closer, he realized that some of the smaller birds nearby were becoming agitated, proof that the magnificent, white-headed creature really existed.

He felt her drawing away from him. As she continued to watch the eagle, envy surged through him. She had something to believe in, a spirit. And he had—what?

His horse shied. He spoke softly to the startled animal but couldn't take his eyes off either Luash or the eagle. They were becoming one again, the eagle risking dashing his body against the ground, she exposing her flesh to those killing talons. When the eagle moved its wings, Jed heard a heavy rustling sound and thought he felt a sharp push of air. Birds squawked and rose off the lake; his horse again tried to break free.

And Luash swept her hands over outspread wings.

The eagle didn't stay long. It seemed that it had no sooner come close enough for her to touch than it lifted its head to catch some invisible wind current into the sky. She continued to stare after it, her body a long, motionless, and utterly graceful line. When, finally, she lowered her arms and pivoted toward the watching man, the wind blew her hair across her face until all he could see were her eyes. They glistened with tears, with love and awe, and despite himself, he lost himself in them. He wanted to run his hands over the white streak at her temple, wanted to feel its silk on his lips. Most of all he wanted to make love to her until who they were didn't matter.

"He is still here," she whispered.

"Did you think he might not be?"

A shadow touched her features; she didn't try to hide its existence from him. "I see more and more soldiers. I listen to braves boast like small children who run to their parents when they are frightened."

Was she saying that she no longer believed the Modocs to be invincible, despite their string of successful surprise attacks? But although he desperately needed the answer, he didn't try to form the question—couldn't think how. She had a feather in her hand, a long, gloriously white tail feather nearly as broad as her palm. When she handed it to him, he couldn't remember how to breathe. "Thank you," he managed, using the last of his air.

"Do you understand?" she asked. "Eagle wants you to have this. It is his gift, his message to you."

"Message?"

"He hopes you will know what this land means to me and my people. If you share my belief, you will."

What belief? She'd given him a feather from a creature that sanity said didn't exist. But he'd seen it, felt the wind of its passing. Overburdened by what he was thinking, Jed tucked the feather under his shirt. The moment it touched his chest, his flesh felt warmer, more sensitive somehow.

Aware of how closely she was watching him, he indicated the stronghold. "I didn't want to come here," he told her. "There were some who bet I wouldn't leave alive. I was inclined to believe them."

"Because the Ma Klas are savages?"

"Ma Klas?"

"That is our ancient name, one fitting for people no better than animals."

He wanted to insist that they were neither savages nor animals, but he'd spent so damn many years of his life thinking of Indians as just that. He wasn't sure he wanted to change, because if he did, he would have to admit he'd been wrong all those years. "Can you blame me for wondering if my life's in danger? I'd be a fool not to realize they might hate me enough to kill me."

"They?" She rocked away from him, the movement once again

allowing the wind to pull the fabric away from her throat. "I am *they*, Jed. And I am not a savage."

"I know that."

"Do you see that there are no animals among the Modocs? Only a few men, women, and children with food in their bellies but without a place to build their wickiups."

"You had one. On the reservation."

Fire ignited in her expressive eyes. Sweeping her arms to take in the land in all directions, she said, "Before the white man came, all this was our home."

She was right, so damnably right that he had no words with which to try to argue. Besides, how could he speak when he had never seen anything that looked as exquisite as she looked at this moment. Like her eagle spirit, she was half flesh and blood, half magic. Behind her lay a lake so large that he couldn't see to the other side, a lake that supplied her people with much of what they needed to survive—or would if the army wasn't trying to keep them from it. She'd told him about those on their vision quests who climbed a distant butte so they could watch the morning sun touch the center of the world. Today it was easy, very easy, to believe that nothing existed beyond this beautifully barren place.

"What do you say to that, Jed? Should we not live on the land that has nourished us since the beginning of time?"

"Things change, Luash."

"I have seen your peace person, Meacham," she said. "He is not a wise or strong-talking man. When he tried to convince us to return to the reservation, his words were weak. Do you think that will change now?"

"He won't be alone. General Canby might be part of the group and probably Colonel Gillem."

"Gillem? Who is he?"

"He's supposed to be in charge of the war effort now."

"You do not like him."

"No," Jed admitted. "I don't. The man doesn't know what he's doing, but then I'm not sure anyone does. It's such a—I can't say who all's going to be involved, Luash. What I can say is that nothing's going to happen fast."

"My uncle is not a man who makes decisions quickly. And he does not trust the army men."

Jed sighed and she wondered if he was as weary as he sounded. If he still cared so little for his life. "What will you say to your general?" she asked. "Will you tell him the Modocs are like starving dogs? We are not. Spring will soon be here. Then we can again make cider from manzanita berries."

"I hope you're right."

She hadn't expected that. Or maybe the truth was, she'd seen the answer already in his eyes and had no defense against her reaction. When he held out his hand, she stared at it for a long time while she memorized the fine lines in his palm, the short, clean nails, the strong fingers. "Don't be afraid of me," he whispered.

"I am not."

"You haven't let me touch you; that tells me something."

He was right, but how could she tell him that if he touched her, she might shatter like a fine layer of ice? "It has been a long time since we last spoke. We have become strangers again."

"No. No, we haven't."

"How can it be otherwise?" she asked in a desperate attempt to keep barriers between them. "We are at war."

"We're also human beings. A man and a woman. I haven't stopped thinking about you. You wouldn't be here if it had been any different for you."

"My uncle—"

"Your uncle spoke of lightning and thunder between us. Maybe he hopes I'll tell you some military secrets; I don't know what he's thinking. What I do know is that I don't want to ride away with things the way they are between us."

He shouldn't have said that. How could she go on telling herself that he belonged to a different world when he spoke words that touched her heart? "I wish we had never met."

"So do I. That way I wouldn't be forced to reevaluate what I've believed for years."

She didn't know what *reevaluate* meant, didn't want to ask. "This must be the end of us," she told him even though she had to force out every word. "When I think of you, my mind becomes like tangled rabbit fur."

"Tangled rabbit fur. I like that."

He liked that. She'd felt so inadequate trying to tell him how she felt. Now she believed he understood what was happening to her heart and mind. Whether that was wise or dangerous she couldn't say. "What do white men say about"—she tapped her forehead —"about what happens inside them?"

"It doesn't matter, Luash. Nothing does except that I have to leave."

"Now?"

"If I don't show, the general or Gillem will send troops after me." Trembling, she slid her hand into his.

"You're sure about this?" he asked as he drew her close.

"No; no." The words came out a whimper.

"I won't force you to do anything you don't want." She felt the warmth coming from his legs, thought about hard muscle under worn fabric. With his free hand, he gently brushed her hair off her forehead. "I could never do that to you."

"I—want to believe you."

"Do."

"We might never see each other again, Jed Britton."

"I know."

She saw only his face, deep gray eyes the color of a coyote's fur, the white scar curving into his hairline, straight nose, and flared nostrils. His flesh was lighter than hers but not by much; she wondered if the summer sun would put an end to that difference. He was much larger than her, all broad shoulders and powerful arms and legs. What was male about him fascinated her, swirled around her and touched her veins and heart and breasts and belly and the woman part of her that no man had ever invaded.

He was inviting her to kiss him, challenging her as she'd never been challenged before. She remembered a doe she'd frightened out of its resting place the other day. Now she shared that deer's emotions. Knowing she could do nothing else, she stood on tiptoe and pressed her lips against this man who was both danger and promise. His arms closed around her and she felt, not like running, but as if she could press her body against his until they became one.

The shivers the wind had awakened on her back and shoulders turned into something ignited by this army man with an eagle's feather flattened against his chest. He held her tight, his breathing as quick and ragged as her own, his strength now no more than hers and yet greater than Kumookumts's had ever been.

Do not leave, she wanted to beg him. *Stay here with me. Show me—help me understand what it is I want.* Fear of what would happen to her if she spoke held the words in check, but there was nothing she could do to stop her pounding heart, her need to fold herself into him.

He became a living blanket, lips that melted against hers, a whirlwind of sensation. She stopped thinking.

11

Jed stared into what he could see of General Canby's deep-set eyes and wondered if the man was as old as he looked tonight or if the weight of his responsibilities had aged him. Maybe it was nothing more than the dim lighting inside the tent. "They've got enough arms and ammunition to hold out for a long time," Jed stated somberly. "As for the fortifications—they've piled up rocks in a number of places to increase their security, but for the most part, there's enough natural shelter that it would take a direct howitzer hit into one of the caves to dislodge them, and the chances of that happening are nil."

Canby ran his leathered hand over his long, thick beard. "I take it our scouts are right then, and the Indians can see anyone coming long before they get there?"

Jed told Canby about the manned outposts he'd seen, then explained that the clefts in the lava formed deceptively deep crevasses capable of hiding both Modocs and their few horses. "It's a fortress. The best damn natural defense system I've ever seen."

Canby leaned back in his wooden chair and swept his eyes over the tent's dirty walls. "Better than this by far, then. All right, so there's no way the men we've got here can roust them out?"

Jed thought he'd made that abundantly clear. The Modocs believed in their shaman's power, so much in fact that if Curley Headed Doctor told them to remain in the caves, they might even as the army cut them down to the last child.

Luash. Although three hours had passed since he'd seen her, he could still feel her lips on his. His body still remembered her heat. And, as if to contradict the way she'd pulled herself free and run, the feather she'd given him remained pressed against his chest.

Gillem, not surprisingly, was arguing for additional troops. If the Modocs saw even more soldiers coming in, he insisted, they would become disheartened and surrender, or if not that, at least take the forthcoming peace talks much more seriously. General Canby angrily retorted that he'd already received a number of cables from the secretary of the interior warning him not to spend any more money on the Modoc campaign. "The president wants a peaceful settlement. That's what I'm going to give him."

"Peaceful!" Gillem snorted. "That's because he's been listening to those ignorant liberals he allows to surround him. They don't know what they're talking about. If he'd come out here—"

Canby cut him off, reminding him that it wasn't up to them to debate their president's policies any more than it was their business to decide whether the Mormon settlers had been right in trying to outlaw all shaman activities. That order had caused deep friction between settlers and Indians and played its own role in the war. In the past, Jed hadn't cared about the politics or religious sentiments behind Indian policies; Indians like Red Cloud and Sitting Bull believed in war and he believed in giving them what they wanted.

A Modoc woman had altered his thinking.

"I suppose the president wants Hooker Jim and the other murderers to receive a pardon," Gillem challenged. "Probably'll invite them to the White House."

Jed's thoughts slid to his short exchange with Hooker Jim. He'd been surprised by the Modoc's youth, but not by his militancy. Hooker Jim was hot-blooded and hot-headed all right, and if Captain Jack—Kientpoos—was wise, he wouldn't for a second turn his back on the man Luash called Ha-kar-Jim. "I told them nothing's going to happen until Meacham arrives, and probably not for awhile even then," he explained.

"And in the meantime, they go right on frightening folks and making fools of us," Gillem grumbled. "The soldiers don't have enough to do. They're drinking too much and gambling; they want to be fighting. If they don't get some action, they're going to walk away from this."

"No fighting! You know the president's orders," Canby insisted. After glaring at each other for a full minute, Canby and Gillem began discussing how well the Modocs would receive Meacham. Jed sat in silence for awhile, then asked for and received permission to get something to eat.

As soon as the cold night air entered his lungs, he began to feel better. The tent stank of cigar smoke and unwashed bodies, a sharp contrast to the clean tang of sage he'd breathed while with the Modocs. For maybe two seconds, it was all he could do not to walk out into the dark and make his way back to where he'd last seen them—her.

The smell of beef distracted him. He waited while a cook working inside a three-sided wooden lean-to filled his plate with something he couldn't identify and then headed toward the miserable excuse for a tent he shared with Wilfred. Van Bremer's ranch, despite the house and barn, now looked like a full-fledged army encampment. Not only had eating tables been set up for the soldiers, but logs had been driven into the earth and ropes strung from them to act as permanent horse corrals, complete with guards. Other men guarded the howitzers, making Jed wonder if anyone really thought the Modocs would try to sneak in and steal the unwieldy weapons.

Although some of the soldiers were still indistinguishable from the nervous local residents who'd gravitated here, a large number wore regulation uniforms. From the looks he was getting as he headed for his tent, Jed guessed word had gotten out about his trip to the Modoc stronghold. He was in no mood to voluntarily repeat what he'd just told Canby and Gillem, and no one among the soldiers was foolhardy enough to question an officer. Not only that, a large group to his right seemed more interested in passing around a couple of jugs.

Wilfred was stretched out on his stomach on his bedroll, his head close to the lantern so he could read. His long legs hung over his cot and brushed the tent wall. "You're still alive," he declared the moment he spotted Jed, relief clearly visible in his eyes. "I'd heard rumors to that effect, but I wasn't sure. Bets were better than even that you wouldn't make it back."

"I'm here, all right. I hope you didn't lose." He pointed at the newspaper Wilfred held and tried to remember the last time he'd had anything to read. "What do you have there?"

"The *Sacramento Union*," Wilfred explained as he shifted into a sitting position, an effort which caused his cot to squeak in protest. "A teamster brought it with him from Yreka, and it isn't even a week old—not that that makes much difference. As mixed up as they are about what's going on here, you wouldn't know they have a correspondent living with us. The paper's calling this Gillem's Camp. I wonder how that sets with Van Bremer, or with the general. I thought if you really had gotten back in one piece, you'd be stuck with Gillem half the night. That's why I decided to wait and see if you'd show up instead of wasting time looking for you."

Jed shrugged, set his plate on his cot, and pulled off his heavy overcoat. It felt good, damn good, to be with Wilfred, where he no longer had to weigh his every word. He started to scratch his chin where he needed to shave, then his hand trailed lower. He stuck his hand under his shirt and drew out the feather Luash had given him.

Wilfred stared. "Where'd you get that?"

"An eagle."

"I know that." Wilfred's eyes narrowed. "You think I'm stupid? I don't know what I'm going to do with you, boy. What I want to know is, does that feather have anything to do with that Modoc woman?"

"Her name is Luash."

Wilfred carefully began folding his newspaper. "And you saw her today, didn't you? I thought you were going to try to talk to Captain Jack."

"I did. She walked part way back with me."

"Did she?"

"On her uncle's orders. I guess he figured I'd be safe if she was with me."

"And you had no complaints. I swear, this business between you and that woman is the damnedest thing I've ever heard of. What'd she have to say?"

Not enough. Too much. "We didn't have a whole lot of time, and it didn't seem like there was much to be said. We both know how it is."

"Yeah, I'm sure you do. So, how did you get that little keepsake?"

Even now the experience seemed unbelievable. "She called her eagle to her, and he left this with her." He indicated the feather. "She wanted me to have it."

"The hell you say." Wilfred said that whenever he didn't understand—or didn't want to understand—something. Jed knew he shouldn't let it get to him, but he already had too much on his mind. "I can't explain it, all right! *It happened.* Either you believe me or you don't. I don't give a damn."

Wilfred, obviously not at all taken aback, grunted, then drew the feather out of Jed's hand. "I've never seen one bigger, I'll give you that. What's she like?"

"Young. Good looking. She's Jack's niece."

"Jesus. You want to play with fire or what?"

He didn't want to have anything to do with her ever again. At the same time, he wondered how he would get through the hours and days until—if—he felt her body against his again. There'd been an almost desperate quality to the way she'd held onto him, and when she'd pulled away, neither of them had said anything. He'd seen tears in her eyes; she hadn't been able to hide that from him. She'd trembled. It wasn't the cold that had gotten to her; she was reacting to him—reacting to how she felt about him and what he'd done to her.

And he felt the same way.

"Jed? You listening to me?"

"What?"

"I asked if you like playing with fire."

Maybe he did.

It snowed for the next three days, one storm piling against another until Lush felt that the lulls between them vanished. Although it took all her energy to join the other women in a seemingly endless search for firewood, at least the storms kept army scouts close to their camp, which made it possible for the Modoc braves to reach Juniper Butte, where they shot a couple of deer. As Luash and Whecha returned to the stronghold one afternoon, wood strapped to their backs, they pondered whether the army tents might collapse under the weight of the snow. If that happened while their leaders were in them—

"Maybe they are not smart enough to dig their way out." Whecha laughed. "They will stay there until the snow thaws, like hibernating bears. Only, unlike bears, they will freeze."

"They will be covered by mud then. No one will have to bury them."

"I would love to see that," Whe-cha admitted. "Soon there will be nothing except bones sticking out of the mud."

Although she laughed, Luash's heart felt heavy. They were talking nonsense because they didn't want to think about a storm in their faces and branches sticking into their backs, about the never-ending disagreements between Kientpoos and Cho-ocks over whether they would meet with the peace commission. If a tent collapsed while Jed was in it—what was she thinking about? No one died from the weight of snow. Jed might have to sleep beside a campfire if his tent was destroyed, but except for not being able to leave the army headquarters, the storms would cause him no great inconvenience. Maybe if it snowed long enough, he'd forget the heat and humidity of where he'd grown up.

Whe-cha's shout of greeting pulled her out of her thoughts. Two girls had called out to the returning women. She waved to them, then turned around so the girls could see how much wood she'd gathered. She helped Whe-cha shed her load, then bent over so her uncle's wife could lift the pile off her back.

"I want it to be spring," Whe-cha groaned. "To hear songbirds and see flowers pushing through the ground—I would be happy then. Except for"—she pointed west—"except for the army. Sometimes I pray the earth will open up and cover them with hot lava."

Luash said nothing, trying to concentrate on what she was doing. Whe-cha touched her arm. "You do not want them burned?"

"It will not happen."

"I know. It is only a foolish girl's thoughts. But if you could kill them, would you?"

"I do not want death for anyone."

"Maybe you do not want death for the man who came here a few days ago." She looked sharply at the younger woman. "I saw the truth in your eyes. I watched the way you looked at him, how close you walked to him. I even felt the thunder and lightning my husband talked about. This was not the first time you have been with him."

The girls had passed out of earshot. She was tired of the questions hammering inside her head. She admitted the truth of what Whe-cha said.

"An army man? Why would you talk to him?"

"Maybe because a deer watches a cougar so it will know its enemy," she explained, then shook her head as if denying her own words. She reminded Whe-cha of the time when Lieutenant Jed Britton had kept her from running into a burning wickiup. It was harder to explain why she'd allowed him to see her and Eagle together.

"Luash!" Whe-cha gasped when she'd finished. "Eagle is not for the eyes of our enemies."

"I know," she said, then sighed. "My thoughts are that the army is not a cougar, which must kill in order to live. Maybe, if we looked at them not as our enemy, but as people with the same thoughts and hearts, this war would end."

"The same hearts? They say we are cattle to be herded where they order. When I hear they will send us elsewhere if we surrender or are defeated, my heart breaks."

So did hers. To never again watch the sun touch distant Mount Shasta or watch shy rabbits hide under a low-growing sage—or to feel Eagle's wing on her cheek . . . "But if they know what is inside us," she pressed, "that our children mean as much to us as theirs do to them—that is why I let the lieutenant see me and Eagle together. I prayed that he would understand and take his understanding back to the army."

"And has he?"

She couldn't answer that. He didn't look at her with hatred; he wanted her as a man wants a woman, but whether he had told his general about the tule doll he'd held the other day, she didn't know. Although the rock near her was snow-covered, she sat on it, her attention drawn to the dancing flakes settling around Whe-cha's head. "The more distance between two people, the less one knows about the other."

"Maybe. Who is to say how it is with them."

"I say we have to try. The army men call you Lizzie. Have you told them your real name?"

"Ha! They did not care; when we were at Lost River and they came, I was afraid to talk to them."

"Maybe it is not wise to let fear rule us."

Whe-cha stared down at her, her features slightly blurred by the storm. After a moment, she clamped her hand over her reddened nose. "I do not want to talk to soldier men. I want it to be spring so I can watch fawns chase after their mothers. I—I want a baby in my arms and to think of nothing except holding it to my breast."

So, although she'd never told anyone, did Luash.

Heart beating erratically, Luash walked beside one of Kientpoos's sisters, Ko-a-lak-a, who the whites called Queen Mary. The women and several men were traveling from the stronghold to Gillem's newly moved camp near Antelope Bluff. The journey had taken the better part of the morning because, although the distance wasn't long, the group had followed the shoreline, stopping more than once so one of them could dig for clams while the rest kept watch for soldiers.

Despite the sun's welcome warmth, she felt chilled and barely aware of the mud that was replacing the earlier frozen ground. With her and Ko-a-lak-a were Ha-kar-Jim, Cho-ocks, and five other braves. If her uncle hadn't told her he needed her knowledge of English, her understanding of Ha-kar-Jim and Cho-ocks, she gladly would have remained behind.

Three times more in the two weeks since Jed had been there, white men had come to the stronghold to make promises of what would happen if the Modocs surrendered. Although Kientpoos didn't trust their words of amnesty, Ha-kar-Jim and his followers insisted on going to the army general to hear more. And because she loved and feared for her uncle, she had agreed to accompany the young braves. Maybe, she prayed, there was truth behind this thing called peace talk. As they neared the army camp, with its dirty tents sprinkled like piles of sand between Antelope Butte and the lake, she felt hostile eyes on her and prayed Jed was among the soldiers. If he would speak for her, she would be safe.

Ha-kar-Jim, dressed in a calico shirt, ragged pants, and the work boots he'd taken from one of the ranchers he'd killed, laughed as he looked around. "I will demand many horses," he boasted. "The army men must pay me well if they do not want me to put my bullets in any more settlers."

Earlier Ha-kar-Jim had said he was tired of hiding behind rocks and was ready for life to go back to what it had been before they fled to the lava beds. Surely he didn't believe he would be treated as if he was nothing more than a naughty child. But he must; otherwise, why would he come here, when so many whites wanted him to hang for his crimes?

Before they reached the first tent, they were surrounded. Luash was overwhelmed by the sight of more soldiers than there were winter eagles. Someone called out in English for them to stand where they were. They obeyed.

The eagles were gone, migrated, all except for Eagle.

A tall, sad-eyed man with a full beard stepped toward them. Both by the way the other soldiers stared at him and his fancy uniform, she guessed he was a high-ranking officer. He introduced himself as General Canby, then demanded to know what they were doing here when a group of his men had been dispatched to speak to Captain Jack at the stronghold. When her aunt and some of the braves looked puzzled, Luash interpreted for them.

"I have listened to your talking men," Ha-kar-Jim announced

in halting English. "Their words made my heart glad. I want to surrender."

"Now?"

Ha-kar-Jim threw out his chest. "Your talking men say that if we agree to go to a reservation, maybe I will not be punished for what I did. This I will talk about."

General Canby's eyes narrowed at that. Muttering from the armed whites left no doubt that everyone, even those who had never been face to face with a Modoc, realized that a suspected murderer was in their camp. For a moment Luash thought they would all be killed, but although the soldiers continued to grumble, no one lifted a weapon. Instead, they watched their general.

"For a long time I heard talk of taking us to the coast," Ha-kar-Jim continued, obviously loving the attention. "Then the talk was of Arizona. I would like that; they say it is warm in this Arizona. Only now I hear that we must go to a place far from here called Indian Territory. It does not matter."

Not matter? She could barely concentrate. She and Ha-kar-Jim had grown up together; she'd once believed they looked at the world through the same eyes. But maybe it was different for a man. Maybe a man thought only of staying alive, not where that life— and the lives of his children—would be lived out.

The general was saying something; she struggled to catch up. "What about Captain Jack?" Canby asked. "He's willing to agree to this?"

Ha-kar-Jim shrugged. Translating for the Modocs who didn't understand English, she waited for Ko-a-lak-a to say something, but Kientpoos's sister only stared, first at one soldier and then another. "I do not know what is in my uncle's heart," Luash told General Canby, reluctantly calling attention to herself. "He believed Ha-kar-Jim simply wanted to talk to you, not give himself up."

"Maybe it does not matter," Cho-ocks interrupted before she could say anything else. "Without his warriors, Kientpoos will become a lonely old man. No one will care if he spends the rest of his life in a cave."

Alone in a cave? This from the tribe's shaman!

"Then what you're saying is, you braves are interested in amnesty?" General Canby prodded. "It doesn't matter to you what Jack does?"

"Kientpoos speaks for himself," Cho-ocks insisted. "I am here to receive the army's peace gifts."

General Canby's heavy eyebrows shot up at that. "I don't know what you've heard or not heard, but nothing final about terms of surrender has come from me. Wait here. You'll be safe."

Calling several soldiers to him, he turned his back on the Modocs and started toward his tent. Maybe, she thought, the general was no different from her uncle in that both men needed time with their thoughts and the words of others before making a decision. She also wondered if it was any easier for the general to know his mind and heart than it was for Kientpoos.

"Luash."

Although it was all she could do not to spin around, she forced herself to turn slowly. Still, she guessed that if anyone looked into her eyes, they would know that her heart now beat like that of a trapped bird. Jed, wearing a fine-looking uniform that followed the lines of his body, stood so close that she could almost reach out and touch him. If she hadn't been so intent on hearing what the general and Ha-kar-Jim and Cho-ocks had to say, she already would have sensed his presence.

"I have to go with him," he said, gesturing at the general's back, not seeming to care who might overhear. "Stay here with the others. Don't do anything that'll make anyone uneasy."

Did Jed really think these stern-faced army men were afraid of her? But when his features remained grave, she realized he was warning her that a sudden or unexpected move on her part might result in bloodshed. He continued to look at her long after he should have gone with his general, his eyes dark and—she be-lieved—touched with concern for her.

Finally, though, he headed toward the largest tent, and al-though she tried not to stare, she couldn't pull herself free until he'd gone inside. She heard Ha-kar-Jim laugh and say something to the shaman, heard Ko-a-lak-a admonish him. Ha-kar-Jim only laughed again before turning his rifle over to the nearest soldier. Once he'd shown everyone he was unarmed, he walked over to a huge fire pit where several men were roasting a cow and held out his hand, in-dicating he wanted to eat.

Was this a game to Ha-kar-Jim, and to Cho-ocks, who was now handing his rifle to another soldier? They believed no one would make them pay for killing settlers as long as they agreed to go to a reservation? Maybe they'd simply wanted an excuse to see the army camp. And maybe Cho-ocks had done magic to protect both him and Ha-kar-Jim.

Luash didn't want to be near the others, but when even Kient-poos's sister joined them, she hurried after them. Although she held her blanket tight around her, she was all too aware of the way many of the men looked at her. Eagle wasn't here today; Eagle couldn't protect her from a man's strength. Only Jed might be able to, but he was with his general.

"I don't know what they're up to," Jed admitted when General Canby asked for input. "The last thing I ever expected was to see Hooker Jim or Curley Headed Doctor here."

"Maybe there *has* been a split between them and Captain Jack," another officer observed. "If we've managed to divide them—"

"Don't count on it." The words weren't all the way out of his mouth before Lieutenant Gillem, who stood to General Canby's right, nodded agreement. "These people aren't stupid," Jed con-tinued. "They know what will happen if they lose their unity. My guess? Hooker's here to look things over. He's got his shaman with him, so he feels safe, and why shouldn't he, after that fiasco when we tried to take the stronghold. He figures we're so eager to put an end to things that we'll listen to anything he says. You don't see Jack, do you? They know better than to have all their leaders in one place at the same time."

General Canby stroked his beard and nodded, but said nothing. Jed assumed Canby was thinking of other possibilities. Luash and the others might be looking for the horses that had been stolen from them back in November. Jed knew all too well how the soldiers would react to having a good-looking young woman in camp. After months of nothing except the few whores who hung around, more than one soldier would be weighing the consequences of satisfying his needs with an unarmed Modoc woman.

"I have to see this as a positive move," General Canby declared. "Jed, you gave them a clear picture of what the peace commission hopes to accomplish. Maybe, after thinking it over, they decided not to wait for it to assemble. They took your visit, and the ones that came after it, as acts of good faith. What I want all of you to do"—he leaned forward as if about to impart some vital secret—"is to afford them the utmost courtesy. And make sure the men under you do the same."

Gillem insisted that would be all but impossible, since a number of local ranchers were in camp and probably would like nothing better than to spill Modoc blood. Canby's reply was that the ranchers had to be made to understand that their personal wishes and needs came second to ending things peacefully.

The moment Jed and Colonel Gillem stepped back outside, Gillem grumbled that the general was once again allowing his decisions to be dictated by distant politicians who had no inkling of the actual situation. When Gillem began to pontificate about how he would handle things, Jed stopped listening.

Looking around, he spotted Luash and Captain Jack's sister standing near the shore of Tule Lake. A number of soldiers had followed at a not-too-discrete distance and were making lewd comments about what they would do if they got either woman alone. When he called her name, Luash took several steps in his direction, then stopped. Damn, how could anyone dressed in simple deerskin, with a single white feather braided into her long, flowing hair, look so beautiful? "You're all right?" he asked, battling his body's need for her.

She nodded, but her eyes gave away her unease. Not giving a damn what anyone might think, he walked up to her and touched her shoulder, indicating he wanted her to come with him. The last time they were together, she'd kept her distance until he'd taken her in his arms. Today she all but crowded him, her slim legs occasionally brushing against his. He wondered if Queen Mary might join them. Instead, the older woman boldly walked up to a couple of soldiers and began a spirited conversation with them. He'd heard Mary had been mistress to several miners before things went to hell. Obviously, she had no hesitancy about being around whites.

Luash glanced over her shoulder at Mary, then looked up at Jed, her features grim. "You don't much like the way she acts, do you?" he asked.

"I do not understand it. To care so little for her own body . . . but maybe that is how it should be."

"What are you talking about?"

"Her heart does not beat as if it might break from her chest when she looks at so many soldiers," Luash said with a small smile. "She is comfortable here; she understands men."

"Maybe. Maybe not. I have to tell you, Hooker and Curley Headed Doctor's coming here really has people confused."

"Ha-kar-Jim in many ways is still a boy. He does what he wants, then later asks himself if it was wise."

"Maybe. Is he sorry he went·on that rampage?"

"I do not think he cares." She looked slowly all around, small and quiet, more than a little awe in her eyes. "There are so many soldiers; they're like ants climbing endlessly out of their underground home."

"What it is is overkill."

"Kill?"

"Bad choice of words. And, unless someone does something incredibly stupid, that's not going to happen today. Do you want me to show you around?"

He could tell she was giving his offer serious thought, but when she shook her head, he wasn't surprised. Besides, the last thing he wanted to do was expose her to any more vulgar stares.

"This is where I live." He indicated his tent, which had barely survived the last fierce wind. "Where I sleep, anyway. Other than that, I try to be here as little as possible." Without asking if she wanted to come inside, he pulled back the tent flap. He and Wilfred never left a lantern lit when they weren't in the tent. As a consequence, the interior was so dim that Luash wouldn't be able to see anything as long as she stood outside. For a moment she pressed her hand tight against her stomach and he guessed she wanted to turn and run. Finally, though, she stepped through the opening.

"It smells."

"Yeah, it does. I've gotten used to it."

"This is your home?"

Home. Hers had once been the land as far as he could see in all directions. "It's where I sleep."

"And when you are no longer needed here, will you take this tent with you?"

"It belongs to the army. It was issued to me for this campaign."

She hadn't moved since coming inside, but now she stepped to the center and looked up at the ridgepole holding it in place. "The wind does not tear it apart?"

"It hasn't yet, but it's gotten close a couple of times."

"I would not want a home that winter can destroy." Her gaze strayed to his cot and then to Wilfred's. When she asked who else slept there, he told her that as officers he and his friend were afforded more luxury and privacy than the enlisted men. He nearly laughed at the word *luxury*, because other than the cots and blankets, the only other things in the small space were his and Wilfred's trunks and their weapons. The lantern was suspended from the ceiling and he and Wilfred were always having to duck to keep from hitting their heads on it. For heat, they had to rely on the campfires, and as for cleaning up, well, there was always the lake.

"When you go to another place, they will give you another tent?"

He didn't want to talk about going anywhere else, didn't want to think about not seeing her again. "It depends. If I'm on the move, I just take a bedroll and sleep on the ground."

"Blankets on the ground? That is your life, Jed? As long as you are part of the army, you have no place to call your own?"

"I haven't had anything else for so long I don't remember what it was like."

"Once you were a boy, living with your parents in a fine home. You rode swift horses over rich land that gave your family great pride."

"And you used to be able to climb a butte and watch the sun rise. Things change, Luash. We have to change with them."

Despite the faint light, he saw the impact his words had had on her. Her eyes mirrored sadness and regret but also acceptance. He wondered if contemplating the turns his life had taken since childhood might make it easy for her to accept what was happening to her world. Maybe not accept but at least endure.

"Why are you here?" he asked. "Mary speaks some English and Hooker Jim can hold his own; they don't really need you interpreting."

"Kientpoos asked me to come. He wanted someone to study the army camp with honest eyes, not with eyes that see only what they want to."

He nodded, wondering if General Canby or Lieutenant Gillem had any idea how formidable a foe they were up against in her uncle. "He also doesn't trust what Hooker and your shaman might tell him, does he?"

"He knows them," she stated flatly. "I do not like it in here. I cannot breathe."

Neither could he, not with her so close. Still, this was the only place he could think of where they would have any privacy. "You're going to be stared at."

"You will be with me."

You will be with me. Did she have any idea how much it meant to him to know she trusted him? How foreign it was to hear someone say that? "You kept an eye on me while I was in your camp. I guess it's time for me to do the same for you."

She took a couple of steps toward the entrance, then stopped and turned toward him. "Your camp. Mine. There is so much standing between us, Jed Britton. If I was wise, I would not let you into my dreams."

"I'm there?"

Had she really said that, Luash asked herself, then faced reality. She wouldn't be standing inside Jed's tent—she wouldn't have agreed to her uncle's request—if she had not wanted to see this army man. "I should hate you, but I do not. I do not understand what I feel around you."

He didn't say anything, and although the shadows hid much of what was in his eyes, she believed her words were echoing inside him. She wanted their words and thoughts and emotions to blend, yet was afraid that if that happened, she would never again be able to walk away from him.

Yet she had to; they belonged to different worlds.

"I was a fool to come here." She threw the words at him. "A fool to want to be alone with you again."

"I'm not going to hurt you."

He already had, although not in ways he might understand. Before she could think what she should say to him, he locked his hand around her wrist. A part of her said she should resist, but instead of trying to push him away, she flattened her hand over his chest and let his warmth and the beat of his heart seep into her.

"I do not want to be here with you," she whispered.

"I don't want you here."

He was so close now that his features blurred. Only it was no easier talking to a shadow-man than it had been before. "We should have never met."

"No. We shouldn't have."

"I hate . . . "

She was in his arms, his strong, living arms. Tilting her head upward, she waited as he brought his face closer—closer. His breath touched her nose and cheeks, brushed over her eyes and made her blink. She tried to keep her eyes open so she could study this man who should be her enemy, but it was easier to let her eyelids drift shut.

Easier to ready herself for his kiss, easier to press her lips against his with an energy that equaled his, easier to clutch his neck with hungry arms.

This moment was why she'd walked from the Land of Burned Out Fires to the army camp.

And when the moment was over—

No! She couldn't think about that!

"You've got folks wondering what the hell you're up to, you know that, don't you? Wondering where your loyalties are."

Not acknowledging Wilfred's comment, Jed continued to watch Luash and the others slowly disappear from view. It was so late in the day that the Modocs couldn't possibly reach the lava beds before night. Still, he couldn't imagine them wanting to spend the night anywhere else.

"Did you hear me? Taking her in the tent like that—what the hell was that all about?"

"I didn't want her to get raped."

"Raped?" Wilfred nodded, accepting the truth of Jed's statement. "Yeah, you're right."

"I know I am. Canby and Gillem were so busy trying to figure out what Hooker Jim and Curley Headed Doctor were up to that they probably wouldn't have noticed if someone grabbed her."

"So you decided to be her protector."

"Yeah." But that wasn't all, Jed knew.

"What do you think about what happened today?" Wilfred asked.

Sighing, Jed forced himself to face his friend. "I think nothing's changed. Those Modocs came here to see what kind of a deal they could work out. They didn't like what they heard, so they left."

"As simple as that?"

"No, not as simple as that." Thanks to the erratic wind, he caught a whiff of roasting beef. He didn't know whether Hooker Jim had been given anything to eat and didn't care. Right now he was too angry at Captain Jack for jeopardizing Luash's safety to be able to concentrate on anything else. "And don't ask me why those braves took a chance on coming in here."

"It was stupid, that's what it was."

"Was it?" he asked after a moment of thought. "They needed to find out for themselves what the chance was of getting out of this mess without having their necks stretched. I guess now they have the answer to that."

Wilfred nodded but didn't bother to bring up the obvious, and for that Jed was grateful. Curley Headed Doctor had spouted some nonsense about his magic being so powerful that no one could kill him, nonsense that Colonel Gillem had listened to but hadn't accepted. After more than an hour of roundabout conversation, the shaman had finally gotten it through his thick head that escaping justice was going to be a lot harder than he'd thought.

Colonel Gillem could have ordered them arrested then and there; almost to a man, the soldiers were muttering that that should have been done. However, Jed knew why the Modocs had been allowed to leave.

It all came down to politics, to a peace commission that might never get its act together but insisted that no negotiations take place without them.

In the meantime, the standoff continued.

And he would spend the night thinking about the few minutes he'd had alone with Luash.

Luash, who, one way or the other, was going to have to leave the land of her ancestors.

"So we wait, is that it?" Wilfred asked.

"No, that's not the only thing and you know it."

"Yeah, I do. We squeeze them and keep on squeezing until something pops."

12

Spring had begun to arrive, chasing snow from the mountains and waking small animals from their winter's sleep. Luash's days were no longer filled with trying to keep herself and others warm.

Life returned to the winter gray sage and turned it into a pale blue cloud that took her back to her childhood. If she sat without moving, a shy sage grouse might slip out from under the cloud-plant to eat sagebrush buds and leaves. She had already pushed aside the woody old growth to study the delicate flowering vegetation that grew underneath, but if those tiny shoots had any aroma, they were overpowered by the sheltering sage. When there was little breeze, she could hear quail calling to each other as if delighted to be free to move about again. The bucks were growing new antlers.

Yesterday she'd ventured away from the stronghold and picked a couple of bitterbrush flowers, the first she'd seen this season. She'd given one to Whe-cha, who had tearfully confided that she'd once again begun her monthly bleeding and despaired of ever carrying Kientpoos's child. Maybe, Whe-cha had said, constant war talk had taken away her husband's ability to place his seed inside her.

War talk! It never ended!

Why, Luash wondered, was it so easy for the world to keep pace with the seasons when man continued to argue as if time meant nothing? More than two full moons had come and gone since she'd last spoken with Jed. Yes, they'd seen each other since then but because there were always others around, they'd done nothing except look at each other with eyes that didn't say nearly enough, that didn't trust.

The peace commission! How she'd come to hate those words that meant little more than gatherings without end or resolution. She hated even more feeling as if she was a prisoner in land she used to love. Although she prayed to him daily, Eagle did not always come to her, and his absence chilled her soul. Maybe, she forced herself to admit, Eagle disapproved of Jed's hold on her thoughts and emotions. And maybe Eagle's message went far deeper.

Needing distraction, she walked over to the rocks the sentries had piled up as fortification against stray army bullets. Because the sky was as clear as a fast-moving creek, she easily saw where army men had moved over the past few days. Some were now so close that she could make out their wagons and horses, saw that the army too had piled up rocks as protection.

Although the main camp remained where it had always been, small groups were coming closer, shifting from one place to another, always moving and making her feel choked. Frightening her.

They made endless demands upon Kientpoos, and no matter what he requested of the white peace commission members, they said no. Why couldn't they return to Lost River, their home, Kientpoos kept asking. But the white man's president and his advisors wanted the Modocs sent elsewhere—only where that might be kept changing.

These days, whenever someone weary of living like foxes in a trap said they would prefer any reservation to having to spend any more time in a cave, Kientpoos would point to the mountains, a wistful look in his eyes. "Soon all the snow will be gone," he'd say. "Then we will scatter into them where no one can find us."

In the meantime, General Canby who, along with Jed and several others, was a member of the peace commission, was pressuring her uncle to meet once again in the flimsy peace-talking tent that had been set up not far enough away from where the army waited. Maybe he would once again have to sit down with the general and the other white men, her uncle had complained. Otherwise they might guess his true plans.

Weary of her thoughts, her fears, she pushed herself off the chunk of lava on which she'd been sitting. Absentminded, she started toward the lake before she remembered there'd been soldiers out there earlier today. How she longed to be at Lost River!

But Jed. She needed to see him even more than she needed to stand beside the river she'd once called home.

Instead—instead she watched warriors build even more rock walls while Kientpoos and Cho-ocks and Ha-kar-Jim argued and tension took on a taste and feel of its own.

Not sure what she intended, she turned her steps toward Cho-Cho's cave. Earlier, she'd clambered to high ground and had been looking to see if Spirit Butte was visible when she spotted her uncle in earnest conversation with Cho-Cho, who had steadfastly remained by Kientpoos's side. Now, as she approached them, Luash sensed she was being watched. Turning, she saw Ha-kar-Jim near the dance ring. After a moment, his attention shifted from her to her uncle. Even from this distance, Luash sensed the young warrior's hostility.

Drawing near her chief and his friend, she observed, "Ha-kar-Jim is an angry man. Maybe he wants to become chief."

"Not angry, afraid." Kientpoos patted the rock to his right, indicating she could join them. "Despite his boastful words, he fears he will be hung."

"It is a rightful fear," Cho-Cho admitted. He rubbed his hand over his scarred cheek. "The white man's law says murder must be avenged."

"White man's law!" Kientpoos spat. "They say there is no longer Indian law and that we have no right to ask that the ponies the army stole from us be returned, that Aga's death be avenged, that we be given back our land. When I talk about that, they speak of when eighteen whites were killed at Bloody Point. That was before I was born!"

Cho-Cho nodded agreement. "The wrongs between Modoc and white go back a long time."

Luash looked for Ha-kar-Jim, but he was no longer in sight. If her uncle didn't want her to be part of this warrior talk, she'd understand, but neither man seemed to mind her presence. "Now we are rabbits who will be attacked by wolves if we leave our dens," she observed.

"That is what I told Meacham." Kientpoos sighed and stared at the ground. "I placed my hand on his shoulder and asked him what I should do. Yes, our braves were wrong to have killed, but the soldiers should not have burned us out. Meacham talks too much like the others. All he would say was that we must come out of the rocks and that they will find a new home for us. I am to trust! Turn my weapons over to men who touch our wickiups with fire! I said I was born on Modoc land; my father was buried in the Smiles of God; I would go nowhere else."

There was no other place, at least not in her heart. She would rather be blind than never see Modoc Lake and the country around it again.

"Before I left," Kientpoos continued, "I told them I expect to be killed, but my body would not fall on the rocks of the Land of Burned Out Fires. Instead it would cover the bodies of my enemies whom I have killed."

"Uncle! You did not!"

"Do not speak with a woman's heart," he warned. "When I die, I will die a man."

"No." She swallowed so that when she spoke again, it wouldn't sound like a whimper. "I will *not* let this happen."

"What can you do that my braves have not been able to?"

When she had no answer for him, he grunted, then continued telling Cho-Cho of the Modoc woman, Kaitchkana, who had married a white man. Kaitchkana had been to the stronghold several times, carrying messages. The last time, she'd said that the army promised protection for any Modocs who wanted to surrender, but were afraid of Ha-kar-Jim and his followers. When he'd heard that, Ha-kar-Jim had ordered Kaitchkana to be quiet. He said that he and his friends would kill anyone who turned on him. Despite her fear, Kaitchkana relayed the rest of General Canby's message. The army would never leave. The Modocs would leave the stronghold either as prisoners or dead.

Luash, listening, felt her heart skip a beat. Kientpoos dead! No! Gentle young Whe-cha dead? Please, no!

Before she could tell her uncle that the Modocs would scatter like feathers in the wind without him to hold them together, she spotted Ha-kar-Jim and the shaman walking toward them. Kientpoos and Cho-Cho immediately jumped to their feet. Luash stood more slowly, her heart drumming in dread.

"We will meet tonight," Ha-kar-Jim announced. "Everyone. Once it is dark, we will gather at the council grounds and decide what must be done."

"You cannot kill all the soldiers," Kientpoos insisted. "There are too many of them."

"Maybe," Ha-kar-Jim said slowly, "that will not be necessary."

As soon as the short confrontation between her uncle and Ha-kar-Jim was over, Luash hurried off by herself. She wanted to go to the lake, where it had always been so easy for her and Eagle to meet, but she didn't dare expose herself with the soldiers so close. Instead, praying that Eagle still heard her thoughts, her prayers, she left the Modoc stronghold, walking slowly over the stone-hard and nearly lifeless ground.

Lifting her head so the warm spring breeze could catch it, she searched the clean and endless sky. At dusk the air often filled with bats leaving their underground homes, but today only a few hawks and smaller birds were about. She loved the feel of the sun on her cheek, wondered briefly whether Jed was outside staring up at the same sky, thinking about her.

Asking himself how this would all end.

"Eagle!" she called. "Eagle. Hear me. I need your wisdom, your comfort. Speak to me; protect me and those I love. Take us—take us back to what once was. If I must be sacrificed so they may live, so be it."

No response.

"I have thought on this. Searched my heart. You protect me; I am grateful for the gift. But it is better that I join my ancestors so my people can live."

Still nothing.

"Please. I have thought endlessly about why you do not always come to me these days, asked myself if you are telling me that the end has come for us. But if—if I can take the place of my people, I will do it."

She saw him now, a dark dot in the distance. As he came closer, the smaller birds fled. His dark feathers shone so brightly in the sunlight that he looked wet. Arms outstretched, she sent out a silent prayer of gratitude for his appearance. Standing on a rocky outcropping, she almost believed she was on top of the world, nearly believed she could sense her grandfather waiting for her. Her end? Was that what Eagle willed?

Eagle's wings stretched over her, but he was so far overhead that she couldn't feel the wind they created. "Please. I need your touch. What must the Modocs do? What do you want of me?"

At her question, Eagle dipped his head until she found herself looking up into his red eyes. For an instant, her heart raced and she felt like singing. But instead of blessing her with his touch as he'd done so many times, Eagle angled his body upward and caught a wind current. Wing feathers fluttering from the breeze, he nevertheless managed to hover directly overhead until she thought her neck would break from the strain of looking up at him. Then, with a shrill cry, Eagle surrendered to the wind and flew away.

Night brought a chill that nearly made Luash forget how warm the day had been. Wrapped in her blanket, she sat next to Whe-cha and waited for Ha-kar-Jim to begin speaking. She'd kept to herself all day, frequently scanning the sky in a vain hope that she'd see Eagle again. Twice she'd stared in the direction of the isolated peace tent, but it was too far away for her to see it. She'd been willing to end her life so those she loved could live, but Eagle hadn't heard her.

Or maybe he had no answer for her prayer.

"My husband was angry today," Whe-cha whispered. "He again said that Ha-kar-Jim and Cho-ocks and the others should have known a white man does not forgive a wrong done by an Indian, that their killing may kill all Modocs."

"There have been wrongs on both sides since the first white came here," Luash pointed out as she fought the impact of what Whe-cha had said. "What are we supposed to do, go back to the first wrong and point at the one responsible?"

"I do not know. I just wish . . . oh, Luash, I am so weary of living like this! I pray to the spirits, but they do not hear me. The only sound is that of my frightened heart."

Tonight, feeling like an animal in a slowly closing trap, Luash shared her friend's emotion. Had she once spent her days looking for spring flowers and butterflies? It seemed impossible, a foolish child's game. What she was living now was a nightmare that made her thoughts chase in endless circles like a foolish fox kit. The only part that wasn't a nightmare were the all too brief moments she'd spent with Jed—moments when she'd been able to forget how different their worlds were.

Ha-kar-Jim climbed onto the speaking rock and addressed everyone sitting inside the rock wall that circled the council grounds. Dark lights from the campfire played across his face, distorting his features.

"There have been enough meetings. Talk and more talk that leads nowhere," he said. "First the peace commission says one thing, then another. Their general says he must wait until he hears from his president before he knows where we will be sent if we surrender. Cannot this president make up his mind? I say I will not listen to any more words." He looked down to where his companions were grouped. "The army continues to grow stronger, to come closer. Something must be done. Now."

Luash couldn't argue with that. What worried her was what Ha-kar-Jim had in mind. His words confirmed her fears.

"The whites must be murdered. Now."

"Murdered? No!" Kientpoos, who'd been all but hidden in the shadows, jumped to his feet. "They are too strong."

"Not all must die." Ha-kar-Jim leaned forward so he could meet his chief's gaze. "Just their leaders."

When Kientpoos demanded to know what Ha-kar-Jim was talking about, the brave explained that after much discussion, he and his friends had decided that without their leaders, the rest of the army would run away. "Would any of us have left the reservation if we hadn't had a leader? No. We would still be waiting for whites to herd us ever closer to the Klamaths. But you, Chief Kientpoos, you told us what we should do and we followed. Without leadership, people scatter. If their general is dead, the army will not know what to do. They will go home."

"You are foolish!" Kientpoos declared. "Modocs have murdered whites. That cannot go unpunished."

"Who will punish us if they have no leaders?"

Grunting, Kientpoos insisted he too wanted an end to the war. However, after talking to the peace commission until his head ached, he believed the only way that would happen was if all Modocs surrendered peacefully. Because his heart rejected that, he had no choice but to wait until the snows left the mountains. Cho-ocks retorted that the ranchers and other settlers hated Modocs; someone would hang for the murder of their neighbors before they were satisfied—unless, as Ha-kar-Jim had pointed out, the army had lost its leader. As shaman, Cho-ocks promised, he would make powerful magic that would make it impossible for any Modocs to be killed, but for his magic to work, the army would first have to be turned into a headless rat.

By now Kientpoos was all but standing toe to toe with the shaman. He continued to meet with the peace commission, he said, because he couldn't yet lead his people safely into the mountains.

"You are a woman!" Ha-kar-Jim shrieked. "A woman cowering behind her mother's skirts. You are afraid of war, too much of a coward to lift your rifle against the general."

Whe-cha whimpered and Luash drew in a strangled breath, but even if she'd known what to say, this argument was between the men of the tribe. She and Kientpoos's young wife would only be shoved aside if they tried to intervene.

"You want me to kill their general?" Kientpoos demanded. "The others would turn on me. Tear me apart."

"Not if every white in the peace tent was dead," Cho-ocks insisted. Then, before Luash could guess what they were up to, Ha-kar-Jim's followers jumped to their feet and surrounded Kientpoos. Although he struggled, they threw him to the ground. Someone held a woman's shawl and headdress aloft, then clamped them on Kientpoos. He continued to fight, Cho-Cho lending a hand, but Ha-kar-Jim and Cho-ocks had too many friends. They managed to keep the women's clothes on Kientpoos.

"Coward! White-faced squaw!" Ha-kar-Jim taunted. "You are no longer a roaring bull, no longer a true Modoc. Look at you, afraid of a white man."

Finally, sweating and red-faced, Kientpoos managed to fling off the humiliating garments. Trembling, he faced the assembled Modocs. "This is what you want?" he demanded. "A leader in murder? Well, that is what I will be."

"No!" Whe-cha sobbed.

"Uncle!" Luash gasped. "No. Please."

He ignored them. "I am no squaw, no coward. I will do as you say and take a weapon into the peace talking tent, but I say this to you. I will die. Maybe every Modoc here will be killed, but this is what you want. I will show you how a murder must be carried out."

"My husband, no!"

"Yes! Yes because I must!" He thumped his heaving chest. "With my own hands, I will kill the general."

Long after the Modocs had gone to their separate caves, Luash still couldn't believe what she had heard. His eyes wild, his voice shrill, her uncle had continued to insist that he would be the one to kill General Canby, because one leader must end the life of another. Yaihaka, who'd claimed to have murdered as many ranchers as Ha-kar-Jim, would be given the honor of killing Colonel Gillem, who had been at most of the peace talks. Sano'tks would be responsible for Meacham. A Sunday Doctor called Reverend Thomas would also be killed, but not Kaitchkana and her husband, whom everyone expected to be there. After all, Kaitchkana was Modoc, even if she had married a white trapper. Slolux and Barncho, two young

206 // Vella Munn

and simple-headed braves who'd ridden with Ha-kar-Jim during his rampage, were given the honor of being put in charge of the horses.

It sounded unbelievably cold-hearted. Still in shock, Luash sat on one of the rocks that ringed the council ground. With the help of the moon, she made out where Kientpoos and the others had stood earlier. She was alone. Still crying, Whe-cha had hurried into the cave after her husband.

Jed might come to the peace tent with his general. At Kientpoos's insistence, he'd become part of the peace commission, attending most of the meetings. No one had spoken of killing him, maybe because in their excitement, Ha-kar-Jim and Cho-ocks had forgotten about him. But Luash knew if Ha-kar-Jim could murder ranchers he'd traded with for years, he wouldn't spare Jed.

Feeling beyond tears, she stared up at the moon, which had been playing with the clouds ever since it had replaced the sun that evening, and listened to the song of the night creatures. Her choices were so simple, yet so impossible. Either she prayed for her uncle to succeed and regain leadership of his people, or she told Jed of the plot. Either she stood beside Kientpoos or Jed, embraced her people or turned her back on them.

The sound of boots on rock startled her, but she couldn't pull herself away from her twisted thoughts until Kientpoos spoke. "Tell me, my niece. Do you hate me?"

"Hate you?"

"For agreeing to their demands."

She made room for him beside her. Together, they leaned forward and studied the ground. "You should be with Whe-cha," she said softly. "She needs you."

"I cannot be a husband tonight, Luash, not when my mind and heart are so full."

No, he couldn't. "Nothing matters to Ha-kar-Jim except what he wants."

"It is how he hopes to stay alive."

She didn't want Kientpoos to be so understanding; she wanted, what—for him to become as bloodthirsty as Ha-kar-Jim? "You are his chief. He had no right forcing you."

"He speaks with the heart of many."

"What he says will not happen. The army will not turn into a headless snake."

"I know." Kientpoos ended on a sigh. "If I kill General Canby, I will become a dead man."

She'd shuddered the first time she heard that; now she shuddered again. "I will ask Eagle to protect you."

"Eagle is your spirit, Luash. Not mine."

Hers? Maybe—and maybe Eagle had taken away his blessing. "I love you. I want you and Whe-cha to have many years together, many children. Those I love should be safe."

"And we should still be free to roam over the land the gods gave to us. Nothing is as it once was."

"No. It isn't." She wanted to say more, but her chest felt tight and her tears were so close that she didn't dare.

"I do not want this, Luash. I do not want to kill the general because then the hearts of the army men will fill with the need for revenge."

"I know."

"Maybe the hearts of *all* army men."

Not sure what he was trying to tell her, she could only wait for him to continue. "Luash, I told Whe-cha that I would not say anything, that what you do and feel is for you alone. But you have done a dangerous thing. Because I love you, I cannot remain silent."

"Dangerous?"

"You have let a white man touch your heart."

"No. His heart does *not* beat the same as mine."

"Maybe. Maybe not. Think on this, Luash. He will be there when I do what I promised. When I try to."

"I know."

"Will you warn him? That is why I sought you tonight, to ask what you will say to him."

She tried to speak but couldn't find the words.

"Answer me! What does your heart tell you to do?"

"To run. To go to Fern Cave and stay there until I am an old woman."

"Fern Cave? Because no one will find you there?"

"And because what grows there is beautiful and ageless, a gift from the gods, and because the wall carvings make me feel close to our ancestors."

"Our ancestors also left their markings on the mountain Kumookumts left behind after he dug his sleeping hole deep in Modoc Lake. Maybe you should go there. If you do, be careful the hawks do not fly overhead or they may gift you with what they ate that morning."

Her uncle was trying to make her laugh. If they hadn't been talking about murdering white men, she might have. "Please tell me this. Are you afraid you will be killed at the peace tent? If they bring guards—"

"They do not. Otherwise, I would not meet with them. But what I said earlier—it is what I believe. Before our war with the army is over, I will be a dead man."

His final words faded into the night air. She wanted to snatch them back, say something to make a lie of them, but she couldn't— no more than she could promise that Eagle would spread his wings over her uncle and the rest of her people. What good was a spirit that gave safety only to her, and one who no longer understood her need for him? If those she loved were dead or prisoners on some reservation, could she call herself free?

Her questions made her head pound. Pushing herself to her feet, she walked out into the middle of the council ring and stared upward. "All my life I have loved the moon," she whispered, "but

I loved the sun more because it brings warmth. Now I wish night would never end."

"We cannot stop the order of things." Her uncle sounded incredibly old. "Just as I cannot stop what I must do. I ask you: are you going to speak to him?"

"I do not know!" Her uncle was a shadow among all other shadows. "I do not know."

Only, she did, Luash admitted as she neared the army camp. She couldn't say how long she'd sat watching the moon after her uncle left, but finally she'd gone to find a blanket to protect herself from the night chill and then, instead of joining her people, she turned her feet in another direction.

Because the moon continued to dodge in and out of the clouds, it took her most of the night to cover the distance that separated the Modocs from the whites. She expected to find that the army had posted so many guards that she wouldn't be able to slip into camp, but she didn't see any. The deep shadows cast by tents, cannons, horse corrals, and rocks gave her the shelter she needed. She kept her breathing and heartbeat under control by reminding herself that no one would be looking for a Modoc here. Finding Jed's tent was easy.

What was nearly impossible was forcing herself to slip inside. When she finally pulled back the cloth door, it was so dark she couldn't make out Jed's bed. She considered hiding outside until he emerged, but he might not stir before morning and she couldn't risk being spotted by someone who cared nothing except that she was a Modoc. Finally, not knowing what else to do, she pulled an eagle feather out of her hair and left it just inside. Then she hurried away to wait behind a large sage growing at the edge of Modoc Lake.

Morning came slowly, as if the moon was reluctant to give up its hold on the world. She became aware of smoke drifting upward from several campfires and heard the restless sound of horses waiting to be fed. When a bugle sounded, she jumped. From where she crouched, those in camp couldn't see her, but if a group headed this way—

Her stomach was rumbling from hunger when she finally spotted a lone rider. He sat tall in the saddle while he scanned the horizon. Taking an incredible risk, she stepped around the rock. The rider momentarily slowed his horse, then urged it on.

Jed hadn't shaved for several days. His hair was uncombed. He wore, not his uniform, but shirt and pants nearly as old and worn as those the Modoc men wore. He seemed so large, roughened by the endless days he'd spent out here. She had taken care with her appearance before leaving the stronghold, but now wondered if she'd made a mistake. If he thought—if he thought what?

"I saw the feather," he said when he was close enough for her to hear. "You could have been killed putting it there."

"You forget, Jed. I am protected."

"Are you? If that's what you believe, why were you hiding?"

Feeling both hurt and vulnerable, she waited until she trusted herself to speak calmly. "Is that what you want? I should stand outside your tent so all will believe you have turned your back on your army? So they will call you a squaw man?"

He held up the feather she'd left for him and smoothed it with his work-hardened fingers. His eyes became less wary, and she believed he was glad to see her. Maybe he needed this time together as much as she did. "Why did you take the risk?" he asked softly. "Things are so delicate now; everyone's on edge. If some scared kid took a shot at you—" She tried to speak but he shook his head, stopping her. "Eagle can't protect you from a bullet, Luash. I don't care what you think."

"Do you care what I came here to tell you? Maybe I should leave."

His mouth twitched, then softened. "No, stay. You've been all right?"

"I am fine. Jed, will you be there tomorrow? At the peace tent?"

"Yes. General Canby's hopeful. . . . Why?"

What had he seen in her eyes that prompted him to ask his sharp question? Maybe she shouldn't try to do anything except give him the whole truth. Later she could ask herself why she'd confided in a white man and betrayed her people.

"There will be killing," she whispered. Then, before he had to drag the words out of her, she told him what Ha-kar-Jim had forced Kientpoos to agree to.

"They're going to the talks armed?" Jed dismounted and stepped toward her, stopping only when he was so close that she couldn't see the world beyond him. "They're willing to jeopardize everything? I don't believe it. Why? Damnit, why?"

"Because Ha-kar-Jim fears he will be hanged if the Modocs surrender. Because he believes the army will scatter if their leaders are dead."

"Is he crazy?" Jed stared at her so intently that she wondered if he blamed her for the warrior's actions. "That's not the way it works. Damn! Listen to me, Luash. Tell this to your uncle." He ran a rough thumb over the scar on his forehead. "When I got this, eighty men died. An entire command was wiped out. A captain was killed. But those who found them didn't turn tail and run. It's not going to be any different this time."

Although fear that he was right cramped her belly, she shook her head. "A captain is not a general. When the army sees how brave and powerful the Modocs are—"

"When they see how stupid you are, they'll hunt down every last one of you."

"Stupid?" Rocking back on her heels, she stared up at him. Her fingers curled into fists, and it was all she could do not to pound them against him. "Is that what you believe I am?"

"I didn't say—"

"You *did* say."

He was going to touch her. She should turn and run, or if not that, yell that she didn't want his hands on her flesh. "What you are, Luash," he said as his fingers settled on her shoulder, "is brave and wise and beautiful."

Like mist under a hot sun's assault, her anger faded into nothing. This was why she'd come here, not just to warn him that his life would be in danger tomorrow, but because it had been so long since she'd seen him. So long since her heart had fluttered and sung and driven her half insane. "I do not feel wise," she whispered. "I am afraid."

His eyes said he understood and maybe even shared her emotion, but when he pulled her against him so she now felt his strength around her, she no longer cared about anything except ending the loneliness she'd spent so long trying to deny.

Her body wanted him; her heart needed him.

When she tipped her head upward and pressed her lips against his, it didn't matter that she knew nothing about the white man's way of showing emotion. He would teach her. And she would show him what beat inside her.

And maybe, when they fell together on the ground, her eyes would shine as Whe-cha's did after a night in Kientpoos's arms. She'd feel the heat Whe-cha spoke of, make those animal sounds. Forget everything except lashing her body to his.

"I missed—" he whispered. "I missed you so much."

He would be magnificent, strong and possessive, appreciative of the gift of her virginity. Her maidenhood—to a soldier? "There is not a day or night that I do not think about you."

"It'd be easier if it wasn't this way."

"I know." She kissed him again. Although her body felt as if a summer's sun now pressed down on her and she hated the clothes that came between them, she found the strength to continue. "I still wish I had never met you. Never spoken to you or looked into your eyes."

"But you did."

"Yes. I have been changed by you."

"And I by you."

"I do not want—"

He gripped her upper arms and pushed her away until his face came into focus. "I know what you don't want," he said harshly. "Believe me, I feel the same way."

"Then—then you should not have come out here."

"Oh no, Luash. It could never be that way. Don't you know that?" he asked and gently stroked her chin with a finger that caressed despite his rough flesh. "If I thought there was any chance of seeing you, nothing would keep me away."

That was why she'd come here. If he hadn't found his way into her heart, she would have stayed where she was safe. Where the damage to her heart wouldn't become even greater. "You—you believe me?" Her voice was tight with desperation and regret, with fear unlike any she'd ever known. "Your life is in danger. If you go there tomorrow—"

13

Luash was still at the lake when Jed returned several hours later. She'd asked him to take her to the general, but he'd adamantly refused. Given the level of tension simmering in camp, he refused to let her risk her life by walking among all those soldiers. He'd assured her that he'd talk to Canby himself. If the general wanted to hear more, Jed would bring Canby to her.

She'd agreed so readily that Jed understood just how upset she'd been at the prospect of leaving the relative isolation of the lake shore. Now, riding toward her, he faced how much she'd risked. Bottom line, she'd betrayed her people.

For him?

The fair-sized breeze grabbed her midnight waist-length hair and swirled it around her face and neck. She looked almost as if she could join her eagle spirit.

"I thought you would be gone longer," she said.

"There wasn't that much to say." He dismounted. He hoped she would put an end to what little distance remained between them, but she didn't, and he respected her unspoken message. "You didn't see anyone? No one bothered you?"

"Some men brought horses to drink, but they were far enough away that I felt safe."

He nodded, guessing she'd had to fight with herself to keep from running. He was glad, very glad, she hadn't.

"What did your general say? He will save himself?"

"There's nothing to worry about, he says. He can't believe Captain Jack would be that stupid."

"He is not stupid! My uncle believes he has no choice if he is to call himself a man."

"I know," he reassured her, "but there are things you have to understand about the general. He's under an incredible amount of pressure both from folks hereabouts and politicians back East to put an end to this embarrassment. A few people even think whites ought to clear out entirely."

"They think—"

He couldn't let blind hope get the best of her. Barely aware of what he was doing, he wrapped his fingers around her wrists and drew her close, thinking to force her to listen to facts. She resisted but didn't fight, a subtle difference that taught him a great deal about how much she wanted to trust him. "It won't happen, Luash. Not ever. What I'm saying is, that sentiment only adds to the pressures on the general. He's been wiring General Sherman, the president, and the secretary of the Interior that talks are coming along and that he's hopeful of a peaceful end to hostilities before much longer. Four months of stalemate, particularly given the army's vastly superior numbers, have everyone on edge and a lot of people saying the army can't do the job they were sent here to accomplish."

"Hostilities?"

"That's a polite way of saying war." When her eyes narrowed, he realized he'd spoken harshly. "If he doesn't show up for those talks tomorrow, General Canby will have lost as much face as your uncle almost did last night."

He wasn't sure she'd understand, but after a moment she nodded, features sober. "Meacham feels the same way as the general," he continued. "And Reverend Thomas—he believes he's got God on his side and God wouldn't let anything happen to him."

"God is his spirit?"

"I guess that's one way of putting it."

"And you believe his god is no stronger than Eagle, that we both cling to something which doesn't exist."

"I can't say what it's like for the reverend. All I know is, God didn't keep my parents alive or save eighty good men. If you can spend a winter living in a cave and still believe some eagle is going to protect you—"

"Stop it! You and I will always see differently on this."

She was right. Besides, they weren't here to argue about her beliefs or his lack of same. "I tried. I want you to believe that. But the general's not going to change his mind. He'll be there tomorrow."

"Then—" Her eyes became so dark, so deep and pain-filled, that it scared him. "Then he is a dead man."

"No," he insisted, despite the voice inside that said he was a fool. "Damnit, Luash, Captain Jack can't be crazy enough to risk the lives of all his people by doing something so incredibly stupid as killing a U.S. Army general. Whatever he agrees to in public because Hooker Jim's putting pressure on him, I simply can't believe he'd throw away his life, and the lives of his people, this way."

"His honor is at stake."

Jed opened his mouth to tell her that honor had to come second in this when, suddenly, he no longer wanted to argue. If Captain Jack and General Canby were true leaders, they would stand face to face and not give up until they'd worked out a compromise they could both live with. Too bad he had been part of the army long enough to know that such things seldom, if ever, happened that way.

But Luash—he needed to think about her, wanted her to know

she'd turned his life and emotions around. Had she spun some kind of spell around him? If she had, he wasn't sure he wanted to know.

"I've been dreaming about you," he admitted, his voice not nearly as strong as he wanted. "I've never dreamed about a woman before. At least not like that."

"You are with me every night."

He'd touched her as deeply as she'd touched him? It seemed impossible; he was nothing but a hard soldier who'd committed his life to ridding the west of savages—savages like her. Since knowing Luash, he'd begun to forget that he'd once thought of Indians as little more than animals.

"Do not go," she begged, night still in her eyes. "When they meet tomorrow, do not be part of it."

He had no choice in the matter, but that wasn't what he wanted to talk about now; in truth, words held no interest for him. A lifetime ago he'd watched his father greet women by kissing the back of their hands. Some of them had giggled and blushed; all had looked pleased. Although Luash wouldn't understand that such a kiss was a sign of respect and affection among so-called cultured and sophisticated people, he lifted her hand and touched his lips to the strong vein just beneath the smooth, dark flesh. When he gazed into her eyes, he could have sworn he saw tears in them. "Are you all right?" he asked.

"I do not know."

"What I just did, it's a good thing. A way for a man to show respect to a woman."

"Jed, I did not come here to feel your lips on my hand."

"You told me what you felt you needed to about what happened between your uncle and Hooker Jim. There's nothing more you can do."

"I tried to warn—"

"I know. And I appreciate it. Most of all, I'm in awe of your courage."

"Jed, it takes no courage for me to seek you out."

"Because you've got this insane belief that your life's somehow blessed. Damnit, I know all too well how you think. Will you be there tomorrow?"

She started to shake her head, then stopped. "Ha-kar-Jim will say no, but I will ask my uncle."

Fear, which he'd denied himself ever since he heard what Hooker Jim and the others were up to, lashed through him. Meacham and the general knew she was Captain Jack's niece. If they believed it was to their benefit, to say nothing of upping their odds of staying alive, they might make her a hostage.

Running his fingers over hers, he waited until he had her full attention. "Do one thing for me, please. Stay away."

"And will you do the same for me?"

"I can't. I'm expected—"

"Your general comes before me?"

He clamped his hands more firmly around her wrist and held her against him. "It's not a matter of choosing one of you over the other. I have a job."

She opened her mouth; he sensed that she was marshalling her arguments and readied himself to hear her attack his career and his way of life, but she didn't. Instead, she looked down at her trapped hands, then back up at him. There was no fear in her eyes. "We are so different."

"Yeah. We are."

"I want to go home. I want to stop dreaming of you."

"No, you don't."

"Yes. I do. I have always known who I am, Jed. I am proud of being Modoc. But a true Modoc does not dream of her enemy."

If she'd resisted him, he could have forcefully ended that resistance and they would have finished the day as the enemies she'd just spoken of, but he'd felt her smaller body soft and strong and still against his, and it was too late.

Too late for anything except grabbing at a memory.

Maybe she needed the same thing, he thought as he slid his hands up her arms. He cupped her neck with fingers strong enough to kill her. There was still no fear in her eyes, nothing that would shatter this precious and insane moment when the world was reduced to only the two of them and all he wanted was to understand what he felt for her.

Luash's kiss, half gentle and half bold, stole his thoughts. He struggled against his desire for her for maybe a half second, then let it rage over him. His hands, mouth, breath even, gave him away, but he was helpless to hold back. He drew her tight against his body, holding her there while heat flooded between them and he wondered if he might die if he couldn't bury himself in her.

She still didn't resist. He felt her breasts flat against him and her hips melting into him, felt her begin to move in a rhythm he guessed was beyond her control. His blood heated until he thought he might explode, then heated even more. He embraced what was happening to him—accepted it for what it was—the greatest honesty he'd ever given a woman.

He wanted to keep his mouth clamped over hers until he'd pulled everything out of her, but there was too much energy in him and he couldn't be patient. Lost, he touched teeth, tongue, and lips to everything of her he could. She shuddered when he ran his tongue over the side of her neck but didn't pull away, only held on with strong fingers and breathed quick and hard. When he finally stopped long enough to drag in a lungful of sage- and water-scented air, Luash stood on tiptoe and clamped her teeth over the lobe of his right ear.

That stopped him as surely as a lasso would stop a wild horse. Energy continued to build inside him; he focused his entire will on keeping that energy contained. Her teeth—teasing now—made his entire body feel as if it was being stroked by a hot feather. His flesh jumped and trembled, recoiled in a self-protective gesture, came back for more.

She had to know what she was doing to his self-control when she began running her tongue over his cheekbone. She might be an innocent, but just because her body hadn't known a man's didn't mean she didn't have a woman's reactions.

A woman's wisdom.

Fighting her, fighting himself, he shoved her away and held her at arms length. She stared at him, eyes hooded, body tense and soft all at the same time. She breathed only infrequently and when she did, it sounded as if she'd forgotten how to do it. He knew exactly how she felt.

"We set each other off," he managed to say, hoarsely. "Right now, when I should be telling you to get the hell back to your people, I want to haul you back to my tent and keep you there."

"No. Not your tent. Come to the Land of Burned Out Fires with me."

The temptation was so great; he could lose himself in her world with its hearty sage and manzanita and the animals, birds, and fish that lived beyond the worst of the lava flow. They'd learn what it was about each other that kept them coming together when they both knew how insane it was.

"Do you really want that?" he asked. "You would keep me with you?"

"Not keep. I could never do that to you. But if you touched my Modoc heart, you would understand what this land means to me. And to my people."

I want that, he nearly said, before years of fighting and hating everything she stood for kicked in, tore him a little free of the insanity swirling around him. "I have a job to do tomorrow." He spoke through clenched jaws. "A job you say's going to get me killed and I say is going to put an end to this damnable war."

The passion went out of her eyes as swiftly and surely as if he'd struck her. "Oh yes," she hissed, leaning away from him so she could stare into his eyes. "Do your job, Jed. Either you will be killed or you and your general will say and do things that will force me to leave the land of my ancestors."

"It can't go on the way it is; you know that."

She pulled out of his grip because he let her, because he told himself he didn't want to hold her anymore. "And you say it has to be the white man's way. That the Modocs have lost everything that was once theirs. I was wrong. You will never understand my heart. And I no longer want you to." She turned away in one motion.

Luash was halfway back to the stronghold before her anger cooled. Then she walked without thinking, her mind numb. It wasn't until she'd climbed onto a rock and spread her arms so the Modoc sentries would know who she was that she faced what she'd done.

Terrified for his life, she'd struck out at Jed so she would no longer be swamped by her fear for him. She'd left him with her rage, with words she didn't mean—words that, maybe, were the only ones she dared say to him.

She hadn't yet reached her cave when Ha-kar-Jim intercepted her, demanding to know where she'd been. "I seek peace," she retorted. "Unlike you, I do not embrace killing."

"What were you doing?" He reached for her, but she evaded him, warning him not to try to touch her again.

"You do not tell me your thoughts," she accused. "You said nothing to me of the awful thing you were going to do to my uncle. Why should I say anything to you?"

He continued to grumble that she shouldn't have left the stronghold and that he didn't trust her, but when she turned her back on him, he didn't try to stop her. Despite her inner turmoil, she couldn't help smiling. It was good to have a powerful spirit. Ha-kar-Jim, killer of unarmed men, was afraid of Eagle.

Although she immediately went in search of her uncle, she didn't find him until late in the day. From what little he told her, she realized that he and Cho-Cho had walked deep in the lava beds, but what the two old friends had talked about, Kientpoos kept to himself. "Your army man would not listen to you, would he?" he asked. "He believes we would not be so foolish as to kill his leaders."

"Do you understand why I had to try?" she asked around the fear that gripped her. *Kientpoos knew.* "It was not because I have turned my back on you; I love you too much for that. But I do not want any more killing." She sighed.

"He would not listen."

"He listened," she insisted. "But I do not think he believed. Neither did the general."

"You spoke to General Canby?"

"Not me," she reassured him, then told him everything except for the emotion behind her trip. She finished by saying that General Canby had refused to call off tomorrow's scheduled meeting. "Please," she begged, "let me go with you. Kaitchkana will be there, but she should not be the only woman. Men are less likely to fight in the presence of women."

"No!" Kientpoos ordered with uncharacteristic anger. "I have made a promise to my people. I cannot change now."

"But—"

"You say you understand a man's heart, but you do not. I will not go back on my word. I cannot."

Sick, she asked the one question she couldn't turn her back on. "You have said that you will kill the general and that others will shoot Meacham and the Sunday doctor. What about Jed Britton?"

He met her gaze calmly. "That has not been decided."

April 11, 1873

The night had been an agony of horrible possibilities and silent prayers to Eagle and Kumookumts. Luash felt as if she'd been trapped in a nightmare from which there was no escape. She should have pleaded more with Jed, should have insisted on talking to General Canby. But if she did that, and Canby and the others decided to come armed to the peace talks, and her uncle was killed, would she be responsible?

But if Jed took a bullet, would that be any better?

She gave up trying to get any rest when the sun sent its first fingers out over the land. Leaving her cave, she scrambled up to the surface and slipped as close to the lake as she dared. She thought she could see smoke rising from army campfires, but because fog still clung to the ground, she couldn't be sure. The only sounds that reached her ears came from the birds. Always before, their endless chatter had made her heart feel both light and full, but this morning they were less than mist to her. Cho-ocks had done a great deal of magic-making last night, to the accompaniment of chants and dancing, and had boasted that his magic was now so powerful that it could defeat an entire army. Although she'd watched the whole ceremony, she was unable to share the others' belief that the sun would set on a Modoc victory.

"Eagle!" she called out. "You see so much. Your ears tell you many things. Please, tell me what I should do. Let my eyes see into the rest of the day. Will Jed die? Will Kientpoos?"

She spotted a couple of distant hawks; except for them, the sky was empty save for a few clouds building to the north. Empty and unbelievably beautiful. She had no words to describe the intense blue, or her gratitude because snow was leaving the hillsides. Wild flowers bloomed everywhere. She embraced the crisp morning wind and imagined how it would feel if it carried summer's heat. This should be a time of beauty and gratitude, not death.

"I have to know. Please, this killing—this dying—is wrong. I must find a way to make Ha-kar-Jim and the others understand that. What should I say? What can I do?"

Although she continued to stretch her arms upward, she saw nothing; even the hawks were gone.

"Do not desert me! Please. Tell me what I must do! Will Jed live? Please. Will Jed live?" Will my uncle, my people?

Whe-cha was roasting a small amount of meat when Luash returned to the cave. Luash tried to respond to her friend's questioning stare, but the words tangled themselves inside her. Eagle had not come to her this morning.

"My husband has a message for you," Whe-cha said as she tore off a hunk of meat and handed it to Luash. "If you want, you can go with Cho-Cho and watch from the rocks. But you are not to speak."

"Not say anything?"

"The army has had their warning." Whe-cha sounded as if she was repeating word for word what her husband had told her. "If they are so foolish as to want to walk into their death, you are not to try to stop them."

Kientpoos wanted her to simply stand there as someone aimed a rifle at Jed? He thought she could stand the agony of wondering whether the army men would be the first to fire, whether her uncle would feel a deadly bullet? But what else could she do? Staying here, knowing nothing, was even worse.

When she saw Kientpoos and the others walk away from the stronghold, she hurried after them, careful to keep a respectful distance behind. Her uncle said little to those around him. She prayed he would change his mind; at the same time, she hoped he wouldn't, because if he did, the Modocs would be without a leader.

There were no whites at the peace tent, but surely they would arrive soon. Looking at the hills between the tent and the army camp, she had no doubt that soldiers were concealed there. Although the hills were a considerable distance from the tent, it wouldn't take long for any hidden army men to reach the tent. The thought that this might be a trap shot through her. When she saw the others scan the horizon, she knew they were thinking the same thing. Had Jed and General Canby warned everyone? If they had, then she had indeed betrayed her people.

At Cho-Cho's orders, she joined him behind a clump of manzanita on a slight rise overlooking where eight braves waited for the general's party. Cho-Cho explained that he had promised Kientpoos that he would make sure no one tried to kill Kaitchkana or her miner husband. Luash was not to leave his side. When Slolux started two sagebrush fires, she knew he was deliberately using the dark smoke to obscure the view of anyone who might be spying on the peace-talking place. The braves seated themselves on the opposite side of the tent from the bluffs the army men commanded.

"Why are you here?" Cho-Cho whispered. "Even Eagle cannot prevent men who hate each other from fighting."

Her mind full of what might happen today and her helplessness in the face of that made it all but impossible for her to answer. "I am a woman. It is not a woman's way to seek war. I may yet find a way to stop the killing."

"If a soldier pointed his rifle at Kientpoos, would you sacrifice yourself to save him?"

"I—I do not know."

"You love him with a love as strong as any I have ever seen. Your heart must know how you weigh your life against his."

Why was Cho-Cho doing this to her? "If—" In the distance, she spotted several mounted men heading toward the peace tent. "If I believed I could stop any more killing that way, I would, but to simply die—"

"And what if someone else's life was threatened? The life of the army man?"

"I do not know; do not ask me that."

Cho-Cho ran a finger over the scar on his cheek. "You cannot change what will be today; even Eagle's woman cannot stop a bullet."

The soldiers were now close enough that she could make out the general in his dark uniform. Next to him rode the Sunday doctor, Meacham who had once been the Indian superintendent and now was the head of the peace commission, another man she didn't recognize, Kaitchkana, and her husband. And Jed.

The army men slowed. From what Kientpoos had told her, she knew that Modocs and whites alike came to the peace talks unarmed. However, both Bogus Charley and Boston Charley, or so the whites called them, openly carried rifles. Her uncle and the others wore coats. Under them, they'd hidden pistols. Young Slolux and Barncho stood to one side holding the horses, their mouths hanging open.

Fear washed through her like waves tossed up by a storm, and it was all she could do not to turn and flee. Still, she felt rooted to where she crouched, horrified and fascinated at the same time. Jed's uniform looked as clean and well cared for as the general's, and the way he sat his saddle swelled her heart with pride. His gaze was fixed on the Modocs waiting for him, yet she sensed he was very much aware of his surroundings. A couple of times the general said something to him; his answers were short and he spoke without looking at the other man.

When they were finally close enough to dismount, she noticed that Kaitchkana seemed so nervous she could hardly stand. Whether someone had told the Modoc woman of what might happen today or not Luash couldn't guess. What she did believe was that she should be standing with her, not hiding.

General Canby stepped toward Kientpoos and shook the chief's hand. When he did, Kientpoos smiled and said something, but she was too far away to hear. When the general pointed at Bogus and Boston, Kientpoos's smile faded. It seemed to her as if everyone stood looking at each other for a long time, but finally the general sat on a rock near Kientpoos. After a few seconds, Meacham took position behind General Canby. Jed sat beside his general. Now he was the only white man not still looking around him, and she wondered if he'd resigned himself to accept whatever might happen today.

Because she couldn't hear the conversation and much of her vision was obscured by the brush between her and those below, she could only guess at what was being said. If she'd been alone, she would have risked crawling closer. The sun, when the clouds moved away from it, felt hot on the back of her neck, and insects buzzed as if nothing of any importance was happening. Only she knew better, and that knowledge made her half sick with fear.

How long the men spoke to each other, she couldn't say. Her body felt tense from the effort of trying to listen and observe and her right leg, which was curled under her, had started to cramp. No matter how hard she fought it, fear continued to assault her; her mind raced. What could she do to stop any further killing? She'd been unable to change either Jed's or Kientpoos's minds earlier. Why would they listen to her today? She tried to imagine Eagle flying overhead, touching everyone with peace. But every time she called forth his image, it soon faded.

A movement caught her attention, and she leaned forward, straining to see. Ha-kar-Jim had walked over to Meacham's horse. After making sure it was securely tied to a sagebrush, he took Meacham's coat off the saddle and slid his arms into it. She couldn't hear what he was saying, just knew he was speaking to Meacham and that Meacham's answer made Ha-kar-Jim laugh. A few seconds later, Meacham took off his hat and held it out to Ha-kar-Jim. The Modoc laughed. When Meacham looked over at the general, she guessed Meacham wanted the general to say something to Ha-kar-Jim. Instead, General Canby turned his full attention on Kientpoos, who looked as if he hadn't seen what Ha-kar-Jim had done.

After a minute, General Canby began talking. When he was done, the Sunday Doctor got to his feet and said something to Kientpoos. Kaitchkana had started to translate when Kientpoos jumped to his feet and hurried toward some rocks, whistling sharply.

Almost immediately, two Modocs, armed with several rifles, jumped out from behind the rocks. The general yelled; Kientpoos pulled a pistol from under his shirt and aimed it at Canby.

Horrified, she heard a sharp crack, watched the general stagger backward. For a moment, she thought he was already dead; then he lurched to his feet and stumbled toward his horse. When he tripped, another Modoc ran up behind him and shot him again. Kientpoos stood over the fallen general, a knife now in his hand. When she saw him slash Canby's throat, she screamed. She felt Cho-Cho's powerful hands on her arms, fought him, screamed again.

Boston Charley shot the Sunday Doctor full in the chest. Meacham staggered backward, fumbling for something inside his coat. Several Modocs began firing at him, but she didn't know if any of them hit him. All that mattered was Jed.

He held a pistol firmly in his hand, but whether he'd used it or not she couldn't say, because so many guns were being fired. He ran, not toward the army camp, but toward his general. Using his shoulder, he plowed into Kientpoos and knocked him away from Canby. Kientpoos fell to his knees and grabbed Jed's arm, but Jed managed to yank free. Sano'tks ran up behind Jed, a rifle aimed at his back.

She felt Cho-Cho's nails tear into her flesh, but it didn't matter. Somehow she had to save Jed! She tried to rush forward.

Guns seemed to be firing all around her. Men screamed; horses fought their tethers. Jed whirled on his attacker and knocked the rifle out of Sano'tks's hands, then snatched it off the ground and swung it around, hitting the brave. Sano'tks crumpled and Jed stepped over him, sprinting for his horse. Just as she scrambled over the rocks, Jed pitched forward. She wasn't sure whether she screamed again.

"The soldiers are coming! The soldiers are coming!"

Recognizing Kaitchkana's high-pitched scream, Luash froze in an agony of indecision. If the army was advancing, they would surely kill her. But how could she leave Jed?

"Come!" Cho-Cho ordered. He pulled her against him and lifted her off her feet. "You cannot help him."

Cannot help him.

Although she continue to struggle, her attention felt too splintered to allow her to concentrate on the act of breaking free. Below, everything was chaos. Kaitchkana, her features distorted by horror, continued to shout that the soldiers were on their way. Two Modocs were crouched over Meacham; one of them had been scalping the motionless peace officer but he now stared at Kaitchkana. The white man Luash hadn't recognized was nearly out of sight, still running, as was Kaitchkana's husband. Several Modocs had been tearing the clothes off General Canby and the Sunday Doctor, but they too had gone still at Kaitchkana's warning. Jed, motionless, face flat against the ground, hadn't been touched.

A yell from Kientpoos flung everyone into action. As one, they began running toward the stronghold, leaving behind bloody bodies, frantic horses, and discarded weapons. Kientpoos scrambled up the hill, staring first at his niece and then Cho-Cho. His eyes looked wild. His words came in loud bursts, sounds she'd never before heard from him. When Cho-Cho released her and began running after the others, she took a staggering step toward Jed.

"No!" Kientpoos shrieked. "The soldiers come! They will kill you!"

"You killed him!" The words felt as if they'd been torn from her throat. She wanted to pound her uncle's face until nothing was left of it. "You killed him!"

"I am a dead man; what does it matter? No!" he ordered again when she started down the hill. "You cannot help a dead man. Think of yourself; think Modoc!"

Modoc! She whirled away from him, her feet seeking level ground. She thought she heard Jed groan, but with so much noise, she couldn't be sure. Before she could get close enough to touch him, someone grabbed her and threw her to the ground. Her head hit stone with such force that the world blurred. Still, she struggled to sit up. Someone loomed over her; recognizing Ha-kar-Jim, she kicked ineffectively at his legs. He leaned down and she readied herself for a blow. When it came, pain splintered her thoughts. A moment later, she felt hands pulling her to her feet. Although she tried to fight free, she could barely think why she was fighting.

"Luash! Stop!" Kientpoos yelled. "You are Modoc! Only Modoc!"

14

A sharp cry yanked Jed away from the nowhere place he'd been. With an effort, he turned his head toward the sound and blinked until the blur sorted itself into human figures.

Meacham, wide-eyed, lay motionless beside him on another cot. The man's head was heavily bandaged because—damnation!—the Modocs had started to scalp him. For a moment, Jed couldn't remember what had stopped their attackers from finishing the job, but when Meacham groaned again, his memory became sharper. Someone—he thought it had been the female Modoc interpreter—had cried out that the soldiers were coming, and after a few moments of confusion, the Indians had all taken off.

But helping hands hadn't come for a long time. Not until the nightmares—

"So you're awake. I don't know how you figure you're going to get paid this month, sleeping it half away the way you've done."

Jed didn't have to look at the speaker to know it was Wilfred. *His friend.* "Do you have bellow like that?" he asked around swamping emotion, not surprised at the effort it took to speak. "You'd wake the dead."

"Whatever it takes. You all right? Really all right?" Wilfred pressed a cool rag to Jed's forehead, the gesture hauntingly gentle. "I hope you don't remember the trip back to camp. The way they strapped you to that horse, I figured you'd either die from being shaken up or weren't hurt bad enough to merit all this attention."

Yeah, he did remember the pain-filled ride; more and more of it with each passing second. "They didn't get you," he said to the peace commissioner because if he didn't speak, he might drown in the past. "Everything happened so fast. What . . . what about the general?"

"He's dead, Jed," Wilfred answered. "Him and the reverend."

"Dead? Dead." He felt exhausted, still caught in a nightmare. His side burned and he had to work at breathing in a way that didn't make his lungs protest. No matter how hard he tried to concentrate, some aspects of what had happened at the peace tent remained a blur. He remembered hearing shooting and looking around, not for a way out, but for Luash.

Had she been there?

"You're not fading on me again, are you?" Wilfred asked harshly. "You've been doing that ever since they brought you in yesterday; I'd think you'd have had enough sleep by now."

"Yesterday?" He swallowed and tried again. "It's been that long?"

"Long enough for those blasted reporters to get the news out. As soon as that hits the newspapers, there's going to be hell to pay. Damn! Damn."

Despite his still slow-moving brain, he knew what Wilfred was talking about. The Modocs had killed a general. A general! Now no one would be satisfied until every Modoc in the lava beds was either dead or hauled off to a reservation halfway across the country.

Dead or a reservation. Was that Luash's future?

What the hell did it matter? Her people had tried to kill him! Had murdered an unarmed general. War. This was *war!* "What's been happening?" he managed to ask despite the growing weight inside him.

"Nothing. Not a damn thing."

"You can't mean that." He tried to sit up, but someone rammed a red-hot poker into his side and he fell back, panting.

"Will you act like a patient?" Wilfred insisted. "The doctor took a bullet out of your side last night. It bled pretty good, but since it isn't anymore, I guess you're going to live."

Jed already knew that. A man doesn't survive a massacre without learning something about his body. He might be frustratingly weak and a little light-headed, but he was going to make it. He wasn't sure about Meacham. The peace commissioner was horribly pale, and in addition to the bandages covering the aborted scalping, another had been clamped over his ear. Wilfred explained that the peace commissioner had lost part of an ear and had been knocked out. "They said you weren't moving when they found you." Wilfred jabbed a finger at Jed. "A torn up side doesn't make a man pass out."

"I couldn't run; I wanted them to think I was dead. I was buying time. Trying to, anyway." A thought struck him. If Luash had been hiding nearby and seen his motionless body, did she think he'd been killed?

Why should he care? Damnit, her people had signed their own death warrant.

She had tried to warn him.

"Hey," Wilfred insisted, cutting into his splintered thoughts. "No more sleeping. I'm getting tired of talking to myself."

Jed wasn't sure sleeping was what he'd been doing, but it didn't matter. What did was making sure he didn't go back into that dark and deadly place where he'd already spent too many hours.

"Tell me," he ordered, determined to keep his mind clear. "How come nothing's happening? You mean no one's gone after the Modocs?"

Wilfred explained, none too charitably, that Colonel Gillem had been sick yesterday—at least he'd said he was—but that was no excuse for his inability to make a decision. During the attack, no soldiers had been coming to rescue the peace commission; the woman had lied while desperately attempting to stop a total massacre.

What had really happened was that Gillem hadn't sent anyone to see what was going on until Captain James Biddle insisted. They'd found Jed and the others; the Modocs were gone. The bodies of General Canby and Reverend Eleasar Thomas had been brought back to camp and were now resting in hastily built coffins. Despite a cry for action, Gillem was insisting on waiting until reinforcements arrived, in the form of Warm Springs Indians, before making an assault on the stronghold.

"But it's going to happen," Wilfred concluded, his mouth pulled into a tight slash. "No one's talking peace anymore. Folks want to see Captain Jack's body. His and the rest of those murdering Modocs. Nothing else is going to satisfy them."

"No. It isn't."

"It's more than that, Jed. General Sherman just sent a cable saying they should be annihilated."

"Annihilated? There's women and children in there."

"And so far they and their menfolks have made laughingstocks out of the U.S. Army. You, more than anyone except maybe Meacham here, should want them to pay for what they did."

Did he? For years—forever it seemed—Indians had been the enemy. Cunning and bloodthirsty. Ridding the country of them had given his life meaning.

But he'd been given an eagle feather and kissed a dark-skinned woman and listened as she talked about her people's beliefs and dreams.

That woman—she might have been watching as his blood stained the ground.

* * *

Luash sat with her legs folded under her, barely aware of the victory dance going on around her. It seemed as if Cho-ocks had been dancing forever, but it had only been through the night. The general's scalp hung from the medicine pole, proof, the shaman said, that his medicine was powerful. To Luash, the horrible sight served as proof that the Modocs had done something the army would never forgive.

Dark figures lit only by firelight briefly caught her attention. They seemed unreal, almost as unreal as what had happened yesterday.

Was Jed alive?

Sensing a presence beside her, she turned and saw her uncle. She hadn't spoken to Kientpoos since he'd shot the general.

He broke the silence. "You are quiet. A silent woman carries many thoughts inside her."

"I do not know what they are. They tangle—"

"Do you not? Cho-ocks boasts his power will keep the army from us. Ha-kar-Jim says there is no need for more magic-making because they have lost their leader and will wander away. Which man is right?"

"What does it matter?" When Kientpoos continued to stare at her, his eyes glittering red from the firelight and maybe from something deep within him, she forced herself to continue. "I do not care which man makes the loudest boast. I believe the army will never allow us to live in peace."

She expected her uncle to argue; after all, hadn't he agreed to the attack? Instead, sighing deeply, he sank down beside her. For a long time he simply stared at the flames. She did the same, taking a little comfort from what seemed to have a life of its own.

"I am a dead man, Luash," he whispered. "I said that the other day; I say it again. What I do now matters little because the time will come when the white man makes me pay for what I did."

"Then why did you?"

"Why?" He laughed; there was no warmth to the sound. "You are not a man. You do not understand what a man must do if he is to continue to walk tall. Besides, if I cannot live as my father did, maybe joining my ancestors is not such a bad thing."

Dying not a bad thing? Trying to convince her uncle that he should want to go on living would take so much effort, and tonight she couldn't make herself look into the future. She rubbed the back of her head. She had hit it on a rock, stunning herself, when she'd tried to run to Jed's aid. Although the gesture held Kientpoos's attention, she couldn't make herself stop. "I would have stayed with him. If you and Cho-Cho had not grabbed me, I would have remained with the army man."

"I could not let you. You understand why, do you not?"

She did, now. Although she'd fought as he and Cho-Cho dragged her back to the stronghold, she now realized that nothing except her own death would have come out of her attempt to help Jed.

Nodding, she rocked forward and let her thoughts drift into the flames. For maybe a half dozen heartbeats, she found forgetfulness in the fire's erratic movement. Then her mind filled with the memory of what Jed had looked like sprawled on the ground and the question of whether death or imprisonment—which was worse than death—waited for her uncle. For all of them. Feeling sick, she got to her feet.

"You hate me."

"No, never. But—I feel like a storm-tossed leaf. I have lost the shore, lost everything I once knew."

"No, Luash. It is not so for you; it cannot be!" He drew in a long, dragging breath. "I do not want to think anymore; I have done enough of that for this life. When I die, you will take Whe-cha into your heart?"

"I love her," Luash said softly. Whe-cha was already in her heart; did Kientpoos understand that?

"No more than I do." Her uncle returned his attention to the fire. "I regret she is without my seed. Before, I told myself it was better that a child of mine not be born in the Land of Burned Out Fires, but now I wish she had something to remember me by."

"You are not dead," she said, trying to reassure him, but heard the lack of conviction in her voice.

"Not yet. Go, Luash. Be alone with your thoughts."

Although she felt horribly torn, she did as her uncle had ordered and headed into the night, sensing Kientpoos's eyes on her. He was still her uncle; she would always love him. But he had changed—or been changed by forces beyond his control.

Except for one woman who'd just had a baby, all of the Modocs, children and adults alike, were either dancing with the shaman or watching him. She didn't want to be around people who boasted like small, unthinking children. She looked around for Whe-cha and spotted her heading toward Kientpoos. Kientpoos turned from his conversation with Cho-Cho and extended a hand to his young wife.

The night absorbed Luash. Although it was colder tonight than it had been for several days, she didn't go back for her blanket before walking out into the lava beds. Within a few minutes, she reached the red rope Cho-ocks had placed around the stronghold. The shaman maintained that all Modocs who remained within its magic circle would always be safe, but she stepped over it without worrying about the consequences.

Behind her flickered the faint glow of the soldiers' distant campfires. Sometimes, when the wind blew toward her, she thought she could hear some of the sounds the enemy made, but tonight there was only the fading thud of dancing feet on rock.

Guided by moonlight, she made her way around sharp outcroppings formed before the first Modoc set foot on this land. The depressions, some of them large enough to shelter a bear, were black against the lighter surface. The night smelled of sage. If she walked until her moccasins fell apart, she might reach the great mountain where Sun God lived. Then, if she had an eagle's vision, she could look down on Modoc land and feel safe.

Maybe she would see Jed and know whether he was alive.

A teasingly cool breeze fanned her hair and lightly slapped her cheeks. When she lifted her head to draw in the clean scent, she felt her body relax. She wanted to take that as proof that she'd somehow sensed Jed, that her heart knew he was safe, but she couldn't.

"Eagle." She touched her fingertips to the streak of white at her temple. "Please, hear me tonight. End your silence; I need you as I never have before. Eagle. Is he alive? Does he hate me?"

She stopped, eyes scanning the horizon though tonight it was more memory than reality. There was safety in darkness, safety and a serenity that had been a part of her since she'd first become aware of the difference between night and day. She had heard of whites who feared the world after the sun left it, but cloaked in black, it became a great, peaceful blanket that could absorb her every thought. Maybe sometime it would absorb her as well.

"Eagle. You see everything; you know everything. Is he alive? Please, is he alive?"

The sound—like a distant whisper—made itself known. Although she still saw nothing different in the moon- and starlit sky, she sensed her spirit's presence. It had been so long since Eagle had answered her call that tonight's gift nearly brought her to her knees. Behind her, her people sang of war and victory; even further away the army spoke of revenge. But neither of those things mattered now.

Only Eagle did.

Eagle and Jed Britton.

As she'd done many times in the past, she stretched her arms upward and waited. Night wind chased across her flesh. Despite its cool fingers, she felt warmed. When silence turned into a steady whisper of sound, it happened so gradually that she couldn't say when the moment came that she knew she was being visited by her spirit.

He glided toward her, a magnificently dark shape against an ancient background. He seemed motionless, a lifeless and weightless creature borne to her on the wind. Yet she sensed his eyes on her. Straightened and stood proudly so he would be proud of her.

You have been gone so long. I thought—I feared your absence.

Eagle was directly overhead now, a protecting, silent blanket untouched by the forces that kept her rooted to the ground.

Please. Do not leave me. I need—need you so much.

One wing dipped slightly and Eagle began a slow, graceful descent. Arms still uplifted, she threw back her head so her hair would flow out behind her. His shape became more and more distinct and she could see the tiny fluttering at the tips of his wings.

I cannot ask it; cannot say the words. But you must have seen him— the army man. Is he . . . does he . . .

Something fluttered down to be caught on the fabric covering her breast. Trembling, she took the feather between thumb and forefinger and held it up to the moon. With Eagle hovering so close that she imagined she felt his body heat, she understood. The feather was as white as mountain snow; except for a small, dark dot, it was flawless.

"A small wound," she whispered. "Then he will live."

By way of answer, Eagle propelled its body upward in a powerful thrust.

APRIL 14, 1873

Three days after he'd been shot, Jed strapped on a pistol and picked up his rifle. In the past, his pulse had leapt in anticipation of battle and the end to the nervousness that accompanied waiting and uncertainty. This morning however, he felt only dread—not for himself, but for a black-haired, black-eyed woman. A woman he wanted to hate.

The supposedly still sick Colonel Gillem's plan was to move all the troops under his command and the Warm Springs Indian scouts as close as possible to the Modoc stronghold before launching an attack. Because he felt strong enough to be moving around and because his wound had somehow given him exalted status, Jed had been involved in the hastily planned strategy sessions. More than that, Colonel Gillem wanted him to be part of the attack.

The military part of him relished the opportunity to put his years of Indian fighting to work. Though he chafed at Gillem's indecisiveness and the officers' lack of faith in their commanding officer, Jed firmly believed that if the plan—to advance on several fronts—was successfully carried out, the Modocs would be forced from the cover that had served them so well during the winter.

The part of him that was made up of his heart and his memories—of a woman's voice and touch, of a little girl's doll—hated what was going to happen.

Jed marched with Battery E when they advanced on the stronghold, keeping up a steady fire while hurrying from one rocky protection to another. Although the effort winded him, he managed to keep up, spending more time on his belly than standing upright. The battery members either seethed at having to wait for the rest of the troops to get into position or spoke worriedly about what it had been like last winter when the Modocs made a shambles of the army's attempt to overrun them.

Jed reminded the men that they now understood the terrain and that fog no longer obscured the land. Even then, when he should be thinking and acting as nothing except a soldier, a man worthy of General Canby's respect, memories of a dark face and soft voice shattered his concentration and he felt the heat of the feather he kept against his chest.

He was here to attack, to kill if need be.

To, maybe, watch her die.

God!

No. No God.

Sniping fire from unseen Modocs kept the battery's advance at less than a snail's pace. At nightfall, Jed reckoned it had taken the nearly four hundred men a good six hours to advance maybe a half mile. If the reports he'd received were correct, three men had been killed and six wounded, statistics that both sickened and heartened him. It could have been worse, he kept telling himself. Tonight the troops wouldn't retreat as they had in the past. Instead, they would camp here and continue the advance in the morning.

And what would happen then—

He shook off the thought that had haunted him all day. He was a soldier, nothing but a soldier, not one of those bleeding hearts back East who thought Indians had more right to land than whites with their superior numbers and weapons.

But because of Luash, he knew her people had walked this land since the beginning of time. Did that give them no rights?

He couldn't say whether he was glad to see night settle over the lava beds. He was so tired that his legs shook; he probably could fall asleep wherever he dropped, despite the rocks littering the ground—if he didn't spend it thinking about what he was doing.

Who he was doing it against.

Mortar fire began as soon as the men were done with dinner. Although the army was still too far from the Indians for the rounds to do any real damage, the Modocs would be kept awake—and nervous—all night. He kicked a jagged rock; he couldn't suppress a smile. No matter what else the morning brought, it would dawn on bleary-eyed men—both Modoc and white. A little while later he heard a shout that made him laugh. In imperfect English, an unseen Modoc was telling the soldiers that their aim was so poor he could stand close enough to a cannon to touch it and still not fear being killed. The Modoc was probably right.

He might have slept; he couldn't be sure. What he did know was that when dawn finally broke, he was grateful for an excuse to be on the move again, desperately grateful for an end to half-seen dreams that again and again ended in a haze of red. In images of a child's doll.

Despite frustrating breakdowns in communication and an outright refusal by one major to obey Gillem, the troops finally closed ranks at the lake shore, effectively blocking the Modocs from much of their main food and water supply. When he realized that the whole southern end of the lava beds had been left unprotected thanks to incompetence and misunderstood orders on the part of several officers, Jed was unable to share in the general consensus that the Modocs would be beaten tomorrow, when the final advance on the stronghold was made. He knew he should be furious about the tactical error; instead, he found himself on the verge of praying that the army's stupidity might save Luash's life.

"It's a damnable mess, ain't it?" Wilfred observed as they crouched behind a hastily built rock barrier. "I knew Mason had no love for Gillem, but to deliberately ignore a command—if it was me, I'd be ordering a court marshal about now."

"Whose? Captain Mason's or Colonel Gillem's?"

Wilfred laughed. "Maybe both of them. What a hell of a way for us to wind up; we're getting too old for this. Do you think Captain Miller's men will succeed in meeting up with the Warm Springs Indians tomorrow? If they do, and if the Modocs are still in the stronghold, we'll have them trapped."

"Trapped." Jed little more than mouthed the word. "I don't know. I talked to the colonel about it a little while ago. He seems to think Captain Miller won't have any trouble closing off the south end, but he was wrong about Mason's ability to carry out an order. I think he's wrong about Miller too."

"How do you feel about that?"

"I'm army, Wilfred. I know my job."

"Don't snap at me," Wilfred warned. "I' just saying you'd better take a long, hard look inside yourself. You can't have both her and an army victory."

Damn Wilfred, Jed thought. If he hadn't let the man get close to him, back when he thought he'd go crazy from nightmares born of the slaughter of eighty men, no one would know what he was going through tonight.

But maybe Wilfred was right. Maybe answering his friend's question was the only way he'd take that look at himself. Restless, he wandered down to the lake from which the Modocs could no longer take water and watched the rising moon paint it a cool silver.

Once he'd stood near here with Luash. He couldn't remember what they'd talked about, only that she'd felt warm and alive and wonderful in his arms. When he kissed her, he'd forgotten how different they were and that he'd never be the same again.

Now he didn't know what he'd become.

When he could make out the shapes of the birds who'd settled on the lake for the night, his thoughts turned to what she'd said about the countless eagles who chose this area for their winter home but were now gone. Would she ever be able to tell him anything else? That was the question that pounded through him harder than mortar hitting lava; was their time together over?

How could it not be?

Restlessness forced him away from the lake. For a long time he told himself he wasn't going anywhere in particular, just that he needed to work off energy; but even before he faced the facts, he knew. No one questioned him when he climbed over the newly erected rock walls and slipped off toward the stronghold. He wasn't fool enough to walk out in the open or take a direct route to where the Modocs were fortified. Still, heading east, away from it all, he put more and more distance between himself and the army, let the night surround him. Breathed in sage and rock and dirt and spring. If anyone had asked him to explain himself, he wouldn't have been able to. Instinct, he might have said. Following his nose.

Only it wasn't either of those things, any more than it was a wish to get himself killed tonight. Luash was out here somewhere. Maybe no more than a few feet from him, maybe miles away, heading for distant hills and freedom. No, not that. He felt her presence, felt her fingers on him, felt the warmth of her breath and heard the beating of her heart.

He had no business being here. Only a fool would sneak unarmed into no man's land when safety lay behind him. But back there waited a sleepless night and an attempt to figure out how he felt about having been shot by one of her braves.

The moon was as intense and powerful here as it had been back at the lake. He missed the image of the stars reflected in the water and wondered if she'd noticed how close the heavens seemed tonight.

Heavens. That's not the way she saw things, and neither did he. All right, sky then. Was she looking up at the sky and asking herself if he was doing the same? Maybe—the thought froze him— maybe she didn't know whether he was alive.

She could be dead. There'd been no reports of Indians being killed, but enough bullets had been discharged since the army began its assault that at least one might have hit a target.

No. He did not believe that. His heart would have known if something had happened to her.

His knees throbbed from the punishment he was subjecting them to, but he knew better than to stand and risk exposing himself. When he rocked back onto his heels, he pressed his hand against his side to quiet the not so dull throbbing, then scanned what the moon revealed of the world around him.

Despite the occasional fire now far to his left, he was aware of a bone-deep stillness, a kind of peace that defied all logic. Maybe the peace came from somewhere in the past—from that place where her people had begun and in some indefinable way still existed.

He didn't believe in ghosts, laughed at the notion of going on spirit quests or giving human form and meaning to mountains, lakes, and prairies. Shamen were a joke. So was praying to one's ancestors and leaving gifts to appease something no one had ever seen. He'd believed that—until he watched an eagle greet a slightly built young Modoc woman.

Now he didn't know.

From sound and sight, he guessed himself to be a good quarter of a mile from where Modocs and soldiers sporadically fired at each other. Why he'd come here he couldn't say. But it felt right, felt a little like coming home.

Home? Home had been rich earth and hot, humid summers, parents who loved the boy he'd once been, horses to ride and care for, devotion to the land and what it could produce. Digging one's fingers deep into warm soil and feeling a part of the land.

That it had been before soldiers and politicians and an insanity called the Civil War had taken it all away from him. Now home was hard and inhospitable rock thrust centuries ago from deep within the earth.

Where he'd met a woman.

"Luash." He had no memory of having decided to speak aloud. Surely if staying alive meant anything to him, he would have remained silent. But he hadn't—maybe because he'd known he wasn't alone. "Luash?"

"Jed."

The sound, soft as eagle down, strong as a winter north wind, floated to him and wrapped itself around him. He found himself breathing deeply and then not being able to breathe at all. "Are you alone?" he finally asked.

"Yes. I felt you coming."

That was impossible, of course. If he'd been able to avoid armed and watchful braves, how could she know he was here? Still, hadn't he sensed something? When she slipped out from behind a massive bush, she looked more animal than human, a shy and wary creature clad in a shapeless garment that barely touched her knees and was in danger of sliding off one slender shoulder.

Luash felt naked under Jed Britton's stare. He stood, exposed to any watching warriors. Maybe his life still meant next to nothing to him; maybe he trusted her this much.

She came a few steps closer, then stopped. The moon wasn't bright enough to show her what lay in his eyes, but she'd seen enough to believe his wound bothered him little if at all.

"I saw the killing at the peace tent," she whispered.

"I wondered if you did," was all he said. When she explained that she'd insisted on going along but that her uncle and Cho-Cho had ordered her to remain hidden, he nodded but still didn't speak. "When you were hit, I tried to run to you. They stopped me," she finished.

"I heard a woman scream. I didn't know if it was you or Toby."

"Kaitchkana, not Toby. Maybe we both screamed," she said. The stars were like the sun on frozen snow, glittering and sparkling, cold and yet somehow warm. She longed to see their color reflected in his eyes, tried not to ask herself if she would ever look at him in the daylight again.

"You didn't sound surprised to see me tonight."

"No," she admitted, then told him about the feather Eagle had left behind as proof that he'd survived the attack. "What about Meacham?" she asked. "Ha-kar-Jim said he maybe was still alive."

"He's going to recover, no thanks to—it's the end for the Modocs, Luash. Can't you see that?"

She stepped toward him, wondering if she really could feel his warmth or just imagined it, and held out her hands. "Maybe you will capture one tonight. Take me back to the others so you can boast of your courage."

"Damnation."

"What?"

"I didn't come out here to fight with you."

She wanted to shake her head but it seemed like too much effort. Fighting tears she didn't understand, she measured the distance that still separated them. Tonight the wind tasted and smelled of spring, felt like freedom. Only she didn't want to spread her arms and wait for the wind to lift her into the sky.

What she wanted was looking back at her.

15

He wasn't a handsome man. There was too much age and reality in his eyes. His flesh had been hardened by a lifetime of wind and cold and heat and work. The muscles that made it possible for him to survive in an unforgiving land sometimes frightened her, always fascinated her.

Tonight she felt herself being drawn to those muscles like a thirsty deer in search of what she needed to maintain life. Arms hanging limp by her side, a single, short dress the only thing covering her body, she stepped closer to this man she should have hated and feared. This man who'd called to her and somehow brought her to his side.

"Am I safe?" he asked.

"Yes," she told him over the sound of distant fire that echoed like faint sounds from another world. "No one will think that an army man would come out here."

"Except you. I started walking; I had no idea where I was going, just that I had to get away."

"I know." Now she was close enough that there was no way she couldn't feel the contrast between his body's heat and the cool brought to her by the night breeze. She wanted to point out the stars and moon to him, ask if he'd seen them reflected in the lake. But if she did, she might also tell him that his soldiers were keeping her people from what had always sustained them and this pocket of quiet they'd found would shatter.

"You're sure no one followed you?"

"I am sure. You can trust me in this."

When he grunted, she didn't know whether he was agreeing with her or warning her that he would question everything she said. She couldn't change his mind and heart any more than she could change her own; surely he knew that. "I can see the streak in your hair," he said after a long, long silence. "Just make it out."

When she lifted her hand to run it over her temple, he took her wrist and drew her to him. She thought he was smiling, but it might have only been because she needed to see that gesture.

"You're an incredible woman, Luash. Unlike any I've ever known."

"Incredible?"

"Brave and intelligent."

"You did not expect an Indian woman to have courage or know more than how to keep food in her belly?"

When he stiffened, she knew she'd spoken the truth. She wanted to tell him she didn't hate him for his beliefs, that she was glad she'd been the one to show him what it meant to be Indian, but words were for another time. They had only tonight and his body calling to hers in a way she'd never experienced or imagined before and yet understood as well as she understood the need to breathe. He was standing on higher land, which forced her to arch her body back slightly in order to look into the eyes that had been part of her since the first time she'd seen them.

"We are strangers," she whispered, "and yet not strangers. I wish it could be like this for the others."

"That isn't going to happen."

She knew that. Still, for a moment she wanted to throw his words back at him. Then, because he was now touching the back of his hand to her cheek, she no longer cared about anything except him.

Tonight.

The woman energy inside her that had brought her here.

"I want to run," she admitted. "I want to stay. When I look at you, even when I simply think of you, I no longer know myself."

"You know who you are; that'll never change."

But *she* was changing. She had never truly been alone because her family and people had always been around her, all dependent on each other, and yet there'd always been a small part of her that ached for something—that needed something.

Now she was beginning to understand what that was.

"Are you afraid of me?" he asked.

"Afraid?"

"Not because I'm a soldier, but because I'm a man."

What she felt had nothing and yet everything to do with fear. Whe-cha and the other married women sometimes spoke of what took place when they were with their husbands at night. She'd listened, half sick because of what had happened to her mother, half fascinated by the glitter in the women's eyes and note of excitement in their voices. When there was love, something took place between a man and a woman. Something she didn't understand—and yet did.

From the first moment she'd seen Jed, her body had whispered of need and hunger.

"I think of you and I want what I have no words for," she admitted. "I should understand this thing; it is spoken of honestly among my people. But when I see an army man take a Modoc or Klamath woman without tenderness or love . . ."

He ran his hands up her arms, igniting a flame wherever he touched. "I can't promise you love, Luash. But tenderness—"

"No. Not love," she said too quickly. "We are too different, our worlds not the same."

"No. Not the same at all." He spoke just as rapidly. "I want you Luash, the way a man wants a woman. I need you to understand that because if you don't feel the same, I'm going to have to walk away right now."

A cannon boomed, the sound echoing endlessly—part of the night. "Don't leave. Please."

"You're sure?" he whispered, the gentle question first swirling around her and then seeping in through her skin to touch her heart.

She couldn't speak, didn't know if she had any thoughts beyond his presence. With his hands settled heavy and strong on her shoulder, she again looked up. In the distance another mortar shot sounded. When that faded away, she caught the wind's faint song and then the whisper of ducks calling to each other on the lake her people could no longer reach. She licked her lips, aware not of how little she'd had to drink today because the children needed the precious remaining drops more than she did, but of how incredibly powerful another need could be.

He must know what she was feeling. Otherwise, why would he cup her chin to hold it steady and then cover her lips with his own? She wanted to ask him how many times he'd done this with other women, who they were, whether he ever thought of them. Then his warmth, his life and energy began a journey through her body, and she knew nothing beyond this moment. Cared about nothing except him.

Shaking a little, she wrapped her arms around his neck and rose onto her toes so the embrace couldn't be broken. She felt her hips pressing, pressing against him, her breasts tingling and growing heavy. Sheltered by the night, she lost herself in both it and him. Later she would face what was happening. Now—now it was time. . . .

His breathing quickened. She tried to concentrate on that, but her own was doing the same thing, and it was all she could do not to cry out. He held her tightly, firmly, as if he would never let her go, yet she felt no fear. Instead, a song began in her, drumbeats of emotion and desire, heat deep inside her belly growing and building until she felt all but consumed by it. She breathed through flared nostrils as his own hot, quick breath heated her flesh.

Their kiss hadn't slackened, had grown even more urgent. His hands roamed her body, becoming more and more intimate. When she felt them on her hips, she stiffened, then surrendered to a storm-wave of sensation that left her gasping. The heat that had invaded her belly and even deeper, where her womanness was centered, felt like a raging forest fire now, out of control, fascinating in its power.

Barely aware of what she was doing, she tore at the cloth around his throat. It resisted, then gave way with a ripping sound that both excited and embarrassed her. She needed his wisdom in this, needed him to tell her what was happening to her, but before she could think how to ask her question, he pulled her dress up over her thighs and flattened his palms against her naked flesh.

She gasped, half sobbed, tore her mouth free only to fasten it over the side of his neck where a vein pulsed. His fingers were both gentle and rough, exploring and commanding, hot—so incredibly hot. A whimper came from her throat and she thought, briefly, of a frightened child seeking reassurance.

She had no control over what was happening to her and didn't care.

With her tongue, she explored that vein in Jed's neck, taking strength from his strength. When he clamped his fingers tight over her hips, searing her wherever he touched, she knew he felt as gloriously trapped by emotion as she did.

"I think of you," she whimpered as his fingertips began an exploration of her belly that reminded her of the energy she felt when lightning from winter storms shattered the sky. "No matter what I am doing, you are there, half hidden, making it impossible for me to concentrate on anything else."

He clamped his hands around her bare waist and pulled her against him again. She felt his powerful maleness. "Tell me about your thoughts," he said. "Please."

"I do not understand them."

"Don't you?" The question was a challenge. He pushed her away from him and yanked the shirt over her head at the same time. The cool breeze lapped at her exposed flesh, but although the moon revealed a great deal, she wasn't embarrassed. Jed, a man who'd twice nearly lost his life to Indians, had come to her and she wanted him. Needed him.

"There are no words for what I feel, Jed. Only—only wanting."

"You're sure?"

"Sure?"

"That you're ready for this. Because I'm damn near the point of not being able to stop."

For a heartbeat, raw terror coursed through her. Then it became something else that demanded she press her naked breasts against him and grip him with all the strength in her. He answered in his own wordless way by flattening his hands against the small of her back. She felt sealed to him. His hands were everywhere, touching hips and thighs, back and shoulder, always keeping her against him. Her body had begun a restless dance she couldn't think how to control or contain. Crushed against him, she realized how completely their bodies spoke to each other. He was energy, hot and urgent; she felt the same. The hunger inside her was incredible.

It took little effort to pull his shirt off him, but when her fingers fumbled with his belt, he finished what she'd begun. She waited with no more patience than a starving animal, fed herself on the sight of his naked flesh.

He helped by taking her hand and placing it around him. He gasped and shuddered when she closed her fingers over him; she did the same when he cupped his hands over her too hot, too heavy breasts. When he leaned forward, at first she didn't understand what he was going to do, but then he took a breast deep into his mouth and it felt right.

Another distant shot echoed through her. She fought off the message that came with it, felt him embrace her as gently as if she was a small child and knew he understood. "We can't stop what's happening," he whispered.

"What are we, Jed?" There was desperation in her voice. "Tell me. What are we to each other?"

"I don't know." The words sounded as if they'd been ripped from him. He shuddered, or maybe the movement came from her. "That's the hell of it, Luash. I don't know what we're doing here tonight."

She didn't either, but couldn't tell him that because the ability to speak, which had been slipping away from her, disappeared completely now. Once again he took claim of a breast, pushing up from the underside until it jutted toward him. He held her in place while he lapped his tongue over a hard nub. Half sobbing, she threw her head back and tried to breathe. Her hands were on his chest now, absorbing his hard muscles and the whisper-warm flesh she'd never seen before. Feeling somehow responsible for the half-healed wound on his side, she tried to cup her palm around the angry intrusion.

"Don't," he ordered. "We can't hide what happened; neither of us can."

She suddenly, angrily wanted to tell him that what his people had done to hers was far worse than this bullet-made slash. But if she said a word, tonight would be ruined.

And she didn't want that, couldn't stand the thought of spending the rest of her life without knowing his body.

She should, she tried to tell herself, ask him what emotions had raged through him as he lay on the ground wondering when a

Modoc warrior would finish the job he'd begun. But she needed him to think of her tonight, only her.

She wanted neither of them to have a past or to think about the future.

"It's been a long time for me, Luash. I don't know if you understand what that means but—"

"I am not a child, Jed," she told him with her hands still against his chest and his hands resting on her hips. "Where I live there is little privacy. And my mother—my mother kept few secrets from me."

He muttered something she didn't understand, would have had to ask him to explain if she hadn't found the truth in his suddenly rigid body. "Did you want me to remain a child, Jed? I know what my mother was forced to do; that is why I had to leave my father."

"It's not going to be like that for us. If you don't believe—"

"I do," she reassured him even though her body now trembled in anticipation and fear. "I want . . . you."

"It's insane. This is insane." His whisper had taken on a harsh quality as if he hated himself, maybe hated her as well. "We shouldn't be together."

"Do you want me to leave?"

"Damnit, you know the answer to that."

When she said nothing, he pulled her even tighter against him. What made him male pressed against her, challenging her. She should be with her people, listening as her uncle and Cho-Cho talked about whether Cho-ocks's medicine would truly keep them safe, whether the red rope that surrounded their home would repel the enemy.

But if safety mattered to her, she wouldn't be here.

Maybe she was like the birds that got drunk on manzanita berries. Only no sickly sweet berries were responsible for the way she felt. Jed was.

Unaware of anything except him, she tried to force herself to concentrate on a gentle exploration of his chin, chest, arms, and legs. But just touching the powerful muscles of his upper arms made her feel as if she'd placed her hand on a rushing river. The current pulled her along, tossed its energy around her, entreated her to explore its strength.

Surrendering, she could do little more than try to breathe while her body burned as hot as a newly lit fire. Each breath seared her lungs and sent need racing through her veins. When Jed spread his fingers over her belly, she sucked in cold air and waited, trembling like a doe caught in a cougar's gaze.

Only Jed was no cougar, and even if he was, she still wanted to be consumed by him. He began rubbing her shoulders, soothing away the slight tremors. Half frantic with need, she brought his hand back to her belly and covered his fingers with her own.

"You're making me crazy." He ground out the words. "I have to—you have to understand. I won't—I don't know how much self control I'll have."

"It is all right."

"All right?" He laughed briefly. "You've never. You don't—"

"I am a woman, Jed. Not a child. Tonight *has* to be for us; there may never be another time."

His groan matched what she felt. Half sobbing, she inched closer until it seemed that their bodies had already become one. His arms closed around her waist as he pulled her toward the boulder he'd covered with his clothes. Until this moment she hadn't given a thought to how their bodies might join on the unyielding ground. When he sat on the rock and drew her between his legs, she steadied herself by clamping her hands over his naked thighs.

She'd never touched a man like this before, never known such intimacy could be both frightening and overwhelming.

"I wish—" he began. "I never wanted it like this between us."

"You didn't want us?"

"No. Not that. But there are places—" His hands seemed to be everywhere, lighting fires along her hipbones, over her ribs, adding even more fuel to the flame in her belly. "Places back East where men and women make love on soft, perfumed beds. There's candlelight, soft music playing." He leaned forward, kissed her chin, nose, eyelids, laughed a little when a spasm rocked her. "Those people make love because they want to. They're not at war. They—"

She cut off his words by first clamping her hand over his mouth and then replacing it with her lips. He let her; she guessed that he too didn't want to talk about this. *I love you,* she wanted to say. In her mind she saw the words drifting out over them, maybe being heard by Eagle. But Jed would not want to hear those words from her.

He pushed her away slightly, not because he was done with her but to spread her legs. When she again reached for him, she felt utterly exposed.

Utterly a woman.

Once again his hands were everywhere. She loved it when he claimed her breasts, felt like screaming when he trailed his nails over her hips, desperately, mindlessly dug her fingers into him when he explored what was most woman about her.

He angled his maleness between her legs and thrust upward. He gripped her waist so firmly that she couldn't possibly break free.

Not that she wanted to.

He was touching her, tasting her woman place with his hard and insistent shaft, easing into her, spreading her apart, frightening her.

She felt pain, recoiled instinctively, held onto his shoulders for support, and threw back her head, breathing quick and deep. Thought of nothing except them.

"Luash. Luash. I'll try . . . gentle."

He wasn't gentle, not really, although she sensed his struggle to give her what he'd promised. But she didn't care. Pain—

Whe-cha had told her about her first time, how unsure she'd been. How it had hurt but only for a little while and how kind and patient Kientpoos had been. How she'd fallen in love with him that night.

"Jed . . . "

"What?" He sounded as if he was fighting a battle.

"Jed. Jed," she said around the already fading discomfort. She couldn't think how to form any more words, couldn't say why she'd spoken his name. Hoped he didn't expect anything more from her.

There was a fire in him, a fierce winter storm. As he drove deeper and deeper inside her, she sensed he was losing control and fighting that loss. Surrendering to need.

If she'd spent her life on a reservation growing crops and waiting for army handouts, she might have run in fear from what was happening to him. But she'd stood alone and exposed while winter threw its fury at her. Watched her home burn. Eagle, with his awful speed and fearlessness, was her spirit. Tonight with Jed making them one, she faced the storm inside him and absorbed it. Lost herself in it.

Felt fury and need, insanity and abandon.

Held him in the palm of her hand and knew he did the same to her.

"Go back, Luash. You don't belong here."

"No, Jed. You are the one who does not belong."

Jed, dressed again, ran his hand over the boulder that had supported him while they made love. "Maybe I don't." His whisper was deep and yet strangely hollowed out. "They're going to keep on shooting all night," he said as yet another rifle blast shattered the fragile silence. "And they're going to keep on advancing. One day, maybe two, and all of Captain Jack's tribe will have been captured."

She didn't try to tell him he was wrong because if she did, he would only throw her words back at her. Still, what he'd said filled her first with unreasoning fear and then defiance, twin emotions that made it all but impossible for her to hold onto what they'd shared. He couldn't see her tears in the dark and if she didn't let him touch her again, he might not understand how deeply she'd been hurt.

"You are wrong!" Rebellion rode her words. "We are blessed. Cho-ocks has—"

"Blessed! Damnit, Luash, stop saying that. *You* might be protected; I'm not going to say one way or the other about that. But the rest of your people—you don't want them to die, do you? Tell them to give themselves up. Come with me. I'll protect you."

"No. I belong with my people."

"I can force you, you know."

"If you take me with you, I will never forgive you."

"At least you'd be safe."

They had had this argument before. Why now, when they should still be clinging to each other, was he driving them apart? But maybe it was better this way. Yes. Better. Otherwise she would never have the courage to leave him.

"It does not matter if you bring ten times as many soldiers as are here now. Even they will not be enough to make the Modocs throw down their arms."

"Damn you. Your pride's going to kill you."

Before she could tell him he was wrong, he pulled her against him, crushing her to him until she could barely breathe. She didn't fight. How could she, when he'd taken her strength and made it his? "I wish I'd never met you," he said in a rough whisper.

She felt the same way, hated him as much as she loved—no! She wouldn't love him. She wouldn't!

"Let me go, Jed."

"Go? So you can get yourself killed?"

"Maybe you are the one who will be killed."

"Maybe." Still holding her wrists, he leaned down, his body sending a silent question. She answered it by lifting her face and letting her mouth fall slack. When he covered it with his, the anger that might have made it possible for her to leave him without crying seeped out of her.

It was still dark when Jed returned to the troops hunkered down behind the hastily built rock barricades. A few soldiers were curled up on the ground, trying to sleep, but most had propped themselves against anything that might serve as a back rest and were grumbling that they saw no earthly reason why they'd been sent out here to defend land that no one except a few fool ranchers wanted anyway. Jed agreed, then asked himself why it had taken six years of fighting Indians for him to question who really had claim to the earth under their feet.

He'd found a small opening in the rock wall and was staring at the nothing that was the Modocs' home when he received word that Colonel Gillem wanted to see him. The commander, still weak from whatever malady had overtaken him just before General Canby was killed, was hunched over a crudely drawn map lit by a small lantern. What, he asked, did Jed think would happen once the troops had completed their sweep around the south end of the lava beds? Jed ventured the opinion that Gillem shouldn't count on his officers to follow orders today any better than they had yesterday. Gillem, profanity sprinkled through his reply, agreed.

"It is my opinion that I have been saddled with the most inept troops ever brazen enough to call themselves soldiers," he finished. "But we will achieve victory! I will accept nothing less."

Jed didn't bother to reply. Gillem, he'd learned long ago, often asked for advice but seldom took it. Jed could tell him that his officers would follow orders from a leader they respected, but to what point? The colonel was what he was, a career soldier who owed his rapid promotions to political connections, not competence. When Gillem started sending out messengers with conflicting and confusing orders for the troop commanders, Jed clenched his teeth in frustration.

He knew how to fight, how to obey orders; that's all he'd known for the past six years. Hatred had sustained and even nourished him because there'd never been anything to take its place.

Tonight he'd sought out and made love to a Modoc woman and she'd scattered his hatred to the wind.

He was army through and through; it was his life.

And so, now, was Luash.

APRIL 16, 1873

"They're not here! Goddamnit, they're all gone."

Jed could have told the others that hours ago. At Gillem's orders and because he'd been there before, he'd taken command of twenty hand-picked men and led the belly crawling advance on the heart of the stronghold while more troops backed them up with a constant barrage of fire. He'd barely paid any attention to the length of reddish rope he'd crawled over.

When he first faced his task, his still tender side had throbbed, reminding him that no matter what insanity had overtaken him because he'd looked into *her* eyes, his life was at risk. But the Modocs hadn't shot back and gradually his fear and single-minded determination to obey his commander had been replaced by certainty. And awe.

The Modocs had somehow escaped undetected from troops that outnumbered them more than tenfold. Maybe Luash was right. Maybe her people's lives were protected by spirits.

"Wait a minute!" someone shouted as he was taking note of a cannonball he'd found in the middle of their council ring. "I've found one!"

One. Who? Mouth suddenly dry, he joined the others scrambling toward the soldier who'd just shouted. Several were already standing at the entrance to a cave. At his order, they moved aside to make room for him. He stared down into deep shadows, barely able to make out three figures. Two were well-armed soldiers. The third, half naked, lay on the ground, propped up on his elbow.

"It's an old man," one of the soldiers explained in response to Jed's question. "He's hurt or sick. Won't talk to us, won't do nothing. Do you think they just up and left him?"

The Modocs had, Jed knew, not because no one loved the old man but because it was Indian nature not to stand in the way of dying. His thoughts went back to the first time he'd seen Luash, when she'd risked her own life trying to run back into a burning wickiup after an old woman. She had been acting on instinct, reacting out of horror.

Had instinct driven her and the other Modocs out of what had sheltered them since their wickiups had been burned nearly five months ago? Suddenly, overwhelmingly, he needed her. Needed her to tell him what lived inside her people's hearts—and where they would go now.

A shot ripped Jed's thoughts away from Luash. When he stared down again, he saw that someone had killed the old man.

16

━━━━━━━━━━━━━━━━━

"I am not a warrior. I do not want—"

"Luash, stop!" Cho-Cho ordered. "You know what must be done. Kientpoos has said it."

Kientpoos, she thought, images of her uncle distracting her from Cho-Cho's insistence that she accompany him to search for the troops who'd followed them after they fled south from the stronghold nine days ago. Ever since the army had stepped over the red tule rope Cho-ocks had placed around the stronghold and a cannonball had landed in the middle of the council ring, no one had listened to the shaman. Instead, everyone had once again turned to Kientpoos. Whether he wanted that, Luash didn't know.

"Your uncle says no harm comes to those who are touched by Eagle," Cho-Cho explained. "That is why he wants you with me. There is no one else, Luash, no shaman."

"But I have no power over Eagle."

"Maybe you have been given a sign."

In Cho-Cho's eyes, she saw the death of something in which he'd always believed. She felt the same way. Although she'd never been comfortable around Cho-ocks, he had been the tribe's spiritual leader, and now they had nothing.

"It is spring," she said hopefully. "There is food and shelter and maybe freedom here." She swept her arms to take in the lava plateaus and pumice or cinder buttes that made up the volcanic basin. "At day's first light, I looked at the sky and saw not just Eagle but another as well."

"Two? They came to you?"

"Just my spirit," she explained, absently touching the white strand of her hair. "I called to him. He floated close on unmoving wings. Finally we touched, his great claw gentle on my shoulder. The other bird remained high in the sky; then they flew away together."

"Perhaps Eagle has found a mate, and that is why you have seen so little of him."

"I hope so. No one, not even a spirit, should remain alone." Her voice trailed off at the end. The recent days and nights of constant watchfulness, always aware of the army behind them, had worn on her nearly as much as thoughts of Jed had. He returned to her nightly in her dreams, clad not in his soldier's uniform, but with a dark blanket over his shoulders and his feet bare because, he said, he wanted to feel her land. The image always faded with the dawn.

"Why do you not want to do as your uncle says?" Cho-Cho asked after a brief silence. "Is it because you are afraid of getting closer to the enemy?"

"Not for myself. Out here I cannot feel their strength, but when I see their weapons, I ask myself if we will ever be free of them."

"This is our home, Luash. We know its hiding places, and if we decide that this land is no longer safe, we will take to the mountains."

She allowed herself a quick glance at the steep slopes of Medicine Lake range. Today the mountains looked so far away, promising safety, and yet they were unreachable. "What does he want of me?"

Cho-Cho explained that scouts had brought word that a large number of soldiers, a howitzer, mules carrying food, extra ammunition, stretchers, even a doctor were heading toward them. The army moved slowly, looking like frightened children. Still, there was danger in both their number and weapons. If the soldiers could be trapped somewhere, they would make easy targets.

At the word *target,* she fought down a tremor. Yes, the army had treated her people like animals to be hunted down, but for her to be part of an attack . . . "What are you going to do?"

"What I must, Luash. What I must." Cho-Cho looked at his wife, who was sitting on bunchgrass as she tried to repair the settler's boots she'd been wearing. Whe-cha sat beside her. "Will you come with us?"

Although the thought of helping trap unsuspecting soldiers made her sick, she agreed because she was Modoc, because anything was better than not knowing, not helping. Before long, she and Cho-Cho and more than twenty men were moving along the back side of a long, thin lava flow that would allow them to get much closer to the army without being seen. Was Jed with the enemy?

They'd covered less than half of the distance which separated the Modocs from the soldiers when she first heard the squeaking sound made by the cumbersome howitzer's wheels. There were other noises, a mule's bray, a horse's whinny, men yelling at horses, all of which made her wonder how whites could be so proud of their army if it couldn't move silently.

She should be terrified at the thought of getting this close to those who rather see her dead than alive, but she and the others with her knew this land. Although she spent most of the time crawling on hands and knees over nearly level ground, something close to a sense of peace stole over her.

Birds were everywhere, their gentle songs blending with the wind like whispers from a mother watching her child fall asleep.

She'd told Cho-Cho nothing of how she felt when Eagle came to her yesterday. To see him with a mate sent her heart soaring.

Did Eagle know how she felt about Jed?

When Jed's name echoed inside her like an owl's call, she pressed her hand against her stomach, remembering what his touch had done to her. They'd made love, come together in the night while their people fired at each other. Both had spoken of the insanity of what they were doing; both said that their night together shouldn't be.

But their bodies had joined, and for those few precious moments, their thoughts hadn't gone beyond that—hadn't needed or wanted to. And even though they would never have those moments again, the memory would warm her through all the winters of her life. And if a Modoc bullet found him—

A Modoc bullet.

Hating herself, her uncle, everyone, she looked around until she saw Cho-Cho slightly ahead of her. He lay flat on his belly on a slight rise, staring ahead. She joined him, careful not to disturb so much as a single blade of new grass. He was looking at a line of men and horses that reminded her of a disorganized ant trail. "They have many weapons," he said without turning his head. "But they are afraid."

Although the land stretched out forever in all directions, the men were bunched together like puppies trying to keep warm during a storm. All carried their rifles where they could easily use them. "Leave them," she begged. "Please, leave them alone."

"If I do, maybe they will kill my family."

"Not if we go into the hills. Cho-Cho, there are so many of them."

"There will be fewer before the day is over."

Sick, she lay beside the warrior while a tiny spider crept close to her hand. She didn't want this! She wanted to be a child again, running free and happy along the shore of Modoc Lake as she tried to catch the ducks that squawked and flapped easily away from her. Why couldn't she have that world back?

"I remember the first time I saw a white man," Cho-Cho whispered. "He was on horseback, leading two mules weighed down with furs. When he saw me, he motioned for me to come close. I did, because I'd heard that trappers carried gifts. He gave me a bright red headband and some nuts. I thought he was wonderful. That was a long time ago."

Now he saw whites as people who threatened his family's life. They'd already killed Aga and probably had murdered Chiwulha', whose legs were too weak to allow him to leave the stronghold. Ha-kar-Jim had been wrong; killing the army's leaders hadn't caused the enemy to scatter.

Maybe they never would.

Cho-Cho silently directed his warriors to make their way to the top of the small depression toward which the army was marching. If they entered the long, narrow valley, the Modocs could easily trap them there. Luash went with them; perhaps Eagle would spread his protective wings over those she loved. She could see no other way.

Although she hadn't seen him earlier, she wasn't surprised when Kientpoos joined them. After speaking briefly with him, Cho-Cho signaled to some of the warriors to position themselves so they would be on either side of the army.

Several times Kientpoos looked at her, but he didn't speak to her. She remembered, years ago, watching as he stood in Modoc Lake with water lapping around his legs, his fingers around a spear while he waited for a fish to swim close. Today the army was the fish.

On came the soldiers, the noises from animals and wagons rasping her nerves and making her feel as if she'd been caught in a current from which there was no escaping. It seemed impossible that none of the white men heard her breathing, but maybe the strangers were so frightened that all they could hear was the pounding of their own hearts.

Only they might not all be strangers. One might be the man who had taken her body in the dark.

The back of Jed's neck prickled, but it had been doing that so much today that he didn't know what to make of it. For the past hour, he'd been walking some hundred yards to the south and ahead of the rest of the troop, wishing to hell he wasn't the only one who believed closely bunched men presented a damn easy target.

When the almost painful sensation repeated itself, he climbed onto a rock and looked around. Where the hell had everyone disappeared to? They'd been here just—swearing, he jumped off the rock and started running back to where he'd last seen them. Before he'd covered half the distance, he heard a chorus of groans and complaints, interspersed with sighs. As he'd feared, the entire troop had settled down in a shallow ravine. Still cursing, he clambered over the edge and half walked, half slid down to where some of the soldiers were already removing their boots.

The top of the depression was no more than twenty feet above him, but from where he now stood, he could no longer look out at the land around them. Damnit, they were in perfect position for an ambush! Just yesterday he'd seen smoke from Modoc fires near Schonchin Flow, an easy day's walk to the south. Although several Warm Springs scouts had reassured troop leader captains Thomas and Wright that there'd been no sign of Indians any closer than that, he hadn't stayed alive by trusting others' words.

All right, he tried to reconcile himself; they'd sweep through the small valley and quickly climb back out of it, barefoot if that's what it called for. No harm done. No presenting themselves as sitting ducks. Only, from what his dealings with Thomas and Wright had already taught him, the two young officers resented anything that sounded like criticism of their so-called leadership.

Hadn't the Modocs proven time and time again that they were a worthy foe? To discount them this way—to ignore his repeated warnings and do something this stupid—

When Jed spotted Captain Thomas and three others scrambling up an outcropping, he took a more relaxed breath. Obviously, Thomas was going to signal back to Colonel Gillem's camp, which was only a mile and a half to the north. If there were Modocs around, surely they'd understand that the larger army force was within easy reach.

Captain Wright, a piece of hardtack clamped between his teeth, was directing two of his men to climb the little ridge to the east. Jed started toward Wright. He'd just opened his mouth to berate Wright for the location he'd chosen for the noon break when he caught movement at the top of the ridge. The sun glinted off something.

"Ambush!" His cry of alarm was swallowed by the sound of two shots. The two climbers spun around and began running down the hill, as did Thomas and those with him. The Modocs were far enough away that Jed wasn't surprised when they missed. Just the same, an awful coldness seeped into his veins. There were natural rock fortifications on all sides at the top of the ravine. If the Modocs had wanted to trap the army, they couldn't have picked a more perfect site.

"Stop!" he yelled at Captain Thomas. It was vital that they get word of an impending attack to Gillem's troops. Although his shout caught Thomas's attention, the man shook his head violently and continued scrambling downward. Jed started climbing, but he'd gone only a few feet when he realized he'd never be able to reach the top before the Modocs stopped him.

He spun back around, cursing at the sight of the many soldiers not fortifying themselves behind rocks, but running for their lives. Most of them seemed determined to head back the way they'd come. Others simply ran aimlessly, rifles all but forgotten, while they stared up at where more and more Modocs were appearing.

Hurrying to where Thomas and Wright now stood, he yelled at them to gather what troops they could for an assault on the nearest Indians. His explanation was simple and hard-spoken. If they could distract the Modocs long enough, some of the soldiers might manage to escape and bring back help. Although obviously frightened, Thomas bellowed at his men to follow his lead, but only a few obeyed.

Wright managed to gather more men around him, but the moment he started toward the ridge, the Indians emptied their rifles at them. Jed yelled that it would take several seconds for the Modocs to reload, time enough for the soldiers to reach the top. His suggestion was ignored. Instead, almost as one, the men hugged the ground, some crying out in fear.

Jed was wildly looking around for the mules carrying the extra ammunition when he saw Captain Wright clutch his chest and fall. Wright had barely hit the ground when his followers turned tail and ran.

Jed yelled for the men to stop and find cover, but there was so much noise that only those closest to him could hear. Tense with more than a little fear, Jed dove for the nearest boulder. He had his rifle and a fair amount of ammunition, but if he was to have a half chance at hitting one of the Modocs, he would have to step out into the open.

Closer and closer the Indians came, their progress almost leisurely, their bullets finding one human target after another until Jed felt sickened by the sound of screaming men. Thanks to the endless lava outcroppings, only rarely did one of the Modocs expose himself. When they weren't shooting, they yelled insults at the helpless soldiers.

Ambush! The word slammed him into the past. But he didn't dare stay there. Captain Wright hadn't moved; Jed vowed to break the news of her husband's death as gently as possible to the captain's young wife.

The scent of fear far overshadowed the other smells of battle. Everywhere around him, wounded men cried for help. He was forced to admire the Modoc who had masterminded this attack. They'd waited until their enemy had boxed themselves in, just as had happened at Fort Phil Kearny.

When memories of that other time threatened to swamp him, he forced them away by taking close note of what he could see of his surroundings. The Modocs, although still firing, had stopped advancing; obviously they believed themselves to be in control. They were right. The sight of their wounded or dead companions, sprawled where they'd fallen, had stripped the young recruits of what little courage they'd had.

Damnit, he'd tried to warn Colonel Gillem and captains Wright and Thomas that the men under them couldn't be counted on to remember what little training they'd had if they found themselves in a confrontation with the Modocs. His warnings had fallen on deaf ears. The men were proud and brave soldiers, he'd been told. They were committed to clearing the land of savages, and wouldn't give up until the job was done.

Well, Gillem and the others had been wrong. The men trapped around him were little more than scared kids, shooting wildly at nothing or desperately trying to protect themselves behind whatever barrier they could find.

Some had managed to escape when the shooting began. Jed concentrated on that. As soon as they reached Gillem's camp, reinforcements would be sent out.

But six years ago, when eighty good men had been cut down, help hadn't come until it was too late for anyone except him.

Night fell. The shooting stopped. Grateful for the darkness, which allowed him the freedom to move about, Jed left where he'd spent too many cramped hours and crawled among the sprawled bodies, the journey taking a long time because the soldiers were widely spread. The moment he touched Captain Wright, Jed knew the young soldier was beyond help. The same was true for Captain Thomas.

For a moment he couldn't do anything except crouch beside Captain Thomas as grief overwhelmed him. He didn't want to care; hadn't he spent years without close ties to anyone—except Wilfred—so he wouldn't have to feel the awful wrench of loss? He'd barely known Thomas; his death shouldn't make Jed question the reason for his own existence.

A groan to his left distracted him. He cut his hand getting to the man because in the dark he couldn't see the sharp rocks. The soldier, a kid really, had been shot in the thigh and had lost so much blood that he was barely conscious. Still, even when his head lolled to one side, he continued to clutch Jed with vicelike fingers.

Jed spent hours beside him, talking when it seemed that the kid needed to hear the sound of a human voice, simply holding and rocking him when nightmares made him shriek in terror.

Throughout the endless night, he fought to keep his mind in a nothing place where emotion couldn't reach him, but failed dismally. It was more than trying to comfort a frightened teenager. At the edge of his thoughts, constantly invading, was Luash. He wanted to hate her. Damnation, he wanted to condemn her and the rest of her people to the hell he no longer believed in.

But he'd been inside the cold, dark cave where she'd spent her winter. She'd been just as trapped as he was tonight; maybe she'd fought the same nightmares.

"They'll be here by morning," he tried to reassure the boy, who'd told Jed his name was William. "The rest of the troops. If the Modocs are still around, they'll chase them away."

"No, they won't. They're everywhere. Savages. Don't—please don't let them scalp me!"

"I promise," Jed said, touching the hilt of his knife. If the unthinkable happened and the Modocs returned to finish the job they'd begun, he would make sure William never knew what they did to him.

It was getting colder, both sky and earth seeming to have lost all warmth. Whimpering, William burrowed close to him, but although he did everything he could to keep the kid warm, there simply wasn't enough cover here to cut the wind. In the absolute darkness, Jed didn't dare try to move him.

Wind. Not the icy blasts of winter, but mind and body numbing just the same. Jed began shivering, and although he lay down beside William so they could share their warmth, it made little difference. The night went on forever, a monstrosity of fitful sleep, violent shivers, William crying, clawing fear spreading from the other trapped men to lap at Jed until he couldn't remember being anywhere else or feeling any emotion other than hatred.

Hatred. It was back, as strong as it had been when he'd realized what the Sioux had done all those years ago. It fed him, allowed him to survive the horrific night filled with sobs and curses and prayers and terror that the Modocs might attack again as soon as night surrendered to day.

Day. Please, let it be day.

"Morning's coming, William," he crooned when it seemed that the night had gone on forever. "Hang on just a little while longer. Colonel Gillem's troops have to be on the way."

Damnit, where were they? Surely someone had escaped the ambush and made his way to the larger force, hours and hours ago. There was no excuse, no excuse at all to put these boys through this hell. "Stay with me. Just stay with me. You're going to be all right. All right."

William didn't answer. Finally life had seeped out of his young body, and he sagged against Jed, who clutched him to his chest and cried bitter tears.

Three days after the attack on the men who'd sought to capture and kill them, Luash climbed down into the small valley and stepped onto the abandoned battlefield. The smell of blood, fear, and death still permeated the air, making her wonder if even another winter storm would kill the stench, the memories.

Jed had been here. She hadn't seen him, because Cho-Cho and Kientpoos had ordered her to remain back, away from where the warriors had positioned themselves. As dusk had started to fall, Kientpoos had come to her and told her he'd spotted the lieutenant crouched beside a fallen officer. No, Kientpoos had said, he didn't think Jed had been shot. Why did that matter so much to her, he pushed. After everything that had happen between their people, could there still be thunder and lightning between her and Jed?

She hadn't answered, but her eyes must have given her away, because Kientpoos hadn't said anything after that. If her uncle knew where she was now, he would insist she was risking losing Eagle's power by coming to the place of their enemies' death.

She wasn't. Eagle was strong inside her, giving her the courage to stand where men had spilled their blood and cursed her and the rest of her people.

Jed didn't have Eagle, didn't have faith in his people's god, she thought as she dug her moccasins in the sand and stared up at the walls ahead and on both sides of her. What had it been like for him to crouch here, knowing he was trapped?

Had his curses joined those of the others?

Had he known fear so strong that it stripped him of the ability to think and move? Jed had told her how little he valued his own life. Death, he'd said, would simply end days and nights without true meaning.

But they'd stood hand in hand, kissed and embraced, made love. Had their lovemaking changed him, made him feel more alive? Shown him that living could be a wonderful thing?

The army men had spent the night trapped here. The next day, finally, soldiers sent from the main army camp had found them, but Cho-Cho, who'd stayed behind to watch, had told her there'd been no doctors among the rescuers and only a handful had risked their lives to come after those whose legs couldn't take them to safety. Night had fallen again while the rescuers were readying the wounded for the journey back to camp.

It had snowed that second night, dark clouds playing a sick joke on the strangers to the Land of Burned Out fires. Luash had found a small cave to hide in, but unless Jed had left the wounded behind, he'd spent the night at the storm's mercy.

Two nights of fear and cold and hunger. Two days of waiting for attack, burying the dead, and trying to help those who cried in pain and fear.

Although she could only guess that Jed was in one of those distant tents, the hatred he'd unleashed against her people swirled around her like a living force.

"I cannot help what you feel," she whispered, "what is in your heart." She imagined the words rising into the air, drifting out over the dark and seemingly endless lava, reaching Jed. "I cannot change you, just as you cannot change me."

Her voice belonged to a stranger. She vowed not to say anything more. This was a place of death, of hastily dug graves and discarded weapons and even a dead horse.

Why had she come here? She should be with Whe-cha, who wept because her husband had become a stranger to her. There hadn't been enough food since they left the stronghold; she should be digging for roots.

But Jed had endured two nights more horrible than she could imagine, and she couldn't stop thinking about that. Despite her sense of horror, she forced herself to walk the same ground he had. Maybe she was here because this was where she hoped to find that compassion and understanding had become part of him, that he realized her people had attacked his because the Modocs clung to hopes of survival and the only way they knew to do that was by stopping the army.

Head throbbing, she clamped her hand against her forehead and fought tears. She had never wanted anything except to be Modoc. Maybe that was why Eagle had come to her, because he had seen her pure heart and understood why it beat. And yet she'd fallen in love—no. Not love. But she had been touched by an army man whose hatred of what she stood for went deeper than the deepest cave. She'd sensed what was good about him. She'd given herself to him, body and heart. And he'd done the same. That she believed.

The battlefield wasn't deserted after all. Realization of that came slowly but steadily, like fog drifting up from a lake. Still, she wasn't afraid, felt no need to run.

He was here.

The spring storm lingered in the air. She wore a blanket over the hide dress he'd taken off her the other day. Maybe he wouldn't recognize her.

No. She'd heard Eagle's cry this morning; she was strong.

"Jed," she called out, "I am alone."

For several minutes, there was only the sound of the hawks who made their homes in the distant buttes. Then he showed himself bit by bit, a shadow slowly separating itself from other shadows. As happened too many times when she thought of him, she shivered a little. The death-place continued to exert its powerful influence, but she managed to keep it from overwhelming her by not taking her eyes off him.

He was armed, a pistol at his side, a rifle held in his hands. His uniform was dirty and torn in several places, and the wind had chased his hair until it massed around his head like a bird's nest. His chin was blurred by unshaven stubble, but it was his eyes that caught and held her.

They were no longer gray. They'd been touched by night and what he'd experienced since they'd last seen each other. "You shouldn't be here," he said when he drew close to her.

"Neither should you."

"I had to come back." He took a few more steps, his boots making soft thudding sounds on the hard ground. "It's called facing one's demons."

"Why? The others did not."

"They're kids, Luash. Most of them, anyway. That's what your men killed. Boys."

"Your men chase women and children. Cut us off from water and force us to leave our only home."

"Damn." He set the end of his rifle on the ground and gripped it with chapped fingers. His other hand was looped around his belt, near the pistol. She thought of her only weapon, a knife dulled from cutting sage. "Damn."

"I do not want your anger, Jed," she ordered, although saying that wouldn't change what lived inside him. "If you have come here to throw it at me, I will not stay."

"I told you; I returned because that's how I face my nightmares. I didn't know you were going to be here."

"You did the other night."

He blinked but gave no other sign that he'd heard her. Today he reminded her of a wolf with nowhere left to run. Was that it? He was a wolf and she an eagle? Wolf and eagle—two creatures with little need to acknowledge the other's existence. Confused by her emotions, she couldn't think of anything to say.

"Were you there?" he demanded. "Did you see?"

Head high, she told him that Kientpoos and Cho-Cho had both

278 // Vella Munn

wanted her near them because they no longer believed in Cho-ocks's medicine, but once the warriors were in place, she'd been sent away. She'd heard shots, but just those of her people. "When it was over, they told me they had killed many."

"Bragged. That's what they did, didn't they?"

"They want to be left in peace."

His eyes told her that wouldn't happen. Caught in their spell, she couldn't think how to argue with him. "You are alive," she whispered. "I asked Eagle for a sign that you were. He sent me his voice."

"Did he? Let me tell you what it was like." His mouth tightened as did his grip on his weapons. "I spent the night trying to keep a wounded kid warm. Talked to him until I couldn't talk anymore. Filled him full of false hope. He died in my arms."

A whimper of pain escaped her lips. "I am sorry. So sorry."

"Are you?"

"Yes," she told him although she was unbelievably weary of try-ing to make him understand the beating of her heart. Did he think she could stand here and not be pulled into the nightmare, not feel what he had when that young soldier died? "Jed, I see the look in a woman's eyes when she is terrified her newborn will know noth-ing except war. I share my people's fear and sorrow when the enemy's weapons strike our sacred council ring, when the enemy steps over what our shaman promised would keep us safe. I un-derstand why my uncle does not want another child because he fears he will not be alive to raise it. And I hear the spirit cries of the men who died here."

She readied herself for his anger, his denial of her emotions, but those things didn't come. Instead, he bent over and set down his rifle. He raked his fingers through his hair.

"When I came to the stronghold," he said, "and you and I waited inside that cave, all I could think about was what it must be like to know you have no other place to live. There weren't any spirits there, at least none I understand. But the cries here . . . "

He looked so weary, so confused, that it tore her apart. She would have understood his anger; maybe she wanted fury from him so he would stop haunting her. But this emotion . . .

"I knew what was going to happen when the warriors hid themselves here," she told him. "I wanted to warn you; I want you to know that. My heart cried out to *you*."

His look of exhaustion faded a little, but she didn't understand the emotion taking its place. "It wouldn't have done you any good. If anyone had seen you, they would have killed you."

"I felt as if there were two of me, one Modoc, the other—I do not know that other person."

He nodded slowly and for a moment a little of the tension went out of him. "I wish I'd never met you, Luash."

She pressed her hand over her heart, not caring how much the gesture told him. "I wish our feet had never walked the same way."

"It's too late. Too damn late. I don't want to ever be here again." He indicated his surroundings. "The ghosts . . . "

"A death-place," she whispered. "Just as the caves will always hold sorrow for what we lost."

"Death and sorrow. What the hell are we going to do?"

He was asking the impossible. If she'd known any way of carving out a peace between their separate people, she would have done so long ago. "Go away," she told him, even though the thought of him turning his back on her nearly tore her apart. "Take your boy soldiers and leave."

"It's not going to happen. Damnit—"

"What do you want from me! Our shaman was unable to keep your soldiers from attacking. Do you think I am more powerful than him?"

"No," he said quietly, sadly. "Damnit, let me take you to the reservation. It's not too late—"

"You want me to sit in the same house with my father, who would sell me for whiskey? This is better."

"You're going to die out here."

"It is you who almost lost your life at this place. It loves me; it hates you."

Jed thought she was incredible—more uncivilized than the racing wind and yet gifted with a wisdom and gentleness that staggered him. He wanted to hate her. He sensed she knew that, but she would never run in fear. Instead, she was presenting her woman's body and ageless eyes to him, killing his hatred with a look.

"You *heard* Eagle?" he asked, still battling her impact on him. "You didn't see him?"

She shook her head, hair sliding over her throat. His fingers ached with the need to feel her silky flesh. "He has found a mate. I sense his happiness. He will make a good father."

"Happiness? He's a bird, Luash. He doesn't laugh or cry."

"You do not know him; I do."

"What's to know? Damnit, there's no wisdom in him. When the hell are you going to see that?"

"Your anger sorrows me, Jed," she said so softly that the whisper nearly tore him apart. "All the hate you have allowed to grow inside you—a man cannot laugh or embrace spring if his heart is frozen."

His heart wasn't frozen; far from it. With the rocks that had held so many warriors clearly visible behind her, it should have been easy for him to wrench free of her, but she reminded him of laughter and spring and, damnit, he needed that. Needed it so much that his heart ached.

"He wasn't alone the last night of his life," he said. "William. A boy, a soldier. At least I gave him that."

"Jed, I never wanted that, for him or anyone. You have to believe me."

He did, completely and without reservation. But it made no difference. He was a soldier; it was the only thing he knew how to be.

"You know what's going to happen, don't you?" he asked. "There's no way your people can kill more than twenty soldiers without having to pay for it."

"Twenty," she said with a small, choked sigh.

"The army is going to run you into the ground."

"We had to protect ourselves."

"And so do we, Luash."

"Then why are we here?" Her voice caught. "You and me." She started to extend her hand toward him, then let it drop. "What brought us to this place where no one else stands?"

"I don't know."

"You said—you said you had to return to where your demons live. But maybe it was more than that. Maybe you knew you would find me."

"Maybe."

Tears slid out from under her lashes, ripping at him.

"Don't cry," he told her. "It won't change anything."

"I am not ashamed of my woman's heart."

Woman's heart. Was there any difference between what a man and woman felt? A sound briefly distracted him, but it was only a shriek from a hawk circling above the dead horse. He and Luash were the intruders here; the hawks and eagles belonged.

Looking at her again, with rocks and hills all around her, the wind in her hair and the sun setting in her dark eyes, he knew he was wrong.

This was her home. The land that held her heart.

The land she was going to lose.

17

The sun burned the back of Jed's neck, and from his horse's labored breathing, he knew the animal was in need of a drink. Water had been hard to come by in the past few days, but Jed barely felt his own thirst. The same couldn't be said for the ten men accompanying him and Wilfred this morning. Their complaints, along with the squeak of saddles and thud of shod hooves, echoed around him sounding like an angry, yet weary, hornet's nest.

He hadn't seen Luash in over a month. During the whole of May, the army had chased one rumor after another about where the Modocs were holed up, run roughshod over folks' ranches, and, because someone said the Modocs had taken off for their sacred, snow-capped mountain, stared south until their eyes ached.

Still, despite the never-ending military bumbling, Jed knew the end was near. In a few days, maybe even today, he, or someone else with the authority to accept a surrender, would stand face to face with Captain Jack. Curley Headed Doctor, Hooker Jim, and their followers had already turned themselves in, Hooker hiding out until he'd seen that the others weren't going to be killed before sauntering in full of his usual bluster. Now the man most folks believed had gunned down innocent settlers and been instrumental in the slaughter at the peace tent was leading the army to where his leader hid.

Jed didn't understand it, didn't like it one bit. But he wasn't the one in charge.

The battles at Scorpion Point and Dry Lakes had turned the tide. For the first time since this damnable war began, the Modocs had lost more than the army had. True, only one Modoc had been killed at Dry Lake, but soldiers had managed to round up a fair number of Modoc horses, some ammunition, even food. Jack and those still with him were on the run, but how much longer could people without food, water, or bullets run?

"You're going quiet on me again," Wilfred observed. "Been thinking about her, haven't you?"

"Every time I'm not yammering away like some black crow you decide I'm thinking about her."

"Because you always are. Don't lie to me; there ain't no reason to."

True. "She doesn't owe Jack her life. Just because he's scared to turn himself in is no reason for her to sacrifice herself."

"Scared?" Wilfred wiped sweat off his forehead and went back to studying the land around Horse Mountain, south of Tule Lake, where Hooker Jim insisted Jack was. "That chief doesn't know the meaning of the word."

"Yeah, he does," Jed insisted. "Just like he knows what it's like to be tired and hungry and thirsty, same as anyone else."

"Maybe he'll die out there." Wilfred indicated the deceptively flat-looking land that hid endless depressions and caves. "Wouldn't that be something. People have come here from clear across the country, wanting to see how this war plays itself out. They'll never be able to gawk at Captain Jack because the buzzards got him."

It was possible, he thought. Possible, but not too likely, since every buzzard sighting would be explored. Still, even if Jack handed over his guns, there was no way the rebel chief could escape justice. The settlers and ranchers, the ones who'd been putting up such a fuss about how inept the army was, wouldn't settle for anything less.

And if Luash was by her uncle's side—

No. There was no reason for her to suffer the same fate, whatever that might be. She'd be sent off to a reservation.

Wilfred grunted, distracting him. When he looked where his friend was pointing, he saw a squaw climbing down a rock and bunchgrass-choked hill toward them, one hand lifted in a pathetic gesture of greeting, the other clutching a baby to her breast. Several soldiers aimed their rifles at the woman, causing her to shrink back. Cautioning the men not to fire, Jed dismounted and slowly approached her.

Her eyes widened slightly, making him wonder if she recognized him. Maybe she'd been in the stronghold when he went there. He tried to tell her he'd take her to the others who'd surrendered over the past few days, but she obviously didn't understand English and he had no translator with him. He made a show of putting down his weapons before reaching for her infant. Her mouth began to tremble and tears formed in her dull eyes.

What he said didn't matter, just that he spoke softly and gently. The woman, looking haggard, let her free hand drop by her side. The gesture drew his attention to her stained and faded linsey-woolsey skirt. Whether her husband had bought it for her or she'd bartered for it with her body back when she could freely walk among the Fort Klamath soldiers didn't matter. Her baggy shirt wasn't in any better condition and she was barefoot.

Did Luash look like that now?

"I won't hurt him." He indicated the whimpering baby. "We'll get him some decent clothes and you some food and shoes."

The woman cocked her head, trying to watch him and the soldiers behind him at the same time. In an effort to make himself clear, he pointed first at her feet and then at his boots. Finally he rubbed his belly and made eating motions. Still she stared, tears now running down her dry cheeks. He could have grabbed her and forced her with him; there wasn't a damn thing she could do about it, no one would stand up for her. But she'd defied the better part of a thousand soldiers for over six months, giving birth somewhere out in that godforsaken land. She deserved some dignity, some consideration.

When he began removing his shirt, she tightened her grip on the baby. Again her eyes widened. Shirt held out, he took several slow steps toward her. She drew away from him but didn't try to run.

While he draped the shirt over the baby, she continued to stare, mouth trembling, face bleached of color. Then, slowly, she sank to the ground and folded herself over her child, sobbing.

Please, don't let it be like this for Luash.

"He is gone."

Luash, who had been resting under the shade of a sagebrush to escape the heat, propped herself up on her elbow. Her legs ached. Her mouth was dry. She hadn't had anything to drink today, and she knew that if she got up too quickly, she would become dizzy, because she also hadn't eaten. Kientpoos stood over her, his shoulders still proudly squared despite the lines of exhaustion around his eyes and mouth.

"Who?" she asked dully.

"Cho-Cho." Kientpoos stared at another sagebrush where Whe-cha was sleeping, then dropped to his knees beside Luash. "He is gone. My friend, gone. His heart must have told him it is time to surrender."

"Uncle, I am sorry. So sorry."

"He does as he must, as Cho-ocks and Ha-kar-Jim did. I do not hate them for it. The soldiers treat us like dogs! I think they would chase me to the end of the Earth."

Maybe they would. The days since she'd last seen Jed blurred together in her mind until she couldn't remember whether it had been one moon or two. What she did remember was constant moving, hiding among endless lava, sage, low hills, trying to get close to Modoc Lake or a creek for enough water to keep going. Never enough food.

Two days ago Ha-kar-Jim had shown up, boasting that after he'd surrendered, the army had given him five days' food ration so he could find his chief and tell him to give himself up. Barely containing his fury, Kientpoos had ordered Ha-kar-Jim to go back to his captors and tell them that the chief of the Modocs would never grovel before his enemies. But now Cho-Cho was gone and Kientpoos's lips were dry and cracked. Whe-cha had aged ten years and barely spoke anymore.

"I am weary," Kientpoos said. "So tired of running."

She and her uncle hadn't really sat alone together since he'd killed the general. Much of the time he'd been busy with his braves, planning attacks, retreating, hiding, occasionally hunting.

But there'd been quiet moments; she should have approached him before now. What could she say to a man she loved but who had shot an unarmed man and then ordered an attack on unsuspecting soldiers while they sat eating their noon meal? "What will you do now?"

"Do?" He drew out the word, made it last a long time. "My legs are played out, Luash. My men are gone, captured. My wives cry with hunger and my daughter—I cannot bear her tears."

This wasn't the chief who'd defied an army through a frozen winter. The Kientpoos she knew would never confess such things to a woman, not even to her. But she understood the exhaustion in his eyes and voice; she felt the same way. She was too tired and heartsick to care about anything. "Ha-kar-Jim says we will be treated with kindness and given food and water. So did the doctor they sent to talk to us."

Kientpoos stared at the ground, saying nothing. Yesterday Kientpoos had promised the slow-talking doctor that he would turn himself in along with what remained of his followers. Then Cho-Cho had snuck away in the middle of the night, taking a few Modocs with him. The army doctor might believe Kientpoos to be a man who didn't keep his word, but Luash knew the truth. Her uncle simply couldn't bear to watch the rest of his people surrender.

With shaking fingers, she pulled a eagle feather out of the rope she'd tied around her waist and handed it to him. The black tip was broken and it had been flattened in the middle, but it was still glossy, still held warmth throughout its length. "Eagle left this for me during the night," she said quietly.

"He came to you? I did not hear him."

"I did not see him," she admitted. "I called for him, over and over again, but . . ."

"As you have many times since we began running."

"Yes." The admission clogged her throat. Where was Eagle? If his absence was a sign— "I did not hear him. But when I woke this morning, this was near my head."

"A broken feather," Kientpoos whispered. "That is how I feel, bent by battle. Luash, this land, the Smiles of God, was given to us by Kumookumts and we were right in fighting for it, but what a man believes and what truly is are not always the same things."

She barely subdued the whimper building inside her. The same thoughts had been pounding at her for weeks, even while they were still at the stronghold. There, she'd been forced to ask herself if she could face living the rest of her life in a cave instead of the wickiup of her ancestors. Eagle protected her and brought peace to her heart; he couldn't take her back into the past.

"I do not want this for you. To become a prisoner—"

Kientpoos shot her a look that froze the rest of her words before they could escape. "If you hide now," she whispered, "maybe no one will find you. A man alone casts a small shadow."

"You ask me to leave my people? My wives and daughter—to never see you again?"

"When I came to live with you, I knew I might never see my parents again. I did what my heart needed so it could hear the song of freedom."

"The sight of your father makes you sick. You are unable to speak your mother's name without great sorrow. Your heart needed to be free to live as our ancestors did; it also needed peace from what you felt when you were around your parents and the soldiers."

Shaken by her uncle's wisdom, she could only squeeze his hand. "The army men will never understand you, my uncle. They see a chief and a warrior, a man who makes war with them."

"A man who kills."

"Yes. And for that they must have their revenge—unless you escape into the mountains." When he said nothing, she went on, her attention on the bent feather and what it might mean. "In years to come, will anyone speak of you with wise words? Will they know what lives inside your heart?"

"My family does; you do. Maybe that is enough."

She couldn't agree; those who came after them and stood at the Land of Burned Out Fires and spoke of Captain Jack should understand why honor and freedom meant more to him than life itself. But no one would listen to her any more than the army had to the leader of the Modocs. They both would end their lives in silence.

Eagle still carried wisdom within him. As long as he flew free and proud over this land, people might look up at him and sense a warrior's heart beating.

"We will wait here," Kientpoos said softly. "Soon they will find us and when they do, I will hand my rifle to them. There is nothing else for me to do. Nothing."

He reached down and picked something off the ground. Luash watched, grief stricken, as he rubbed pitch over his cheeks as a sign of mourning.

Tears stung her eyes, but she didn't beg him to reconsider. Her body felt as if she'd been alive since the beginning of time; Kientpoos had to be just as weary, feel just as broken. The only thing that kept her going was knowing that her uncle was still alive. Despite his belief that he'd ended his life by killing the general, his heart continued to beat. "I will walk to them with you."

"You do not have to do this. Alone, no one will come after you. And with Eagle beside you, you would be safe."

If Eagle still protected her. "My heart does not beat only for me, my uncle." Holding out her hand, she waited for him to place some of the pitch in it. "You are my family. You and Whe-cha and Cho-Cho and all other Modocs."

"There is another in your life, Luash. One who is not Modoc."

Jed wasn't with the men who accepted Kientpoos's surrender. Luash was grateful that she didn't have to look into his eyes and half sick because the soldiers whooped and shouted that they had won the war against savages; they pounded each other on the back. These hard-eyed strangers—how could any of them possibly understand what having to give up meant to Kientpoos?

Whe-cha cried the whole way to the army camp, and Kientpoos's young daughter seemed frightened half to death. Luash rode behind her uncle, refusing to look at the armed men pressing around them. Like Kientpoos, she held her head high. If their captors thought themselves great fighters, she couldn't do anything about that. What she did know was that she was Modoc, that she had chosen to spend a winter deep in the Land of Burned Out Fires because freedom meant that much to her.

Several tents had been erected at the army camp at Clear Lake, and she and Kientpoos and the others were directed toward the largest one where, they'd been told, Colonel Jefferson C. Davis, the man who had replaced General Canby, waited. As the tall, slender colonel stepped out of his tent, Luash's attention was drawn to the man beside him, the fierce, brave man who had turned her from a girl into a woman.

Jed's face carried no expression. If she hadn't learned to look deep into his eyes and from there to his heart, she might have thought that today meant nothing more to him than all those that had gone before it.

This was a man sent here to help end a war. His features should be alive with triumph. Instead, he no more than glanced at Kientpoos before walking over to her and holding out his hands, indicating he wanted to help her off her horse. She should have refused; after all, she and her people were at his mercy.

But his eyes spoke of understanding.

"You've lost weight," he said when she was standing beside him and his body heat seeped into her. "And you look tired."

"A deer running from wolves has little time to eat." She kept her voice low.

"The wolves won, Luash."

"Because there were ten wolves to each deer."

Colonel Davis was shaking hands with Kientpoos, who barely looked at him and said nothing in reply to whatever the colonel was saying. Kientpoos's wives and daughter were still on horseback. Luash couldn't stop watching her uncle, not even when Jed slipped his arm around her waist. "He'll be treated fairly," he whispered. "You don't have to worry about him."

"His heart is broken." Many eyes were on them, but if it didn't matter to Jed, she would continue to stand beside him—at least until she understood her emotions.

"I wish it didn't have to be like this."

"Do you?" He seemed old today, his eyes cavelike. Although he was dressed in a fine uniform that reminded her all too much of what he was, he seemed unaware of anyone except her. They had been through so much together, distant and unsure at first, finally finding a kind of understanding she could put no words to. She couldn't think of him as her captor. Her enemy.

"At least they didn't strip him of his dignity," Jed was saying.

How much dignity does an unarmed man have when he stands surrounded by those he has fought? Suddenly, she could no longer keep her thoughts on Kientpoos. "You were in the leader's tent. I thought you would be out looking for us."

"I was. Yesterday, I found a woman and her baby. They—" Breaking off, he gripped her and held her firmly at arms' length. "I've been so scared for you," he whispered. Then, as if regretting his words, he began pulling her toward another tent. She stumbled, then regained her balance, wondering why she wasn't fighting him and why he thought he had to hold onto her.

This camp, although hastily assembled and temporary looking, was alive with both soldiers and the reservation Indians who'd helped hunt the Modocs. She felt buffeted by their presence, exhausted by the heat their bodies gave out. Beyond them lay the hills and mountains her great-grandparents had known.

No one was inside the dark, stale-smelling interior of the tent, which wrapped itself around her like a trapper's steel trap; still, she could sense the presence of the men who spent their nights here. This was not Jed's tent.

"This is where the reporters have been staying," he explained briefly. "You and I are in the middle of a war, and people are following us around, writing about what we're doing, so people across the country can read about it."

She didn't care about that any more than she could keep her thoughts on what might be happening between her uncle and the man who'd taken the place of the one he'd killed. The air in the tent smelled as if it had never been touched by a fresh breeze. It was strangling her. Feeling slightly nauseated, she considered sinking onto one of the cots, but if she did, Jed would loom even larger and stronger.

"Are you not needed with the others? With your kind?"

"There aren't *kinds* here, Luash. Only the end to something that should have never happened. Should have never run on the way it did." He released her but didn't move far enough away. "Are you sure you're all right? You look so tired."

She shrugged to let him know it didn't matter. Awareness of the difference between them washed over her. He carried a pistol, wore sturdy shoes that didn't feel the hard ground underneath. Someone else prepared his meals for him and if he wanted, he could walk away from everything. Still, a Modoc sun had tanned him and Modoc wind had left its mark on his flesh and hair. "What will happen to us now?" she asked.

"Things haven't been settled. Until today, we weren't sure Jack would turn himself in."

"Turn himself in? How easy you make that sound."

"What do you want me to say?"

"Nothing." She caught the word before it could become a cry. Still, speaking took all her strength, that and battling her unwanted surroundings. "This morning my uncle told me his legs were played out. A warrior should remain proud, not be driven to the ground like this."

"I can't help what happened, or the way you feel about it. I wish to hell I could, but I can't."

"Why did you bring me in here? There is nothing left for us to say."

"The hell there isn't. I've got to know how you feel about this."

"Why?" she challenged even as tears pressed at her until she thought she might explode. She heard the muffled sounds of men and horses, wagons and weapons, but they didn't matter. Nothing did except for the stench and heat of this tent, and the man who shared it with her. "Would that change what is going to happen?"

The muscles around his mouth tightened. "No. But damnit, we've been through a lot together. I want—"

"I want to be left alone. To mourn the loss of everything I hold dear. To try to find the strength to face the rest of my life."

"Oh, God."

"You do not believe in a god, remember?" Why was she attacking him? Was this the only way she could keep from falling apart?

"It doesn't matter, Luash. Nothing does except what's going on inside you."

He cared. Of course he did. He wouldn't be here with her if he didn't. But his compassion frightened her. She was standing at the edge of a cliff with no room to turn around and only blackness ahead of her. If she couldn't find her courage, she might cling to Jed and sob out her fear for the future, but eventually his arms would no longer be enough and she would have to face that darkness again. Alone. "What I feel, Jed, does not concern you."

She thought he was going to strike her. For little more than a heartbeat, she saw rage in him. Then anger was replaced by something she lacked the strength to explore. "You can't believe that," he said. "After everything we've been through, you can't."

"What have *we* been through? Have you spent the days and nights since we last saw each other running, hiding, afraid on the very land that should have brought you peace? Did you fall asleep knowing the man you had given your body to was among those hunting you down?"

He reached toward her, then stopped, looking like a wolf who senses danger. "I was afraid it would be like this between us. Either that or—or you would be dead."

Dead? He'd feared that for her? But Eagle— "I do not want to talk to you, Jed. I hurt . . . my heart . . . I belong with my people; I was wrong to come with you."

"Were you?" he asked, the question so gentle that she couldn't hold onto her anger, her grief, her hatred of her surroundings. "I don't think so, not if we're ever going to resolve what's tearing us apart."

"You ask me to forget who we are, to believe we were both born today? I cannot. I do not want to."

"I don't believe you."

How did he know her so well? Desperate to keep her growing despair concealed, she opened her mouth to remind him that they'd been already ripped apart and nothing would ever put them back together. Instead of arguments and anger, only a whimper slipped past her lips.

"I'm sorry," he whispered as he drew her into his arms. "I'm so sorry."

He couldn't change what had happened to her ancestors' world. Why did she think that blaming him would take away the pain? "I hurt, Jed," she moaned from the shelter and danger of his chest. "My heart, my spirit—all I want is the wind in my face. Is that too much to ask for?"

He didn't answer, and she felt herself drowning in the silence. No, he couldn't give her the wind or mend her heart. All he had to offer were his arms. And maybe his understanding.

But to turn to him instead of one of her own kind? To have walked away from her family because a white man asked her to—

Why couldn't she think?

Why did she feel as if she was dying?

18

Fort Klamath had changed in the nearly three years since Luash had last seen it. The collection of crude wooden buildings were still sheltered by evergreens, but a new stockade had been built from heavy, fresh-cut logs driven into the ground and the fort now pulsed with life and white man's power.

Sitting next to Whe-cha, Luash thought only briefly of what her mother had endured at this place. The long wagon ride from the Land of Burned Out Fires had numbed her, stripped her down until only fear and heartache and resignation remained.

During the journey, Jed had been a silent and brooding man whose eyes said endless things Luash didn't want to acknowledge. The chasm-deep differences between them, which had always simmered beneath the surface, had burst forth to swamp her. He was captor, she captive.

It didn't matter that he hadn't put a bullet in her or thrown a rope over her. He was part of that terrible and massive thing called army and she couldn't forgive him for that. Neither could she forgive him for the chains around Kientpoos's ankles and the four helpless Modocs who'd been gunned down right after their capture. The day was clear and bright and warm with birds singing and the wind playing; in her heart it was winter again.

When the wagon stopped, she and the others were immediately herded into the small, high-walled, shadowed stockade. In the distance, mountains and trees beckoned, but in here there was barely room for her to lay down. Once again she was forced to fight the sense that the teeth of a steel trap had closed around her. Heat reached her, heat and dust and sometimes the smell of pitch and pine, which helped a little; but because there was so much noise, she no longer heard the birds, and the stockade walls blocked out the wind she'd embraced her entire life.

Kientpoos had been hauled off to a small, solid building with only a single window. Her heart wrenched at the thought of him forced to sit in there, separated from his family and Mother Earth, heavy chains on his ankles, waiting for white man's law.

Eagle, she thought bitterly. Eagle hadn't heard her pleas! Swamped by despair, she stumbled over to Whe-cha. Always before, she had felt like an older sister to her uncle's wife. Today, however, it was Whe-cha who comforted her.

For most of that first day, she and the others stood in small, frightened groups asking useless questions about what would happen to them now. No one knew what a trial meant, just that it was something Kientpoos and other braves had to endure; they had no idea where they would be sent once their time at Fort Klamath was over.

She was a prisoner. Over and over again she struggled to make sense of the word, but every time it began to invade her heart, she recoiled. She could think of only one thing at a time—how would they be fed; would they be given sleeping blankets; would the angry settlers make good on their threats of more killing? Most of all, she thought about the man outside the stockade, the gray-eyed man who'd once shared his body with her and now might be meeting with those who wanted all Modocs to live like cattle.

* * *

The captives had been at Fort Klamath for three days when Jed first walked into the crowded stockade with its smell of unwashed bodies and fear. For a moment it was all he could do not to turn and leave, but if she could survive these conditions, so could he—at least briefly.

Already, the Indians had begun to turn the enclosure into a home of sorts by arranging their few belongings in separate, mostly neat piles. After the way they'd spent the winter, they were used to sleeping in close confinement and, he reassured himself, took comfort from each other's presence.

But Luash trusted in Eagle. Eagle had given her strength at a time when many might have given in to despair. Her spirit couldn't reach her in here. What was that doing to her?

Aware of hostile and frightened eyes on him, he walked slowly past small knots of ragged Modocs until his senses told him she was near. Stopping, he looked around, his hand a deliberate distance from his handgun even as he cursed the soldier in himself that wouldn't allow him to remove it. These were mostly women and children; the few warriors who hadn't been separated from them had no fight left in them. For too many, only their eyes remained alive.

At last he saw her. She was almost unrecognizable. Her hair hung limply over her shoulders, which slumped slightly, aging her. She wore the oversized deerskin shirt he'd once taken off her, now caught at the waist with a short length of rope. Her bare feet were dusty, her legs scratched from trudging through brush during those last days of running. Her hands hung useless at her sides. Still, she met his gaze boldly and made no attempt to hide from him. Her eyes were magnificent, alive and angry.

Now that he was standing face to face with her, he realized he had no idea what he was going to say to her. A thousand things had crowded his mind when he had finally been allowed to leave

Colonel Davis's side, but now, seeing her deplorable condition and sensing her still-simmering fierce pride, nothing mattered except adding fuel to that pride and keeping her eyes alive.

"Have you had enough to eat?" he forced himself to ask. "Enough water?"

She shrugged. "What will happen to him?"

"Jack?"

"Kientpoos."

"Kientpoos. There's going to be a trial." He looked around but there was no place they could go for privacy. "I need to talk to you alone. As long as you're with me, you can walk out of here."

"Because I am your prisoner?"

He should have been prepared for her hard question. He thought he was; still, the words stung. "Call it what you want, Luash. What I'm saying is, if you want to understand what's going on, the only way you'll get the truth is from me."

For an instant he thought she was going to turn and run, hide from what she couldn't possibly want to hear. Instead, trembling so faintly that maybe he only imagined it, she nodded and waited for him to lead the way. He told the guard she'd be back later, not caring what the man thought of his behavior.

Once they'd stepped outside the stockade, he pointed toward the thick pines that surrounded Fort Klamath. He told Luash that if she decided she couldn't live as a prisoner of war, he wouldn't try to stop her from fleeing.

Her gaze went to her surroundings, and he sensed her spirit, her soul, something, clinging to the trees, taking nourishment from them. "Where would I go? If our enemies see me, they will kill me."

He nearly reminded her that she believed Eagle had blessed her life, but just in time he noticed that she no longer carried an eagle's feather in her hair and instead said, "I don't want it to be like this." They'd reached the first of the trees; he could see her taking long,

deep breaths. When the sun hit her full in the face, her features gen-
tled and the lines around her mouth softened.

She hadn't looked at him since walking out of the stockade.
Now she turned toward him, shoulders no longer slumped but
fiercely squared. Behind her grew countless trees that could easily
swallow her. Irrationally, that was what he wanted. Even if he
never saw her again, at least she would be free.

But she was right. What kind of life would she have, alone, and
in constant danger of being hunted down? Damn, he hated his job!
Hated everything that had happened here since the first trapper discovered the Land of Burned Out Fires.

Shaken by his thoughts, he began telling her what she needed
to know. The Modocs had been removed from where they'd been
captured because he and the other officers feared that agitated
whites might grab Jack and the other Indian leaders and kill them
before justice could be served.

Now Colonel Davis was waiting for final word from the president before proceeding with that justice. About the only thing that
had been decided was that since no one could positively identify
those who'd killed the settlers back in November, Hooker Jim and
those who'd been with him would not be put on trial.

In fact, because he'd helped the army find Jack, Hooker was free
to move around the fort. On the other hand, Curley Headed Doctor, who'd tried to escape during the journey to Fort Klamath, was
being kept locked up. Scarface, who'd been identified as the leader
behind the Thomas-Wright massacre, had become a kind of folk
hero because of what he'd accomplished with only a handful of warriors.

"It's not so much folks around here," Jed admitted, "but people back East, protesting that the Modocs haven't been treated fair.
They want someone to root for; that person's going to be Scarface."

"Ha-kar-Jim free? His hands are covered in blood! He betrayed my uncle! If he had not called him a squaw woman, Kientpoos would not have killed General Canby."

"No one put the rifle in Kientpoos's hand, Luash. He acted of his own free will."

Her look said he couldn't possibly understand what it was like to be chief of the Modocs; she was right. "Cho-Cho is healthy?" she asked, abruptly changing the subject. Jed had seen little of the scarred warrior because his duties had kept him with Colonel Davis nearly every waking hour, but told Luash that the man seemed well.

"What does the colonel want from you?"

"We're trying to decide what's going to happen to all of you."

"You are deciding my life? It is no longer mine?"

He hated having to weather her anger and try to answer questions that weren't really questions; yet wasn't that better than the apathy, the quiet despair that surrounded her uncle? "That's the way war is. The victor makes the decisions."

"And the loser is a dog on a rope. How proud you must be."

Proud? Sick was more like it. "This isn't getting us anywhere. Neither of us can change what happened and what's going to happen."

"You are an army chief. You meet with the commander; he must listen to you."

Instead of trying to explain how complicated such things were, he simply waited her out. "There is much fear among my people. Are we going to be killed? the children ask. The women want to know if they will be turned over to the army men and the braves— some say they count their lives in days. While you and your leaders meet and decide our tomorrows, we are trapped deer, waiting for bullets."

That's what had put the age in her eyes, he realized, wondering whether Modoc children would live to become adults. His need to reassure her that one day she'd again have land to call her own became almost more than he could bear, but what could he say?

Until her uncle's fate had been decided, she and the others would remain penned up like the deer she'd just mentioned. If it was in his power, he would give her feet wings so she could run, so she could—

But she didn't want to be alone, and he didn't know if he could go through the rest of his life without seeing her.

"No one's going to kill babies or women."

"You can be sure of this? There are many whites who wish the Modocs were no more."

"They're not in charge, Luash. The U.S. government is."

Her look said she couldn't trust something that had done nothing except fight her and her people. "I am so tired," she said, "so tired of being afraid and angry and helpless."

He'd come to her determined not to stare too deeply into her eyes or get close enough to hear her heartbeat, but he'd only been lying to himself. How this had happened, how he'd come to care so much about someone he thought he'd spend his life hating, he couldn't say. All he knew was that she was the most beautiful, sensitive, intelligent woman he'd ever known; he'd do everything within his power to end the pain in her eyes.

When he held out his hands, she stared up at him for so long that he felt as if he'd been stripped naked, then, silent, she slipped into his arms. He was right; she had lost weight. Her frame had no more substance than that of a newborn fawn, and if he hadn't sensed her courage and determination, he would have been terrified for her.

"You're going to be all right," he promised, an empty promise that burst from him nonetheless. "Wherever you're sent, at least you'll have your people with you." *And me? Where will I be?*

"Not all of them."

He pulled her tight, then, stumbling a little, led her into the woods. Surrounded by trees, drinking in the deep, rich scent of a summer-heated forest, he wondered if she'd said her good-bye to the lava beds, wondered if she truly understood that she'd never see them again. "Talk to me," he whispered. "Tell me what you're thinking."

"You have done your job, Jed. Brought the Modocs to their knees." Before he could gather his arguments, she took a deep, shuddering breath. "I am afraid for my uncle. He is never far from my thoughts."

"You can't help him, Luash. Think about yourself." He struggled against the man in him that wanted to make love to her until neither of them thought of anything except need and satisfying that need. "Take care of yourself. Concentrate on what you can do."

She tried to pull away, but he continued to hold her. "You made me listen to a white man's words," she said. "Showed me that you are more than someone trained and paid to kill Indians. I do not want to care about you. I do not want to care!"

But she did. That was the hell and the wonder of it. "I didn't either," he admitted. "You came into my life and turned me inside out. I could hate you for that."

"Then do. It is easier that way."

Maybe he could still hate her, if they hadn't made love; if he hadn't seen her spirit eagle; if he hadn't told her how lost he'd felt when his parents died. "I can't."

He watched her lips form the word "why," asked himself how the hell he was going to answer. Then she shook her head and blinked back tears. "Neither can I. I want—but I can't."

He nearly told her he would walk away from here with her. They'd find a place deep in the mountains where none of this hell they'd been living could touch them. He'd learn how to hunt and trap and she'd pick nuts and berries and leaves and make meals for them. They'd—maybe they'd go to Crater Lake and she'd tell him the Modoc legend of the crater's beginning.

He'd stop being a soldier.

She'd stop being a member of a vanquished tribe.

"I do not want to be here," she said abruptly. "To smell earth and trees, to hear birds sing and know I cannot join them—it is too hard."

"You'd rather be locked up?"

"My heart is in prison. My body does not care." She pulled free of him. Then, before he guessed what she was going to do, she grabbed him around the neck and kissed him, a hard and desperate kiss that tore him apart.

He came at her with equal strength and desperation, all but ripping her dress off her in his need. For a moment he was afraid that she would fight him—if she did, he knew he would let her go. Instead, she continued to cling to him, hands and mouth possessing him until it felt as if he might explode.

The soft ground was littered with generations of pine needles and the wind was hot and full of summer. He lay her down, all dark and moving beneath him, and yanked at what was left of his clothes. He didn't try to meet her eyes, didn't want to know what he might find there.

When she reared up to clamp her hands around his neck again, he grabbed her to him, rocking, his heart full of silent agony. Hurting as he hadn't hurt since he stood over his parents' graves. Wanting her as he'd never wanted anything since the last time he'd walked on what had once been his family's land.

Luash sensed his battle, not just because they were sealed together and he was breathing as if he'd been running for his entire life, but because the same insane desperation claimed her. They didn't belong together, were ruled by different forces. Still, her body screamed and begged until she no longer heard any other voice.

No longer knew anything except needing him.

The trial of Kientpoos and five others who'd been identified as participating in General Canby's murder was set to begin right after the Fourth of July. Jed accepted that decision with a sense of resignation that was almost relief. If nothing else, at least the endless wrangling was over.

No one other than he thought it important that the Modocs have legal representation. He'd unsuccessfully argued the point with the six men who made up the military commission that would try the case. At least the commission had agreed with him that the prisoners deserved an interpreter, since some of them spoke only a few words of English.

"You know who should do it, don't you?" Wilfred asked as he and Jed left Colonel Davis's barracks. "Luash understands English better than most; she'll make sure Jack knows everything that's going on."

"I don't want Luash there. Toby can do it; Jack trusts her."

"Now you're making Luash's decisions for her? No matter how hard it is on her, she'd want to be on hand. You said—"

"I know what I said! But you and I both know how this is going to turn out. Why put her through any more hell than she's already in?"

"Why protect her now; it's a little late for that, isn't it?"

Jed was careful not to look over at the stockade where Luash had been held for nearly three weeks. He'd seen her occasionally since their frantic coupling in the woods, but they hadn't spoken a word. He'd told himself it was best this way, that there was nothing for them to say to each other.

"You know what I'm seeing here?" Wilfred continued after a too brief silence. "All right, I'll tell you. She's got a hold on you that you can't possibly break."

"You're wrong." Even if Wilfred was right, it did not matter. "As soon as the trial's over, Custer wants me back in the Black Hills. I got the word yesterday."

"Shit. Are you going to go?"

They'd nearly reached the oft-moved tent where he and Wilfred lived. If he kept a firm grip on himself, he might be able to enter it without first looking at the stockade. "What concern is it of yours?"

"I'm making it my concern. If you get your marching orders, will you leave?"

She won't be here much longer; there won't be anything to keep me here. Despite his best efforts, he couldn't keep his legs moving. He stopped, started to turn toward Wilfred, wound up staring at the walls that held Luash prisoner and separated her from the sky, sun, and land she loved. "I don't know. Things have changed for me. I've changed."

"Because *she's* gotten to you. And once her uncle's fate has been decided, she'll be forced to go somewhere she's never been before. Maybe alone. Have you told her about that part? Does she know what the president's considering?"

Bile rose in Jed's throat. "No."

"The Modocs are going to hear about it sooner or later. Wouldn't it be better if she got it straight from you?"

"That information's under wraps and you know it. How could I tell her that the president's thinking of spreading the Modocs over every damn reservation in the country so they'll never constitute a threat, or even the possibility of a threat again? She's got enough to worry about with the trial coming—and what the hell do you care, anyway?"

Wilfred nodded in the direction of the stockade. "Strange thing about a war that goes on for more than half a year. It gets a man to thinking."

Jed waited for Wilfred to continue. His stomach felt as tight as it had when he first saw the president's cable detailing the reasons behind what he was considering—the devastating ripping apart of a once-proud people.

"They're folks, Jed," Wilfred said, "just like us. They don't want much, just a place to be. Only it's been taken from them. That's not something I'm proud of."

Neither am I. "You're right," he admitted. "She has a right to be there. A need. Maybe that's the only thing I can still give her."

Luash stepped inside the dark, thick-walled building, careful not to breathe too deeply of the stench of many bodies. One of the guards had brought her a white, nearly new blouse and skirt this morning, saying that they were from Jed Britton. For too long she'd simply clutched the clothes to her while Whe-cha silently regarded her. At that moment, Luash wanted nothing more out of life than for Eagle to leave wherever he'd hidden himself and touch her with his courage. But these garments were from Jed, not her spirit. She couldn't hide from Jed's challenge, his understanding. If she had the courage to attend the trial, he wanted her to feel proud of her appearance, but all he had to give her was this.

Using some of the Modocs' precious water, she'd scrubbed at her hair and flesh, then discarded her too-loose, too-short deerskin dress and put on the strange garments. She had no shoes but it didn't matter. She was doing this difficult thing because she loved the man whose life was at stake, and because it was a way to be near Jed—Jed, whom she never wanted to see again. As she was leaving the stockade, Whe-cha had hurried up to her and pressed a bead necklace in her hand. "Please," she'd begged, "give this to my husband. Tell him—tell him I have not forgotten him."

The sparsely furnished and ill-lit room was already full of soldiers in newly cleaned uniforms, settlers sitting off to one side muttering among themselves, six shackled prisoners, and a long table with six stern-faced men sitting behind it. Ignoring everyone, she hurried over to Kientpoos and dropped to her knees before him. A sob clawed at her throat; she felt a heartbeat away from screaming. In a choked whisper, she told him she loved him and had prayed to Eagle for him.

"I do not want my wives and daughter to see me like this,"

Kientpoos said, indicating the chains around his legs. "If they ask, tell them nothing."

Although she didn't know how she could possibly keep her emotions locked within her, she nodded. When she clutched Kientpoos's hands, they felt dry and soft—the hands of a man without enough to do. One of the guards tapped her on the shoulder and ordered her to sit with the spectators. She stood, but before she obeyed the guard, she slipped the necklace Whe-cha had given her over Kientpoos's head. "You are loved," she whispered. "Never forget that. Whe-cha loves you."

Ignoring a rickety, straight-backed chair, she settled herself on the floor a few feet from her uncle. Only then did she look around for Jed. After a moment, she spotted him, sitting next to Colonel Davis. The room was like a disturbed bees' nest, all restless sound and movement. Only Jed sat perfectly still, his attention on her and not the army leader, who'd just said something to him. Jed's eyes took her back to the wild, impossible moments they'd spent drinking from each other's bodies.

She wanted to hate him; she knew it would never be that simple.

The trial barely had begun when she realized that something was horribly wrong. Not only did the men behind the table speak so rapidly that Kaitchkana could barely translate, but the shackled men had no one to speak for them. They were asked if they had someone to act as something called defense counsel. When Kientpoos said they didn't, one of the counsel men said it was fine with him and his companions if the Modocs acted as their own lawyers. Slolux and Barncho, men with the minds of children, looked around them uncomprehendingly, then went back to staring at their shackles.

She shot Jed a sharp glance, but he only shook his head. Rage boiled through her with such fury that it was several minutes be-

fore she could concentrate again on what was happening. She
didn't understand these things called defense counsels and lawyers;
what she did know was that if her uncle had to speak for himself,
he would speak like a Modoc—and none of these white men would
listen. The same was true of those the army called John Schonchin,
Boston Charley, and Black Jim. Slolux and Barncho were only interested in the chains around their ankles.

Kaitchkana's miner husband, who had been there when General Canby was killed, was the first to speak. After talking at length
about what had happened from the moment the disastrous peace
meeting began, he admitted he'd started to run away when the
shooting started and hadn't seen anything.

Kaitchkana, speaking first in English and then Modoc, came
after her husband. She had, she admitted, seen everything and
could point with certainty at those who'd killed the general and the
Sunday doctor and who had tried to scalp Meacham.

Although she'd seen the fight from a distance and had heard
about it endlessly since then, Luash felt both spellbound and heartsick by Kaitchkana's somber tale. If only she'd been able to convince Jed of the danger to General Canby, if only he'd been able to
make his leader listen—

When the commission men pushed back their chairs and people began moving about, she realized she'd seen sitting without
moving for most of the day. She scrambled to her feet, trying to remember what had been said last. Something about the prisoners
being able to give their testimony tomorrow and hoping to wind
things up soon after that.

Ignoring the guards' objections, Luash again pushed her way
to her uncle's side. Showing him the bedraggled feather she'd carried next to her breast for weeks, she told him it was her last gift
from Eagle. She tried to give it to him, but a soldier knocked it from
her hand. She stooped quickly and picked it up, but not before
someone stepped on it.

"Let it be, Luash," she heard Jed whisper. "You can't change what's going to happen."

"You are wrong!" Her outcry died on a strangled whimper. When Jed pushed her toward the door, she briefly resisted, then, spent, did as he ordered. Behind her, she heard the rattle of chains as Kientpoos and the others were led away.

"I didn't want you here," Jed said, "but Wilfred was right; the decision had to be yours."

"I cannot help my uncle." She still clutched the flattened feather.

"No one can. You don't have to go back in there." He indicated the stockade. "Come with me; we'll talk."

"Talk? Will that change what is going to happen?"

He didn't answer, but it didn't matter, because she knew what he'd say. The last time they'd been together, she'd fallen on him as if by making love with him she could make the world go away. Now she knew better. "My people will want to know what happened. Whe-cha, I must—"

"Later." Walking beside her, not touching, he began moving toward the trees that had sheltered them before. She didn't think anyone was watching them this afternoon; the others were too busy talking about what had happened at the trial to pay attention to two quiet people—two people as different as winter and summer.

"When this is over," Jed began and then stopped. "After the trial—there's something you need to know."

"What?"

"About—about what's going to happen to me. Custer knows things are winding up here. I have no reason to stay."

"No," she made herself say. "No reason at all."

"Besides." He held the word for so long that she imagined it drifting slowly out on the wind. "You won't be here much longer either."

"I know." She wouldn't look at him; she couldn't. "We will be sent to a reservation."

"Maybe more than one."

A warning like the rifle shot which brought them together so many months ago ricochetted through her. She tried forcing herself to ask him what he was talking about, went as far as opening her mouth. Then she made the mistake of looking up at him. In his eyes lay darkness.

Near terror, she shied away and stared up at the late afternoon sky. It was blue today, a clean and flawless color that made her want to weep. How many times had she seen Eagle on a day like this? The sight of him drifting almost lazily toward her had always filled her with joy; she needed that joy with a fierceness that nearly brought her to her knees.

"Tell me what you're feeling," he said softly.

"Alone," she told him after a long silence. "I feel alone."

"I'm here."

"It is not enough."

"I know." His voice caught.

Any anger she'd had toward him died. She couldn't say what replaced it. "I want to be a child again, but I cannot. I must find the courage to face what will come . . . alone."

He waited a beat before speaking and she knew how much he wanted to rip that last word from her. "You still have Eagle."

"No," she said with an honesty that should have torn her apart but came easily. Too easily. "He is no longer with me. I think . . . maybe he has seen inside my heart and knows it is dying. He knows the Modocs are a broken people."

19

Luash was back in the stockade before dark, telling everyone about the trial. When she said that others might attend if they wished, they simply shook their heads and asked her more questions. As night quieted Fort Klamath, she watched what she could see of the stars come out, slowly at first and then one upon another like joyous children after a storm.

Something about what Jed had said had left her stomach knotted, but when she tired to find the source of her fear, it slipped away, along with the comfort his presence had given her.

Honoring Kientpoos's request, Luash told Whe-cha that his thoughts were of her and that he now proudly wore her gift. She said nothing of the shackles still around his legs. Then, although Whe-cha wanted to hear more about the trial, she sought a distant corner of the stockade, hoping she would be left alone.

Again the sky called to her, whispered its summer song and brought back memories of her childhood, when she'd first become aware of how much a part of the Earth she was. Eagle lived in that night sky, claimed it for himself. She knew that because he always carried its essence with him when he came to her. Although her heart felt wounded, she sent Eagle a painful message.

Be free. Even when I am gone, spread your wings over this land and find another to comfort. Fly with your mate; catch the wind and ride it to where the other spirits live. Settle yourself over your children and teach them your wisdom. Give them your courage. And, please, please—leave me a little of that courage so I can face what I must.

Tears streaming down her cheeks, she sank to her knees, eyes still on the cool, distant shards of light, and waited for the moon. Waited for an answer.

A shadow. Maybe an illusion. No. There, just beyond the trees that clung to the mountain behind the stockade. For a moment, her thoughts caught on fragile memories of what she and Jed had done there, but they soon faded. Tonight, Eagle was everything.

The shadow took on more form, became a living, breathing essence. Great wings outspread, Eagle rode the wind. She thought her spirit might come closer, hoped he would seek her out in this place that was surrounded by white man's walls, but Eagle didn't and her tears became hot.

Still, her guardian spirit didn't leave. Instead, moving so slowly that she couldn't believe he didn't feel the Earth's pull, he drifted over the trees. Her heart felt as if it had been shattered and yet a spark of warmth remained and began to grow. Eagle hadn't deserted her. Yes, the wordless connection between them had become less, might never again be strong and clean and pure, but tonight Eagle touched her heart with his freedom.

And she understood something else in the way he slowly circled a rocky outcropping near the top of the mountain.

The trial continued for nine days that bled one into another and made it impossible for Luash to concentrate on anything else, even Jed, who was there the entire time. Although it all but destroyed her to have to sit in that close, white-man-smelling room every day, it would be harder not to go.

Not once did she speak, not even when Ha-kar-Jim told the commissioners he didn't understand why Kientpoos no longer considered him a friend. She wanted to scream at the young brave that he was a traitor, that he should be the one on trial, but because her words would change nothing, she simply glared at the man who'd forced her uncle to murder a general. Finally the man who called himself a judge said that when they came back in the morning, he would tell them what he had decided.

As she got to her feet, Jed stopped her, whispering that there was something he needed to talk to her about. She stared at him and shook her head, muttering "not yet" over and over again. He nodded, brushed his fingers against the back of her hand, then walked away. The memory of that feather touch stayed with her through the endless night.

"It has been decided that you will be hung on October third," the judge said, nodding at the six prisoners. "That date, nearly three months from now, has been chosen because certain arrangements must be made first. The president and secretary of the Interior are involved in that process. Decisions must be made; those decisions take time."

The harsh-faced man talked on, his attention not on the Modocs whose lives he had just ended, but on white men who either nodded agreement or grumbled about the long delay. *You will be hung.*

You will be hung.

Eyes burning, Luash stared at her uncle but he sat staring down at his shackles. It was as if the spark of life had already left him, and he was simply waiting for his body to go to wherever his spirit now lived. She sensed people getting to their feet, heard voices without meaning, watched as the condemned Modocs stood and slowly shuffled out. She longed to run after her uncle and clutch him to her breast. To have the power to send him to live with Eagle.

"Luash. It's over."

Over. Hanged.

"Do not," she warned when Jed tried to help her to her feet. "I do not want you to touch me. Not ever again."

Pain and something else, maybe understanding, etched his features but she couldn't think about him. Instead, barely able to control the storm building inside her, she fell in line behind those waiting their turn to step outside.

It was another sun-flooded day. The breeze brought the scents of sage, pine, and earth. Of life. A few clouds, sharply white against the pure sky, drifted overhead, teasing her with their false promise of freedom.

Jed joined her. "Talk to me," he insisted. "Tell me what you're feeling."

Didn't he know? "I want to be alone." Her attention slid to the distant rocky crag where she'd last seen Eagle. "I will not weep in front of you—or any white man."

"Crying won't change anything, Luash. He's going to die."

"He does not care; his spirit has already been stripped from him. Without freedom"—she pointed at the mountain—"without freedom there is no life. His soul—it is our belief that a Modoc's soul leaves his body through his head at death. A rope around his neck will trap it, allow it to die with him."

Jed took a ragged breath. She glanced at him, then jerked away, unable to absorb the dark emotion simmering in his eyes. Once they had spoken of many things—of traditions, of generations of Modoc belief, of how losing their land had killed his parents. She remembered all that and mourned the loss. But now, "There is nothing left to be said. After my uncle and the others have been hung, the Modocs will be taken from here. When that happens, you will go where the army sends you."

He took another ragged breath. "I already have my orders."

They were no longer near the courtroom where Kientpoos had been condemned to death. Somehow Jed had led her through the settlers, army men, Modocs, and loud-talking newcomers who filled Fort Klamath, until they stood at the edge of the fort. The trees called to her.

"Custer wants me back with him as soon as I can get there."

Custer. The Indian fighter. Rage, like a violent river attacking its banks, surged through her. She whirled on Jed and struck his cheek with all the strength in her. He staggered back but did nothing to defend himself.

"Go!" she screamed, not caring who might hear or what punishment might be meted out to her. "Go to him then! Pick up your rifle and kill again."

"No."

No? She felt as if she was being split in two, wondered if there would be anything left of her once their time together was over. "Tell me." Blood trickled from Jed's nose but he didn't seem to notice.

"I've asked for an extension; there's something I have to do first." He paused. "Let's get the hell out of here."

When she looked in the direction he indicated, she realized that many of the settlers and soldiers were staring at them. Half stumbling, she hurried into the woods, sought the protection of deep shadows. Jed kept pace with her, a powerful presence that lingered quietly within her even though she'd thought herself consumed by Kientpoos's fate—by her people's fate.

"Don't run from me."

His words stopped her. She spun toward him. Like her, he was now sheltered by the shade cast by countless trees. The woods were alive with sound as birds, insects, and animals went about the task of living, unaware that the people who had always shared this land with them could no longer call it their home.

She turned her fear and grief on Jed. "I wish I had never met you, never shown you my world."

"I don't believe you."

He didn't know her heart. Did he? Wondering how long she could keep from crying, she pressed her finger to her lips to ask him to be silent. To listen.

"I know these sounds," she told him. "The smell here. That knowledge lives deep within me and flows through my veins. This is where our spirits will always live because it is truly the Smiles of God. What will happen to us now? Will our hearts find peace on another land? Without our leaders, what will become of us?"

Midnight was back in his eyes, spearing her. "Don't do this to me, Luash. Not now."

Jed began walking again and after a moment she fell in line behind him. She didn't belong here. Her place was beside Whe-cha and Kientpoos's daughter as they struggled to accept what the white man had decided. But what lurked in Jed's eyes kept her with him.

Deeper and deeper they went into the woods. The air became cool and damp, the ground soft from generations of fallen pine needles. Great green branches all but blocked out the sky, sheltered her from the world beyond this place, brought her in touch with herself and the only emotion left to her.

How many times had she denied her body's hunger for Jed? How many tears had she fought when thoughts of what they might have become if they weren't enemies pounded around her? He, a soldier, had a gentleness to him that touched her soul. When she spoke of Eagle or the gods who live on the top of the great snow mountain, he listened. And when he told her what it had been like for a seventeen-year-old to watch the men around him die, she'd cried for that terrified boy.

Finally Jed stopped and waited for her, his features blanketed by green depth. Behind him, she could just make out the steep, barren rock where she'd last seen Eagle.

"I don't know what we're doing coming clear out here," Jed told her. "I guess I had to be doing something and there wasn't anything except walking. I had to put what happened today behind me."

She waited for him to say more but he didn't. Something was building inside him, something that might be fury but perhaps was sorrow. Maybe both. She should be caught in a whirlpool of agony, but her mind had closed itself to everything except him and the incredible impossibility of their being together.

"I don't want to go back," he said. "For the first time in my life, I don't want to be a soldier."

How horrible it must be to be afraid of what went to the core of him. Thinking to give him distance from his thoughts, Luash pointed at the knifelike rocks that seemed to stretch into the sky and told him that she'd seen Eagle land up there. "Maybe that is his new home," she whispered. "I want to believe he is here because he wants to remain near me, but maybe he has chosen those rocks to shelter a nest."

"Maybe. Luash—"

"I want to go up there. To climb to the top and see if Eagle is a father."

"We'd never make it before dark."

We. "But we would be closer to my spirit; maybe Eagle will come to me even if you are with me."

"Maybe," he said. After a moment she walked around him and began climbing. Before long, her fingers stung from gripping sharp edges, and her calves ached from the strain. Sometimes she was forced to crawl on hands and knees, but she couldn't stop. Ahead was Eagle's home. If she saw it, touched the massive nest that she prayed sheltered his offspring, maybe she would find the courage for tomorrow.

On she went. Jed warned her to slow down, to be more careful, but she could not. The closer she came to the wind-beaten mountaintop, the greater her sense of urgency, her belief that she *had* to do this thing. Finally, when she wasn't sure how much strength was left in her, she spotted a familiar movement high overhead. Even though her eyes were blurry from fatigue, she knew she'd found Eagle, her Eagle.

"There," she whispered in awe as the great bird pointed its sharp talons toward the top of the crag and pulled its wings close to its body to aid its descent. "That is where he lives."

With a sharp cry, Eagle swooped downward and disappeared. In her effort to see where he'd gone, she nearly lost her balance, would have if Jed hadn't caught her. "You've done enough, Luash. It isn't safe—"

"No! Not yet. I must touch—"

She thought he would try to stop her, but he didn't. Instead, he placed his hands around her waist and lifted her onto the next ledge. She extended her hand to help him up beside her, but he shook his head. "You're not strong enough. Besides, there isn't room for both of us there. Can you see anything?"

She couldn't, but to her right was another ledge and beyond that several more. Leaving Jed, focusing on nothing except what her heart told her to do, she kept moving. Something gouged her palm. Her legs, trembling from weakness, couldn't carry her much further, but she was so close. So close.

Eagle's nest was still above her, perched on the crag's tip like a reckless man's hat. Dizziness assaulted her and she had to hold onto a sharp rock to keep from losing her balance.

"Are you all right?" Jed called from below. "Please, don't go any further."

She didn't have to. As she blinked and carefully lifted a hand to shield her eyes, she saw there was something in the nest. Two birds, huge black- and white-feathered mounds. Her heart told her this was Eagle and his mate. Beneath them, nestled safely in the bottom of the nest, she prayed, were the eggs.

For a long time after she returned to him, Jed didn't say anything. She wanted to tell him everything she'd seen and express her hope that there would soon be eaglets, but the experience remained a warm and wonderful pocket within her that she wasn't yet ready to share with anyone, even him.

Finally though, they were back where the fort sounds fought with those of the forest. She would have to return to the stockade and face Kientpoos's family. She would have to ask unanswerable questions about what would happen to them once their chief and five other men had been hung.

"Wait."

She stood with her shoulder a scant distance from his, increasingly aware of the heat radiating out from him. For a little while she would stay near that heat, would not allow herself to look beyond this moment. "How do you feel?" he asked. "Seeing Eagle, did that make it easier for you?"

"Maybe. I do not know."

"I hoped it would."

"It did, for awhile." Jed seemed more spirit than man now. The realization reminded her of the secrets she'd seen buried in his eyes earlier. "But Eagle did not come to me. I do not understand . . . maybe I don't want to understand."

"Why not?"

How she hated his hard questions! "A Modoc who has lost her heart has no need for a spirit."

"You haven't lost—"

"You do not know what is inside me."

"Yeah, Luash, I think I do."

Of course he did. Not only had he lost the land of his childhood, but as a boy had had to bury his parents. Then he'd entered a world filled with killing and tried to make himself one with that world. If he had succeeded in that, he wouldn't be with her today.

Overwhelmed, she pressed her fingers over his throat, smiling a little when she found the strong pulse there. "You may have believed you had no feelings for anyone except yourself; after what happened at Fort Phil Kearny, that way was safer." She didn't try to plan her words, only let them tumble from her. "But it was a lie. When you hear crying, you cry yourself. When—when my uncle hangs, you will feel my grief."

"Stop it."

He spoke so gently that she was able to wash the words under her. "Just before my people left the Land of Burned Out Fires, you found me in the dark. I think maybe you heard my heart beating. That is not a man who can go back to Custer and aim a rifle at a Sioux."

"Stop it."

"Do you not want to hear the truth?"

His features contorted, making him look first stricken and then angry. "It doesn't matter, Luash. What I do once I'm no longer needed here doesn't matter."

"Yes, it does."

"No." He covered her hand with his, slid her fingers under his uniform so that she now felt his flesh and the strength beneath that. They had done this before, tried to touch each other's hearts. "It doesn't, because . . . because soon there won't be a Modoc tribe."

No! she tried to scream but the word wouldn't come.

"I hate this. *Damn,* I hate this! But President Grant wants the Modoc families scattered."

"Scattered?"

"I'm sorry."

Feeling as if she was dying, she yanked free and stumbled backward. He stared at her, his eyes no longer holding anything inside him. One glance told her that he spoke the truth.

Shattered, she whirled and ran, not caring where her legs took her. The growing night whipped around her, sending messages of dark and quiet, of peace. All lies! Finally she came to a stumbling stop because her frantic flight had brought her to the stockade walls. Screaming silently, she began pounding the logs with her fists.

"Don't! For God's sake, don't!" Jed was right behind her, had stayed close throughout her race.

"Leave me alone! Leave me alone!"

"I can't. Luash—"

"No!" If he hadn't held up his hands to protect himself, she would have dug her nails into him. Locked in battle, a battle she knew he would win, she tried to hate him, tried to imagine him dead. "Not scattered. Together we are Modoc. Apart—no!"

"Grant's the president. What he says is the law."

"The law?" Her wrists felt on fire where he gripped them. "Are you its slave?"

"You don't understand."

She understood everything, at least the only things that mattered. "I will die," she whispered. "Alone, we will *all* die."

20

"You're fixin' to go clear across the country? What does Colonel Davis say about that?"

"All he cares is that he gets final word on what he's supposed to do with the Modocs. If I can accomplish that, he'll say I'm a miracle worker."

Wilfred's skeptical look came as no surprise, but Jed didn't care. It had been nearly two weeks since he'd watched Luash try to destroy the stockade door singlehandedly. The day after the trial ended, he'd been dispatched to the site of the Thomas-Wright massacre to make sure everything with any value had been recovered. Once that wrenching chore was over, he'd taken a small troop to the Modoc stronghold, where they'd collected what few belongings the Indians had left behind. He'd asked Wilfred to let Luash know where he was, but when he returned, his friend told him she'd refused even to acknowledge his presence.

Although he had tried talking to her several times in the two days he'd been back, she remained silent and unresponsive. Whenever he walked into the stockade, the captives' fear and disbelief assaulted him and it was all he could do not to tear down the confining walls himself. Was she right? Would it kill her people to be scattered across the country?

"Davis made it perfectly clear that what happens to the Modocs once they leave here doesn't interest him," he told Wilfred. "Just as long as they're no longer his responsibility."

"But you trying to change the mind of the president of the United States."

"Not just him. The secretary of the Interior too. According to what I heard, President Grant and Secretary Delano have been receiving petitions from people like the Quakers, who say the trial was a farce. That reporter, Atwell, told me the eastern newspapers are full of editorials about how Jack didn't get a chance to defend himself, how they all ought to be pardoned. That kind of pressure isn't going to go away. Someone needs to remind politicians of the outcry they'd have to put up with if they order the Modocs torn apart."

"Why should the president of the United States listen to you if, so far, he's ignoring the tide of sentiment against what's happening here?"

"I think it'll be hard for him to ignore a lieutenant who came clear across the country to make his point—a lieutenant not at all opposed to talking to the press, the Quakers, anyone who'll listen."

"Damnation. Jed, you're putting your neck, not to mention your career, on the line. Going against army policy—saying you're questioning something the army did—"

"What do you want me to do? Sit back and let the Modocs have their souls sucked out of them?"

Wilfred rammed his thumbs into his belt and rocked forward. "You concerned about the whole damn tribe or just one of them?"

Good question. Good and hard and a hell of a lot more than he wanted to face right now. He shrugged and shook his head. "I figure, I'll ride down to Redding and then take a train east. I talked to Meacham. When he went there, last winter, the trip took him just shy of three weeks. That'll give me more than enough time to do what I have to before the Modocs are shipped out. Before Jack's hung."

"What about your responsibility to Custer?"

"I'll send him a wire."

"Saying what? That you'll go back to hunting Sioux once you've pleaded for the Modocs?"

All through the hard two-day ride south to Redding, Jed kept his mind on what he would say to the most powerful man in the country—if he could get an audience with Grant. When he bought a train ticket and settled himself in for the long, muscle-jarring ride east, he told himself he wouldn't, under any circumstances, think about Luash, but it was a damned lie. The train had no sooner pulled out when he realized he wasn't looking at the scenery.

Instead, he remembered the look in her eyes when he forced her to listen to what he had to say. He was going to travel three thousand miles for her, he'd told her. He was going to sit down across from the president of the United States and tell the man that he couldn't break the Modocs apart as if they were stale bread being thrown to chickens.

"A powerful man three thousand miles away cares about a Modoc heart? It will never be," she'd said.

He hadn't bothered to try to argue her down. Instead, he'd stood with her, just outside that damnable stockade, and fought his body's demands. She wasn't his to take. She didn't want him anymore, if she ever had.

He was making this trip to settle his conscience; it wouldn't be like that if she hadn't shown him her world, hadn't given him a feather to carry next to his heart.

Jed reached the capital during the second week in August. Trying to ignore the heavy heat that made him long for a mountaintop, he checked himself into a hotel room—for the first time in his life—and then began making inquiries. Thanks to contacts made available to him as an army officer, he was granted an audience with both the president and secretary of the Interior. However, arranging for that appointment had eaten up ten days. While waiting, he met several times with officials of the Quaker church and the Universal Peace Group who'd petitioned for clemency for all Modocs. He talked to the press.

He also sent several cables to Wilfred asking about Luash. Wilfred's replies came sooner than he expected: Luash and the rest of the Modocs were fine physically. Although there'd been a lot of wrangling about it, the Indian Bureau finally had been assigned responsibility for providing the prisoners with new clothing. Many of the soldiers brought in for the war effort already had been deployed elsewhere or were being released from service. Those left were being kept busy with endless marches and the fort had been policed until it looked as clean as a parson's parlor.

"No one minds that the Modocs roam all over the fort these days," Wilfred concluded. "The ringleaders are still locked up of course, but Luash is free to go wherever she wants. She spends a lot of time in the mountains."

Looking for Eagle, Jed concluded. He no longer questioned the connection between the bird and the woman; he wasn't sure he'd had any doubts after the first time he saw them together. If it was in his power, he'd rope and hogtie that creature so it would always be there for her.

Only tied up, the eagle would probably die.

Just like her.

The thought of Luash losing her will to live sent a shudder through him and forced him to concentrate on the argument he needed to present to Grant and Delano. Despite the closed-in smell of the little hotel room, he remained bent over his notes until he'd done the best damn job he could. He went to bed that night with the window open to catch what little breeze came his way. There was no ignoring the contrast between the hot, still air here and the wild wind that claimed the Land of Burned Out Fires.

A little before noon the next day, he was ushered into a high-ceilinged, dark-paneled room in the nation's capital. Despite his nervousness, he was glad this moment had come. No matter how things turned out, at least he would have fulfilled his vow to Luash—and to himself.

Behind a desk that looked as if it weighed as much as a train car sat a somber-eyed man with a full, graying beard and receding hairline. In the man's firm expression, Jed easily found the former Union general who'd defeated Robert E. Lee. At the side of the desk sat Columbus Delano, sweating in the dark suit that was a near twin of the one worn by the president. There was another man in the room, obviously brought in to record whatever was said.

Jed began by explaining that he'd been assigned to the Modoc campaign just before the Indians had been driven from Lost River back in November. If the renegade Modocs had been treated with respect by an organized, thinking army, instead of having their homes burned, he insisted, there wouldn't have been a war.

"You haven't seen the Modocs," he pressed. "I have. I've kept an eye on them for months, crawled into one of the caves where they were forced to spend the winter. I watched their homes go up in flames and was myself wounded when General Canby was killed. As I said when I petitioned for this meeting, I know firsthand the worst that an Indian is capable of." He ran a finger over the scar along his hairline. "If I, who have spent my adult life fighting Indians, believe the Modocs should be shown some basic human concern, I trust you will feel the same way."

When neither man said anything, Jed took a deep breath and continued. He first outlined what it had cost him in terms of time and expense to come here, his conversations with the various groups concerned with the Modocs' welfare, his interviews with the press. Then he detailed the Modocs' present conditions. His eyes fixed on the president, he described the exhausted woman and baby who'd surrendered to him.

"There are fewer than fifty able-bodied men among them and none have any fight left in them. They're beaten, Mr. President. All they want is to try to rebuild their lives."

"They went to war against the United States," Delano said. "They have to be punished, so other Indians won't try the same thing."

Jed had prepared himself for that argument. "Thanks to the reporters assigned to cover this war, folks know what happened, at least the reporters' version of what happened. Yes, people were outraged when a general was killed. They also laughed at the notion that it took nearly a thousand bumbling soldiers to break no more than a hundred Modocs, women and children included. If you rip the tribe apart now, will it bring Canby back? Will voters applaud your decision, or will they see this as a deliberate and cruel attempt to destroy what's left of a once-proud people?"

"And what happens if this so-called vanquished people decides to arm themselves again?"

It was all Jed could do not to laugh. "I've done everything but lived with them, Mr. President. I spent hours with Captain Jack's niece while she told me of their heritage, their beliefs, their dreams. They don't want guns—they want something to believe in. I'm absolutely convinced there's no fight left in them. If you scatter the families, you'll rip what's left of their hearts from them. They might not die as fast as they would from smallpox or malaria, but they're going to die. It's one thing to face a warrior in battle. It's quite another to have to tell an unarmed man he's never going to see his father or mother again."

Grant and Delano exchanged glances but didn't speak.

"I'm not a religious man, Mr. President. I lost whatever faith I had a long time ago. I'm not going to quote the Bible at you. I'm simply here to tell you what I've seen, and that's that the war is over. All the Modocs want is a chance to live. I believe they deserve it."

"Are you saying you want them set free so they can go back to living the way they did before the war?"

With Luash's eyes haunting him, that was exactly what he wanted. "No," he forced himself to say. "The way of life that once sustained them is over. The land they buried their ancestors on and took courage from, the land they think of as their mother's breast has been taken over by whites; there's no going back. What I'm saying is, if they can't have that land, the least they deserve is to be surrounded by the people who mean the most to them."

President Grant asked if those at Fort Klamath knew how much pressure he was getting from religious groups and others to commute Jack's sentence. Jed acknowledged that he had heard some rumors before he left, but it was hard to keep in touch from a train. Delano reminded Jed that, as secretary of the Interior, he had ordered the Peace Commission to be formed and had directed its operation throughout its attempts to end the war; thus he knew a great deal about the situation.

"With all due respect, sir," Jed said, "you weren't there. I was. I've buried soldiers who shouldn't have died. And I saw Captain Jack's people react when they realized their leader was going to hang. The Modocs are no different from you and me. They cry; their hearts can be broken. They're also people who want to get on with the act of living, wherever that might be."

"They lost the war; they're prisoners of the U.S. government, subject to its laws and wisdom," Delano said.

Wisdom? So far he'd seen precious little of that. "You're talking about a family here. Men, women, children. Newborn babies and old folks. People used to depending on each other for survival and companionship. Take that from them and there's not going to be anything left for them to hold on to. They'll die."

"You're convinced of that?" Delano pressed him.

"Absolutely. Sir, it's one thing to hang Jack and the other ring-leaders for war crimes. It's quite another to rip their souls from women and children and old men." *Souls.* "I don't want to think about the outcry that'll take place if there aren't any Modocs left in a few years."

The meeting, Jed guessed, lasted no more than a half hour. When the president stood up, indicating he'd heard enough, it was all Jed could do not to demand to know what had been decided. But the government, he reminded himself, was a lot like the army. Nothing happened without everything first being laboriously weighed and debated. He asked what message he could take back to northern California and was told that any presidential orders would be wired to those in charge of carrying out policy.

Luash stood outside the guardhouse where Kientpoos was being kept, trying to imagine what was happening inside. Although her uncle and the five others who'd been condemned to death remained locked up, they were allowed visits from their families.

Whe-cha had gone to see him right after breakfast. Now it was afternoon and she was still in there. Luash prayed they'd be able to laugh together, to find a few moments when their thoughts weren't on the chains still around Kientpoos's ankles.

Sweat ran down the back of her neck, and her throat felt dry. After looking up at the hot, heavy sun, she headed toward one of the water barrels. Her shoes—white man's shoes—slapped dully on the dust; the sound settled into her heart to add to her lethargy.

She hadn't seen Jed for nearly two moons. His friend had told her he'd had a conversation with his president and was now on his way back. One day soon he would ride into the fort and she'd have to look at him, somehow conceal from him how unbelievably hard the days and nights without him had been.

After drinking from the wooden dipper, she turned her gaze toward the mountains. It was too late in the day to climb up to the eagle's nest, and even if it wasn't, the heat pressed down on her shoulders and stripped her of energy. Still, she would love to be where she could hear baby eagles' loud demands for food and watch patient parents in their never-ending quest to feed them. Maybe if she swept her heart clean of all sorrow and regret, Eagle would bless her with his presence.

And maybe he would simply go on caring for the winged family she had gone to see time and time again while waiting— endlessly waiting.

She'd caught the white strand of hair at her temple between her fingers before she realized what she was doing. Gallows were being built to hang her uncle and the others. For two days now the awful hammering had found its way into her dreams. If only Jed would return—

But his presence wouldn't tear down the gallows or put dirt back in the six mocking graves that had been dug in front of the guardhouse. All Jed could do was momentarily distract her from reality by covering her hungry flesh with his man's hands.

Sick, she turned her back on what the carpenter was doing, but there was nowhere she could run—not unless she was willing to spend the rest of her life alone.

When she became aware of eyes on her she couldn't say. It began like a slowly developing storm. First she had only the faintest awareness, then she grew more and more certain until she knew.

Jed was here.

He rode into the fort on a dark brown horse that had white front legs and a short tail. He sat tall in the saddle, looking not at all like a man who had spent days traveling. He wasn't wearing his uniform. Instead, he was dressed like many of the civilians who hung around the fort.

Only, she prayed, Jed hadn't come here because he wanted to watch white man's justice be served.

He came so close before dismounting that she could have reached out and touched his horse. Waiting for him to speak, incapable of doing so herself, she traced with her mind and eyes the lines and angles of his face. He hadn't shaved for several days, but instead of looking rough and unapproachable, he seemed somehow vulnerable. She liked seeing him without his uniform, told herself to never forget what he looked like now.

Memories. Was that all she would have?

"I missed you," he whispered.

Her eyes burned, but she refused to blink. "I missed you."

"You're all right?" His voice sounded like pieces of gravel being rubbed together. "Wilfred said you were, but I heard so little from him."

"I am fine." What did he think of her white woman's blouse and long skirt? The shoes she discarded when she climbed up to Eagle's nest because they didn't know how to cling to rocks? "The days are too long. Waiting . . . "

"Waiting for your future to be decided. I know."

"Not just that." She nodded at the gallows. The effort of not shivering made it nearly impossible to hold back her tears. He hadn't had to return. He could have sent his messages to the fort commander and gone—gone back to fighting Sioux.

But he was here.

"I need to talk to you," he said, his hand so close to hers that she felt the hairs on the back of it brushing against her flesh. "But I have to see Colonel Davis first. You'll be here when I'm done?"

No. "Yes."

It was nearly dark before she saw him again. Although the other Modocs had gone into the stockade for the night, she remained outside, seated on a log not far from where the forest began. Soldiers had been coming and going from the commanding officer's quarters ever since Jed arrived, and she guessed he had much to tell them. It hurt and angered her that his news, which deeply concerned the Modocs, was told to whites first.

Finally he emerged, Wilfred beside him. The two had their heads close together, maybe not wanting anyone to hear what they had to say. She thought about standing—fought the urge to run—but instead remained where she was.

When he paused, glanced in her direction, then shook hands with Wilfred before walking toward her, she concentrated on trying to remember how to breathe. She wanted to tell him so much, ask so many questions, yet she was afraid.

"The meeting took longer than I wanted," he said. "Everything about this damn army takes so long."

"You hold my life in your hands, my people's lives; I have a right to know what happened in there, what happened when you were with your president."

His nostrils flared, but he said nothing. When he briefly looked into the woods, she understood. Leading the way on legs that had sought the wilderness daily while he was gone, she slipped into the trees, their cool darkness insulating her from the day's lingering heat.

"It's good land here," he said softly. "Much more productive than what's at the lava beds all right. Plants grow; animals flourish."

"What are you saying?"

He grunted low in his throat, then placed his hands on her shoulders and turned her around toward him. "You know me pretty well, don't you?"

Not well at all, she nearly said, but maybe he was right. "Tell me. What is to become of us?"

"I don't have any answers; that's the hell of it. The president promised he'd decide before the hanging but—"

"The hanging! The president believes the trial was fair?"

"Whether he does or not, he's not going to reverse the decision. But as for what happens to the rest of the Modocs once it's over . . . "

She waited for him to finish, told herself she had the courage to hear what he'd brought her here for, but when his silence stretched on, she gradually forgot there needed to be words between them. Despite the unrelenting heat of summer, she'd felt strangely cold ever since he rode away. She'd tried to tell herself that being a prisoner was the reason, but the army men allowed her a great deal of freedom—maybe too much, because each day she had to fight the need to remain in the woods.

Tonight she was warm. It was almost as if Eagle had returned and spread his great wings over her, touching her heart with his strength and courage. Only this touch came from a man, not from her spirit.

"Not knowing how you were, I felt as if I was on the other side of the world from you." He took a ragged breath and although his hands were still on her, he now held her at arms' length, as if he didn't dare get any closer. "You wouldn't like it there. Too many people. Smells—smells that are nothing like what's here."

"Jed? You said the president would soon say what is to become of us, but surely you know what he is thinking. What did you say to him? Did he hear your words?"

"I told him what it's like for your people now, asked him—begged him. . . . It's out of my hands, Luash. I've done everything I can."

Everything he can. "Then while my uncle and the others live, we will not know whether the Modocs will be allowed to remain together?"

"I'm sorry."

Such simple words, spoken with so much emotion. In a desperate attempt to keep her balance, and because she'd gone without touching him for as long as she could, she ran her fingers up his arms until they rested on the sides of his neck. His features, so harsh sometimes, softened.

"I prayed for you," she admitted. "Every time I went to where Eagle lives, I asked him to look out for you, to give your words courage and compassion."

"You've seen him?" He'd lowered his head until his lips were both an invitation and an incredible risk.

"Yes. Caring for his children."

"Children. Good. But he hasn't sought you?"

Sick despite Jed's presence, she shook her head. "He is free; I am not. Our hearts no longer sing the same song."

She wanted to tell him how incredibly hard it had been to face the loss of her spirit, but he was drawing her closer and closer, the pressure so slight that if she fought, she could easily escape.

His body pressed against her, legs against legs, her breasts flattened against his chest. With her arms locked around his neck, she slid up onto her toes and parted her lips to receive his. Nothing mattered—not a future with no answers, not the bedraggled eagle's feather she still wore in her hair, not what would happen to her uncle when he stepped up onto the gallows. There was only Jed. Only putting an end to the long and horrible days and nights without him.

Without breaking their kiss, she gently ran her fingertips over his unshaven cheeks, then up into his hair. When she brushed his scar, she allowed her fingers to rest on it for a time, committing it to memory. Making it part of her.

Jed held a strand of her hair, sliding his palms over it as if awed by its texture. She tried to concentrate on the sensation, but she was being bombarded by him, caught up in him. Losing herself. When he released her mouth to run his lips over her throat, a hot shiver chased throughout her body until she felt as if she was on fire.

Twisting, not to free herself but so she could spread the fire to him, she slid her arms under his and arched her back until the tips of her breasts were just touching his chest. Moving to a silent rhythm, she rocked from side to side, aided now by his hands on her hips, his body dancing to the same beat.

Together they moved like slender trees caught in the wind. Her fingers became those of a craftsman as she traced his form, wondering at each canyon and mountain. His strength—the pure strength of him . . .

With fingers as deft as hers, he slowly drew off her shirt and let it rain down on the ground. "God!" he groaned, then took first one and then the other breast into his mouth. He wrapped his body down around her, his spine so bowed that when she touched it, she could feel each and every bone.

Her legs gave out. She sank to her knees on the ground, taking him with her. He knelt beside her, just far enough away that the sight of him remained sharp-edged. With him guiding her, she did to his shirt what he'd done to hers.

How perfect he was! Despite his scars, she could believe him invincible—needed to believe that of him.

Leaning forward, she touched first her lips, then her tongue, to his chest. When she began feathering her fingers over him, he shuddered and reached out as if to stop her. Reckless, she placed his hands over her breasts and arched back, giving him full access. *Was this her? All hot and wild and needful?*

Yes. Yes!

When she forced her eyes to focus, he was looming over her. Understanding the unspoken message, she laid herself back on the ground and lifted her hips so he could tug off the hated skirt. It took only a moment for him to remove what remained of his clothes and then he was over her. Coming closer. Spreading her legs with his knees, sliding between them.

Becoming one with her.

She clamped her hands as best she could over his broad shoulders, closed her eyes, embraced the growing storm inside her. She felt his teeth rake over her throat; then his mouth was on her shoulder, wet and strong. A moment later the same strength gently clamped around a nipple. Head tossed to the side for breath, she lifted her back off the ground and danced with him—danced until the dark world inside her exploded into uncounted stars.

When it was over and his sweat-drenched body lay beside hers, she struggled for the courage to tell him that she needed more than for their bodies to be one. That her tomorrows couldn't remain a trackless cave.

But she couldn't.

21

"Damnation!"

"What is your objection, Lieutenant Britton? When the president gives an order, it's my responsibility to carry it out."

"And by doing so, you're putting the Modocs through needless hell."

Lieutenant Colonel Frank Wheaton, who, as far as Jed could determine, had recovered from the humiliation of being relieved of command following the disastrous attack on the stronghold, shrugged, then tugged at his uniform. "I'm doing as my president dictates. If he doesn't want Slolux and Barncho to know their sentences have been commuted until just before the execution, then I'll abide by it."

Jed clenched his teeth and curled his fingers into tight fists, but that did nothing to kill the rage thundering through him. "And in the meantime, those two boys believe they're going to die today."

"Boys? They're full-grown warriors."

He had no intention of wasting time debating the point with his superior officer. From the moment he'd heard that only the Modocs directly involved in the killing of General Canby would be brought to trial, he'd argued that Slolux and Barncho, while present, had raised no arms against the peace commission. Apparently he wasn't the only one who felt that way. The question, the damnable question was why the two were being treated so cruelly.

"All right. All right." He swallowed and took a deep breath, then tried again. "If the president has sent orders regarding Slolux and Barncho, then I take it he's *finally* made a decision about what's going to happen to the Modocs afterward."

"As a matter of fact, he has."

The question built inside him like a volcano on the verge of eruption. Still, he wasn't sure he wanted to speak it, let alone hear the answer. He'd been back little more than a week and during that time, he and Luash had spent hours together, saying little, making love only occasionally. He hadn't expected it to be any different. After all, the unknown in her future remained a great dark cloud that followed them everywhere.

"Someone must have made a pretty powerful case for keeping the Modocs together," Wheaton said. "Maybe you can take credit for that. The president wants them sent to Fort McPherson in Nebraska, at least temporarily."

"All of them?" He barely breathed the question.

"All of them. Only the president doesn't want them told anything until they get to Wyoming."

Jed recoiled. "What?"

"For reasons of security, neither they or anyone else are to know anything."

"Not even that they're *not* going to be split up?"

"That's right. Do you hear me, Lieutenant Britton? If you want to take credit for keeping the tribe together, that's fine with me. But you are *not* to say a word about this until you're given permission."

Luash stood surrounded by Modocs, all of them ordered to watch the hanging. She'd placed her arm around Whe-cha's shoulder but couldn't think of a thing to say. Like her, Whe-cha remained silent while a breeze tinged with the taste and smell of early fall swirled around them. The gallows, with six ropes hanging limp in the morning air, held her attention as firmly as if she herself was tied to the monstrous contraption.

All yesterday, people had been arriving at the fort, some of them having traveled the same three thousand miles Jed had. It seemed as if every settler who had taken a piece of Modoc land was here, as were a number of reporters, all the remaining soldiers, even Klamath Indians. The sound and sight of them made her want to bolt and run.

A few minutes ago, Kientpoos, Bostin-Ah-gar, Te-te-tea-us, and Skonches had walked up the ladder leading to their death-place. Their shackles had been removed and although the thought of what was to come sickened her, she struggled for calm by concentrating on her uncle's now-free legs. When she saw the rope being placed around his neck, her courage nearly failed her.

Desperate, she looked around for Jed, but he was nowhere near. The court sentence was read aloud; somehow she managed to translate the horrible words for those around her. Whe-cha shuddered but said nothing.

When she heard that Slolux and Barncho would spend their lives in prison instead of being hanged, it was all she could do not to scream in outrage. Until this moment, the two had believed themselves dead men. Barncho, maybe not comprehending, continued to stare slack-jawed at nothing. Slolux, however, locked his gaze with Kientpoos. She couldn't say what passed between the two men, just that Slolux was now crying while her uncle's features remained impassive. She paid no attention to the roar of disbelief and outrage from the assembled ranchers.

A black-dressed Sunday doctor standing on the platform near the condemned men muttered something, but not enough of his words reached her for her to be able to translate. Suddenly a handkerchief waved, an axe flashed, and the floor dropped out from under the four Modocs.

Someone sobbed. The sound held in the air like a floating eagle, and after a few horrible seconds she realized she had made it. Her uncle's body jerked and spasmed. Skonches went rigid, looking as if he would shatter from the strain.

Whirling, she collided with Whe-cha, who clutched her so tightly that the younger woman's nails broke through her flesh. Whe-cha trembled violently, making Luash fear she would collapse, and despite the image of her uncle's death now seared into her brain, she clutched her dearest friend to her, turning her so she could no longer see her dying husband. She desperately wanted to say something to comfort both herself and Whe-cha, but no words came. Tomorrow, the army men had said, the Modocs would be forced to leave their home.

"I hate them!" Whe-cha sobbed. "They have killed my husband and I hate them!"

A young brave standing nearby warned Whe-cha to be quiet. Despite the horror crawling through her, Luash forced herself to look up at the gallows. The four men, all motionless now, swung at the end of their ropes. She'd told Jed that her people believed that a Modoc's soul could not escape if its path to the head was cut off. Why had the army men chosen that way to put an end to her uncle? Why?

The young brave drew Whe-cha out of her arms and began guiding her back to the stockade, speaking softly, cradling her. Luash took a stumbling step, but when she tried to rest her weight on her right leg, it gave out and she sank to the ground.

She didn't cry. The act that might have released some of the grief and horror trapped within her was denied her; all she could do was cover her face with her hands and rock slowly back and forth. *Eagle. Eagle! Please!*

"Luash?"

At the sound of Jed's voice, she struggled to pull herself out of the whirlpool of her thoughts. Still, she wanted to remain where she was, caught safely within memories of the years when Eagle and everything he stood for had been her companion and support.

Feeling Jed's hand on her shoulder, she looked up at him with blurred vision. He was as he'd been the first day she'd seen him, powerful and remote—part of the great force that controlled her life. Someone began crying; she recognized the voice of Kientpoos's daughter.

"It is over," she whimpered. "The Modoc are no more."

"That's not true. Luash?" He dropped to his knees in the dirt beside her, took her face in his hands, and forced her to look into his eyes. "Listen to me. I'm going to tell you something I'm not supposed to, but—damnation, sometimes they're dead wrong; this is one of those times!"

She didn't know what he was talking about, didn't know or care anything except that life had been forced from the chief of the Modocs and tomorrow they would be herded into wagons and taken from their homes.

"You aren't going to be separated. The tribe will remain together."

"Together?"

"It's an order from the president, Luash. The same kind of order that saved Slolux and Barncho's lives."

"Not scattered?" The tears she couldn't tap a moment before pressed against her temple and the backs of her eyes with such strength that she was afraid she would start to scream and not be able to stop. "Why were we not told? Why did Slolux and Barncho have to face a hanging rope if they were to be spared?"

"Because that's the way the president wanted it."

She hated this white chief she would never see, the hatred a black snake that threatened to curl itself around her heart, squeezing until nothing was left. "Does he think we are animals incapable of feeling? He says it is right for us to believe we are to be ripped apart?"

"I can't see inside him, Luash. I don't know what led him to that decision."

She couldn't listen to any more of this. If she did, she would say things that neither of them could ever bury. Only what did it matter? Tomorrow she would be sent from here and he would return to the Black Hills.

"I wasn't supposed to tell you," he said, helping her to her feet.

"But you did. Why?"

For a heartbeat, his features remained immobile. Then, slowly, the shadows lifted. "Because it's not right. Because Modocs are human beings. I can't say where you'll be sent eventually; I'm not sure anyone knows."

"But together? You are sure?"

"Yes."

She nearly told him she could hear her heart beating again when she thought it had ceased to exist, but was stopped by what remained in his eyes.

Her world had fallen apart when Kientpoos surrendered, when she saw the chains being placed on his legs. This morning, maybe, the same emotion swamped Jed. They stood so close that she felt his breath skitter across her temple to disturb the white hairs there.

"Your president listened to you," she managed. "You pleaded with him to spare Slolux and Barncho and he did."

"Life in prison—they may wish they were dead."

She shuddered at that, then took Jed's hands and placed them on either side of her neck. She thought he would look around to see who might be watching, but when he only continued to stare down at her, she realized she hadn't yet pulled him out of the dark place his emotions had taken him.

"Listen to me. Please," she begged. "Once I believed Eagle

would spread his wings over everyone I love. I was wrong. He—maybe he no longer hears my heart beating."

"Don't say that."

It was hard to speak. Still, she forced herself to continue. "Eagle loves his mate and children; he has forgotten the Modoc woman he once knew. Jed—a seventeen-year-old boy alone in the world needed to belong to something. He chose the army. When he nearly lost his life, he vowed to hunt those who scarred him and left death around him. But you are no longer seventeen."

He blinked, his eyes now glazed. The emotion she'd been battling since a rope was placed around her beloved uncle's neck rose in her like a storm wave. Fighting it, she pressed Jed's hands even tighter against her and waited until he was looking at her clear-eyed again.

"Once Eagle gave my heart peace, but no longer."

"You're turning your back on him? Damnit, Luash, you can't!"

"I do what I must." She longed to touch her hair to see if the lone feather was still woven through it, but to do that she would have to release Jed. "I do not own my life. It is in the hands of your president, your army."

He stiffened. Her pain, become stronger with each breath she took, would soon force her back to her knees. The sound of a woman crying tore her thoughts from Jed. Turning, she saw that Whe-cha had run up the ladder leading to the scaffold and was trying to stop an army man from cutting off Kientpoos's hair. Agony, horror, and outrage tore through her.

Before she could stumble after Whe-cha, Jed grabbed her and jerked her hard against him. "Luash! Stop!"

"No! They cannot—they cannot . . . " The warrior who'd tried to comfort Whe-cha a moment before scrambled up the scaffold and clutched her to him again. This time Whe-cha didn't try to pull away.

"He's dead, Luash. It doesn't matter. Listen to me!"

The force of Jed's words spun her back around. He was strength and dark power, a hated uniform and gray eyes that had found a home inside her. "What I told you about the Modocs staying together? I broke a soldier's promise by saying what I did. You can't tell the others. Do you understand me? You can't say anything!"

"No." She barely got the word out.

"I countermanded an order. I wouldn't have if I didn't love you."

Love? Shaking violently, she stared up into Jed's eyes. What did he mean? She couldn't think; the fort pulsed with the presence of those who'd come to see her uncle die. And Jed wore an army uniform.

"You want my silence?" she managed. "I am to say nothing to my people of what is to become of them?"

"Not until you reach Wyoming. That's the president's orders."

She yanked free, then doubled up her fists. "Love? You say love! And then you order me to allow my people's hearts to go on breaking?"

He said nothing, did nothing. Instead, his face now bleached of color, he simply stood before her.

"I hate you, Jed! You and your army! If I had a rifle, you would be dead!"

"No."

"Yes."

Somehow a day had passed. Luash remembered turning her back on Jed, watching Whe-cha and the brave walk away from her husband's body. Watched as arm in arm, Whe-cha and the brave returned to the stockade.

The day had beat on, one precious second after another. She tried not to look over the top of the heavy walls that held her prisoner to the trees and mountains beyond. Over and over again she'd prayed to Eagle until the strength for that too left her. She'd thought there'd been a shadow, the distant shape of a great bird high overhead, but that might have been only in her mind.

She'd forced herself not to think of Jed. Instead, doing as she was ordered, she'd pulled together her few belongings so she would be ready to leave her ancestors' home. She'd mourned with Whe-cha, holding on to Kientpoos's young wife with a strength that frightened and sustained them both through the long night.

Now she sat on a hard wagon to which four horses had been harnessed. Whe-cha, silent and red-eyed, sat near her, her shoulder resting against the brave known as Son of Schonchin. Cho-Cho was in another wagon with his wife and several others. Ha-kar-Jim and Cho-ocks, both silent and sullen, were in a third wagon surrounded by their families. She didn't know what had happened to the dead Modocs' bodies, or to Slolux and Barncho.

Her people wouldn't be ripped apart. Jed had said so and she believed him. Only he'd begged her to say nothing of that because if she did, all would know he had gone against his commanding officer's order.

Why should she care?

Because—the answer pushed its way through the blanket she'd tried to wrap around her heart—because he had said he loved her.

It wasn't enough. As long as he wore his uniform and stood beside the man named Custer, his words were nothing more than a high, thin cloud.

The wagon at the head of the line jerked and began moving. Numb, she stared at the Modocs in it. As one, their eyes scanned their surroundings. No one spoke, not even the soldiers who'd come to watch them leave or those who would be traveling with them. She told herself not to look around for Jed, but her heart wasn't easy to control.

With her fingers clamped over Eagle's mark in her hair, she

stared into one pair of enemy eyes after another. They kept secret from her whatever they might be thinking. She told herself she was glad, that it mattered not at all what those who had vanquished her people thought, but if Jed could care enough to fight for the lives of two Modoc boys, maybe there were others who didn't hate.

Maybe.

Someone was coming toward her. Despite the distance between them, he stood out, different from all those staring faces. Although she knew it was Jed, for too long she couldn't make sense of what she was seeing. Then he was so close that there was nothing to see except the truth.

He wore, not yesterday's uniform, but the clothes he'd had on the day he returned from his long trip. He hadn't shaved and something had scuffed and dirtied his boots.

In his arms he carried an eaglet.

Her legs felt so weak that she wasn't sure they could support her weight. Still, she climbed out of the wagon and followed him to a quiet place near the edge of the woods. She couldn't take her eyes off the mound of fluff resting quietly against his chest.

"I've resigned," he said simply. "Turned in my uniform last night."

"Why?"

"Because I can't condone what the army's doing to you, the hell our government is putting your people through. The incompetence. It's been there for years; I'm just now seeing it for what it is. I've decided . . ."

His words drifted on the wind, making her think of feathers. She hadn't cried yesterday because she was afraid that if she once gave in to tears, she would never be able to stop. Now emotion raged in her, all but robbing her of speech. With unsteady fingers, she touched the top of the eaglet's head. When he grew up, would he have his father's mark? "How . . ."

"Why do I have him?" Jed stared down at her, his eyes soft and clear. "I saw Eagle last night; he flew over me, hung there for so long—I went climbing first thing this morning. I don't know what I was doing, what I was thinking. I'm not sure I had any choice."

"No choice?"

"I wanted to see you, to tell you what I'd decided. Instead, I wound up on that crag looking up at the nest. Luash, Eagle came to me."

She wrapped her arms around her waist and began rocking back and forth.

"Then he returned to his nest. The next time I saw him—Eagle left his child at my feet."

Crying, she could only stare into Jed's eyes, and believe.

"I don't understand." He shifted the eaglet in his arms, glanced down at it, then carefully lowered it to the ground. The bird stared up at her, its beak slightly open, eyes bright and unafraid. "But I believe Eagle wants his son to go with us."

"Us?" Had the day suddenly turned cold? Was that what was responsible for her violent shivering?

"I've decided to come with you and your people."

Could he hear her silent question? She prayed he could because she couldn't force out a single sound. "Someone has to speak for the Modocs." His voice sounded rough, as if he too had come to the end of his ability to talk. "I've been talking to a religious group, the Quakers. They're willing to pay me to look after Modoc rights."

"You would do this thing? Work for Quakers?"

"Yes. If that's what you want."

What she wanted was to spend the rest of her life wrapped in Jed's arms. To watch Eagle's son grow until his wings were strong enough to lift him into the sky. "What are you saying?"

"That I love you."

Love. The word filled her until she felt as if she might burst from it. The unknown that made up her tomorrows still terrified her, but

Jed was willing to speak for her people, live with them, with her, do what Kientpoos no longer could.

Eagle had trusted him with his son.

"My heart is full of you," she whispered. "You touched it that first day; it has only become more so since then."

"You never told me."

"I did not understand. I believed that a Modoc heart and a soldier's could not beat as one. But you are no longer a soldier. You are a man and I, a woman. Maybe—maybe that is enough."

"What are you saying?"

Not sure whether she had the words for this, she took in her surroundings and tried to absorb enough memories to last for the rest of her life. Although she hadn't seen the Land of Burned Out Fires for months, the image remained strong and clean inside her. Even now, she imagined she could smell sage, feel the clean wind that always blew there, see—

Eagle.

Barely able to keep her feet under her, she riveted her attention on the gloriously dark shadow now drifting high above her. She knew Jed had seen it too, but they would talk about this later— later, when she no longer felt part of her spirit. Was no longer drinking in the silent message radiating out from Eagle.

Let your heart find peace, her spirit told her. *Keep peace with you always. Peace and life and belief in tomorrow.*

Tomorrow.

I cherish the gift of your son, she sent back her own message. *I will keep him, and you, in my heart for as long as I live.*

Jed wrapped his arm around her. Grateful for his strength, she sagged against him as Eagle's scream filled the air. Before it had finished echoing, his son spread his immature wings and answered Eagle's call.

"My God," Jed whispered. "My God."

Eagle was gone; the wind and wilderness had claimed him. And yet Luash remained strong, content. At peace for the first time in months. "Jed. I . . . "

"What, my love?"

My love. "I—I love you."

"Oh, God."

Did he know what he had just said? It didn't matter, not now. Clinging to him, she looked over her shoulder at Fort Klamath and beyond that toward the Land of Burned Out Fires. She would take her memories with her. Eagle had given her and Jed his son and she cherished the gift. Jed would sustain her and she would live.

Learn along with her people how to walk into tomorrow.

With Eagle in her memory and Jed in her heart.

Author's Postscript

After a number of moves, a year after the beginning of the war, the Modocs were settled at Seneca Springs, in Oklahoma, under close supervision. Cho-Cho served as chief until he was replaced by Bogus Charley, who had participated in the attack on General Canby but escaped hanging because he helped the army hunt down Kientpoos. At Seneca Springs, the Modocs built their own barracks and farmed wheat and corn. Their children were sent to school there. Most of the Modocs eventually took white names. Unfortunately, almost fifty of the 153 exiles were dead by 1880, most from malaria. Both Cho-Cho and Cho-ocks died in 1890. Ha-kar-Jim, who outlived his son—who was killed by a white—died in Oklahoma in 1879. Barncho died in prison, but Slolux was pardoned after serving five years at Alcatraz and lived until 1899.

In 1909 the government gave the Modocs permission to return to their original reservation near the Land of Burned Out Fires. Some of their descendants are still there, many dedicated to preserving what remains of their culture.

Although much of Modoc Lake, now Tule Lake, was drained

to create farm land, the stronghold and other sites remain virtually untouched. Many visitors to Lava Beds National Monument say they sense the ghosts of those who lived and fought there. I am one of them.